DEC   1992

IN MY FATHER'S HOUSE

IN MY FATHER'S HOUSE

....

HUNTER WILSON

THE JOHNS HOPKINS UNIVERSITY PRESS
BALTIMORE AND LONDON

Printed in the United States of America on acid-free paper

The characters and events in this book are fictional. Any similarity to real persons, either living or dead, is purely coincidental and not intended by the author.

The Johns Hopkins University Press
701 West 40th Street, Baltimore, Maryland 21211-2190
The Johns Hopkins Press Ltd., London

LIBRARY OF CONGRESS CATALOGING-IN-PUBLICATION DATA
Wilson, Hunter.
    In my father's house / Hunter Wilson.
        p.   cm.
    ISBN 0-8018-4337-5 (hc)
    I. Title.
    PS3573.I45695515   1992
    813'.54—dc20   92-5596

To my mother and father,
whose undemanding love, integrity, and courage
made all things possible

ACKNOWLEDGMENTS

Several people have generously given me their time and assistance in the writing of this novel. I wish to acknowledge their help and to thank them sincerely: Thomas Hardie, for his enthusiasm, encouragement, and astute advice; Jackie Baldick, for her kindness and unflagging confidence in the book; William Grose, M.D., for his patient reading and wise comments on historical and medical elements in the story; Jack Goellner, director of the Johns Hopkins University Press, for seeing all possibilities and making them happen; Jane Warth, for her precise reading and resolution of script problems; Talbot and Anne Bond, who gave sustenance, both physical and spiritual, during the writing of the book; and finally my wife, Valerie, for her patience and warm support always, especially when the going was slow. To all of these my humble thanks for cheerfully made contributions.

IN MY FATHER'S HOUSE

PROLOGUE

Saturday, May 11, 1985

Dr. Clayton Hallam, professor of neurosurgery at the Johns Hopkins Medical School, was retiring. Furthermore, he was doing it damn soon. In about an hour and ten minutes, he calculated, after glancing at the digital clock on the middle shelf of his office bookcase, he would march himself down to the time-honored auditorium known as Hurd Hall and present, and then rest, his career. He would stand up before a host of peers, associates, students, friends and family, and tick off the platitudes that would, like Burma-Shave signs he used to see along a highway, define his life. There would be some honors, perhaps a silver tray, hopefully a rare first-edition copy of Osler's *A Way of Life,* which had been hinted at, and a lab facility in the hospital was to be named for him. He had to accept them, onerous though it was to do so, and then walk off graciously into the dusk. *Professor emeritus!* Easy as pie.

He was ready for the occasion. He had his speech well in mind, with prompter notes stowed in the pocket of his long white lab coat. He had worked on it long enough and carefully enough to know that it was adequate. The problem was that it didn't say anything. Not really. Not what was in his heart, not the pains or the guilts that lurked there; not how ill-deserving of honors he felt. Professor un-emeritus, or non-emeritus, would be more appropriate.

The speech addressed his curriculum vitae, all right, in an abstract, bloodless, philosophical way, touched on a few of his accomplishments, his insights, the innovations that bedecked his career in neurosurgery. But it didn't get down to gut level to talk about the dark memories that pervaded his consciousness and threatened even now to overwhelm him. The world thought well of him, he reflected, but the world didn't know everything. If it did . . . if it did. . . . Well, the hell with it!

Abruptly he broke off his musing, rose from his desk and went to a small gray file cabinet under the bookcase. He unlocked a file drawer and drew out of it a small glass vial from which he poured a mound of whitish powder onto a piece of filter paper. He locked up the vial in the cabinet, made sure his office door was secured, and returned to his desk chair. Then, deliberately, he raised the powder to his nose and snuffed it up into each nostril, in avid inhalations. He settled back and glanced at the clock—forty-five minutes to speech time.

CHAPTER 1

Saturday, May 11, 1985

Spring comes suddenly to East Baltimore. There are no preliminaries, no warnings. It simply arrives one morning in April in the guise of a warm, light breeze with a fresh smell in it that does not bite the nose or chill the lungs, a blue sky with clean white clouds that soar above the tenements, and a bright sun that lightens and softens, in alleys and narrow streets, the shadows that have lain there heavily all winter. Signs of its advent are particularly human, there being relatively little of the floral element in East Baltimore to either foretell its coming or respond to its arrival, and suddenly the previously winter-muted streets are filled with the blare of automobile horns, the chatter of countless small children spilling out of schools and three-story row houses, and numerous other intonations and cadences that accompany the yearly rejuvenation of this section of the city.

In the midst of the area, sprawling over the top of a mild rise in the topography, lay the irregular Victorian shape of the Johns Hopkins Hospital, an edifice that, because of its size and height and relative elevation, seemed like a giant father figure to the lower habitations surrounding it in all directions.

It was on such a spring Saturday at about quarter of nine in the morning that Jim Gallier hastened down the steps of the Welch Medical Library and across Wolfe Street toward the rear entrance of the Hopkins Hospital. The warm sunlight sparkled on his starched white uniform, and the soft wind, which turned up the leaves on the few trees growing in sidewalk plots, tugged at his lapels and raised a cowlick in his well-combed hair. His pace slowed as he reached the dark hospital entrance, and he lingered outside for a moment. He leaned against the iron picket fence that separated the hospital walls from the sidewalk, having first ascertained that to do so would not soil his white jacket, and, tilting his head back, closed his eyes and lifted his face toward the sun.

Noting him, a casual passerby would have seen a slender figure of medium height whose face seemed surprisingly youthful for the authority implied by the white uniform he wore. His features were small and delicate, with high cheekbones and a sharp nose that turned up a bit at the end. His lips were full to the point of bowing, and thick brown eyebrows made a quizzical statement as they arched over his squinted eyes. The jaw line was clean-cut and would someday undoubtedly be jowly, but today ended in a forward and precise chin. It was a face that was not quite handsome but could be called nice-looking, a puckish, Tom Sawyerish kind of face that also seemed to reveal thoughtfulness and intelligence. There was nothing casual in his aspect even in this moment of relaxation. His uniform was spotlessly white and sharply creased, looking as if it could have stood there successfully even if he had not been in it. He presented, therefore, a very revealing self-portrait.

Jim suddenly broke off his reverie, glanced around guiltily to assure himself that no one had witnessed his stolen moment, and headed into the hospital entrance. The great corridor, a major thoroughfare in the hospital, was bustling with life at this hour on Saturday morning, but Jim moved familiarly through the traffic, past the elevators and corridors leading off to the neurological institute and obstetric wards on his left and, farther on, those to the public medical wards and outpatient clinics to his right. His pace did not slow until he drew opposite the large bulletin board that hung on the wall next to the imposing entrance to Hurd Hall. Automatically he paused to scan the notices that were posted.

There were the usual memoranda that adorn any hospital bulletin board: the daily operating room schedule, a list of specialty conferences and lectures, a calendar of events for the preceding week that had not yet been changed. But Jim's attention was directed toward another announcement, one that stood off by itself in a glass case usually reserved for affairs of special interest. The large white letters stood out from the black background: "Retirement ceremony: Dr. Clayton Hallam, 11:00 A.M., Saturday, May 11, Hurd Hall."

Jim glanced briefly at his wristwatch and was about to continue on his way when a heavy hand descended on his shoulder from behind, and its owner spoke simultaneously.

"Hop to it, intern. You can't learn any medicine standing there!" The voice was laced with southern drawl.

Jim smiled as he turned to face the speaker. "Well, Jonas, where do you suggest I should go then? Mick! Idy." He nodded to the other two white-clad youths who accompanied Jonas. Without hesitation, Jonas replied, "Why, with me, of course, to have a cup of coffee in the canteen. Just the other day two professors told me that having coffee with me was the biggest event of their day."

"Professors of psychiatry, no doubt," retorted Jim. "Well, I can't pass up this chance, but it'll have to be fast—I have to do ward rounds before going to Dr. Hallam's speech."

"Tut-tut, not to fret, my child, just come along with me." Jonas hooked his arm under Jim's and drew him down a side corridor toward the canteen.

The hospital canteen was a brightly decorated enclosure separated from the corridor by a wall that was partially glass, which exposed the coffee drinkers to the passersby and occasioned many a chance drop-in conversation or consultation. There was much business that morning in the canteen, so while the other three commandeered one of the remaining small tables, Jonas stopped behind the counter, winked familiarly at the occupied waitress, and drew off four coffees with which he returned to the table.

"Enjoy, boys, you won't find service like this elsewhere!"

"Very true, Jonas. In fact, I think you may have found your true forte, not surgery, but waiting on tables," said Idy, grinning.

"Two years of cafeteria work at college does pay off sometimes," replied Jonas, as he tried to settle his thin, six-foot-four-inch frame into the cramped chair space at the table. "Handling four cups of coffee through this crowd without spilling a drop takes training."

"You can have a job here anytime you want it, Dr. Smith," interrupted the waitress, who appeared at the table and left their check. "We're always looking for good men!" She was in her mid-fifties, scrawnily thin, her face like a starved hawk's but somehow managing to have a nice smile, and she had been in the canteen for years. The group gave her considerable recognition, and she departed satisfied.

"You guys going to Dr. Hallam's affair?"

"Sure, everybody's going," said Jonas, answering for everybody. "After all, it's not every day that you hear a world-famous neurosurgical professor sing his swan song, even at this illustrious place. It'll be something to tell our grandchildren about. They'll say, 'Granddaddy, did you ever know that Dr. Hallam who did that pioneer work on the cerebrum?' and I'll say, 'Know him! Why, children, I was there when he gave his retirement address and stepped down as professor of neurosurgery at Johns Hopkins.' "

"Praiseworthy!" grinned Mickey, "but I think it's much more likely that they'll ask if you ever knew Marilyn Monroe or Hulk Hogan."

"That is, if they're normal, which seems unlikely in view of their granddaddy," laughed Idy.

"You all raise your grandkids the way you want," answered Jonas defensively. "Me? I'm going to raise mine on the nursery version of *Radiography of Brain Tumors* by Hallam."

"Gag," said Mick, as he rose from the table, "I'm leaving in case your enthusiasm is infectious. Thanks for the coffee, Jonas—see you at the lecture." Idy wandered off in Mick's wake.

"Jonas, you scared them," bantered Jim. "They were afraid you were going to ask them if they had read that book."

"Naw, both of them read it—a standard book in neurosurgical radiology, as you know. Trouble is that I am here to praise Caesar and they are content to see him buried."

"Well, you have a momentary audience of one, so lay on—is Hallam really such a star?" Jim worked on his coffee.

"Few brighter, in my opinion. Bregel, up in Boston, and Penniman, in Montreal, are probably of his magnitude. But if you look almost anywhere in the field of neurosurgery, you'll find some mention of a contribution he made. He's been a beacon here for a lot of years—drawn a lot of able people here to work under him—he's a first-rater . . . but then, they don't let you stay if you're not."

"He's getting on a bit though, isn't he? Seventy or so—ancient by active professors' standards."

"You're right. He stepped down as department chairman six or seven years ago, but he's continued on the active staff, and he's still on top—surgeon, teacher, still a very inspiring guy. . . . Gives us a lot of years to look forward to, doesn't it, James? A career that long?"

Jim smiled. "God does not deduct from thy allotted time the hours spent in doing medical research. Isn't that the saying around here? Looks like it might be true in his case. Have you ever met him?"

Jonas shrugged and downed the last of his coffee. "Nope, not really. Been to a lot of his lectures, of course, and assisted on some of his cases when I was in neurosurgery rotation—not time to form a relationship—too bad for me . . . and, of course, very too bad for him. But I'd love to have known him."

"Me, too," mused Jim. "It'd be interesting to hear what his life has been like—hard work to stay on top like he has. I wonder if it's been worth it to him. I wonder if he's enjoyed his life."

"As Numero Uno? I would imagine. Ask me in twenty years and I'll tell you." The two hastened out of the canteen and threaded their way up the busy corridor as far as the surgical building elevators.

"See you at the lecture maybe," called Jonas as he headed for the elevator. "You on duty or off this weekend?"

"I'm on."

"Me too—good for . . . " Jim couldn't hear the rest as the elevator door closed on Jonas's last sentence.

Jim continued on his way toward his current ward assignment in the Marburg Medical Building. He hadn't caught Jonas's last remark, but he was sure it was amusing, for Jonas had been amusing him ever since the chance hospital internship rooming assignments that brought them together as roommates almost a year ago. However, he remembered that his first reaction to Jonas had been one of quiet distaste.

Jim had arrived in the room first and was unpacking his suitcase when he heard the high-pitched voice with the broad southern phrases rising up the stairs and coming through the narrow corridor, transcending the murmurs of other voices, and he remembered even now the disquieting apprehension that swept over him at the thought that this might be his roommate for a whole year. He had glanced up at the doorway just as the owner of the voice proceeded to fill it, and beheld there a tall, angular, stoop-shouldered figure, dangerously overloaded with suitcases, cameras, books, and other gear, whose attire included a brown-checkered sports jacket and shining silk tie as blue as the sky itself. Surmounting all of this, on a neck that was long and thin, was a large, dome-shaped head with a forehead already enhanced by premature recession of the straight red hair, and eyes even bluer than the tie.

"Jim Gallier?" accused the figure, extending a long arm with a camera on a strap hanging from it. "Is it 'Galli-á' or 'Galli-er'?"

Jim acknowledged his name, while grasping the large hand placed in front of him. "Galli-er."

"Jonas Smith," came down from the heights. "Your new roomie. I got your name from down below."

"Ah," said Jim. "Come in. Let me help you with your things."

They succeeded in getting Jonas unloaded and settled the question of beds, desks, and bureaus, whereupon Jonas said, "Might as well bare a few facts, I guess. I'm from Powellville, North Carolina. I'm twenty-five years old, University of North Carolina '80, and Duke Med School. I've come here as a surgical intern. I'm not married or engaged or anything, not that I don't like girls, but I don't let myself think of them yet."

Jim, who had listened to this accounting with quiet distaste, gave a start as he realized it was now his turn.

"I'm from New York City, I'm twenty-six, Princeton, Johns Hopkins Medical School. I'm a medical intern. I—uh—prefer girls, too, and I think about them a lot."

Jonas grinned and went on, "Good enough, only so far the last point seems the only thing in common between us. My father's a doctor, a general practitioner."

"Mine was a broker. He passed away several years ago."

"Oh—I'm sorry. Well, now tell me something about yourself." Jim, who was beginning to enjoy the game of exploring how many things they didn't have in common, had been braced for some comparatively inane remark, and the question actually asked made him think for a moment and eye Jonas with amusement.

"Well," he said finally, "I'm an only child, I grew up . . . "

"No, no—I mean, do you have epilepsy, diabetes, or a rheumatic heart? Do you snore or walk in your sleep? I had a roommate once for three months, and one night he walked over to the light switch to turn the lights off—and he didn't come back! I lay there in the dark for a while, waiting for him to get into bed, but not a sound. I called out to him a couple of times, and nothing happened. I began to get panicky and, finally, got out of bed and groped over to the light switch, and there I found him, bolt upright and sound asleep. Found out that he had narcolepsy, but he scared me to death for a while."

Jim laughed, largely because he didn't know what else to do, but at length admitted that to the best of his knowledge he was free of all the afflictions Jonas had listed. This confession appeared to have lifted a great weight of responsibility off Jonas's shoulders, for he then said the story reminded him that he hadn't been able to get much sleep on the train coming up, and that he'd like to catch a little nap before dinner. He lay down upon the bed, put shades over his eyes, and within the space of some three to four respirations was in the arms of Morpheus, as Jim sat silently on his bed looking on, the bright four o'clock sun streaming through the open window. It wasn't until that night, when both were lying in their beds with the lights off, after dinner and long after Jim had wandered down to the Rooming Office and tried unsuccessfully to find one of his friends who might need a roommate, that Jonas admitted to him that he had come to Johns Hopkins to learn how to become the best general surgeon in the country.

Jim's first impulse on hearing this revelation from this gangling, unsophisticated, but unabashed southerner was to laugh, though not outwardly, because there was no mistaking the sober manner in which it was made. But during the ensuing days and weeks, as new routines and procedures gradually became automatic and exposure softened what at first were jagged edges in new personalities and new habits, it gradually became apparent to Jim that under Jonas's un- tutored exterior there dwelt an exceedingly clear intelligence, a pro- digious memory, and a great fund of medical reading. It also became increasingly evident that, although he could drop off to sleep at will in the flicker of a light bulb, Jonas possessed a frenetic, wiry energy that allowed him to drive on for days at full speed without pause. And, although he talked incessantly, one could do worse than to lis- ten to him, for his words contained much good sense imparted with an abundance of good humor. It was not long, therefore, before Jim came first to tolerate him, then to view him with affection, and, fi- nally, to feel a friendship and respect for him that he had had for few others in his young life.

The ward was quietly a-hum with complacent Saturday morning efficiency, like an engine that had been reduced to idling speed for the weekend, when Jim arrived. The sound of Bertram Harper's fat little feet impatiently tapping on the floor was the only discordant note. Jim found Harper sitting back in his chair in the doctor's office, an expression of displeasure on his rounded visage. He was an assistant resident of two years' standing, and, considering the comparative venerability of his station, which he never lost sight of, nothing that the two interns under him did on the ward really pleased him. Of the things that definitely displeased him, to be kept waiting by either of them was definitely high on the list. Viewed with a dispassionate eye, Harper was a product of the system that taught him, and the blame for his more intolerable faults was to be laid to others under whom he trained, and for them, still others who were their tutors, and so on back. The system. But it was hard to view Harper with a dispassion- ate eye; at least it was for Jim, who saw in his immediate overseer's pudgy features one more reminder of the unrest that had been gnaw- ing at him in recent weeks.

"Ah, Jim!" Harper began. "Top of the morning to you, or is it still morning? I seem to have forgotten, I've been waiting here so long."

"It's 9:05, Bert," retorted Jim calmly, sitting down. "I'm sorry if I've kept you waiting."

"Oh, it's not me, Doctor, it's these poor patients I'm thinking of," Harper continued sarcastically. "They're the ones who suffer—there's poor Mrs. McKenzie whose i.v. has infiltrated and who is waiting for you to restart it. And there's Mr. Grodek, waiting with his sleeve rolled up for you to draw a blood culture. And Mrs. Stanberry, whose sugar has to be checked before she can get her insulin, and last of all come I, to make weekend chart rounds with you so I can leave for my day and a half off. But please, consider me last!"

Jim hesitated a moment, then stood up. "In that case," he said, "I'll go get started on those other things, and we'll make chart rounds when I'm finished."

"Sit down!" Harper almost screamed. "We'll do no such thing! We'll do these charts, and then I'm leaving. One trouble with you is you won't admit when you're wrong."

"I said I was sorry, Bert, what more can I do?"

"I'm not just talking about today," replied Harper, in a calmer voice, "I'm speaking generally. I'd always heard you were a cracker-jack intern, and I looked forward to working with you. But since you've been on this ward—what's it been, a couple of months?— you've been strictly run of the mill, always a little late, always a little foggy on things. I don't know what's eating you, but you'd better crank it up a good bit. This ward's my responsibility, and I'm going to see it done right or else!"

He turned to a steel rack standing nearby, which was equipped with rollers, and, pulling it toward him, rapidly began selecting from it the metal-bound charts that contained the medical histories of the patients on the ward who were assigned to Jim. As he brought out each chart, Harper spoke rapidly and to the point, usually not even looking at its contents, outlining the pertinent features in the development of the patient's medical record and progress thus far and indicating what needed to be done and watched for over the weekend. For the most part, Jim sat silently, now and again jotting down notes in a black notebook he carried in his pocket and occasionally interjecting a comment or question. Fifteen minutes or so passed in this way, and thirteen charts lay neatly on the table by the time Harper's clipped voice dispatched the last case. It was a masterful demonstration, much like a violin virtuoso plucking thirteen compositions from his memory with only an occasional glance at the scores, and Jim was impressed despite his personal feelings about Harper—especially because he realized there were twelve charts remaining in the racks assigned to the other intern which Harper had already been through. It represented hard work, close attention to detail, and a sense of responsibility for each patient, and indicated what Jim already knew, that Harper was a competent assistant resident and deserved his position of authority. Jim also knew that he probably could not have duplicated the feat.

"Well, that's that!" said Harper, as he rose from his chair and prepared to leave his office. "You'll be responsible to Harris until 8:00 A.M. Monday. I expect to find everything shipshape when I get back." He left abruptly, and Jim watched his pudgy figure recede down the corridor.

Glancing briefly at his watch, which registered 9:20, Jim set swiftly to work. Moving efficiently and smoothly, he located a vein in Mrs. McKenzie's thin arm and started her intravenous solution running. He carefully drew a sterile blood culture from Mr. Grodek in 114 and sent it to the lab, then checked Mrs. Stanberry's capillary sugar level and ordered her insulin. Jim recorded each activity in the appropriate chart and finally, after checking quickly through his notebook, realized that the rest could wait until after the lecture. His watch said 11:05.

Hurd Hall, the large, tiered amphitheater, was filled to capacity when he arrived. Seating space had long since vanished, and people were standing in the rear. Jim took his place by one of the great marble pillars that lined the sides of the balcony. Glancing around, he estimated that some three hundred people were present, a fair number of whom wore the white lab coats and uniforms of medical students and house staff. Most of the assembly, however, was more senior and consisted mainly of such "personalities," as Jonas put it, who only come out of their labs and offices to give special lectures or receive honorary awards and then withdraw. Most of those seated in the first three rows Jim recognized as professors and as heads of the various departments of the hospital. He could see Dr. Gehrig, the silver-haired professor of surgery, world-famous for his work on cardiac surgery, placidly inhaling smoke through a long cigarette holder, and next to him, in remarkable contrast, the black-haired, heavy-featured figure of Dr. Mendel, professor of medicine, with whom few could boast close contact. The others were there, too: Renz, professor of pathology, a small, bent man, whose work on tuberculosis and the pathology of allergy had won him an international reputation, and Meyerbeer, professor of obstetrics, and so on.

Jim never failed to experience a stir of excitement at any event that drew the attendance of these men, simply because their presence lent an atmosphere of heightened importance to that happening. Although four years of medical school and almost a year of internship had gone far to humanize them for him and to expose their various frailties, their vast medical knowledge, their accomplishments, and their implied capabilities as Hopkins faculty were never lost on Jim. He no longer stood in awe of them, and he disagreed with some of them on occasion, but in the end he respected them all, and that was enough.

" . . . privilege of knowing and associating with Dr. Hallam for over forty years, I am cognizant of that privilege and am grateful for the honor of being asked to come and talk about it today."

The speaker had a slow, deliberate manner of speech, delivered in an almost falsetto voice peculiarly lacking in tonal range or changes in pitch. Indeed, the voice did not seem appropriate to the face, which was long and heavy, although narrow. It brooded up at the audience, and the reading light from the rostrum upon which the speaker leaned accentuated his high cheekbones and the somber hollows of his eyes. His remaining hair was graying, and a thin mustache had the odd appearance of a second mouth. He looked to be in his late sixties. Jim leaned forward to ask who he was.

"Dr. Warren Bregel," he was told in whispered tones, "professor of neurosurgery in Boston."

" . . . since we were medical students and then interns together on the surgical service of this hospital, in 1938. Since then Dr. Hallam's career has been amazingly varied in both experience and achievement, and I would like to sketch it briefly for you. After his internship, he went to Philadelphia for a year as assistant resident in general surgery. This proved a turning point in his career, for it was then, I believe, that he decided to enter the field of neurosurgery. He returned to Johns Hopkins as assistant resident in neurosurgery. Here our association was renewed, for at the time I was assistant resident on the same service.

"Two years later Dr. Hallam entered the armed forces and served as neurosurgeon in the Johns Hopkins Unit stationed on Fiji. After three years of distinguished service in the army, he returned to Johns Hopkins. One year later, having completed his residency, he accepted a two-year research fellowship in England, where he began his studies on the mapping of subcortical brain centers, which became so important later on as a standard of reference for anyone working in this field.

"He returned to the U.S. to accept the Covington Prize for Neurosurgical Research and entered a post as assistant professor in Boston. There he remained for some ten years, while his name became increasingly well known in the neurosurgical world as one identified with sound, dependable, and imaginative research and consummate surgical skill. He advanced to the rank of associate professor and, following the publication of his work on limbic dysarrythmias, was called to the chair in neurosurgery at the Medical Center in New York.

"The next fourteen years added continued luster to his name, as his department earned the renown it continues to enjoy. He pioneered in the new field of radiography of brain tumors. Finally, in 1970, upon the death of Dr. Horace Browning, then professor here, he was asked to return to Johns Hopkins, his alma mater, as professor of neurosurgery and chairman of the department.

"One might have thought that, having attained this pinnacle, he would have been content to rest his oars for a bit and let the tide carry him along, but he was not. In the fourteen years he has been here, he has continued with sustained freshness of thought and vigor of mind to strike out at all boundaries of neurological and neurosurgical medicine. His magnum opus, *Cerebral Dysfunctions,* was published in his second year here, and he has currently made advances in the use of refrigeration techniques applied to neurosurgery."

The speaker paused for a moment and, glancing up from his notes to the audience, cleared his throat self-consciously in the manner of one about to make some personal pronouncement.

"So much for the facts of his career. They speak for themselves and need no gilding from me. The only thing that is needed from me today, I think," and here he paused and glanced toward the front row of seats, "is an apology."

He waited to let this sink in and then continued. "Time, in the neurosurgical sense, is a very tricky paradox, because it is stored in the brain not as minutes, hours, or years, but as proteins, or crystal memories. As one grows older, the crystal-forming process becomes less sharp, so the earlier youthful memories tend to be much clearer and are more easily recalled than those that are more recent. Thus, the remote past overtakes the recent past and may, in certain cases of advanced age, entirely replace it, as if the recording protein of the brain runs short on ink as time passes and can't print as clearly.

"Well, this hasn't happened to me entirely as yet, but certain events in the distant past are very clear to me, as if they had just happened yesterday. One of these is of a particular night, forty-five years ago, in the Accident Room of this hospital, when I said to a fellow intern, 'Get out of surgery, you're not right for it.' Furthermore, I believe I repeated these sentiments three years later, when the same individual was my junior assistant resident in neurosurgery. The individual I spoke to was . . . Dr. Clayton Hallam."

A soft gasp of surprise spread through the audience.

"Every man is entitled to be wrong sometime in his life," confessed the speaker, "and it is certainly obvious that I was wrong. I have followed Dr. Hallam's career very carefully since then, more carefully, I fancy, than he has followed mine, and I must say that I have known I was wrong for many years now. This, however, is the first public chance that I have had to tell him. And so, I would like now to apologize, Clay, for that mistake, and I might add that I'm glad I was wrong."

Applause rippled throughout the audience as Dr. Bregel solemnly gathered his papers and left the rostrum to take a seat in the front row. Whispering spread through the hall, and Jim concluded it had been a most unusual laudatory address. It was bound to be, he thought, as he contemplated the poetry of this moment, when the threads of two lives, starting from the focal point of their medical schooling and internship, diverged and then ran parallel across a span of nearly a half-century to come together again at this point, at the very summit of the neurosurgical field. It occurred to Jim that the tableau he was watching was like reading the first and last pages of a novel; he would never know exactly what happened in the chapters between, but at least the story had a happy ending.

Dr. Gehrig followed Dr. Bregel to the podium and, after a brief introduction, invited Dr. Hallam to speak. Jim watched his tall, erect figure rise and walk carefully to the rostrum. Although Jim had been familiar with his appearance since medical school, Dr. Hallam's still handsome face, with its crew-cut gray hair and penetrating green eyes, always pleased him. It was, he thought, the way everyone would like to grow old. But Dr. Hallam did look older today.

He began to speak in a husky baritone voice.

"Dr. Gehrig, colleagues, friends, ladies and gentlemen, I would like to begin by thanking Dr. Bregel for his remarks. I, too, remember the events to which he alluded, and in his defense I want to say that time is also paradoxical in that while it occasionally makes one sad in remembering former happy moments, it also heals the sting of former unhappy ones. At the time I began, I probably deserved what was said, and your words, Warren, as you perhaps knew they would, proved to be a great stimulus for getting my life on its track. I want to thank you for them, and I thank you for today.

"I have been in a quandary over what I was going to say today. It seemed to me that by the time he is seventy-two a man ought to have already said everything he had to say that was worth listening to. Finally, I mentioned the problem to my wife, and she said, 'Say what you want to say!'

"Well, that put a different light on it. You see, it doesn't have to be important, just what I wanted to say. Gentlemen, never underestimate the power of a wife."

A chuckle that became a laugh spread through the crowd, and then it slowly subsided.

"And so, with this help, I arrived at two conclusions. First, I wanted to keep the theme philosophical, rather than scientific. You all are gummed to the teeth with science anyway, so a little light philosophy should be a relief. Second, I wanted to say something to the students and house staff—the ones who are just embarking on their life in medicine. After all, I am supposed to be a teacher, and if I can say something to these young minds that will be of value to them, that they can carry with them, then all this fuss might be worth it."

Dr. Hallam smiled up at the audience. "But again, what to say— what lesson could possibly derive from my life and experience that would apply to their new world of scientific gadgetry and technical advances that are beyond even the dreams of those days when I was their age. One way a person knows he's aging is to see his children mature. Well, look at the children, in addition to my own daughter, that have been born since I was married, so to speak, to neurosurgery—microsurgery, radioscopes, scanners, MRI's, laser endarterectomy—why, some of them have grown and are having children of their own by now."

Another low-pitched laugh arose from the audience. "And yet, maybe this is where lesson number one might come in. Fostering children such as these is usually not a single-parent affair, although it may begin from a single inspirational thought, so to speak. But for those of you who are interested in research and teaching, if you can look back thirty or forty years later at these children, who have grown and matured and proven their worth, and say, 'One or two of my ideas went into that technique or that treatment advance,' then whatever effort and time you put into it becomes worthwhile. At least it seems so to me, especially when one adds the excitement, the rich associations, and the closeness of human effort that are a part of it.

"But lesson number two, for that majority of you who will go into the practice of medicine when your formal training is over, remember that children and grandchildren keep you young and give you pleasure. Therefore, let me admonish you to keep up with these new babies, the new ideas, the new approaches, as they come along, because to neglect them antiquates you, but to associate with them keeps you fresh and increases your happiness in the field you have chosen."

Dr. Hallam paused and looked down at his notes. Gradually, the pause lengthened, and Jim, leaning forward in the silence, saw his face suddenly turn white and become slack. He slumped back slowly from the rostrum. Half of those seated in the front rows jumped up and leaped forward to assist him. Dr. Gehrig, suddenly comprehending the situation, rose quickly and requested the stunned audience to quietly leave the auditorium. Jim's last look down on the scene was at a cluster of people gathered around Dr. Hallam, prostrate on the floor. He spied Jonas among the murmuring crowd that now began to fill the corridor outside the hall, and the two walked quietly up the hall.

"Coronary, don't you think?" asked Jonas.

"Most likely," answered Jim in a low voice. "What a sad thing. Was he gone? Could you tell?"

"No—too many people around him."

The two stood irresolutely at a corner in the corridor, somehow depressed and drawn together by the event they had witnessed.

"Going back to the room?" Jonas asked.

Jim nodded, and the two strolled silently up the hall toward their quarters. They had progressed almost to the Main Residence, in the south wing of the hospital, when Jonas exclaimed, "Hey, can't you hear? They're paging you."

Jim hurried to a nearby desk phone and dialed the paging operator. Jonas saw him listen for a moment, and then Jim turned to Jonas. "It's a stroke, but he's alive. They've taken him to my ward. I've been assigned to take care of him."

CHAPTER 2

Saturday, May 11, 1985

Tension was in the air on Marburg I. It was evident in the small group of people gathered in the corridor near the entrance to Room 112; it hovered over the nurses' station, where there was a flurry of activity concerning orders and equipment being assembled for use in the new patient's room; but it centered in Room 112 itself and immediately absorbed Jim as he entered. It was one of those moments in medicine now familiar to him, when the crisis of a new arrival, or a precariously ill patient, galvanized the ward into an active team in a concerted effort to save a life. These moments were thrilling to Jim, one of the compelling aspects of medicine, almost like an immense game being played between the forces of life and those of death, the red and the black, in which he was a part of the red team, the team of life. Now the excitement was augmented by the importance of the patient, the fact that he was a professor on the staff of the hospital, and by the eminent doctors in attendance.

Dr. Hallam was propped up in bed with nasal oxygen in place, and Jim could see that an intravenous infusion had already been started.

Reggin, the chief resident on the private medical service, was bent over an electrocardiograph, which whirred intermittently as he manipulated the dials, while behind him, standing silently, were Dr. Mendel and Dr. Andres, professor of neurology. The room was silent but for the whir of the EKG and the hum of the oxygen machine. Dr. Hallam lay with his eyes closed, his face as pale as the pillow. He scarcely seemed to be breathing. Jim started forward, but an arm restrained him from behind, and he turned to see Harris, the assistant resident, who drew him out of the room.

When they reached the resident's office, Harris turned to him. "Let me give you a rundown on what's going on, Jim, since he's going to be yours. We've decided to keep him here rather than in the ICU. He's fairly sick. He seems to have a slight left-sided weakness, which Dr. Andres feels is probably a thrombosis, but it's hard to be sure. He'll be going up for a CAT scan soon. His blood pressure has fallen, and Dr. Andres decided to start a Decadron drip; in addition, he's been started on heparin, so you're going to have to stay by him and watch him pretty closely today and tonight. He's been sedated because he was quite restless and agitated, so your main job will be to keep an eye on his pulse and blood pressure and adjust the drip. I'll be available, so if you notice any changes for the worse don't hesitate to call me, no matter when it is. Okay?"

Jim nodded.

"Meanwhile," the assistant resident continued, "here's a catheterized urine specimen we drew from him. Take it to the lab and get a start on it and then come on back."

Jim took the tiny bottle and hastened to the ward laboratory. His fingers shook slightly as he opened the specimen bottle and then steadied as he settled down to work. It took him ten minutes to finish and return to the office on Marburg I, where Drs. Andres and Mendel were finishing their analyses of the findings, as Reggin and Harris looked on.

"It's a puzzling one," said Andres. "Very slight left-sided weakness, if any, and no lower-facial involvement. State of consciousness out of proportion to the findings. Could be a hemorrhage, but more likely a thrombosis. The CAT scan should tell." He was a short, well-built man, whose silver hair, glasses, and high forehead made him the perfect picture of a distinguished professor.

Mendel was a study in darkness. His hair was black, his complexion swarthy, and his features settled in well-worn grooves, all downward. His personality matched his physical appearance, dark and obscure, and he guarded his speech as if it were a treasure he expended only when forced.

He nodded at Andres' statement, and then there was a silence. Finally, Mendel said, "Should we do a spinal puncture?"

Andres thought for a moment. "I think I'd say wait for the scan. What do you think?"

Again a silence.

"I agree—I'd wait!"

Another silence. Andres looked over at Reggin.

"We'll wait on the spinal puncture."

"Right, sir," replied Reggin, while Harris nodded.

All stood, lost in thought, the younger men watching the professors respectfully.

"Can you think of anything else?" asked Andres at length.

Mendel shook his head. "I think that ought to do it—except, what about the cardiac monitor?"

Again Andres turned to Reggin. "Of course, we'll want him monitored constantly. I assume you've already ordered that? Good. The intern should stay on the ward tonight, I think—have you a good one? All right. We'll be going now. We'll drop back in a few hours—uh . . . take care of him, Jeff, he's been one of the great ones."

Reggin nodded as the two men left the office, and then he turned to Harris.

"Who's the intern on the case, Jack?"

"Jim Gallier, here."

"Okay, Jim, sorry I didn't notice. Now listen up. Forget your other duties; Fishbein'll take 'em. We'll want the works on this case: cardiac monitoring, blood pressure and pulse charted every fifteen minutes, rates of heparin drip, continuous oxygen, heart sounds. But first, send these other blood specimens to the lab."

As Jim left the room, he overheard Dr. Andres talking to a small group gathered around a bench just outside the door, on which were seated two women. It was they whom he addressed.

"Hello, Anne, Charlie."

In reply to their questioning looks, he continued, "He's doing as well as can be expected. I won't hide from you the fact that he's seriously ill, but every moment we gain is in his favor. Everything possible is being done for him—of that you can be sure. Now I suggest you stay around this afternoon and evening and, if everything is the same, go home and try to get some rest."

The older woman spoke for the first time. "Can we . . . see him, John?"

"You can look in on him occasionally. He's been pretty well shocked, so he probably won't be conscious. I'll drop back later on."

Both women rose to voice their thanks and then sat back down on the bench.

Despite his haste, it was almost twenty minutes before Jim could complete his work in the laboratory and return to the ward. He found that the crowd had thinned and that the only remaining people in the corridor were the two women he assumed were Dr. Hallam's wife and daughter and several men, among whom he recognized Dr. Bregel. Jim walked past the group and felt their eyes following him down the corridor. He entered the office. Harris, who awaited him, received the laboratory report with a nod.

"Okay," he said, "let's go to the room, and you can get started. I think I'd better introduce you to Mrs. Hallam and the daughter, though, because they're going to stay for a while, and maybe you can give them an occasional word of comfort during the day. Also, you better try to get Dr. Hallam's medical history from them, if they're up to it."

The introductions were brief. Mrs. Hallam was pale and composed, but moisture glistened in the daughter's eyes. She was introduced as Charlotte, and the hand that she extended to Jim was cold. She was taller than her mother by several inches and had black hair, whereas her mother's was light brown and graying. Both were fashionably and expensively dressed. Oddly enough in this hasty meeting, it was their dress that registered in Jim's mind, leaving him with the impression of two thoroughbreds who looked marvelously like they should have looked—Dr. Hallam's family.

After promising Mrs. Hallam that he would report to them frequently on Dr. Hallam's progress, Jim entered the room, leaving Harris to escort the four to the lounge at the end of the corridor, where they could wait more comfortably.

After ten months as an intern, Jim was not unused to responsibility, but even though his present role was mainly that of observer and reporter, he felt a sudden twinge of apprehension as he found himself in the room for the first time without a higher authority beside him. He glanced at Dr. Hallam, who seemed as before, and then turned to the special duty nurse to introduce himself. To his relief, it became apparent to him within a few moments that she was excellent. Her name, she told him, was Mrs. Jennings, and he judged she was about forty years of age. She told him the latest pulse and blood pressure readings, which seemed satisfactory. He approached the bed and gazed down at his silent patient.

The oxygen device hummed in the background. Sunlight streamed in through the partially open window by the bedside, and somewhere on the distant streets an automobile horn sounded. There was a peace, a tranquility, a springlike quality about the scene which seemed incongruous with the life-or-death struggle being enacted in the middle of it, as if someone had provided the wrong setting for a drama. The two main essentials of reality being motion and change, and both seeming impossible in the calmness of the room, the ultimate realities of living or dying likewise seemed suspended. Jim bent down and, reaching out, applied his stethoscope to the patient's chest. Dr. Hallam breathed heavily, regularly, and then stirred. The heavy gray clouds of narcosis and cerebral shock that whirled thickly over his consciousness parted for a moment as if drawn by some chance wind, and the eyelids trembled and then opened. Jim looked down into the eyes, glassy and opaque, which gazed up toward him, and he smiled but could not be sure that he was seen or, if seen, that the picture registered, for there was no adjustment of irises or lenses to focus on him, and no change in the facial muscles. Large, gray-green eyes, intelligent eyes without intelligence in them at the moment, beneath long lashes and graying brows, in a face that was pale and damp and lined but still agedly handsome.

Clayton Hallam awoke for an instant. He had no feeling, was aware of no sensation, and yet when the dull clouds closed over him once more, and he sank again into unconsciousness, he carried with him the image of this face he had seen looking down at him. He saw it framed against the curtain of gray that separated him from wakefulness.

"Young," he thought, "young . . . " And the picture flickered, changed, shifted, and transformed into a series of views without a particular sequence, flashing at random through the inner consciousness from the vast storage places of memory, lacking the central control that might have sorted and arranged them, and expressive outwardly only in an occasional groan or stir of the body, which Jim noted as he listened carefully to the heartbeat. But if they could have been ordered and sequenced, as if some master editor in the cutting room could have put them together, it might have come out like this.

• • • •

In June 1938, three young men walked along Monument Street, which bordered the Johns Hopkins Hospital and School of Medicine. Their steps were springy and swift. All were clean-shaven, and they were attired in the long white laboratory coats familiar in these environs as the traditional garb of the medical student. They maintained close ranks as they walked along the busy sidewalk, parting now and then to dodge a passerby and then coming abreast again, oblivious to all but what each other was saying and totally unaware of the frequent glances bestowed upon them.

They were ranged in order of descending height, and Bart Mateer, who was nearest the curb, rose up like a mountain bluff. He was six and a half feet tall, but the impression of height was increased by the spareness of his frame, his narrow but square shoulders, and his deep chest, so he seemed to get larger and more overhanging as he went up. His features were regular, his brown hair tousled. His walk displayed the ungainliness of the very tall, and he leaned down in the direction of his two companions, as if to prevent the winds of his higher altitude from interrupting communications between them.

"I know I flunked," he was saying animatedly. "I could see it in Harrison's face as I left the room."

"You always flunk, Bart. To the best of my knowledge you've flunked every test you've ever taken. It's amazing that they've let you get this far."

"But this time it's different, Clay. I got locked up. I couldn't even talk!"

Clay, whose full name was Clayton Garrett Hallam, snorted and turned to his right, to the third member of the trio. "What do you think, Dan? Shall we listen to him or shall we turn on the tap and drown him when we get home?"

Dan Forrester was the shortest of the three, although he was almost six feet tall. His hair was brown and curly, his eyes shone, and he exuded health.

"Well, Clay," he said, "in my experience drowning one's sorrows is a bad habit to get into, and, besides, we don't have anything big enough to drown him in. I think we might listen until we fall asleep."

"Lemme tell you about this," broke in Bart. "You know how nervous I was this morning? When I got to Harrison's office, I had to wait ten minutes while he finished with Don Bernheim, and by the time he came out I was almost climbing the wall. I went in, and my mouth and throat were dry as a bone, I was so scared. Old Harrison was sitting there behind his desk, writing. He didn't say anything, just waved me down into that inquisition-style chair, full of blood and other stains."

"Come on, Bart, cut the allusions."

"Okay, okay. So after a minute or two, he looked up at me with those ice-blue eyes and shot me a question. Now here's the sad part. I knew the answer, knew it cold, but I couldn't get it out. My mouth was so dry that my tongue had stuck to my palate, and I couldn't get it loose. All I could do was gag."

"Bart, now I've heard everything! I've heard of swallowing the tongue, biting it, the cat getting it, and so on, but I've never heard of having it stick to the roof of the mouth," said Clay disgustedly.

"Yeah, Bartie," put in Dan, "you're wasting your time in medicine. You should be on the radio—'Mateer's Hairy Fairy Tales' or something of the sort."

"Wait a minute—I haven't finished. Old Harrison finally figured out what was wrong and gave me a glass of water to loosen things up. And then he had the nerve to ask me to explain the physiologic processes involved in producing dryness of the mouth during times of stress."

"A very dry tale, Bart, and all I can say is that if Harrison really wanted to loosen you up, he gave you the wrong lubricant," said Dan. "Maybe he was trying to drown you. How did you make out, Clay?"

"Oh, all right, I think. I had Dr. Falls, and he was fairly straightforward. I'm just glad they're over. Do you fellows realize our last examination in medical school is over? We're finished!"

The three grinned at each other and hurried up the white steps of one of the row houses, marked 726, that lined North Broadway.

There was nothing, except the numbers, that served to distinguish the exterior of this building from those of its neighbors on either side. Indeed, it was not even an individual structure, for, like most of the houses in this section of the city, its façade was continuous with that of the rest, and on both sides of the street the monotony of two- and three-story red brick fronts with windows was broken only by the monotony of regularly spaced sets of white steps leading up to individual front doors. An occasional alley or street or store temporarily disrupted the pattern, but the ranks of houses soon closed again and continued their march.

As one of the main north-south thoroughfares in this section of the city, Broadway enjoyed the distinction of two lanes of traffic, separated by a broad lawn of grass with a paved walk up the middle. Here and there a tree fought its way up out of the sidewalks on either side of the street. In this manner, Broadway ran south from the 700s past the red brick cupolaed front of the Johns Hopkins Hospital on one side of the 600s and the nurses' home and medical fraternity houses on the opposite side, through a seedy business district possessing the dubious comforts of the Broadway Hotel, to end finally at the oily water of the Patapsco River. Despite its derelict termination, however, it was really not a bad-looking street, its structures for the most part being well-kept, and its grass median lending it a pastoral aspect absent in the narrower avenues surrounding it. It was a desirable address in East Baltimore—which was why most of its houses and businesses were tenaciously held by whites against the encroachments of blacks.

Clay Hallam thrust his head out of the second-story front window and surveyed the scene below him. A group of younger medical students clad in T-shirts and shorts was playing catch with a tennis ball in the middle of the median, with the traffic streaming by on both sides of them. Farther down the block two black children were locked in a half-hearted wrestling match. A warm June sun beamed on the city. Clay gave a wave to the students and, drawing back into the room, flopped down on the spare bed near the window.

Nothing seems changed out there, he thought. My God, it's over. I've finished medical school.

A light breeze wafted in through the window, and the house was quiet. He lit a cigarette and leaned back against the pillow. He felt at peace with the world and his own existence. His mind, ranging at random over his circumstances, the completed examinations, his upcoming marriage, his family, could not find a single jarring note in the whole survey. He was advancing in the career that he had envisioned since childhood, and he was graduating from one of the foremost medical schools in the country and secured his internship there. He was marrying a lovely young woman who fascinated him completely and who was from a medical family herself. His father, a general surgeon, was not wealthy but was well-to-do, so Clay had finished medical school without being in debt. His parents and older brother and sister were well. In future years from time to time Clay would hark back to this moment and this summation as the pinnacle of his age of innocence.

For up to this point in his life, his passage had not been complex. The struggles of adolescence in the small West Virginia town of Bloomington had been negotiated with success, and sometime during those years, after watching his father operate and being taken on rounds with him, he began to develop interest in becoming a physician. His father did not discourage him.

By the time he went off to college in 1930, at age seventeen, he had reached six feet, three inches in height. He played forward on the Princeton basketball team for three years. His popularity was thereby assured on campus, and it was certainly enhanced by his excellent mind and his attractiveness.

He had inherited his father's tall stature and bearing and his mother's olive complexion and large green eyes. His family did their best to play down his striking looks, so he remained unaffected by them, and vanity never became one of his faults. He accepted his college successes on the basketball courts, in the classrooms, and in the social areas with surprise and pleasure, took none of them for granted and, except for developing a growing confidence in himself, was not otherwise affected by his accomplishments. Medical school had proved a smooth extension of his college career except for having to surrender athletics and study longer hours. He had not finished in the top part of his class, but by the same token he had not been fired with the need to do so. With his roommates, he had led what they felt was a balanced medical school life. Now it was over, and he foresaw no problems.

He had fallen asleep, and evening had spread across the sky by the time, hours later, he strolled up Broadway toward the fraternity house. The street was tranquil in the cool spring air. Traffic had thinned, and the streetlights had just come on, although traces of day were still visible above the western skyline. The restaurant and drugstore on the corner were brightly lit, while the façade of the hospital across the street was beginning to fade into ranks of lighted windows. The scene was so familiar and friendly to Clay that he found it hard to realize that his days as a student were over. Weighing this in his mind, he could find no regret, and he was only passingly aware that there were memories of the past four years that would someday be pleasant to dwell upon. Now he felt only exhilaration.

He dropped into the restaurant to buy cigarettes and exchange good-byes with Bouaris, the owner. Bouaris was a Greek who had operated his establishment almost as long as the hospital had been in existence. He called everyone "Doctor" from the moment they first started medical school, and consequently his business thrived.

"Well, Doctor, I must be getting old, because I was pretty well along when you first came here," he said to Clay.

"You haven't changed a bit in four years, Jake," replied Clay. "You'll be here when my children come to medical school."

"Nah, nah, Doctor," said Jake, shaking his head, "maybe my sons, but not me. My liver'll get me before then—it's in the family."

"Well, Jake, as a new doctor, let me tell you how to help it. Make a habit of eating that Brunswick stew you serve here. That stuff's so powerful it wouldn't let anyone lie down long enough to croak."

The party was already in progress by the time Clay reached the steps of the fraternity, and he could hear familiar voices and laughs even before he pushed open the battered green door.

There were twenty or thirty people gathered in groups about the large room, which, because of its high ceiling, dark furniture, and mahogany-stained walls, never seemed brightly lit. The dimness was fortunate, for stronger light would have revealed age and hard use in the walls and furniture. As it was, the room had an air of aged warmth without appearing shabby.

Clay's entrance was hailed by loud greetings from corners of the room, to which he responded in kind. Someone placed a drink in his hand, and he moved across the room to join the group that was gathered around a huge red divan in front of the empty fireplace. The cracked mahogany mantelpiece had been burned with countless cigarettes. Along the base was the inscription "Given in memory of many happy evenings spent with the boys," and below that the famous name "Trudeau" with the date "1909." Over in the corner, a wind-up phonograph was working scratchily on "Amapola," and a few couples were already dancing in the passage leading to the dining room.

Clay stood leaning against the mantelpiece, watching the swirl of activity and listening as the murmur of the party built into an ever-increasing roar of sound with the steady arrival of new guests. He missed Anne and did not feel like losing himself in the gathering waves of the party, but was content to watch as they whipped from one side of the room to the other, in a burst of laughter here or a flutter of activity there, breaking into ripples as individuals moved from group to group, where they gathered again for another plunge. He realized that this was the last such party, and the last time for years that he would see many of those present. He wondered what they would look like in twenty years, and where their futures lay.

During his four years of medical school, he had come to know them all fairly well—their idiosyncrasies, their personalities, their abilities and habits—and in between his second and third drink he decided to go around and shake each one of them by the hand and tell them he was sorry to see them go. He began to feel blurrily that he loved them all, that each of them was "a piece of England, a part of the main," and he wanted them to know. Fortunately, or unfortunately, he was waylaid by the first group he encountered. With his fourth drink a few moments later, he had forgotten his original purpose.

This group was engaged in anecdotes, and Zimmer, a squat student with a crew-cut, was embarking on the story of Russ Black and the pigeons. "Old Mountbatten, our physiology professor," he was saying, "has a favorite lecture on the cerebellum that he gives every year."

"What's the cerebellum?" asked one of the women.

"Off with her head for not knowing what the cerebellum is!" cried a voice.

"The cerebellum," pontificated Zimmer, "is the part of the brain that controls balance and muscular coordination."

"Oh, like whiskey," the woman replied happily.

"When the time came to give us the lecture," continued Zimmer, "Mountbatten asked Russ Black to help him. All Russ had to do was to bring in a box, containing this pigeon that Mountbatten had removed the cerebellum from, to demonstrate that without the cerebellum a bird can't fly or walk or anything. Well, Russ brought in the box all right, but either on purpose or not he got the wrong pigeon, so when old Mountbatten opened the box, the pigeon flew up beautifully, made a few passes around the room, and then sailed out through the door with not a sign of incoordination, and the class broke up. Old Russ nearly didn't get through physiology."

"And what about Schmidt and the tiger?" spoke up a blond student with babylike features.

"Tiger!" screamed his date.

"Sure. Dr. Schmidt is professor of comparative anatomy and likes to operate on animals. One day this big circus with a sick tiger came to town, and Dr. Schmidt decided he had appendicitis. So he had him brought in a special cage over to the Anatomy Building, gave him a shot to put him to sleep, and strapped him down to the operating table. Schmidt had two other professors to help him, and he asked our classmate Bill Kaiser to scrub with them. So there were four men and a nurse anesthetist who was to hold an ether cone over the tiger's mouth in case he woke up.

"They made the first incision in the abdomen, and the tiger woke up and let out with a tremendous roar, and all four men made a dive out the door and slammed it, leaving the nurse in the room with the tiger. The roars finally died away, and they opened the door enough to see the nurse sprawled over the tiger with the ether cone over its mouth, and the tiger was fast asleep."

"Bravo for nurses everywhere!"

"Schmidt still blushes when anybody mentions it."

"Hey, Clay, tell us the story about Hubert Tapper, you saw it all happen."

Clay smiled a little foggily and complied. "Well, Hubert Tapper is the mildest, most conscientious guy in our class, but a little on the innocent side, at least he was. One day in biochemistry lab, we were studying the composition of our own feces, and . . . "

"Your own *what*?" screamed one of the women across from Clay.

"Feces . . . you know . . . feces!"

"Oh," she replied, blushing. "Of course."

"The experiment called for dissolving the specimen by boiling it in water over a Bunsen burner, and we were all boiling away when Hubert got called out for a minute, leaving his pot boiling, as it were.

"While he is gone, Lou Chan, who works next to him, empties Hubert's kettle and substitutes a rubber facsimile. He replaces the water and puts the pot back on the grid, and by the time Hubert gets back his specimen is boiling away, just as he left it."

"Oh, that's mean!" said a woman who was immediately hushed by her escort.

"Well," Clay continued, "time passed by and gradually everybody was getting his specimen dissolved and going on to the next stages of the experiment, while Hubert kept peering into his kettle and adding more water as it boiled down, but his specimen still seemed as solid as ever.

"By this time everyone in the lab knows what's going on, and we're all holding our breath to see what would happen. In a little while Hubert sidles over to the lab instructor and asks if it would be all right if he stirred the specimen a little bit. The instructor was busy and didn't pay much attention except to say that it was okay with him. So Hubert goes back to the boiling kettle and begins stirring and every once in a while gives a little jab with the stirring rod.

"Then Hubert sees that Lou Chan is finished with his Bunsen burner, so he walks over to Lou and asks if he can borrow it. At this point, everyone in the lab is about to explode, but we're so curious to see how it will turn out that nobody says anything, although we almost forget about our own experiment.

"Without a change of expression, Lou lends Hubert his burner, and Hubert adds it to his own so that he has two flames going under his grid—and a little while later he adds a third, so that he has three in action. You talk about steam—you could hardly see Hubert at all!

"Well, the lab instructor strolls over, having been attracted by the sight and smell of burning rubber coming from Hubert's pot. He immediately turns off the flames and empties the remaining few drops of water out of the kettle, and all that's left in the bottom is a mound of melted rubber."

Amid the laughter, one of the women said, "But I don't understand why Hubert didn't catch on sooner."

"Well, that's the point," Clay said. "I said each was working on his own . . . uh . . . specimen. Hubert was so afraid that something was terribly wrong with his own digestive system that he couldn't bring himself to take a closer look!"

Another wave of laughter, and then more stories. The noise and the momentum gradually built to a crescendo, as groups began singing, and someone started burning old notebooks in the fireplace. People glided up to Clay, saying good-bye, pledging reunions, wishing good luck. He played the game with them, enjoying it, his mind full of fuzzy warmth, feeling that never had a better group of people been assembled under one roof.

"Hello, Clay, how goes the celebration?" The voice at his elbow was neither loud nor forceful, but the words were so precisely spoken that they cut through the blurry background of noise like a knife. To Clay both the voice and its owner seemed out of place because they were the only things in the room that were in focus.

"Great, Warren. How about yourself?" He looked into the brooding eyes of his classmate and felt a sudden gathering of his senses.

"I probably don't feel as good as you do, but good," replied Warren, grinning with thin lips. "There's someone here I'd like you to meet. This is Nell Hargrieves. Nell, Clayton Hallam. Nell has just consented to be my wife."

Clay could not keep amazement from his face as he looked down at the small, dark-haired young woman beside Warren. She was plain, but she had soft lips that smiled broadly up at Clay in answer to his congratulations.

"But when did all this happen? I never even knew you—uh— were dating each other," said Clay, choking off just in time a remark that he had never known Warren even to have a date.

"Oh, just recently," replied Warren, still grinning. "We haven't really seen much of each other, but I knew when I met her that she was the one. You're getting married yourself, aren't you, Clay?"

"Two weeks," acknowledged Clay, smiling at the allusion to Anne.

"Well, well, big change for both of us. I hear we'll be interning together, too. The paths of fortune seem to be leading us in the same direction. I'm glad—it'll make the race more interesting."

"Which race do you mean?" asked Clay, glancing at Warren curiously and noting for the first time by a slight slip of the jaw and a glaze in the eyes that he had unmistakably been drinking, too. I'll be damned, he thought, amused.

"Why, the race we're all in—you know, the one to the top," said Warren, and giggled. "Oh, that race," answered Clay, glancing around at the crowd. "Well, that's one that you can have all to yourself. I'm not in any race."

"Oh yes you are, Clay, whether or not you know it."

"How is that?"

"Well, the whole Hopkins medical staff program is built on competition—you know that. Each year the number selected to stay on as residents is halved, so in the four years after an internship group starts, only one, the best, is chosen to be the chief resident. That's what I aim to be, and I think you do, too." Warren grinned without mirth.

Clay gaped at him for a moment, and the party eddied about them.

"Well, I'd rather face it then than now, Warren, but I'm glad you warned me . . . I guess." Clay's eyes were moving elsewhere.

"Sure, Clay, and I just wanted to add that I think it's a contest I'll win."

"Oh? And why is that?"

"Because you don't know how to work hard for something. You've never had to. You don't know how to give up things, nice things, pleasant things, in order to get something more important. I, on the other hand, do know how. That's the difference. There's nothing wrong with your mind, Clay, but you've got a lot of fat on your soul!"

Late in the evening Clay left the party, surfeited, to have a final bottle of beer before retiring. He was joined at the small sidestreet bar, first by Dan and later by Bart.

"I knew I'd find you here," said the latter as he entered. "Couldn't stay away, could you?"

"No, and we've been expecting you. Did you take Betty home?" asked Dan.

"Of course I did. Did you think I'd let her walk?"

The three sat in a booth drinking beer and smoking, as they had hundreds of times in the past.

"A great party," said Dan. "I told the same joke six times and got six laughs."

"Seven," said Bart. "I laughed once at the joke and once at you."

"You didn't laugh at me—you didn't even see me. As far as you were concerned, the party consisted of seventy blobs and Betty."

"You're wrong—I saw many weird and unnatural sights at that party. Sights like Jerry Phillips trying to show his date how to ski down Tuckeman's Ravine by pretending they were both on the same pair of skis, and like you singing 'K-K-K-Katie' to your date with your mouth full of ice cubes—what was her name, anyway?"

"K-K-K-Mary!"

"I see. But the queerest thing I saw all evening was Clay having a serious conversation with Warren Bregel. Clay's face looked like he was sitting on the john with one hand in the oven—maximum effort with maximum pain. What were you talking about anyway, Clay— *The Origin of Species?*"

"Close," smiled Clay. "He introduced me to his fiancée."

"His what?"

"His bride-to-be in two weeks."

"You mean that nice little student nurse? She's going to marry him? What a shame—can't she see what she's getting into?"

"Yeah, maybe it was a blind date or something," said Dan.

"Also," said Clay, "he told me I was too fat!"

"You're not fat!" exclaimed Bart. "Dan's fat, but you're not." Dan grimaced at him.

"You can't see it—he says it's on my soul."

"Soul-talk from him! Strange source! But what made him think he was in any position to judge?"

"I don't know that he did. I think he only wanted to tell me not to expect any help from him even if I do need it. He seems to think that next year we'll be in competition with each other."

"Well, you will be that, won't you?"

"I don't know. I guess so, in a sense, but I never thought of it that way."

"You probably want to stay here, don't you, to take your residency?"

"I'm not sure yet. It's four more years here, you know, the longest in the country. At this point all I know is I'd like to be good. If that means staying here, maybe that's what I do want."

"The thing about guys like Warren is, they take everything personally. To him, you won't be trying to get good surgical training, you'll be fighting against him."

"Well, maybe there's something to be said for his viewpoint—he finished number two in the class, didn't he?"

"Yeah, but what's he got now except a class standing? We maybe didn't do as well, but we came out all right, we have our degrees."

"But maybe that's not enough," said Clay thoughtfully, "and

maybe we'll find that he got more out of medical school than we did. Maybe he learned more than we did. Anyway, it'll be interesting to see."

"Well, gentlemen, here's to medical school! Because of it, we'll never forget each other," said Dan.

"You're right, Dan," said Clay. "I'll never forget the smell of your socks on laundry day, once a month or two."

"Nor your snoring, Clay. On occasion it's symphonic. It'll ring in my ears forever."

"Well, now we'll go out and learn how to be good doctors and recognize our limitations," said Bart Mateer.

"Well, we haven't found ours yet," put in Dan. "Maybe there'll be a sign like on the ski lifts: 'Doctors with limited abilities get off here.'"

Clay laughed. "Let's just hope they let us stay on the lift past the novice level."

. . . .

Dr. Clayton Hallam stirred in his bed in Marburg I. His eyelids fluttered, and blurred consciousness returned. Where the hell am I? he thought. And what is this thing in my nose?

CHAPTER 3

Saturday, May 11, 1985

The visitors' lounge on Marburg I was nicely appointed. There were tall french windows, but the sun shone in unkindly on the fake oriental rug and featureless orange sofas and chairs. Tables offered magazines, and Anne Hallam was reading from an old *Reader's Digest* that had happened to be on top of the pile.

She glanced up from the sofa at her daughter, who was standing by one of the windows and gazing thoughtfully into the courtyard.

"You all right, Charlie?" she asked softly. Her voice was low and soothing and still retained traces of the southern accent that had marked it more heavily in earlier years. She was not a large woman, but her upswept gray-gold hair and level blue eyes increased her stature. There was a felicity of expression in her features that was at once charming and childlike. On seeing them together one would not have guessed that she and Charlotte were related, except for this elusive quality of expression that had somehow been passed on to the daughter without concomitant similarity in looks or coloring. She looked at Charlotte searchingly, and only her small hands twisting nervously at the end of the rope belt of her fashionable black dress indicated that anything in her world was amiss.

The sound of footsteps approaching the lounge caused both women to turn and face the open doorway, and when Jim entered the room he found them awaiting him expectantly. "He's just awakened, Mrs. Hallam. I think perhaps you could see him now for a few minutes." As both women started for the door, he added, "It might be better to go in one at a time."

Charlotte smiled at her mother and turned again to her post at the window as the two left the room. She felt relieved that her father had regained consciousness, for the possibility that he might slip away without seeing her again had been her greatest fear. Their relationship had not been close. Her father was much older than she and, as long as she could remember, had been increasingly absorbed in his work. He seldom discussed his work with her. For years, especially since her brother had died, she had made sporadic attempts to bridge this gap, but she was defeated not only by the inadequacies of her own knowledge but also by the geographical restraints imposed by her attendance at college and her father's frequent traveling as a neurosurgeon of world-wide renown. In the beginning, defeat had frustrated and disappointed her. She felt an almost intended rejection by him, but later a conscientious analysis had led her to conclude that such rejection was only partial and that, while certain aspects of his life remained obscure, as a father at least she knew him better. She remembered him to be capable of warmth and kindness when she was a child, and patient as she grew older. And as she did so, her regard for him increased. She could remember her jealousy of her brother at one point for his apparently closer relationship to her father, but as she matured she learned to accept what gender kept from her. If someone had told her that with this acceptance she also found a measure of her own independence from him, she would not have believed it.

A sound behind her broke in on her thoughts, and she turned to see Jim standing in the open doorway.

"I hope you'll excuse me, Miss Hallam," he said. "I've left them for a few minutes, and thought perhaps you might like a cigarette."

"Oh, thank you, yes," Charlotte nodded, and gazed at him for a moment as he lit it. "How is he?"

Jim paused before answering, balancing the inadvisability of raising her hopes too high against his desire to encourage her.

"He seems to be doing fine for this stage of things," he said. "Everyone thinks he's going to make it, all right."

She gave a relieved sigh, and ground out her cigarette.

"I hope you'll forgive me—I guess I really don't feel like smoking."

"Of course," he responded. "I'd better get back anyway. I just wanted you to know that everything possible is being done for him and that meanwhile, if there's any way that I can help you or your mother, any questions, or messages, or anything, I hope you'll let me be of service."

She looked at him quickly, full of gratitude, and in this instant their eyes met and they became more fully aware of each other.

The moment ended, and Charlotte was able to answer Jim's offer. "Yes, I . . . thank you, Doctor . . . "

"Gallier—Jim Gallier, Miss Hallam." He hesitated a moment longer and then turned and left the room.

Anne Hallam leaned forward and gazed down at her husband. He was so still he seemed not to breathe, and her heart lurched as the possible significance of his quiet occurred to her. She glanced hastily at the nurse, but at that moment he stirred, his head turned slowly on the pillow and his eyes opened and looked up into her face.

She smiled at him, while two tears that she hadn't known were there slipped down her cheeks. "Hello, Clay," she whispered.

The light of recognition burned dimly in his eyes, and his hand rose feebly off the bed and then sank back, as his lips formed the word "Anne."

"Anne . . . " And the mist formed again before his eyes.

· · · ·

The wedding invitation read "Saturday, June 15, 1938." Clay had arrived in Richmond with his parents four days before, as had been suggested by Mrs. Grier, Anne's mother, in order to allow plenty of time for preparations and to give the families a chance to "really get to know one another" before the wedding. "Hmmph," his father had snorted when news of this plan first reached him. "If I'd gotten to know that woman as many times as she's suggested it since you and Anne were engaged, I'd know her better now than I know your mother."

"Clayton! She's only trying to do the right thing," Mrs. Hallam had remarked.

"Well, Martha, in my experience there are two ways of doing the right thing. One way is to do it, and the other is to overdo it. And I think she tends to do the latter."

Clay grinned as he listened to this repartee. His father was a tall, portly, silver-haired man with the outspoken ways and forthright opinions of one who is used to having his advice sought. He always claimed that half his wife's time was spent in chiding him for what he had said already, and the other half in trying to prevent him from saying anything like he was going to say next. The truth was, however, that he took pleasure in the gentle scolding. Thus, both were prone to exaggerate the opportunities in order that the ritual be repeated. With them it was an act of love that grew out of his natural propensity for frankness and bluffness and hers for shyness and reserve. Both had the luxury of understanding that fifty-odd years of married life had never revealed any serious division between them.

Nevertheless, before they had departed Dr. Hallam had drawn Clay aside and in his direct manner had spoken to him on subjects that both were to remember later on.

"Now, Clay," he began, "I want you to understand that what I'm going to say casts no reflection on Anne. I think she's a wonderful girl and will make a splendid wife. She's been brought up by her parents, however, and that's a little bit of a different matter, which is why I wanted to speak to you.

"As we've already discussed, I'm prepared to provide reasonable financial assistance for as long as you need it . . . "

"Dad, you know Anne and I have already worked this out. We'll receive room and board from the hospital, and we figure we can make it if you could let us have about one hundred a month. I expect to pay you back."

"Fine, son, fine." Dr. Hallam smiled. "And I think it's good that you have a financial plan worked out. But I just wanted to suggest that you not be too hard on Anne if she occasionally steps beyond the budget. She's been brought up to have whatever she wants, and the adjustment may be difficult for her for a time. Has she considered part-time work?"

"Yes, we've discussed it. Her parents, of course, are dead against it."

"Hmm. Well, it's for you two to work out, and I'll have no hand in it. Personally, though, I think it would be a good idea just from the standpoint of giving her something to occupy her time, because you're going to be mighty busy.

"Now, about her parents. As you know, her father is a lot richer than I am, and I expect that he will try to force money on you, or at least on Anne. How you handle this will be your problem, but personally, I wouldn't take it. It would obligate you, and perhaps open the door for other incursions."

"Like what?" answered Clay.

"Oh, on your future, maybe. Your future's your own now, yours and Anne's, and I'll be hornswoggled if I'd let anybody else decide it for me."

This ended the discussion, but it seemed to Clay an indication of something he already knew, regretted, but had come to accept—that there could never be any close relationship between Anne's parents and his own. He had seen the differences between them from the first, but even now he could not see that it really mattered so long as their superficial associations were harmonious. After all, he and Anne were the ones who were getting married, and they understood each other. Beyond this application of his father's words, therefore, and an appreciation of them as well meaning, he attached to them no particular significance and especially no sense of danger.

The trip to Richmond, in Dr. Hallam's conservative black Dodge, was a pleasant though lengthy one, and their greeting by the Griers when they arrived at the imposing colonial mansion was in the best tradition of southern hospitality. The ensuing days before the wedding turned into a whirl of social activities, for the Griers produced to meet the new in-laws a whole host of the elite in Richmond society, plus numerous near and distant relations, only one of whom Clay could later remember with any degree of clarity.

This was an uncle of Anne's whom he met at an afternoon reception given for them by the Griers on the rolling lawn that stretched away for several acres at the rear of their home. The day was bright and sunny, and multicolored umbrellas, chairs, and tables had been scattered about. The guests had assembled, filling the green lawn spaces among the tables and chairs. It was not until he had been in the receiving line for almost an hour that Clay managed to head toward the bar, which had been set up in the shade of one of the great elm trees near the house. It was here, while awaiting the production of a mint julep, that he found himself standing by the side of an elderly man with a very pink face, who looked vaguely familiar. The two shifted uncomfortably in each other's company for a minute, undecided as to whether to speak or to walk off as fast as possible in opposite directions. Clay at last broke the silence.

"A very pretty scene from here, isn't it, sir?" he said tentatively, indicating the tableau that sloped gently downward from their vantage point in a series of terraces to where the main body of the party was located. The chatter of mingled voices and the music of a small string ensemble were muted as the sounds reached their ears. Groups of ladies with parasols escorted by perspiring gentlemen from umbrella to umbrella lent the scene an aspect reminiscent of an impressionist painting.

"Wmm!" said he of the pink face. "Where the women come and go, talkin' of General Lee and Shiloh," and he looked at Clay shyly, as if for signs of approval or disapproval of his paraphrase.

Clay parried the remark with a smile. "But they manage to look mighty attractive while they are about it," he encouraged.

"Delightful! All the lovely ladies and men. But then they've had a lot of practice, and, after all, practice plus training adds up to that euphemistic term of human behavior called breeding, which is one of Richmond's largest exports. Why, that's really what you're watching here today—a Richmond breeding session. Look at 'em! Not a flaw, not a simple loose end, not a discordant note. Everybody takin' part, everybody knows his lines. Men shake hands with each other and bow to the ladies, who talk to each other and walk with the gentlemen, who bow to the ladies and shake hands with each other. The dance of life—the summit or the depths of social achievement. I've watched 'em for years like this, seen 'em get better and better at it—in fact, used to be in it myself at one time, until one morning I woke up, or went to sleep, and vaporized myself. But that's another story. And I imagine it would be pretty hard to distract you today, wouldn't it?"

Clay, who had listened with fascination to the man's remarks, suddenly laughed. "I guess you're right. I'm Clay Hallam, and probably nothing could carry me too far off today."

"I'm Randolph Grier, Dr. Grier's brother—his older brother. Welcome to the family."

Clay gripped his hand in surprise, for he could not recall Anne having referred to an older uncle on her father's side. He remembered two younger brothers of Dr. Grier, as well as a number of other relatives, but never this particular gentleman, Clay was sure. He studied him more attentively.

He was of medium height, but so slender that he appeared fragile. He had a high brow and a bulbous head, and his remaining hair was fine, light brown, and streaked with gray. His features were small, the nose sharp and almost recessed under the forehead. His speech and bearing were soft, even effeminate, a characteristic that he evidently tried to counter by occasionally hitching his trousers or pulling his nose. His resemblance to Anne's father was more in coloring and accent of speech than in similarity of features. Yet these points alone were sufficient to establish them as brothers.

"Thank you, sir," answered Clay. "I'm glad to join the family."

"I'm happy to tell you that you've chosen the best of all entrances into it. Anne has always been my choice of all the Grier clan, perhaps as the one with the best chance of—uh—departing it."

"Oh, are you welcoming me in only to invite me to leave?" asked Clay, not certain how to take this new-found relative, but hoping he was attempting humor.

"Not at all," said Mr. Grier, eying Clay a little slyly. "I was merely alluding to what I call 'Grierism,' or the condition of being a Grier. But perhaps you are already familiar with it."

"No, I'd like to hear about it," said Clay slowly. He watched him take a deep draught from his mint julep and realized that Mr. Grier was tight.

"You will, you will, Clay, and soon—I know," said Mr. Grier, looking about him a little nervously and eying his watch. "Well, well, I must go—sorry. Glad to meet you. Every happiness. Remember, it's most important being a Grier—was one myself once, before I vaporized." His voice trailed off as he backed away just as Anne appeared at Clay's side.

"Was that Uncle Randolph you were talking to, Clay?"

Clay nodded assent. "Unless it was the rabbit from *Alice in Wonderland*."

Anne laughed. "That's him, all right. What did he say?"

"Well, he was a little tight, and maybe a little bitter, although it wasn't really an angry bitter, more of, sort of . . . uh, wry bitter, I would say. And it seemed to be mainly about the family."

Anne smiled and nodded. "Yes, that's Uncle Randolph when he's had one or two drinks, which he does do very often, actually."

She paused but, in answer to Clay's questioning look, continued.

"He's always been sort of the family eccentric, different from the rest, and left out of many of the family affairs. He's been what I suppose you might call ineffectual. You see, most of the Grier men are what Daddy calls producers. They all do things that are significant and contribute to the general welfare of the family. For example, there's Uncle Louis over there, he's a stockbroker, and Cousin Horace with him is a banker, and so on. It's sort of expected of a Grier man to go into some line that will help the family, and this will in turn help him, because then he gets to handle the family business."

"Very good. Kind of an ingrown community."

"Oh yes, very organized. They even have family meetings once a month or so, I suppose to sort things out and see what the family interests are. Grier ladies are not invited to the meetings, so I don't know for sure."

"And what about Uncle Randolph?"

"Well, he's still a bit of a mystery. To begin with, he's the most cultured and most highly educated of the Griers . . . unless you want to count Daddy's four years of medical school as an education." She smiled as Clay grunted. "But it usually comes out only when he has had a few drinks, or if you are on close terms with him, as I once was. You see, I have always found in him some of the qualities I think of as yours, dear, a kind of broad-mindedness, tolerance . . ." Their looks met warmly for a moment. "But he withdrew from me, a few years ago, as he already had from the rest of the family. His great sin, if it is a sin, is that he has been a nonproducer, a noncontributor to the family."

The party caught them up in more introductions and pleasantries, separated them and reunited them and parted them again, but Clay found himself returning again and again to the personality and comments of Randolph Grier. Later, after the guests had departed and evening was quietly coming to Richmond, when he and Anne and Dr. and Mrs. Grier and Dr. and Mrs. Hallam were sitting in the hammock and chairs under the elms and discussing the party, he reintroduced the subject.

"One of the people I enjoyed meeting the most, Mrs. Grier, was your brother-in-law Randolph."

"Oh, poor Randy," Mrs. Grier said, laughing. "The whole family worried about him for years, but now we've just about given up on him. I'm surprised he even came today."

"What do you mean, given up on him?"

"Why for years we waited for him to accomplish something, to do something with himself. He's very bright, you know—he graduated from the university and then went to Harvard Law School and got his degree. But he came back to Richmond and has done nothing ever since but, guess! . . . play bridge!"

"Play bridge?" Mrs. Hallam said.

"Can you imagine it?" Mrs. Grier continued. "Never married, never worked, just played bridge for the last thirty years. And the opportunities he had." She shook her head and sighed, telling the story with polish as if she had told it many times that way. "Why, he plays bridge four, if not eight, hours every day. He keeps a little notebook with his bridge engagements in it, and he stays booked two to three weeks in advance." She shook her head again. "A great waste— but, of course, he is a good bridge player, they say," and she laughed.

Mrs. Grier was an attractive, carefully coiffured woman whose features and manner were already showing the constant strain of maintaining her prominence in Richmond society. Capable of kindness and great generosity, she was nonetheless ridden by the idea of who she was, and therefore the thought of who she must be—not only because of her name but also because her husband, her family, her world, expected it of her—was a continuing challenge to any quiet moments she might have had. To Clay, who viewed Anne as one of her attributes, Mrs. Grier was mildly amusing, but to his parents, who had a somewhat more dispassionate view, she was a little too frenetic for comfort.

A candlelit dinner was served to the immediate family in the tall-ceilinged dining room: iced tea and cold fried chicken, fresh corn and grits, served on silver and French bone china. Mrs. Grier commented on the merits of good, simple food. Clay suspected that what she was saying was how marvelous it is that such fine, wealthy people will eat such simple food. He would probably have said this to Anne, but never had opportunity to in the light of a subsequent event.

Dr. Grier presided at dinner. As Clay observed him, he seemed a man at the very height of his power, energy, and charm. He was of medium frame, not an ounce overweight, and had aristocratic good looks with an abundance of dark and graying hair. He was in his mid-fifties. His most outstanding attribute, however, was an intimation of absolute coordination in everything he did, as if in this man, at least, all the machinery, both mental and physical, was working smoothly and together. His bearing and motion were easy and graceful, his speech and manner were urbane and polished. He looked effective in the white dinner jacket he wore this evening, but Clay had no doubt that he was just as effective in his surgical garb. Clay could also see that his parents were impressed despite themselves by the charm and easy worldliness of Dr. Grier.

After dinner, he invited Clay and Dr. Hallam into his spacious study for a cigar.

"Well, only two more days to the wedding," Dr. Grier began, selecting a thin cigarillo from the silver box and passing it to Dr. Hallam, "and time we all sat down and had a talk. Clay, what are your plans for the future? Are you going down to join your father?" He looked at both of them pleasantly.

"Oh, I doubt that he'll want to do that when the time comes," Dr. Hallam said lightly. "He'll be a little too high-powered to join an old general practitioner like me, and I doubt if either he or Anne would want to live in Bloomington."

"It's . . . too early to make any decision yet," Clay said. "I've a lot more training ahead."

Dr. Grier drew on his cigar and looked at Clay. "How much do you know about our setup here in Richmond, Clay?"

"Well, more or less just what you and Anne have told me, plus what a few people on our staff at Johns Hopkins said when they learned I was marrying Anne—that you are the head of the Grier Clinic, which is one of the largest privately owned hospitals in the United States, and that it's well run and well thought of everywhere."

Dr. Grier nodded and seemed pleased. "Yes, the hospital was started by my great-grandfather Dr. Darcey Grier, and carried on and expanded by my father, Randolph, and his brothers, and more recently by me.

"It's entirely family-owned and -operated, and the corporation, of which I'm the president, hires the doctors who staff it. Let's see now, at present we have 160 beds and fourteen doctors on our staff, including surgeons, internists, obstetricians. Our annual payroll is about one million dollars, and our annual gross is around four million."

Both Clay and Dr. Hallam whistled at these revelations.

Dr. Hallam said, "I've heard a lot about the clinic, of course, but I had no idea it was on that scale."

Dr. Grier smiled again. "The figures are not for common knowledge, of course. But you can see how big the operation is and can therefore imagine the size of the problems in running it. It would take a large family to do it."

Here he paused for a moment and sipped his brandy. "Fortunately, we have the family that can do it. Through our family connections in banking, business, manufacturing, and so forth, we get the very best in equipment, food, services, at the lowest possible rates, which gives us a large advantage over other hospitals. With myself as head of the hospital and also president of our family endeavors, a high degree of coordination of all activities is possible. In all modesty, I must say that we have been very successful to date. Again, our family name and connections in business bring us a large supply of patients. And the cost of hospital labor in these times is cheap."

He paused again and looked at Clay and Dr. Hallam. "However, like you, Clay, I have to look at the future. I'm fifty-four now, and I think I'm in reasonably good shape. But one never knows, and there may be a day coming along soon where I may want to retire!

"There are two other family members on the medical staff at the clinic. These are my Uncle Laurence, who is almost eighty, and my younger brother Kit, who is an internist and who really isn't equipped to lead. Besides, I think a surgeon should be the head of the Grier Clinic—it's primarily a surgical hospital, and also that's where the money is!"

He smiled confidentially at the Hallams.

"But Anne told me about a cousin of hers who is in medical school," Clay said.

Dr. Grier continued smiling. "Yes, Kit's son is in his second year at the Medical College. But, just among the three of us, it was political pull that got him in, and I don't think he's the timber I'm looking for.

"Now, as you know, Anne is my youngest child and third daughter, and frankly, if she had been a boy I would have made a surgeon out of her, come hell or high water." He got up from his chair in his earnestness and leaned against the edge of his desk. "But the next best, and possibly the best, thing has happened, for her and perhaps for you and also for the family, which is that she is marrying you, Clay."

The wedding was lovely. Saint Peter's Episcopal Church was garlanded with heliotrope, hibiscus, and gardenias, and the five hundred guests agreed that the church had never looked prettier. The bishop himself conducted the wedding ceremony. Bart and Dan performed their duties as head ushers flawlessly, and the lawfully wedded couple leaving the church entered into a bountiful sunny day with white puffs of clouds in the sky and the air full of the gardenias Anne carried because they were her favorite flowers.

In the limousine on the way to the country club reception, Clay took Anne in his arms and pressed her close.

"At last, we can do it in public. But what price, legality."

Anne smiled. "You were magnificent. You should get married all the time . . . but I hope you didn't mind it too much—all the excesses, that is. Mom and Dad."

"I know, sweetheart, you don't have to say anything. I wanted us to have a great wedding, and a happy one, and it is. It's as good as a meadow by a brook would have been."

"I'll love you always," Anne replied.

Seven hundred and forty-two guests had been invited to the reception, and approximately that many came, the only notable exception being the governor, who had other commitments but sent a representative. The afternoon was well advanced by the time every hand had been shaken and the photographs taken, but the orchestra was very good, and Bart seized Anne away from the receiving line and led her onto the dance floor. As they moved among the other dancers, accepting humorous comments and greetings as they went, Bart smiled down at Anne.

"Well, we brought it off!" he said.

Anne smiled up at Bart, and she swayed a little dreamily with the music as she replied, "Yes, you and Dan were magnificent."

"Well, you two made it easy, it's so obvious that you belong together."

With a little laugh, Anne said, "I think so, too. I'm only sorry we won't be able to be there next week when you and Betty are married. But we'll still be away."

"We'll miss you, but we understand—and we'll be seeing you a lot during the next year. As you know, I'll be interning at Hopkins on the Eye Service. We'll be living not far from you."

"That's right, we're counting on that—my love to Betty," she said as she turned to greet the man who had cut in on them. There followed a steady stream of new partners until, as happened to her occasionally, when she was happy and had had just the right amount of champagne, or Kentucky whiskey, she became almost mesmerized by the music, became one with it, so her body and mind and the music moved as if joined. She felt herself changing partners again and heard Dan say to her, "Ah, I can see you're ready for me, now!"

The music had suddenly increased in tempo, and, as Anne looked at the challenge in Dan's grinning features, she smiled back and said, "Okay, boy, let's see!" She kicked off her shoes, and suddenly they were soaring on the music, apart, their hands joining only occasionally, feet off the ground more often than on, to the applause of the crowd gathering around them. Anne had to lift her long white gown above her ankles, and she had long since doffed her veil. As she danced, her fair complexion gained color, and tiny beads of perspiration formed along her hairline and slipped down her cheeks. On they danced until, at almost the limit of their endurance, Dan suddenly pretended to weaken and collapse onto the floor, while Anne turned and sank back breathless and laughing into the arms of Clay. He looked down at her half-turned in his arms, flushed and warm and with the scent of her body accentuated by the heat, and he thought he had never seen anyone so lovely.

"God, I love you, Anne!" he said, and she laughed up into his eyes.

Two or three people assisted Dan to his feet, and he came over to Anne and Clay, still breathing hard and mopping his face with a handkerchief.

"All I can say is, Clay, you'd better stay in shape if you're gonna live with her."

Clay and Anne laughed. "I'll see to it," she said.

Finally, they were away, the last good-byes said, the last tearful hugs exchanged, the last whispered advice given. The last hand that Clay gripped, almost blindly among many thrust out at him as he was hurrying from the club, was that of Randolph Grier—a warm, soft handclasp that made Clay look into his face. Clay had the distinct impression that Randolph was very shyly and very quietly, but very definitely, laughing at him.

"Good luck, Clay," came his mellow voice. "We'll be seeing you." And then Clay moved past.

The chauffeur drove them to the Richmond train station, where they boarded the Pullman and found their private compartment for the five-hour journey to North Carolina. It was during the trip that they made love for the first time.

They hadn't really thought of it, at first, sitting close together watching the late-afternoon shadows lengthening across the green Virginia countryside, and talking. They discussed the details and incidents of the wedding as a new kind of excitement increased subtly in them, the excitement of the growing awareness of each for the other in the permissiveness of their new relationship, the heady license of feeling and experiences it implied, and the intimacy of their small compartment, until every lurch of the train seemed designed to press them together, and every breath Clay took seemed full of the scent of Anne. Their speech became murmurs, and their eyes glazed with the hypnotic effects of their growing sensation, as their hands sought for more and more intimacies, until Clay said, "Darling, darling," and Anne whispered, "Oh, now, dear, now." They came together like two highly charged energies, and in the end found themselves in a new world, wiser, and awed and cleansed. That night, after they had left the train and ferried across the bay to the Outer Banks, then gone by road to the tiny hotel in Hatteras that was to be theirs for the next two weeks, they lay in bed listening to the sound of the surf roaring in upon the beach.

Anne said, "No going back now, is there? I mean, once you've crossed the bridge, there's no return to the old ways, the old life."

Clay smiled. "We've grown up. But I'll try to see to it that you never want to get back across that bridge."

Thus they spoke in all innocence in the year 1938, when he was twenty-five and she was twenty, in their room overlooking the Atlantic Ocean.

Clay had been to the Outer Banks years before with his father on a short fishing trip, and even then he had felt it was the most wildly romantic spot he had seen. A small four-car ferryboat delivered to the island every day or so, depending on demand, and the drive up the barely paved road from the ferry landing to the only hotel covered more than fifteen miles of empty surf-filled beach on the left and Pamlico Sound on the right. The hotel was a small three-story clapboard and shingled affair with a wrap-around porch and an upper walkway for viewing the ocean. It could accommodate twelve guests. Mrs. Daniels was the proprietress, and when Clay had written her about reservations for him and Anne, she had agreed to meet them at the ferry in her old Ford and convey them to the hotel, which she did. She was a large, active woman in her sixties, who did most of the carpentry, most of the plumbing, and all of the painting required to keep her establishment going. She conspired, however, with the aid of a black cook and several vintage maids, to serve good food and keep the rooms clean. Her mind, therefore, as Clay put it to Anne, was entirely at home, and did very little visiting in other spheres.

The hotel was near the southern tip of Hatteras Island, and at the tip itself was Hatteras Village, a small fishing settlement, consisting of weatherbeaten houses, a general store, and a tiny restaurant.

To be alone, determinedly alone, was the goal Anne and Clay had set for themselves, and mostly they succeeded. They breakfasted together in the small dining room, were smilingly civil to the six or seven other guests, and then, with a load of books, a picnic basket, blankets, and fishing gear, made off for some remote point along the empty beach, where all day long the cries of the seagulls and the roar of the surf were the only sounds that came to them. They made camp in the lee of some of the huge dunes that lined the beach, erected a battered old beach umbrella lent them by Mrs. Daniels, and felt the awe of being alone at one of nature's venting points. The weather was warm and the sun usually bright, but some days the wind would drive the clouds across the sky, and the air above the surf for miles in both directions would be full of the spray of the agitated sea.

In this setting they read, conversed, made love, slept, and walked for long hours through the day. They swam a little, and Clay fished in the surf, but mostly they touched and were together. Free from the stress that plagued most of the world at this time, and confident in themselves, in each other, and in the "rightness" of their marriage, their minds roamed at will over their universe. Anne was the more imaginative, inventive, and willful, all of which were qualities Clay found compelling, while he was more logical, better read, and pragmatic. They considered themselves liberals and discussed the need for

social reform, for government aid to the poor and needy, and for the
stronger measures for relief being brought into action by the Roosevelt administration.

"I wonder how it ever happened," said Clay one day as they sat
eating lunch at the small restaurant in the village, "that you, who
were raised in wealth and never really knew the ills of poverty, could
have such great feeling for the poor."

"Maybe it's because I'm so selfish," answered Anne thoughtfully.
"Perhaps I so like the things that money can buy—comforts, beautiful objects, even social standing—that I think doing without would
be terrible, and that's why I feel so sorry for those who have little. I do
feel great empathy for them. Rest assured that Mom and Dad have
talked to me often enough about the advantages of being rich."

"It doesn't seem to have registered, or else you wouldn't have married me, a poor aspiring physician."

Anne smiled. "My father has said that sometimes he thinks I'm
not his child. He says sometimes he thinks that a little of Uncle Randolph rubbed off on me." She looked at Clay. "By the way, did Uncle
Randolph say anything to you about being 'vaporized,' as he puts it?"

"Yes, he mentioned that." Clay smiled. "What did he mean?"

Anne replied, "That he suddenly and inexplicably renounced his
position as head of the family enterprises. He gave up his law practice, totally, and withdrew completely into an entirely frivolous career
of playing bridge. He fully realized at the time, and has said to us
since, that he became of no further use to the family, and thus he
vaporized himself as far as the Griers were concerned."

"But how about as far as he himself is concerned, and the rest of
the world? After all, your family, great as it is, is not everything."

"Oh, of that I'm not sure. I was much closer to him when I was
younger, and he did have considerable influence on me. But he told
me once that he had awakened one night with a terrible sense that
something was wrong, and then he had a sort of revelation, in which
he became suddenly aware of the hypocrisy of his life. Within a week
after this, he resigned his law practice, moved out of the great house,
renounced his family and friends, and began his new life. Of course, I
was quite young at the time, but it caused a huge furor, not only in

the family but I think through the whole state. Whether he accomplished anything by doing it, or justified himself, I don't know, and could never ask."

"Do you think he's had second thoughts?"

Anne shrugged. "The last time we talked about it was a year or two ago, and I remember him saying that when he had made the decision he suddenly felt free as the wind, but then, a little later in the conversation, he reminded me that the wind has very little substance."

"Fascinating! But speaking of wind," said Clay, pushing his chair back and looking for the waitress, "let's go rent a sailboat for tomorrow. We might see just how little substance the wind really has."

So they left the sounding sea and sailed instead on the vast sound that separates Hatteras from the mainland, in a little sailboat Clay was able to obtain from the son of a local fisherman. The day began beautifully with a bright sun and a sparkling breeze that was fully as much as Clay, whose seamanship was limited, wanted to handle. Anne was a more experienced sailor than he was, and they spent an exciting morning tacking the stout little boat back and forth across the wind, taking the spray as it came over the high side of the bow with gasps at the cold shock, and then enjoyed drying in the sun.

At first Clay was careful to stay fairly close to the wharf area, but gradually his confidence grew, and as their spirits soared he set out on a close reach with the wind and the sun over the starboard beam, his right arm around Anne, sitting beside him in the cockpit, and his left hand holding the tiller, which took them far out across the sound toward the mainland. He was vaguely aware of the passage of time, but his senses were so filled with the touch of Anne's warm skin against him, the occasional scent of her blown on the wind in their faces, the sun and the cool spray, and the sound of the wind in the rigging and of the hull chunking the water that he could not have changed course even if he had wanted to, for fear of breaking the magic.

He was a little perturbed when the mainland appeared before them, so much closer, and on putting about, to see how far was their return. And then, as if their turning about affected natural events in some way, the sky almost lazily began to cloud and the wind's edge sharpened. It also shifted a little to the north, so before long Clay found they were running before it.

"Could be a storm coming up. Maybe we should put in on this side instead of trying to get back."

He looked at Anne and saw that she had already appreciated the change in weather. Her color had heightened, and a new light was in her eyes, and even her voice was pitched with excitement as she shook her head.

"Oh, let's go on—we can make it—what a run it will be!"

So on they tore in front of the muscular wind, on a darkening sea whose swollen waves now sent them planing on top for twenty yards at a time, and then dropped them to wallow briefly in a trough before swinging them up again. Clay was severely extended to keep the boat on course and to avoid a jibe that might have snapped the mast or boom and, after several close calls, asked Anne if she wanted to take the tiller. She declined, saying he was doing fine, and seemed to feel that they were considerably less close to disaster than he would have thought they were. Clay had not seen her like this before, calm and yet full of an intense excitement that was almost palpable.

It began to rain lightly, and Anne brought out of their duffel two light windbreakers she had taken to protect them from the sun, and she tied her hair back with a soggy piece of string. Then, suddenly, they slipped into a trough and yawed violently, and the boat surrendered its starboard stay. The mast bent ominously, but, as Clay came up into the wind, Anne was able to snare the loose stay and tie it to a cleat with an end of rope she had found under the deck. At her advice, they lowered the sail a bit, yet they drove forward under the gradually increasing pressure of the wind. Occasionally, a gust would wrench the sails and boom violently and snatch at the rigging, and Clay was sure the whole ensemble was going to be torn from the boat, but somehow it held.

The rains began to increase, and Clay could no longer see the shoreline or their own little dock. This scarcely mattered, however, because there was very little choice except to run on full before the wind as they were doing, for to attempt to head up at all would have either turned them over or swamped them by taking one of the waves broadside. As it was, they were taking quite a bit of water, which Anne, sitting up ahead of Clay, was bailing continuously with a tin can.

The sensation of a deepening fear for Anne was a new one for Clay. He wanted to touch her, to communicate with her, and to reassure her, but he kept his grip on the tiller. As he looked at her back, wrapped in the faded slicker, hunched down in front of him resolutely bailing water into the scuppers, he felt very proud of her. His own apprehension was diminished by her resoluteness.

Miraculously, the wind began to abate, and in front of them they could see the shoreline and then their own small jetty, which they had missed by only a few hundred yards. When Clay finally brought the boat up into the wind, he saw that the whole family, except for the fisherman himself, was awaiting them on the dock. They stood silently on the bank, shrouded in the driving rain like Druids, until Clay and Anne luffed the boat up to the jetty and lowered the sail, and then the fourteen-year-old son came down to them. "We was about to come look for you," he said. "It's beginnin' to blow up pretty good." He nodded at the boat, saying, "You can leave her now. I'll do the rest."

"Well, take good care of her," Clay said gratefully, "she got us through out there. It's not blowing as hard now as it was."

"Oh, that's cuz you're under the banks," replied the boy, helping them up on the jetty and stepping into the boat himself. "Outside it's blowin' frightful, and the fleet's just comin' up the inlet—bet they're havin' fun. I'd be down there now 'cept for you all."

Clay and Anne paused only long enough to dry themselves and change clothes, then headed in their old rented Ford for the inlet. They were tired from the arduous sail, yet exhilarated by their success, and neither felt ready for the day to end.

The Hatteras Inlet is never quiet even on calm days, for it is narrow, with extensive shoals that funnel and increase the run of the tide through it. The fishermen that use it and its sister channel to the south, Ocracoke Inlet, as their gateways to the ocean from the quieter, protected waters of the sound, are aware of its vagaries, however, and are usually able to steer their ships in groups to enter between the strongest pulls of the wind and tide. There is a hook in the direction of Hatteras shoreward just above the inlet, so when the wind is in the north, and especially of any force, it takes a very strong motor and a knowledgeable skipper to warp his boat up through the channel without being swept off course and onto a windward shore.

On this day, the fishing fleet had been caught out by the storm, and although most of the boats had already beaten their way through the inlet by the time Clay and Anne arrived, and were heading for their safe berths in the sound, at least three or four were still fighting their way, single file, up the foam-lashed channel. The lead boat was almost directly between the two sides of the inlet, and from their vantage point on the rough stone jetty overlooking the water's edge, the Hallams could see the captain straining forward on the rudder line to keep the bow up into the channel. Spray erupted under the bow and shot back over the cockpit, driven by the gale, as, with motor open full and propeller lashing the water astern, she inched slowly forward, as if in defiance of natural law.

"It's going to be close," said Clay, "especially for the boats behind this one." Anne squeezed his arm. "That engine had better hold out," he muttered.

Suddenly two other oilskinned figures appeared in the cockpit of the boat, leaning out red-faced and grimacing into the wind. They stretched long grappling hooks toward the water, and it was only then that Clay, following their eyes to his right, saw what they were attempting.

A battered but rugged tugboat had appeared just at the inside of the mouth of the inlet and, facing into the wind, had backed itself into alignment with the fishing boat, and the distance between them was narrowing. A thick black line had already been extended from a winch at the rear of the tug into the water and was swept greedily by the wind and tide down to the embattled fishing boat. Expert arms grappled the double-headed line out of the water and laboriously made it fast to both port and starboard stanchions. Hand signals passed between the two boats, and, with a loud blast of its horn, the tug simultaneously began winding in and moving forward up-channel toward the quiet of the sound. Its huge rear propellers took hold of the water and exploded under the stern, the line between it and the fishing boat sprang taut out of the spray, and the fisher, whose own engine was now turned off, began to move miraculously forward against the protesting elements. Only the experts on land could see the battle waged by the helmsman against the yaw and pitch and the careful play of the winchers to ease or pull on the line to keep the bow of the fisher from being pulled under by the line.

In minutes the feat was done, and both boats had disappeared out of the channel and around the headland on their right. Only moments later, the tug was back in the channel to pick up the next boat in line.

Oblivious to the wind that heaved at them and the rain that drove at any opening in their slickers, Clay and Anne hunkered together, spellbound at the brawny drama of the rescue operation, and watched until each fishing boat had been plucked and hauled in by the foaming tug. Then, numbed and exhausted by the tensions of the last several hours, they walked in from the jetty and over to the small restaurant beside the harbor. They could see that the tug was just putting in.

The restaurant was a haven of warmth, and the rich smell of coffee revived them almost as soon as they entered. Finding it empty, however, their eyes soon went to a window in the rear, through which they could see that a crowd had gathered on the dock beside the tug and that something was being carefully passed from tug to shore.

"Someone's been hurt," said Clay. He and Anne hurried toward the restaurant's back door, which led out to the dock, but as they reached the door it exploded in upon them, and they were swept aside by burly rain-slickered fishermen, who carried between them a similarly attired man.

"Put him on that table there," cried a voice at the rear of the group. "Now stand back—and keep the rest of the crowd outside—give him air!" The owner of the voice turned toward the crowd that was beginning to enter the doorway. "Out—out!" he shouted, and forced them back and closed the door. Moving back to the table quickly, he whipped off his own rain gear, saying, "Off with his clothes—careful—quickly—get off that slicker—okay, the sweater. Put something under his head!"

The voice was that of authority, and it was obeyed, but the figure that emerged from the rain gear was much less so, a small, portly man

with graying hair who was dwarfed by the burly figures of the fishermen. Clay and Anne, totally ignored, stood silently watching as this
little man approached the victim, who was in his early thirties and
obviously in great distress, gasping for breath and barely conscious.

"What happened?" the examiner demanded.

"He was on the winch, Doc, and somehow the gear slipped. The
handle gave him a wham in the chest—knocked him back against
the rail. He said it hurt and appeared okay for a while, but on the way
in he began to get dizzy and short-winded, and then he just
collapsed."

"Let's get his shirt and undershirt open," Doc muttered as he did
so. "Oh yes, see the red mark forming up on his chest there—right
over his heart—let me look now."

He put his ear over the man's heaving chest, listened for a moment,
and then straightened and shook his head.

"Can't hear a thing!" he announced to the hushed group. "Can't
feel his pulse—he's bluer than a spring peeler's bottom and gettin'
cold. Guess his heart's been hurt. Only thing I know to do is to get
him in the car and try to make Manteo Hospital."

The group of men stood numbly considering this opinion. One
said, "That's an hour—hour and a half—at least, Doc."

"Yes, and it's still an hour and a half, but twenty seconds have
passed since you said it, so let's get going."

Men shuffled forward to carry out his bidding, when suddenly another voice, tight and clipped, said, "Wait!"

During the examination Clay had edged his way forward until he
had an unobstructed view of the victim and, listening to the examiner's words as his eye moved over the patient, was about to agree with
the summation given by Doc when his eyes fastened on something
that caused his whole body to snap to attention. The spoken word
"Wait!" was pure reflex. Clay was surprised to hear his own voice, and
it was with great uncertainty that he stepped forward. "I don't want
to interfere," he said deferentially to Doc, "but I thought . . . may I
ask, are you an M.D.?"

Doc stared at him. "Nope—not me. I'm just the closest thing to it
hereabouts. Why, are you one?"

"Well, I just graduated from medical school"—Clay wanted to

add how inadequate that made him—"and I could take a look if you like?"

Doc stepped a bit aside and said, "Hurry."

Clay bent over the man, trying to muster his thoughts and to recall his medical school training. He was young and green, and his movements were not grooved or routine as they would be someday, but, as he forced his mind to focus on the patient, he noted the bluish color of the man's lips and fingers and chest, the ominous coldness and wetness of his skin, the now strident respirations. Clay took these in quickly and then turned to the things that had caused him to step forward in the first place, and they were still there, at close range, just as they had appeared to be from across the room, the greatly distended neck veins.

With growing excitement, Clay placed his ear to the man's chest and confirmed Doc's statement that the heart sounds were almost inaudible. He listened to the lungs and found that there was good air exchange and that neither had collapsed. He felt the abdomen and found it normal. Bent over the heaving body, Clay closed his eyes for a moment and tried to recall the details of the magnificent class lecture in medical school which had engraved in his mind the telltale clue of swollen neck veins. There was something else . . . another clue . . . yes, it occurred to him. He felt desperately for the pulse, just at the wrists, and failed there; then the antecubitals and failed again; and, finally, the great femorals, and there it was, the clue, the sign: the fall in pulse volume as the patient inhaled. Clay made up his mind.

He straightened and said to Doc, "Is there an emergency kit?"

Doc nodded and produced a battered case that was Hatteras's traveling emergency supply.

"Is there a hypodermic needle?"

Doc's eyes widened, but he nodded again, opened the case, and extracted a large syringe with needle attached, which was used for glucose administration.

Clay grasped the syringe, separated the needle, and returned the syringe to Doc.

He looked at the group gathered around him, frozen as myths, silent, expectant, ready to be hostile to his youth, his demotion of their local authority, yet aware of their own impotence.

"I ought to tell you," Clay began in as strong a voice as he could muster, "that I think this is a condition called hemopericardium. Blood collects around the heart and pressures it, so the heart can't work. I can't be certain—I've never seen a case—but all the signs are there. He may die if we don't ease the pressure . . . by letting the blood out. So that's what I'm going to do. Does anybody object?"

There was a low murmur, and Doc finally said, "No, go ahead, if you think it may save him. He's about to die anyway."

Clay took the needle at the haft with his right hand and, feeling the patient's moving chest with his left hand, found the proper spot at about the fifth rib and breastbone juncture. He took a deep breath and slowly plunged the needle into the chest up to the hilt. The group gasped, and cold sweat appeared on Clay's face as the needle sank in. He could feel it pass through one tissue plane—then another—then another. My God, I'm wrong, he thought. Then suddenly there it was. A veritable geyser of blood spurting out of the needle under such pressure that, clearing the end of the table by several feet, it splashed among the spectators and caused them to shrink back in surprise.

For an endless second Clay thought that he had punctured the heart itself, and he was momentarily light-headed with dread, but then, as he looked desperately at the stricken fisherman, miraculous changes began. The previously absent pulses suddenly returned full and bounding under his exploring fingers, respirations became deeper and more regular, and he watched with joy as the skin color changed to a warm and reassuring pink. Within a few seconds more, the glazed and unseeing mask was leaving the man's face, and awareness returned to his eyes. He moved his head slightly and looked up at Clay.

"What the hell happened?" he demanded. Clay looked at him, as tears of emotion filled his eyes. "You're going to be all right, fella. Now just stay quiet while I get this needle out of your chest." He withdrew the needle, from which blood was no longer spurting, and, looking up at the awed crowd, said authoritatively, "Now let's get this man to the hospital fast."

Later that night, long after Clay had made the long ride to the hospital, watching for any signals that would indicate a repeat buildup of blood around the fisherman's heart, and finding none, and after they had freed themselves from the grateful solicitations of the family and other islanders over what the latter regarded as a miracle, Clay and Anne lay in bed listening to the distant surf through the open window.

"God, what a sturdy group of people they are," Clay said in the dark, "living on this little finger stuck out in the ocean, no medical help for miles of land and water, and fighting that"—he indicated the ocean—"every day of their lives."

"I think I understand them," said Anne after a moment. "That sound fills me full of fear at times, full of excitement at others, even loneliness at others . . . but at least it fills me, moves me, makes me feel alive. I think that's why they stay here—the sea gives them life as well as a living."

"Mmm, maybe they do get kind of attuned to it. I really like them. I could easily settle down here."

Anne laughed. "You're funny." She snuggled reassuringly against him. "Now that you're the king here, and I'm sure the most popular man on the island tonight, why of course you want to stay. I'll bet they love you almost as much as I do."

Clay laughed and drew her closer. "How about it then, shall we stay?"

Anne looked up at him and then shook her head. "I like them, and I like their values, but we're not them, and we could never be them." She laughed. "So we'd better get the hell out before they find out about us . . . ."

"Aye, about what sex maniacs we are," Clay finished as he kissed her.

Later that night, they lay awake in bed and smoked silently.

"I was so proud of you today," Anne said.

"I was very lucky," Clay replied. "I could have just as easily been wrong. But you know, darling, the feeling that it gave me, when I

saw I was right, and he was coming around, was the most intense joy
I've ever felt, and it filled me with such a sense of limitless power, as if
there were nothing I couldn't do, and suddenly I loved . . .
everybody."

Anne whispered, "Christ raising Lazarus."

Clay looked toward her in the darkness. "Yes, I suppose . . . like
he must have felt, except for one difference, that Christ *knew* he could
do it, but I—I was overwhelmed that I could do it. Maybe"—he
leaned toward her—"maybe that's what medicine and being a doctor
is all about—that intense joy and love and power. . . . All I can say
is, that if there are more moments like this coming . . . it's going to
be quite a life."

And so their idyll ended. Tomorrow they had to return to Baltimore, where Clay would begin his internship. They lay together in
the dark that night, fatigued but too elated by the day's excitement to
sleep. They were pleased with themselves and each other. Each had
lived up to the other's hopes and expectations of what they thought
they had seen in the other. They faced the future with confidence that
they had kept the sacred trust of their own god, and they were not
afraid.

CHAPTER 4

Monday, May 13, 1985

". . . so as you can see," the lecturer intoned, "the pathophysiology of shock is extremely complex and involves not only volume determinants, and small vessel tone, but also oxidation processes at the cell molecular level.

"Now, there are multiple causes of the shock syndrome in man, as you will see on the following slide." As he spoke, he pushed a small button on the rostrum, causing the room lights to dim and the projector to pierce the dark to show a finely printed slide on the screen at his left.

Staring at the screen, Jim Gallier's eyes began to burn mercilessly. He leaned on his elbow, cupping his hand over his eyes, and was grateful to the darkness for keeping others from seeing him. Gradually, he capitulated to the boredom, and his eyes closed completely, freeing his mind from the lecture and allowing it to roam free.

He imagined playing a tennis match against a fellow intern which was to be played the coming weekend. Then, magically, the figure of Charlotte Hallam appeared before him, as if lurking there in the shadows and simply waiting for a chance to appear.

64

He opened his eyes with a start and looked guiltily around, relieved to find it still dark and yet another slide being projected. He looked down at the lecturer.

"Septic shock is quite different, therefore, from cardiogenic shock or hypovolemic shock, although elements of either or both of the latter can be present in any given case of septic shock." Jim closed his eyes again.

Charlotte Hallam. He thought of her as she had been yesterday when he had tried to outline her father's progress for her—where the blood clot had interrupted the circulation in his head and what outcome might be expected. He had watched her glistening brown eyes as he had explained which nerve pathways were damaged and what was taking place in the damaged area. Some of her questions were quite routine ("Will the clot dissolve?" and "Can you bypass it?"), but others showed some unexpected insights, due in part to remembered conversations with her father. Jim had thought her one of the loveliest women he had ever met, a seeming combination of the quiet poise of the mother and the startling good looks of her father. He found that he felt sympathy for her, for while there was no end of supporters who came forward to cheer her and her mother, he remembered that her brother had died and that she was now an only child.

With those last ruminations, Jim opened his eyes again just seconds before the room lights went on.

". . . and so, in the treatment of shock, get your i.v. catheters in, get the O_2 going, give your Ringers Lactate, and have your Dopamine, your Lasix, and your appropriate antibiotic ready!"

There was a scattering of applause, and the audience broke up for the exits.

In the corridor Jim found Jonas, and they headed up the corridor together. "How'd you like it?" Jim asked perfunctorily.

"Torture," was the response. "Pure torture—but we finally got the truth out of him, that shock is still an unsolved mystery. Are you heading for dinner?"

Jim glanced at his watch and shook his head. "I ought to check on Dr. Hallam first. How about joining you in the cafeteria in about a half-hour?"

"That seems possible. By the way, how's he coming along?"

"He's doing very well for his second day into it. He's awake and seems vaguely aware of what's going on. He's got a bit of dysarthria, so it's hard to tell about his sensorium exactly—only a questionable left hemiparesis, though. The CAT scan was negative."

"Well, it sounds like he's going to survive—due in large part to my roomie's good care, I have no doubt. Hey, you're looking a bit seedy, though." Jim felt Jonas eying him as they paused for a moment along the wall of the corridor. "What's the deal, pardner? Is anything wrong?"

"Oh, I got a little sleepy in the lecture," Jim replied. "I guess I'm tired . . . and actually maybe a little discouraged."

"Oh? What about? Family problems? Love problems?"

"No, nothing like that. Uh . . . to tell you the truth, Jonas, I've been wondering lately whether—well, whether I really belong in this place at all. Maybe I ought to take a year off and sort of think things out."

"Holy mother, that is serious!" Jonas exploded. "Especially to drop on me in the middle of the corridor on our way to dinner on a routine Monday evening! How long have you been feeling this way? Why haven't I heard of it before?"

Jim smiled. "I'm sorry, Jonas. I didn't mean to lay this on you now." He realized that he hadn't really meant to bring the subject up, but suddenly it was as if all the words had been gathered and waiting there at the back of his throat, needing only Jonas's presence to release them.

"I've been thinking about it for several months now, but I'm here trying to reason it out myself. I mean, it's my problem."

"Not as long as you've got a roommate, it's not just your problem. It's our problem. Maybe you've just got the intern blues. Many a strong spirit has wilted after nine or ten months of internship life."

"I thought of the possibility," Jim said, "but it's deeper than that. It seemed to begin at the time I got accepted to stay on as assistant resident next year. Now, you know that's a great compliment, and ordinarily even a tired intern would feel elated about it, but I didn't feel elated. In fact, the idea of staying seemed to depress me, and my work hasn't been as good lately—my mind's been wandering, I don't know."

"Hmm," Jonas nodded. "Well, we can't solve it standing here in the hall. I tell you what—you go on up to see Dr. Hallam, and then I'll meet you for supper, and then we'll go up and talk it out tonight. After all, two heads are better than one, especially . . . "

"I know," interrupted Jim, "especially when one is yours. Okay, I'll see you at supper."

Jim headed for the ward feeling better for having told Jonas of his dilemma, but soon found that speaking out had raised his misgivings even more disturbingly. It was not particularly that he was misleading himself by keeping them inside him, but rather that revealing them seemed to make the need for decision and action more imminent, and he did not feel ready for such a momentous confrontation.

He had sailed through four years of medical school, getting good grades and enjoying its camaraderie, with never a doubt that he was happy. The intellectual challenge of understanding the workings of the human body and the aberrations produced by disease seemed totally worthwhile and involving, and it satisfied his natural bent for reading and scientific curiosity. Then, in the middle of his fourth year, his father had died, and with his death Jim soon realized that a measure of his own enthusiasm for his work had died also. His father, a successful stockbroker, had always been immensely proud of the career of his son and took great interest in his accomplishments.

It was natural, therefore, that Jim should miss his support but, nonetheless, he finished medical school and entered his internship year with enthusiasm at putting into practice the knowledge that he had absorbed during his schooling. The erosion of this enthusiasm during this past winter and spring had surprised him, once he became aware of his discontent, and he had spent much time mulling over its cause and extent.

Boredom, he realized, was not a factor. The limitless subtleties of disease and the innumerable variations in diagnostic approaches and treatment were fascinating to him. He realized that this tremendous field for learning might itself be part of the problem. There was so much to know, so much to keep up with, that he couldn't really do it no matter how hard he tried, and this disturbed the perfectionist in him. As long as he could remember, he had heard his father say, "Whatever Jim does, he does well," and no matter which had come first, this statement or his performance, he had found a need to be thorough. In medicine, however, it was impossible to learn it all.

Jonas had once said to him, in one of their early conversations, that "the properly educated doctor is the narrowest guy in town," a remark that he had always disputed until now. In his internship year he had learned that the medicine's educational need was daily and that what medical school had provided was only a basis on which to lay future learning. Between this need and the daily routines of patient care, Jim found that he was extremely constricted in his activities, but only in recent months had he felt the yoke.

He had come to the point of doubting not only the life he had chosen but also himself. He made the error of comparing himself to Jonas and others on the house staff who seemed to have no reservations or problems about dedicating themselves single-mindedly to their work, and in so doing he invariably came to a dwindling opinion of himself. He was, he decided, too shallow, too superficial, to be happy in a field as complex as medicine. Medicine appealed to him as an intellectual exercise, but now to immerse himself in it, to give his life to it, in other words to become serious about it, was more dismaying than he had imagined. The cause for his disquiet, he reasoned, was not simply a difference but a real flaw in his personality, and, in searching even deeper for sources, he conjectured that it was possibly genetically endowed.

Harry Gallier, Jim's father, had inherited both wealth and a seat on the New York Stock Exchange and, being a man of intelligence with a natural acumen in matters of finance, had with little effort managed to increase the sum of his inheritance several-fold. It was his misfortune, however, that his interest in these affairs never measured up to his ability, and, though he spent most of his productive life in manipulating stocks and making money, his approach to the occupation was always more that of the dilettante than the devotee. The uncommitted portion of his time he gave to different activities all aimed at finding what he really wanted to do with his life. All fell, after a short while of fierce burning, into embers. Harry had been a member of the Greater New York State Thoroughbred Racing Commission and the treasurer of the United Church of Unique Salvation, but most recently had been the owner of a small repertory ballet company. All of this, of course, made him a very interesting person; but he was still an unfulfilled and restless one.

His marriages were undoubtedly another expression of his uneasy spirit. After the first had failed due to lack of care, Harry, at age forty, had fallen thrall to the enthusiasm, warmth, and beauty of a nineteen-year-old college student, Sheila Ellender, whom he met when she applied for a summer job with his firm. He married her. Strangely enough, the marriage survived, for, though there were vast differences of age and experience between them, each appreciated what the other contributed to the union, and each liked the effect of marriage as a brace to their disparate interests.

Jim was born not quite nine months after their marriage and grew up pampered by and loving his parents, but he was puzzled by his mother's occasional diffidence and his father's oft-voiced malcontent. In his late adolescence Jim made the decision to become a doctor. He couldn't remember exactly when the inspiration came to him, but he did know that it hadn't emerged overnight but had seemed simply to seep into his awareness. Perhaps a curiosity about scientific matters and his studious bent had some influence on his decision, but he concluded that something even more important was that his maternal grandmother had been a nurse for a short time before she married his grandfather. During his early childhood he was frequently left with "Nanny" when his parents were traveling, and he loved her dearly. He had been terribly distraught when she had died in an automobile accident years before, and he vividly remembered their times together, which included games in which he played "doctor" and stories about doctor-heroes she had known or made up.

When he finally accepted his own decision to become a doctor, his parents were pleased, and his father was particularly enthusiastic, undoubtedly happy that his son had picked a field that promised fulfillment.

Now, however, with his father gone and the internship year slipping by, large questions had begun to appear about the life he was leading. He was, he decided, in need of some guidance.

The nurse looked up as he entered Dr. Hallam's room. She rose to greet him. "Oh, Dr. Gallier."

"Hello, Mrs. Jennings, how're things going?"

"Very well, I think. He was awake a little while ago, but now he seems to have drifted back to sleep. Vital signs are all okay."

"Good. How about intake and output?"

"Doing fine. He's taking fluids well, and his output is good. He hasn't eaten much yet, but that little swallowing problem seems to have improved."

"Maybe we could start giving him some liquid protein supplement now. How's his speech?"

She shook her head slightly. "Still hesitant and a little garbled, although possibly some clearing."

Jim was about to reply when he heard a sound from a corner of the room, and for the first time he noticed Charlotte Hallam sitting in a chair by the window. He reddened slightly as he saw her.

"Oh, Miss Hallam, I'm sorry, I didn't see you sitting there." He stepped toward her.

She rose and extended her hand. "I don't want to interrupt. How are you?" She smiled, and her hand was cool and smooth.

"I'm fine, thanks. How do you think your dad seems this afternoon?"

"I think he's definitely better—more awake, and he did speak a few clear words."

"Do you think he's aware of things?"

"Oh yes! He smiled at me when I came in and tried to say something and, when he couldn't get it out, kind of shrugged and pointed to his head."

Jim smiled. "That may be good—a possible sign that his mind is clearing and won't be impaired. As a neurosurgeon, he may even have diagnosed his own case by now." He gazed at his drowsing patient. "And if so, he knows it's just a question of giving himself more time for this to resolve."

"Do you still think all this may clear—even his speech?"

"I'm very hopeful, and so are all the senior people who have seen him. It usually takes four to five days to get through the worst of it."

They were silent for a moment, gazing at Dr. Hallam, and then Jim asked, "How long have you been here?"

"Just a few hours. I was just getting ready to leave. Mother will be here later."

Jim hesitated a moment and then said, "Look, it's not much of an offer, but how about having dinner with me in the hospital cafeteria? Then you could come back and meet your mother here."

"Well, I . . . Why, that would be lovely. Are you sure it fits in with your schedule?"

"It fits in just splendidly. Mrs. Jennings, we'll be back in an hour."

They turned to make their exit, scraping a chair on the floor as they moved past it. Dr. Hallam awakened to see their retreating figures as the door closed behind them. Once again, in the jumbled circuitry of his brain, as natural processes moved toward repair and recovery from the shock to millions of brain cells, the clear-cut distinctions between past and present were subdued, and perceptions and recollections of the past returned. He remembered . . . he remembered.

• • • •

On the way back from Hatteras in that June of 1938, they had stopped briefly in West Virginia to see his parents and then in Richmond to be with Anne's. Once again, her father had made a point of conducting Clay on a tour through the Grier Clinic and had arranged for him to meet members of the board of directors, visit the operating rooms, and witness the internal workings of the clinic, much of which seemed to center on the billing department.

"The heart of the hospital, Clay," mused Dr. Grier as Clay inspected the well-staffed area. "What comes in and out of here lets the whole clinic function. A lot of my own ideas in here, and I don't mind telling you that the Grier Clinic has one of the highest accounts-receivable returns of any hospital in the whole United States. A lot of it, of course, is because of our clientele. The clinic's reputation and connections permit us to be selective, and we send most of the charity work down to City Hospital, unless of course we need it for occasional public-relations purposes. Also, we tend to send the long and involved surgery, the vascular stuff, Whipple procedures, and so forth, on down to the university, simply because those operations aren't cost-effective. They simply aren't worth the long hours and long recovery periods that are necessary—unless, of course, the client is rich." He smiled and looked at Clay a long moment. "I don't know whether you're ready for all this money talk at your stage of the game, but it's important and, believe me, Clay, gets to be more important as life goes on, as you have children, position, responsibilities."

He glanced away. "I'm being frank with you now, Clay. There was a time when I was young when I visualized this thing as largely a charity clinic, turning away nobody. Fortunately, my daddy and the others were able to show me that this was wrong thinking, because if it became a charity clinic our revenues would go down, and our best patient sources would go down, and our medical staff would go down, and, in short, the clinic would go down."

He stared at Clay. "The clinic is good. It does excellent work. It helps many people go through illness in the most tolerable way possible. And it bestows handsome rewards, financial as well as others, on the doctors who are lucky enough to be on our staff. Will you try and remember all that, Clay, when you go back to Johns Hopkins to intern?"

Clay promised readily that he would, not imagining that it would ever be much of a problem for him and not realizing until much later that, while nothing had been either affirmed or solicited, a point had nonetheless been delicately made.

During this visit to the clinic Dr. Grier had remarked off-handedly that Randolph Grier was in it, recovering from a mild heart attack. Dr. Grier seemed pleased when Clay expressed a desire to see him.

"Yes, I think he would like that. He seemed to enjoy talking to you at the reception." Clay found Uncle Randolph sitting by his bed in a pair of pink pajamas and looking over some old bridge scores. He did indeed seem pleased to see Clay, although exhibiting so much shyness and embarrassment that anyone would trouble to come to see him that Clay at first could not be certain of his welcome.

"I'm delighted to come and see you, and Anne will be in too, soon as she learns you're here. But what happened?"

Randolph shrugged a little. "My heart. I shouldn't have doubled—it was two no-trump bid, but I had nine points and was sitting over her clubs . . . and I was feeling overly bold that day." He smiled quietly at Clay.

Clay stared at him a moment and then sat down. "You mean your heart attack came on during a bridge game? You got that worked up about it?"

He nodded. "It began coming on when she made her book, but I was able to hold out until the hand was played." He looked shyly at Clay as if to see if he was following. "You see, I really wanted that set."

"That much?" Clay asked lightly.

"How can man die better, than facing fearful odds, / For the aces of his partners and the temples of his odds." Randolph smiled wryly. "I think I probably should have died that day. You see, Clay, defense is my forte, my passion. The great Jacoby once told me that I was the stingiest person on defense that he had ever known, which I consider my highest attribute. And on that day, against very improbable odds, against Marcia DuChamp, I arranged to make her misplay—in short, I set the bitch. Oh, I should have died then. Imagine! defeating two no-trump, doubled and vulnerable, then dying—wouldn't that have made a stir?" He sighed as he contemplated the event.

"I'm sure there are a lot of good hands left in your life, Uncle Randolph," ventured Clay, surprised to hear himself using the adoptive title for this slight, pink-faced man for whom, for some reason, he felt a great measure of affection.

"Oh, thank you, Clay, thank you, I hope so indeed!" Randolph added, as though Clay had just given him a gift. "I'm feeling fine now. But how are you? How was the honeymoon?"

"Great," Clay replied, and briefly told him about it.

"It sounds wonderful," said Randolph, "and now you're heading back to start your internship. That's going to be a change."

"I know," Clay grinned, "but Anne and I have talked about it, and I think we're ready."

"I'm sure you are . . . tell me, has my brother said anything to you at all?"

"Dr. Grier? Well, he's shown me around the clinic, introduced me to some people, but no. Nothing special. What do you mean?"

Randolph looked down. "Stuart can be very persuasive if he chooses, and, as most people will tell you, he usually gets what he wants."

Clay waited. "Yes?" he said finally, when nothing more was forthcoming.

Randolph seemed to be growing rapidly tired. "Beware Number Ten Rotary," he said in a voice almost indistinct. "You must excuse me, Clay," Randolph said, drifting off. "Come again, will you? Best to Anne."

"I will, Uncle Randolph, I will, and it's good to see you. Is there anything I can do for you before we leave for Baltimore?"

"No . . . well . . . yes, in a way, there is." Randolph perked up a bit. "I've always felt very close to Anne, and now I do to you, too. The rest of my family kind of looks down on me . . . as a failure, a black sheep. I . . . have this diary, that I've kept for the last thirty years, of my bridge games, scores, who played, where, comments on the hands, how much I won or lost. It's almost a record of my life. If anything happens to me, I'd kind of like for you and Anne to take it. It's not important or valuable or anything, but it's my lifework, in a way, and no one else in the family would care about it." His voice diminished to almost a whisper. "Would you and Anne accept it, if anything should happen?"

"You'd have thought we were accepting his child to take care of," Clay said later as he and Anne were packing for the trip to Baltimore. "When I said yes, tears formed in his eyes."

"I'm afraid Uncle Randolph is beginning to feel a little sorry for himself," answered Anne, "but he did bring it on himself. He pulled away from the family and has lived his life entirely as he pleased. It's no wonder he has to rationalize . . . but I'm glad you told him we'd take his diary. I don't ever want to forget him."

"Nor do I," said Clay, "but what could he have meant by saying, 'Beware Number Ten Rotary'?"

"Number Ten Rotary," said Anne thoughtfully, "is the Rotary Club my father and most of the family belong to. I think they kind of control it."

· · · ·

The heavy hand of summer was already on Baltimore when they arrived by the overnight train on June 30th. They could feel its hot, humid grasp on their compartment as they prepared to get off the train, and it closed over them even more tightly when they exited the station.

"Good old Baltimore summers," gasped Clay in the taxi as he loosened his tie and shrugged off his jacket. "I'd almost forgotten them."

"Shall we turn around and go back—now, while we have a chance?" asked Anne, laughing.

By the time the old cab had wandered its way through the streets of East Baltimore and deposited them in front of the two-story row house that was to be their home, Clay had perspired through his shirt, and Anne's hair was limp. Even so, they were not prepared for the blast of pent-up, hot air that greeted them after Clay swung open the narrow front door and carried Anne across the threshold into the living room.

"Welcome to our oven, dear," he said softly, looking at her in his arms.

"Clever of you to let us in through the oven, Clay, but I think you'd better get us out now and into the house," she returned, sliding out of his arms. They opened all the windows and the front and rear doors, and got two old electric fans going that they had found in the closet, and only then brought in their luggage from the sidewalk. While doing so, they noted several other couples in the same block who were moving in. It helped for them to know they were not the only ones suffering in the heat of that June morning.

The narrow streets behind the hospital were lined with two-story brick row houses, which the builder had had the foresight to create as half-width, rather than full, in order that twice as many rents could be gathered in any one block. Spotting the advantages of this arrangement, and possibly believing that the house staff would not be spending much time at home anyway, hospital and medical school administrators had recommended that their institutions purchase several of these, or had arrangements with private landlords, in which to install interns and residents for low rents in order to keep them close to the hospital. The houses were furnished, but sparingly, and the hospital was notorious for its neglect of whatever furniture was passed down through the years, so current tenants bought replacements.

The houses were much deeper than wide and usually opened in the rear onto a small stone patio, which bordered on an alley separating it from the rear terrace of the house fronting on the next street. They were hot in the summer, although not unbearably due to high ceilings; and they tended to become hot in the winter due to poorly controlled heating. But the plumbing usually worked. The result of this arrangement was a closely knit hospital community, drawn together not only by common interest and proximity but also by the sense that all were suffering the same humble circumstances of living.

There was, however, an even subtler and perhaps more compelling reason for the feeling of closeness engendered in this medical community. This derived from the belief, never spoken but always felt, that the people who came here to train were special, chosen from among the best that medical schools and medical training programs across the nation could produce. The innate sense of belonging, of having joined this company, created a strong undercurrent of brotherhood and mutual acceptance in those lucky enough to be there. Pride showed not only in the trainees themselves but also in their spouses, producing a harmony of living together under Spartan circumstances and making light of discomforts and inconveniences.

Clay glanced up from carrying in luggage to see Warren Bregel and his new wife arriving at their house down and across the street. Clay waved, and Warren grinned and waved back.

"See you tomorrow," Warren said, his words floating in the still air like an acoustic mirage. Tomorrow would be July 1, 1938.

CHAPTER 5

Monday May 13, 1985

The great cafeteria was a clatter of dinner-hour activity as Jim and Charlotte arrived and made their way slowly through the line. They were searching for a table when Jonas found them and steered them over to the corner he had been saving for Jim. Introductions were made as they sat down.

"Charlotte, this is Jonas Smith. Jonas, Charlotte Hallam. Charlotte, Jonas is my roommate and possibly the most talkative surgeon in the U.S."

"How do you do, Jonas? That's quite a title."

"And poorly deserved, too. But I'm glad to meet you, Charlotte. I'm—we're all—very sorry about your dad. How's he coming along?"

"Better, thanks. Don't you think so, Jim?"

"Oh, much better. He's much more active now. He may come out of this with no deficit at all."

"Hmm, that's good," responded Jonas, as he began to eat. "Funny thing about the human brain is that, so far as we know, we've all got about fifty percent more of it than we ever use. I remember my first day in anatomy class in medical school. Dr. Gold brought in an entire right cerebral hemisphere that he'd just removed from a patient with a brain tumor, and he said that because we've got two brain hemispheres, right and left, the patient would never miss it—and he was right, the patient died. But that's not the point. The point is that we can all spare a little gray matter and really not even know it's gone."

Charlotte smiled. "I hope you're right, for my father's sake, but there are times when I don't feel like I have one bit left to spare."

"Ha, but that may be because you don't exercise your mind enough. Got to keep it active, keep the circuits in use, or they'll shut down. Too many people these days spend their time watching the tube or numbing themselves up with drugs, so no wonder their minds deactivate. My theory is that talking and even thinking are activities no different from doing aerobics or skipping rope—the more they're practiced, the better you can do them. By the way, Charlotte, what do you do?"

"Jonas and Jim, you could call me Charlie—it's my nickname. I'm on the staff of Senator Byron in Washington. I'm a sort of an aide."

"Oh, my Gawd!" exclaimed Jonas, "how utterly predictable! Why in the hell are you doing that?"

"What do you mean?" said Charlotte, blushing.

"Well, I mean, it's so incredibly . . . safe. Proper young woman goes to college, then takes a proper job with a senator to meet a proper young lawyer so that she can lead a proper life. Ugh. . . . Why don't you take a chance and be a nurse or something—something that is really meaningful?"

"Jonas, for God's sake," put in Jim.

"It's all right, Jim," said Charlotte. "You don't know anything about me, Jonas. Maybe I'm not cut out to be a nurse."

"Nonsense," Jonas retorted. "You're an intelligent woman, well-educated. I'll bet your father wanted you to be a nurse, didn't he?"

"Never once mentioned it. Besides, what's so good about being a nurse?"

"Being a nurse is reality training. It gets you down to what life's all about. Gives you a chance to serve, earn your keep. It's getting as close to Jesus as you can get!"

"So, in your opinion, all women should be nurses?"

"Nah, only the special ones," answered Jonas, smiling at her for the first time, as if reassuring her that he was only mildly serious about his remarks.

"But how do you know I'm nursing material?" Charlotte asked archly.

"Simple. You're your father's daughter," replied Jonas, as he stood up. "You'd have to be. I must get back. Great to meet you, Charlotte."

"And you," she said, smiling, "but don't forget one thing, will you?"

"What's that?"

"That I'm also my mother's daughter."

Jonas laughed and nodded, and they watched his lanky figure leaving the cafeteria. They looked at each other and laughed.

"Sorry about that," Jim offered.

"It didn't bother me . . . in fact, it was rather fun. But do you think he believed what he said?"

"Oh, I think so. He may smile, to make it easier to hear, but he generally says what he thinks, and also, what he thinks he generally says."

"He wouldn't call me 'Charlie'—just 'Charlotte,' " she observed thoughtfully.

"Probably thinks it's not appropriate. He has a distinct feeling for the difference between male and female."

He told her the story of their initial meeting.

Charlotte laughed and said, "Initial impressions are almost never right, but in this case, *wow!* But at least there's no question what he's doing here, is there? I mean, to be the greatest surgeon in the country. That's really having a sense of direction."

"I know! There are times when I almost envy him."

"Almost?"

"Well, I mean having a goal like that is a long-term burden, and, besides, it has no end point. I mean, how do you know when you've become the greatest surgeon? Nobody suddenly comes up to you and announces, 'You're the greatest.' "

"Oh, no," Charlotte said quietly. "I think rather it's something you come to know within yourself, something you simply come to feel, or realize."

"Yes," agreed Jim, "and I suppose it also helps when you're given a professorship at a great institution. Your father may be at the top of most lists in neurosurgery."

"I don't think he believes so anymore." Charlotte shook her head. "He told me a few years ago that he knew several dozen people he'd rather have operate on him than he himself."

"A surgeon can pass his peak in terms of operation technique, reflexes, dexterity, and so forth, which is probably what he meant, but those things may not be as important as other assets, like judgment, or experience. At least not in teaching. Your father is a great teacher."

Charlotte nodded. "He loves teaching, probably even more than operating. He's said that there are few things that are more pleasing than dispensing knowledge and truth to a receptive mind."

"It sounds as though he's had a very satisfying life so far," Jim said, with almost a sigh. "He's accomplished so much, and given so much."

Some hint of the sigh must have reached Charlotte, for she suddenly changed the tenor of the conversation. "How about you, Jim? How did you get into medicine as a career?"

"Oh, I just kind of . . . wandered in," he answered lightly, "and can't seem to find my way out."

Just a bit of warmth left Charlotte's expectant smile as she heard the reply. "Oh? Are you looking for out?"

Jim was aware of her disappointment with his answer and was angry with himself.

"No, not really. It was just a figure of speech. It's just that, compared to Jonas, I'm not as sure of myself. But I see I've disappointed you. You expected total dedication."

She hesitated a moment before answering, "Well, you seem dedicated."

"It's possible for a person to be competent without being totally— uh—sacrificed to the profession, even though people are always a little let down to see a doctor who does other things as well."

"You're certainly taking good care of my father."

"Oh," he replied carefully, "I've had a lot of help with your father, from the best authorities around, so my input has been very little. I'm . . . " Distracted, he glanced at his watch. "Look—I think we should get back up to the ward now, but maybe we could talk another time."

She nodded, and they made their way back to her father's room. They stood together at his bedside for a moment and gazed down at the drowsy figure.

"He seems to sleep a lot," Charlotte remarked.

"That's par for the course. He'll wake up more in the next few days." He hesitated and then said softly, "You know, Charlie, I would love to talk to your father someday. I wonder if he would tell me a few things about his life, if I'd ask him."

"I'm sure he would love to, Jim. Anything special?"

"No . . . well, yes," Jim reflected, "I'd like to ask him about . . . significance." His eyes met Charlotte's and found in them interest, as well as what he interpreted as compassion.

They left his bedside, Jim to go about his duties, and Charlotte to sit and wait for her mother. Neither was aware that Dr. Hallam had overheard Jim's query and was forming his response. He thought, significance—significance—well, it may begin with the internship. His mind drifted again, easily, willingly.

· · · ·

Clay and Anne ate breakfast together on July 1, 1938, so he could get to the hospital for the seven o'clock orientation meeting. They had slept poorly, partly due to the heat, and partly due to Clay's excitement about beginning the internship.

"It's nice being so close to the hospital," said Anne. "You'll have no excuse for missing lunch or not dashing over here between patients."

"I don't know about that last part," smiled Clay, "but you can be sure I'll dash over here as often as possible—the cooking's too good to stay away."

Anne laughed. "Cooking indeed! That piece of toast is the first thing I've cooked for you. I think it's the other aspects of the cook that you're interested in."

They said good-bye on the front steps, as close to each other as they had ever been, in their love, and pride in each other, and in their resolution to accomplish what lay immediately before them.

The orientation meeting was held in a classroom on the sixth floor of the surgical wing. Clay estimated that there were about fifty people, all dressed in the traditional white jackets, pants, and shoes of the house staff. Four of the fourteen surgical interns were Clay's former medical school classmates, including Warren Bregel, while the rest were unknown to him.

"I guess we'd better get started," drawled an easy voice from the front of the room. "Will everybody please take their seats?"

As they sat down, Clay saw that the voice belonged to a man only slightly older than the majority of those present, one of the most handsome men Clay had ever seen.

"I'm Tom Burroughs, your chief resident for the first six months this year, and this is Bill Fleming, who'll have the job the second six months. Come to us if you have any problems." Fleming was tall and less graceful than Burroughs, but shared his air of authority.

"It's a good surgical service this year," continued Burroughs. "You're all lucky to be here, and we're all lucky to have you. We've all got something to learn from each other, so don't be shy about speaking out.

"Welcome to the Surgery Department, gentlemen. There are seventeen residents, counting nine in general surgery, and eight in the surgical subspecialties of orthopedics, neurosurgery, and urology. Your schedule for where each of you is to be assigned for each month is posted on the bulletin board outside, but I'll read it out anyway, shortly.

"Each of the subspecialties has its own chief resident, who will explain its independent function to the interns who are assigned to it. Each new intern will serve two months in orthopedics, two in urology, and two in neurosurgery, and the other six months will be spent in general surgery, including two months in the emergency room. With rare exception, these schedules are not subject to change.

"For those interns now assigned to general surgery, the operating rooms run on a tight schedule and usually begin at 8:00 A.M. This means that ward work—drawing blood tests, starting i.v.'s, writing orders—all has to be finished before 7:45 so that you can be in the O.R., with your patient prepared and you scrubbed and gowned, by 8:00 in order that the surgeon can get started. There'll be two interns on each ward, plus two residents, which means that each intern and his resident will have responsibility for about fifteen to eighteen patients, and, if somebody goes off duty, the coverage will be for thirty to thirty-six patients. That's a load, so you'll have to get up early.

"There'll be residents' rounds at 5:00 P.M. every Monday, Wednesday, and Friday, at which you interns will be asked to present your interesting cases and be ready to discuss them. The professors' rounds are on Wednesday at noon and Saturday at 9:00 A.M. Be ready for these. Other rounds and conferences will be announced. Needless to say, we start right away. I'll read out your assignments, and you can go to your floors and meet your assistant residents, and get going."

Looking around the room as each intern stood when his name and assignment were called out, Clay realized that these would be the people he would be working with during the next two to four years. It did not occur to him—nor, had it occurred, would he have thought it strange—that among the entire group there was not one black, not one woman, and only one, an Englishman, who was from a foreign country. At this time, and in this place of competitive selection, only white men were surgeons-in-training.

Clay was pleased when he learned that his first service initiation was six months of general surgery—he had hoped to begin this way, in the field in which he ultimately wanted to specialize. He hurried from the meeting to Halstead 4, the surgical ward to which he was assigned, and found when he arrived that he had already been posted for surgery at 8:00 that morning, to assist Dr. Clemson with a gallbladder case. That gave him ten minutes to get there, get scrubbed, and change clothes, in order not to hold things up.

I'm starting with a bang, he thought as he almost leaped through the corridors toward the operating room. Quick as he moved, however, he found that he had been preceded. Warren Bregel had finished his scrub and was getting into his gown when Clay arrived.

Clay said, "Hello, Warren, what're you doing here?" as he changed into his loose green linen shirt and pants.

"Hello, Clay, I'm happy to say we'll be working together for a while. We're on the same rotation schedule. I think Dr. Clemson is ready."

There was no time for Clay to digest this news other than to give a nod and a quick grunt of acceptance as he pulled the mask over his nose and mouth, accepted the nurse's adjustment of his green linen gown, and pulled on the sterile rubber gloves. He arrived in the operating room to find the patient already anesthetized and the team already in place. He quietly slipped into the vacant space at the table, at the surgeon's left.

"Victory belongs to the swift, Doctor," muttered the silk-soft voice of the surgeon, who sensed rather than saw Clay's presence, for he did not look up from draping the patient's abdomen. "Because of his promptness, Dr. Bregel will serve as my first assistant today, and you will hold the retractors. However, because it's our first day, I'm inclined to forgive your being late." He looked over at Clay, who fancied that he saw the surgeon smile under his mask.

Dr. Joachim Clemson was well known to Clay, as he was to his entire medical school class, largely from the lectures and various surgical clinics that he conducted. Clay thought he was perhaps the most colorless individual he had ever met and, in the fraternity play last year, had introduced the question, "What, besides water, is colorless, odorless, and tasteless?" The answer was "Joachim Clemson." This was based mostly on Dr. Clemson's speech, thin as a knife and seeming to emanate mostly through his nose. His bearing was one of icy calmness, expressionless features, gray eyes behind steel-rimmed glasses, and the drabbest clothes, worn repeatedly, that Clay had seen. Clay believed that Dr. Clemson could walk by so blandly that he would not cast a shadow. He was, however, said to be a highly skilled and unflappable surgeon, as his rank of full professor in the Department of Surgery seemed to attest.

"Well, they always give me two of the most promising interns to begin the year with, gentlemen, so you're starting off in good shape. Anyway, I hope you both have a good year. I'll try to see to it that there are some challenges in it. Well, let's get started. Scalpel, Miss Frei."

In one deft, smooth gesture, he made a long incision into the abdomen under the right rib cage.

"Know anything about the case? Sponge!"

Warren Bregel sponged the incision clear of blood and clamped two bleeders.

"Now, tie."

Clay watched as Warren, with blinding finger work, tied off the two bleeders in the subcutaneous fat and removed the clamps.

"Excellent, Dr. Bregel, I can see you know how to suture. Now let's widen our incision." He glanced at Clay. "Well, do you know anything about the case?"

"Oh, only that it's a gallbladder, sir. I didn't have time to study it."

"Okay, well, never again come to the table without knowing everything there is to know about the case. It won't do you any good, and it sure won't do the patient any good. Sponge! And how about you, Doctor, do you know anything about this case?"

"Yes, sir," responded Warren. "The patient is a fifty-two-year-old black female who was referred to you because of abdominal pain and fever. She's been in the hospital for five days now, and her fever has subsided, but she's still sore and tender in the abdomen. The physical findings suggest tenderness in the right upper quadrant of the abdomen, and x-rays showed the presence of gallstones. Blood tests indicate the presence of an anemia, and her test for sickle-cell trait is positive. Gallstones, of course, are more common in persons with this trait."

"Very good, Doctor, very good. Always remember, to know the case is to know the operation. This patient had fever, fever means inflammation, and inflammation means adhesions, bleeding, and the need for wide exposure, and that's why we used this particular incision, nice and wide . . . so we can help her by getting that gallbladder out. So let's do it. Suction—sponge!" And Warren and Clay leaned toward the incision, sponging and suctioning the bleeding points as Dr. Clemson widened and deepened the incision.

"Blood's a little dark. Is she okay?" he asked the anesthetist, who checked his data and said, "She's fine. Blood pressure 110/80, pulse 88, respirations 14. Is the patient relaxed enough?"

"Seems to be," said Dr. Clemson. "Adjust the light a bit for me, will you?" The charge nurse tilted the great overhead light to give a better angle to see into the incision.

"Now." The surgeon leaned back to allow the interns to look into the incision. "We'll retract that big rectus muscle laterally and *voilà!* What's that?" He leaned back.

The incision was now about four inches long, and at its bottom Clay could see a gray smooth membrane.

"The peritoneum, sir," they answered in unison.

"Very well. Dr. Bregel, have you ever incised one before and entered the abdominal cavity? No? Nurse, if you'll hand my first assistant the surgical scissors we'll let him do the opening. Hold the retractors, Dr. Hallam. Give him a lot of exposure. Remember, elevate it with your clamps and cut carefully, and be sure you're not slicing into anything underneath. Now, Doctor, you are entering the wonderful world of the abdomen. Congratulations! A world of infinite variety"— he glanced at Clay, who was holding a retractor in each hand, keeping the incision open—"due to Mother Nature's great imagination in playing congenital tricks with the anatomy.

"Now, Dr. Hallam, this is where we start earning our pay. Tell me something about the usual relationships of the bile duct, the hepatic artery, and the cystic duct and artery."

Clay searched his memory feverishly. "Um, um, I don't exactly recall, sir."

"Oh?" Dr. Clemson's reply was abrupt. "Dr. Bregel?"

"Well, sir, as the liver is rotated and retracted laterally, the gall bladder and cystic duct become exposed, and the common bile duct becomes posterior and medial, and the hepatic artery appears behind the duct."

"Very well, that's what we expect to find. Now let's see if that's the way it is."

So with Clay retracting the liver laterally, and Warren pulling the intestine and its appendages medially, the operation proceeded, and Dr. Clemson continued giving a running commentary on what he was doing and firing quick questions at his two intern assistants. Nor were the questions restricted to the present operation, but ranged from the embryonic development of the gallbladder and liver, through comparative anatomy of the gallbladder in other species, to the structure and function of the gallbladder system. Clay became aware of the depth and scope of the surgeon's knowledge on the subject, as well as that he and Warren were being sharply appraised as to their training and relative abilities. It did not take Clay long to realize, painful as it was to him, that Warren was much better prepared. His answers were, in general, fuller and more informative than Clay's, and he had an annoying eagerness of supplementing Clay's answers with more detailed, albeit unbidden, elaborations. A sense of strain developed in the air as the differences in their responses and Warren's willingness to demonstrate his superior knowledge became apparent to the entire team.

They were two hours into the operation. Clay was perspiring down his forehead and between his legs, and his right arm was becoming numb from holding the retractors. The circulating nurse mopped his brow to keep his vision clear, and he wanted to ask her to scratch the awful itch in his privates, but of course he did not dare. He was amused later on, however, when Dr. Clemson asked her to scratch his balls, which she did without a blink. Dr. Clemson looked at him for a moment afterward as if to say, "See, anything's okay to help the operation." Clay, however, didn't think he would ever be able to bring himself to make such a request.

The gallbladder, in this case a dull grayish, shrunken, and scarred organ, had been carefully freed from its bed of inflammatory adhesions by Dr. Clemson, and was being retracted with a long clamp on its end by Clay.

"Now we come to the crucial moment," the surgeon said into the cavity as he bent closely over it. "Ligation and division of the cystic artery and duct. What is that bluish structure there, Doctor?"

Clay bent forward and looked down into the operation site. The object pointed out was a dark blue, large vessel that seemed to be coursing behind the other structures.

"The portal vein?" he suggested.

"Excellent," Dr. Clemson answered. "I only point it out so that it can be totally avoided. Accidentally rupturing the portal vein is the worst thing that could happen in this operation, as it's extremely hard to suture once it's opened. Now if you'll give me a little more traction on the line, Doctor, I could see a bit better."

Because his reflexes were numbed from the fatigue of holding the retractors, or because he was simply tired from the strain of the questioning, Clay suddenly retracted not only on the liver with his left hand but also on the gallbladder clamps he was holding in his fingers. Suddenly, blood spurted up from the cavity, covering the face mask and glasses of Dr. Clemson and splattering the abdominal drapes and floor.

Dr. Clemson's head jerked back, and the nurse hurried to him to remove his glasses and clear them. Temporarily blinded, however, he said in a calm voice, "Hepatic artery rupture, Doctor, you'd better stop the bleeding."

Warren leaned closer into the spurting stream of blood, reached down into the incision, and suddenly the flow stopped.

"I think I've got it, sir," he said. "My finger is on it."

"Very good," said Dr. Clemson, his glasses now restored, and coming back to the operation. "Good reflexes, and you didn't panic. Now let's clamp that artery and sew it up."

He said to Clay, "Doctor, you were a little too frisky on pulling those clamps."

An hour later, the artery was repaired, the gallbladder removed, and the operation was over.

As they wheeled the still-anesthetized patient toward the recovery area, Dr. Clemson said, "Thank you, gentlemen. Good job, Dr. Bregel. Dr. Hallam, you'll be my first assistant tomorrow."

It was noon by the time they had written the post-op orders and made final checks on the patient's awakening from anesthesia. Clay felt spent, but realized he was posted for another operation that afternoon, and had to look to the needs of some eleven patients who were assigned to him on the ward. He and Warren left the recovery room at the same time.

"Good job today, Warren. I didn't realize you knew so much about the gallbladder."

"Why, thank you, Clay. I do think it went well . . . and I don't mind telling you how I did it. You see, I came over last night, instead of waiting till this morning, and found out what we were going to be doing this morning, and so I simply took the trouble to read up on it last night. Also, I skipped that meeting this morning, because I'd found out where we were assigned, and I knew Dr. Clemson didn't like to be kept waiting." He grinned at Clay. "See you later."

Clay headed for the cafeteria for a quick snack, but remembered that he had promised Anne to come home for lunch. He went to the telephone and called her.

"Hi, where are you?" she said, her voice bright. "I've got lunch ready."

"Sorry—I've only got ten minutes—put it in the icebox for me, will you?"

"Oh, darn, the first thing I've cooked for you. Oh, well, how'd it go this morning?"

"Busy—a gallbladder operation with Dr. Joachim Clemson . . . "

"And?"

"Interesting. This may be harder than I thought. I'll tell you about it tonight—be home around seven, I guess. . . . I love you."

He concluded, late that night—after his second operation of the day and an emergency procedure in the evening, and residents' rounds and looking after his patients, and while curled up in the hospital library boning up on tomorrow's operations—that several things had become apparent during that first day. First, he would never again characterize Dr. Joachim Clemson as colorless. Second, to stay on a par with Warren Bregel and the rest of the interns and to remain at Hopkins for his entire four years of surgical training, he was going to have to work very hard. Third, the exhilaration of surgery, even in his lowly position, was already greater than he thought it would be, and he realized with startling clarity, even while fighting sleep, that he wanted to be the best that he could possibly be.

He was not able to return home to Anne for three days.

CHAPTER 6

Friday, May 17, 1985

It had been a good Friday, Jim Gallier admitted to himself as he scrutinized his face for shaving flaws in the mirror of the small lavatory in the house-staff quarters of the hospital. For a change, he and Bert Harper had not locked horns over some shortcoming that the resident had observed in his performance. And some of the treatment programs he had been instrumental in initiating for several of his ward patients seemed to be paying off. Furthermore, his star patient in Room 112 seemed much improved today. After six days, Physical Therapy had reported almost complete return of strength and function in the questionably weakened left arm and leg. His speech and mental awareness had been much clearer all day. The drowsiness that had been so much a feature of his illness seemed to be lifting, and the tests of his mental function conducted by Jim were satisfactorily performed.

Jim smiled as he recalled his embarrassment about proposing such tests to the professor of neurosurgery, but when the latter saw what he was doing, he encouraged Jim to proceed.

"This is no time to spare feelings, Dr. Gallier. I'm sure you're as eager as I am to find out how this brain you've been working so hard to preserve is functioning. Fire away."

They had begun with dates, place names, capitals, and so forth. "There was a time when I knew the capital of every state in the Union and of every country in the world," Dr. Hallam had said as he proved his alertness in matters of temporal and physical orientation. He was able to remember and repeat up to eight numbers, backward and forward, fairly easily, and he performed the serial 7's, which consisted of subtracting 7 from 100 on down, very quickly. "As many times as I've administered that test through the years, I ought to do it well," he said. He had been able to recite the names of more presidents of the United States backward in order than Jim could, and, as they progressed through the meanings of a few proverbs and metaphors, Jim became satisfied that Dr. Hallam's intellectual functioning was indeed well preserved.

The testing that Jim usually saved for last consisted of questions designed to examine abstract-reasoning capability, that highest redoubt of mental function, so delicately balanced that even the simplest injury to the brain produced dysfunction. The test that he used was a simple one, a conundrum that even perfectly healthy minds could not always easily solve.

"Brothers and sisters have I none, but that man's father is my father's son! Who is that man, sir?"

He watched Dr. Hallam's face as he came to grips with the problem, and then in the next instant was surprised to see tears filling the elder doctor's eyes and running down his cheeks.

"I'm sorry, Doctor, sorry . . . the answer to your little riddle would be . . . my son . . . my son who died. I haven't cried about him in years." He wiped his eyes and cheeks with his sleeves, but the tears did not stop flowing.

"Dr. Hallam, sir, I'm so sorry, please forgive me. I didn't realize . . . " Jim stuttered, rising from his chair and approaching the bed.

"No, no, it's all right. I'll be fine," Dr. Hallam said, obviously embarrassed. "Why don't you leave me for a while? Come back later. I seem to want to cry a bit longer."

Jim had left him, chagrined and angry with himself for having unintentionally hit upon an obviously painful subject. He was well aware of the tendency toward loss of emotional control in people who had suffered strokes, but Dr. Hallam had seemed so much improved. Who was Jim, however, to say that this was abnormal emotionality? When he returned an hour or so later, Dr. Hallam had a visitor and seemed fine. Jim waved at him from the door, and Dr. Hallam waved back.

"Have a fine time tonight, Dr. Gallier, and make sure those women give you enough to eat."

Jim smiled in return. "I was going to mention it to you, sir. I wish you were going to be there."

"I wish so, too, but I'll join you another time. Have fun, and don't stay out too late."

"I won't. Sorry for interrupting." He glanced at the visitor, who was tall and silver-haired. The two waved genially as he left the doorway.

Jim dressed with some care. He had been pleased when Mrs. Hallam had called a few days before and invited him for dinner tonight, and he found himself excited at the thought of seeing Charlotte in a more private setting than the hospital afforded. He wore the light gray seersucker suit that Jonas called his "spring sincerity" suit, which seemed to fit his sense of the occasion, and he picked up a small bouquet of flowers at the hospital shop on his way out to the car. He felt ready.

The sunset streaked the sky with orange behind the tall oak trees of North Baltimore, and the perfume of blossoming lilacs and wisterias lay in the soft spring air as Jim's Volkswagen nosed its way along the streets. Mrs. Hallam had given him directions, but he was unfamiliar with this section of the city, and he had to go slowly to make out the street signs. He had no time to focus on the individual houses, but he could tell from their masses in the gathering dusk that they were large and surrounded with appropriate yard spaces. The Hallams' house was one of them, the middle house of five on the north side of a one-block street. The outside lights were on to guide him, and he could see that it was the fieldstone house with red shutters that she had described to him. Charlotte came out to the street as his car drew up in front.

"Hello, Jim, you're in good time." She was dressed in a short black dinner dress with narrow shoulder straps and a vee neck, and her black hair was swept up and caught with a simple comb in back. She also, it seemed, had dressed for the occasion, and when he saw her he felt both proud and inadequate. He should have worn his dark blue suit, or at least his blazer.

Mrs. Hallam was reassuring, however, when she met them at the door. Her greeting was cordial, and she led the way through the large central hall into the book-lined study and then out through the french doors onto a small terrace.

"It's such a lovely night," she said, "I thought we could sit out a while."

A Judas tree, with spreading branches, had been incorporated into the middle of the stone deck, and it was under this tree that their chairs were drawn up. In the light thrown out by the yellow garden lanterns, Jim saw that one of the seats was already occupied. Upon drawing closer, he saw that it was the same man he had seen earlier visiting Dr. Hallam. Only when he stood up to greet them was Jim able to appreciate his great height, as he had sat very low in the canvasbacked chair.

"Bart, this is Dr. Jim Gallier, who is taking care of Clay at the hospital. Jim, this is Dr. Bart Mateer, an old, old friend."

"Hello again." Dr. Mateer smiled and extended his hand.

"How do you do, sir? If I'd have known you were coming, I would have given you a lift."

"Oh no, no, you've probably got one of those small cars, and I can no longer fold this bag of bones into them. You've certainly done a good job with Dr. Hallam."

"Oh, Dr. Andres is calling the shots, sir. I'm just a flunky."

They drank light gin and tonics as they discussed Dr. Hallam's progress. The women were pleased when Jim described his assessment of Dr. Hallam's intellectual function that day, excluding the incident of the riddle. Dr. Mateer lighted a cigarette and sank back in the chair with his legs crossed, jiggling his foot.

"He seems to have lost nothing in terms of brain function," Jim continued.

"No. I thought he was occasionally a little slow on a change of subjects, just a momentary hesitation. And he stumbled on a word or two. But otherwise, he seemed fine," observed Dr. Mateer. "Has it been confirmed that he had a stroke?"

"There are still some tests to do. He's to have a twenty-four-hour monitor of his heart and a digital angiogram of his carotid arteries, looking further for a cause of what happened."

"He told me today that he thought those tests should be done," chuckled Dr. Mateer. "He hasn't changed."

"You've known him for a long time, then, Dr. Mateer?" asked Jim, grinning.

"A long time," he confirmed. "We went to college together and were roommates all the way through medical school. By the way, Anne, Betty sends her best—she just didn't feel up to making the trip today."

The talk turned to other things, and before long they were called in to dinner by the elderly black maid, Ona, who had apparently helped the family with "occasions" for years. They dined on shad roe with crisp bacon and on fried tomatoes. They explored Charlotte's job with Senator Byron, heard about Jim's family and background, and learned of Dr. Mateer's retirement two years before as chairman of the Ophthalmology Department of Deconing Hospital in New Jersey.

"Yes, it wasn't an easy choice to make, but, once made, it's amazing how ready for it both of us were. We're growing tropical flowers, and I'm doing some writing. It's nice being home more—and having Betty serve me lunch is a real experience." He smiled and wiped his eyes with his long fingers. "Tell me, Jim, how are you enjoying taking care of your distinguished patient?"

"Oh, fine, sir, very much. I haven't gotten to talk with him very much, though."

"He'll talk your ear off one day soon, if he decides to get started on you, won't he, Anne?" Dr. Mateer looked at her with sly amusement. "He always could."

Anne smiled back at him. "Now, Bart, remember he's not here to defend himself."

"No defense necessary! But when he and I were interns, like Jim here is, why, Clay could talk all night."

"You interned with Dr. Hallam?" Jim asked.

Dr. Mateer nodded, "Well, yes, both interns at Hopkins—1938, it was. He, of course, was intern on the surgical service while I was in ophthalmology, but we'd see each other a bit."

"What was it like, interning then?" Jim asked. "Was it different, do you think, from now?"

Dr. Mateer looked at him a long moment, then glanced briefly at Anne, before replying.

"I think it was more physically demanding then. We had fewer drugs, fewer instruments, and patients tended to be sicker for longer. It took longer to diagnose an illness then, and much more time was spent by the bedside observing the patient and looking for clues and at the course of the disease. As interns we had no scheduled time off, sometimes a week or more would go by before we could get home, even though we lived right next to the hospital. Sleep was a precious commodity and was viewed as only questionably necessary for the house staff. Total dedication was expected."

"Sounds terrible," said Jim. "I wonder why you put up with it, and how?"

Dr. Mateer shrugged. "The answer to the 'how' part is 'barely.' The 'why' part? Curiosity, I suppose. Looking back on it now, I think we were at an institution that had drawn to itself inspired teachers from all over the world. They were lured there by a dream, which was that man was at last in a position to track down disease to its lair and conquer it. Their enthusiasm roused us all to a pitch so fervent that it was almost religious in its intensity. I liken it to a historical educational phenomenon, like Plato's school in old Greece or the Alexandrian school. It was an exciting place, and it brought out the best, and at times the worst, in us." Dr. Mateer eased forward in his chair as if stimulated by his recollections. "I won't say it was easy or pleasant, and the competition was there, but we were proud of ourselves and what we were learning, and many lifelong friendships were formed during wee hours. And . . . those men who survived became some of the best doctors and teachers in the world . . . like Dr. Hallam."

"But, Jim, lest you come away enamored," Anne interjected softly, "the system was hard on any kind of family life. It was, in fact, inhumane . . . it couldn't endure. You don't have it so hard now, do you?"

"No," admitted Jim. "I'm theoretically off every other night and weekends but, in actuality, it's less. There's so much to know, so much to learn . . . it's a bit overwhelming at times."

"Well," said Dr. Mateer, "it's still the same school, still the same traditions—to be the best."

After dinner, Charlotte and Jim strolled back out onto the terrace and sat together on the wrought iron bench under the tree, while Mrs. Hallam and Dr. Mateer stayed in the study. The soft lantern light accentuated the contrast of her clear olive complexion and soft black hair, and Jim felt a flush of excitement at her beauty and her nearness.

He told her how her father wept that day at the mention of his son.

Charlotte nodded gravely. "When Mark died, twelve years ago now, of malaria, it nearly killed all of us in different ways. I was only thirteen at the time, but even I felt lost. And I could see the change in Dad after that. Not that he cried or mourned so much as that he became even more engrossed in his work, put in even longer hours. Mother tells me that this is the way he has always reacted to sadness or pain in his life. I remember seeing him cry only once, at the funeral, but never again."

"I suppose, in a way, you could say he's lucky he had something so rewarding to turn to," said Jim thoughtfully.

"Oh, yes, undoubtedly," said Charlotte, with slight bitterness in her voice, "except that both Mother and I wish he'd been able to turn to us a bit more. After all, we also had grief to deal with."

Jim looked at her, disturbed by this unexpected revelation. "Perhaps his grief was too great to comfort; perhaps it had to be evaded."

"I suppose everyone loves in their own way, and grieves in their own way, but neither can be submerged forever," said Charlotte. "I'd like to have touched him the way you did today, and held him. . . . I hate macho men, don't you? They're so . . . so out of it. You're not one, are you, Jim?"

"Who, me? Hell no. I cry at the drop of a hat!" Both laughed.

Anne saw Dr. Mateer to the door, kissed him fondly, and watched as he folded his tall figure into the cab. She sighed as she closed the door, and returned to the study to clean up. She turned down the light and gazed for a few moments at the two figures sitting together on the terrace. She felt she almost knew what they were saying to each other, so heavy was her sense of déjà vu at the sight, and for a moment she felt carried away by a desire to call out to them and warn them. The feeling lasted only an instant, however, for the present forced its way into her consciousness, and she realized the differences between her circumstances and Charlotte's. First, Charlotte was now twenty-five, whereas she herself had been only twenty when she and Clay had married, and Charlotte was more mature and worldly than Anne had been. Second, times were different now, with different rules and moralities. Nonetheless, as she made her way up the steps and into the bedroom, and changed into her nightgown, her mind sought and fixed on that early period in her life, and she hadn't the will to try to redirect it. Perhaps her thoughts were due to the spring air, the visit of Bart Mateer with the many reminiscences evoked during the evening, and the two young people on the terrace below. She sat down in her reading chair by the open window of the bedroom, turned off the light, pulled a pint of bourbon out of her bureau drawer, poured half a glassful, sipped, and, as if mesmerized, succumbed to the sad sweetness of recollections.

. . . .

The painful uncertainties of those first days, weeks, and months of Clay's internship year at Johns Hopkins Hospital returned to her as if summoned, and the awareness of the life they would be leading seemed real again. Clay had left her in the early morning of that first day, July 1, 1938, saying that he would be back for a quick lunch, which to her novicelike mind, trained in the framework of her mother's southern-cooking concepts, was in no way synonymous with a light lunch.

She visited the small market that served the neighborhood and returned loaded down with the groceries for their premier lunch together under her auspices. She prepared vichyssoise, soft-shell crabs with coleslaw and tomato, and a tossed salad. There were rolls, iced tea, and a sherbet for dessert. It took her several hours in her out-moded kitchen, in which she found that battling roaches was an extra challenge added to fixing the meal itself. The heat in the kitchen caused perspiration trails to run from her hair down over her face and neck, although she wore only a light tennis shirt and shorts. She made mental notes about where to install the new fans after they were purchased. Before lunch, she took a shower and donned a fresh cotton blouse and skirt, swept her hair up behind in a bun for coolness, and put on perfume. She looked at herself in the mirror and did not dis-like what she saw: shining light brown hair, features regular despite a deep-curved nose and high cheekbones, full lips, smooth cheeks still tanned from the North Carolina sun, and warm, adventuresome blue eyes. If Clay had made it home to lunch he would not have found it easy to leave.

But he did not get home, calling on the phone shortly after she had finished dressing to say that he couldn't leave the hospital, but would be there for supper around seven o'clock. She choked off an automatic protest, detecting in his voice that he was upset at not being with her. She put lunch away in the refrigerator and went upstairs and changed her clothes again. She felt let down, but she did not let herself dwell on it. Both of them were aware of the demands to be placed on them by this internship. They had discussed the problem, and so she was in a measure prepared for inconveniences, although they were easier to accept in theory than in fact.

She finished their unpacking and moved the sparse furniture pro-vided by the hospital around to her taste, making notes of things they would need to replace or add. She was aware of their budgetary restraints, but her parents had given her some extra money, and she resolved to make full use of it. List in hand, she charged out into the July sun, wilted momentarily as the hot breezeless air caused her skin to prickle, then set off resolutely for the cut-rate shopping area sev-eral blocks from the hospital. She returned several hours later, pleased with what she had bought. Even though hot and a bit fa-tigued, she set about refurbishing lunch into dinner. She bathed again and, feeling refreshed and anxious to see Clay, noted a decided lift in her spirits. She had just placed the crabs back in the oven for rewarming when the phone rang.

"Mrs. Hallam, this is Rhoda Marmer. I'm circulating nurse in the operating room. Dr. Hallam asked me to call to tell you he won't be home for dinner. We've just started an emergency case up here, a gunshot wound. He said he would call you as soon as he's free."

Anne sat quietly by the phone for a few minutes, trying to take in what was happening. Then she picked up the phone and asked for the Mateers' residence, which was in the same block. When Betty answered, Anne said calmly, "Hi, Betty, it's Anne. I guess we won't be able to go out with you all tonight. Clay's working."

"First of many times, I guess," Betty laughed. "Come with us anyway. We're just going to the movies, and we'll be back by ten o'clock, in time for you to be home for Clay."

The movie, a thriller called *The Double Doors,* was distracting enough, and she felt better during the walk back home.

"I fixed two meals today," she said, "and neither of them produced a husband. What's a girl to do?"

"Two things," answered Bart as they approached the wooden steps in front of her house. "First, don't get upset about it. Things are particularly bad now with all of us new faces coming in. It takes us twice as long to do things now as it will after we get the hang of things, and also we're a bit short-staffed with vacations, and so on. Second, adjust to it. Make your cooking and your own schedule simple and easy—gourmet cooks here at Johns Hopkins live lonely, frustrated lives."

Betty laughed. "Bartie, don't treat her like a child—she knows these things."

"No, you're wrong, Betty. I should know them, but I don't. I'm glad you said what you did, Bartie, it'll help a lot."

Bart shrugged. "We're all in this together, my dear. In four years or so we'll look back on all this as some weird kind of bonding ceremony."

Anne laughed. "I think I'd rather endure a branding iron, but thanks for tonight, you Mateers."

She ran up the steps and unlocked the door. "Lock your door behind you," yelled Bart, as he and Betty went on up the street.

Anne heard the phone ringing even as she locked the front door and went up the steps to their bedroom. She ran to get it.

"Hi, honey, how're you doing?" Clay's voice was so good to hear.

"Fine, dear. Where are you?"

"I'm on the ward. Just got out of that gunshot case. It was a mess. His wife had shot him—ruptured his spleen, mashed his left kidney, and ruptured his diaphragm. He may not make it."

"How awful," responded Anne. "How about coming home and telling me about it?"

"Well, that's just it, honey." Clay's voice became decidedly less vigorous. "The resident thinks I should stay here tonight to be close to this guy. He's very precarious."

"Hmm," Anne finally responded. "Did you tell him I'm precarious too?"

"I did." Relief now sounded in Clay's voice, as he realized she wasn't going to be irritated, or at least show it. "What I couldn't tell him was what you're wearing right now. No, don't tell me. Tell me what you've done today."

Anne recounted the events of the day, " . . . and Betty and Bartie Mateer gave me the best advice of the day."

"What was that?"

"I think it was something to the effect of 'when married to a Roman, behave like a Roman.' "

"I'm really sorry, Anne," Clay said. "I'll make it up to you."

Anne laughed. "Soon as possible, I hope. When do you think you'll get home?"

"I'm not sure. I'll call."

By the time he did get home, three days later, on Monday, the Fourth of July, at noon, Anne had made real progress on the house. Several comfortable wicker chairs were in place, as well as ready-made red cotton curtains and venetian blinds for the windows and some scatter rugs for the wood floors. Four electric fans were now doing their best to keep the warm air moving.

Anne heard his key in the latch almost as a fanfare. She hastened in from the kitchen as he was closing the door behind him, and they looked at each other for one long moment before he shrugged his white hospital jacket onto a chair and they met in a wordless embrace.

"God, you look beautiful," he finally whispered in her ear.

"God, you look seedy," she whispered back to him. "But lovable. Want lunch?"

He nodded. "A shower and shave first, and then I'll join you in the kitchen. Mmm, you taste good . . . do you want a shower? There's room for two."

"No, but I'll go upstairs with you, to make sure you know where it is."

She had been shocked when she first saw him. His eyes were bleary and puffy underneath from lack of sleep, and his face was pale. After the initial appraisal, however, she felt that these changes made him more appealing, sexier, as if adding more character to his already good looks. She suddenly realized how great her hunger for him was. They made love as if it was their first, or last, time together, touch, smell, sight, and sound impacting together. At the end they could only speak softly to each other, and Clay fell asleep.

Anne watched him for a time, thinking about the depth of her love and admiration for him, which made all her inconveniences and sacrifices insignificant, if they could help him in his work. She had always been an independent thinker, had inadvertently been raised as one by her strict parents, who were mostly unaware that it is easier to lead than it is to drive one's progeny to respect and adopt the values their parents hold dear. There were two older sisters, both now married to Richmond businessmen, and Anne was enough younger than them not to have been repressed by their influence.

Anne's father had suggested a Sweet Briar College education, but he had been satisfied when she selected Goucher. As a freshman, she had met Clay Hallam, then a junior in Johns Hopkins Medical School, on a blind date at a medical school fraternity party. They had been so smitten with each other that the marriage was planned for the following year, at the end of his last year of medical school and her sophomore year. She had seen no driving need to complete a college education, and she was not compelled to find or establish a career of her own. She was warm, sensual, and romantic, she trusted her instincts, and when she found Clay, who was a doctor like her father, she knew that marriage was enough of a career for her. She believed that after the several difficult years of internship and residency, they would settle down to the same pleasant, although certainly not similar, life that she saw her parents living—more meaningful, more sentient than theirs, perhaps, but nonetheless abundant and fulfilling. Both she and Clay wanted children, and she felt that bearing and raising his babies would be all the career she would want. She loved him so much, as she lay there watching him sleep, that her only fear was that she would never get enough of him, could never possibly ever be with him to the point of being satisfied.

Clay was off duty that Fourth of July, due to the annual party for the new surgical house staff given at the residence of Dr. Sarnoff, the professor of surgery, at five o'clock that evening. During this time, interns' places on the ward were taken by the senior assistant resident and some assistant professors, who donated their time in order to make the event possible. The annual party was a favorite project of Dr. Sarnoff, who was deeply interested in his house staff and their training. Getting to know each of them on a personal footing was an important part of his program. He was a cardiac surgeon, and his stature as professor of surgery at Johns Hopkins placed him in the front ranks of the surgical world.

Anne found him utterly charming; his silver hair, horn-rimmed glasses, and soft Alabama accent, with its innate courteous manner, were irresistible to her. His home, a big, rambling clapboard house in the Catonsville section of west Baltimore, boasted a large backyard with a swimming pool and barbecue pit, and Clay and Anne were immediately urged to don their bathing suits. They complied, but before Clay could get into the pool he was sidetracked by a group discussing a new surgical technique in breast surgery being developed at Hopkins.

Anne plunged gratefully into the pool and swam luxuriously for a time, finally pulling herself up to sit on the edge of the pool, partly shaded by two oak trees. She found herself sitting beside another woman who was dangling her feet in the water. She was perhaps ten years older than Anne and had dark hair showing some early gray, a roundish, pleasant face already lined with resignation, and a dumpy figure.

"Hello, I'm Anne Hallam."

"Hello, I'm Delores Burroughs."

"Oh, are you the wife of Tom Burroughs, my husband's chief resident?"

"Yes, he's chief resident. Is your husband one of the new interns?"

"Yes," answered Anne, smiling, "and it was your husband who kept my husband from coming home the last three nights because of a critical patient he had to watch."

"Oh," said Delores, giving a wan smile, "the gunshot case, you mean. Well, if it's any consolation, my husband didn't come home either, and he's been here a lot longer than your husband."

"How long have you all been here?" asked Anne.

"Six years, all told," Delores replied. "We came here for this internship from the University of Michigan Medical School."

"Have you enjoyed your stay here?"

Delores looked at her carefully before answering. " 'Enjoy' is a strong word. I think Tom has enjoyed it. I—I guess—have enjoyed it. Oh, it's had its compensations. We have two children, aged three and two, and they're healthy and well . . . but let's face it, for married couples it's more or less a waiting period, until his training is finished. I mean, almost no money, a house you can hardly turn around in, social life mostly house-staff parties, and, on top of it all, hardly any time together. I mean, what's to enjoy?

"They're all crazy, you know, they love it and, if you left it up to them, they'd stay here forever. Their training would never finish. Always more to learn, more to find out—as if the hospital is some sort of primal font they have to stay close to so they won't miss anything. And you know that gunshot case they've worked so hard on? He's a shiftless wife-beater, no job, beat up his wife for years. So she finally shot him. And these guys, our husbands, are eating their hearts out to save him, bring him back. Can you tell me why? But it doesn't matter, the end's in sight. We're leaving after next year to go back home. Tom will be professor of surgery at Kansas, which is big, so I guess it's all worth it. We'll see."

Anne and Clay talked about this conversation that night, after making love again, and were lying in bed sipping coffee.

"You can't do a moral assessment of a human life before trying to save it. All lives are equal under the knife, and that's the way it should be," Clay said. "Besides, what is learned from this case of the wife-beater may help later to save a saint."

"How long do you think you'll stay here, Clay?" asked Anne, studying her cup.

"The training program is at least five years after the internship—two years of assistant residency, a year in surgical pathology, possibly a year of research, and then a year or two as chief resident. However, it's competitive all the way, and each year a guy may get dropped from the program. Only one makes it to chief resident."

"And you'd love to be that one, wouldn't you?"

He looked at her and said, "Honey, it's exhilarating. I've already learned more in three days than in four years of medical school. But it's hard. I may not make the cut. Warren Bregel is . . . tough."

He was gone the next morning when she awakened, leaving a note on his pillow which said, "Love you forever—see you soon."

So she adjusted. She was in the lush, early bloom of life, but she felt that she already had most of what the heart tells one to search for, and she prepared to wait until she had it all. During the first weeks she threw herself into refurbishing their house. She painted the walls, first the bathroom, then the kitchen, and finally the dining and living rooms, a stylish gray, leaving the trim of the windows and doors an off-white. She took on the living room sofa and, after much struggle, succeeded in re-covering it. She beat down the roach population, although she found that a single day's letdown in her defenses would bring them back.

Then, as the weeks turned into months, she expanded her activities. She joined the house staff's wives' club, for book and movie discussions, and she volunteered to teach at the kindergarten on the hospital grounds several days a week. Other days she worked for the patients' library at the hospital, pushing the book cart around to the rooms. She saw Clay periodically, frantically, and, when he was home, he spent much of the time trying to catch up on his sleep. However, she was able to notice a change in him during those months—

increased irritability, less humor, less willingness to put aside his hospital work. She struggled with these changes, unable to find any specific cause for them except too much work. He became much less interested in socializing, and he usually brought medical journals home with him, which he would pore over at night.

Later that fall, Anne's parents came for a weekend visit, saying that they would have come sooner but had not wanted to travel in the heat.

They stayed at the stylish Belvedere Hotel, and at dinner on Friday night they entertained friends who lived in Baltimore. Anne was included in the dinner, but Clay could not get away. The guests seemed upset that Anne had not called or visited them during the summer.

"Imagine! Staying in that hot East Baltimore slum all summer, when you could have been in our pool or at our club every day—it's ridiculous."

Anne had been well aware of those opportunities, but had decided against them. She wanted to stay as close to Clay and his life as possible, and luxury and swimming pools would certainly have been incongruous with this purpose.

She promised, however, to call at her earliest opportunity. She felt how far these people were removed from the life that she and Clay led.

As he drove her back to her house after dinner, her father said, "You look a bit thin, Anne. How are things going? Are you still in love?"

"More than ever, Dad, it's a hopeless case," Anne said, smiling at him. "But he has to work so hard. Did you have to work like this?"

Her father laughed. "Interns are the scum of the medical world—they have to do it all and still shine. It's the next years for you and Clay that are on my mind."

She looked at him. "What do you mean?"

"I'm going to propose to Clay that he come back to Richmond next year and complete his training with us. I want to start grooming him to take over someday as the head of the Grier Clinic, and he can learn all the surgery he'll ever need to know from me and the other surgeons at the clinic. It's a wonderful learning opportunity, and you would immediately begin to live a life together at, I might say, a fabulous salary."

"It sounds like paradise to me, Dad. Why haven't we thought of this before?"

Dr. Grier laughed. "I haven't thought of anything else since you two got engaged. I've just waited for the proper time. I hope Clay will see it my way."

But he didn't. When Dr. Grier put forward his proposal at dinner for the four of them the next night, Clay sat back in his chair.

"That's a wonderful offer, sir, and I appreciate it very much. But it comes a little too early for me. Give me five years to get my training."

"The clinic, and I, can't wait for five years, Clay. We need you soon. Why can't you complete your training with us and, at the same time, have a decent life for you and Anne? Start your family. Make a lot of money."

"It's very tempting, sir, and I'm sure it is for Anne, but, with all respect for you and the clinic, it's not a teaching hospital. I think you told me you send your most difficult cases elsewhere. Here, the most difficult cases are done every day, and here is where the learning is."

"But, Clay," responded Dr. Grier, "at the clinic you'll be doing the most common cases in surgery—the appendices, the gallbladders, the breasts, the colons. It's true you won't come out of it a professor of surgery, but you'll come out very adequate for your needs, and very well-to-do."

"Dr. Grier, all I can say is that at this point I'm just not interested. I want to get the best training I can get and try to be the best surgeon I'm capable of being, and, if I'm lucky enough to be chosen to stay here, I'll stay."

"And if you're not . . . chosen to stay?"

"Then I'll go to another teaching hospital."

The rest of the dinner was quiet and the ride home was silent. Not until Anne and Clay were in bed did they speak.

"I'm sorry your parents came. Things are tough enough without throwing another monkey wrench in the works."

"I'm sure Dad wasn't trying deliberately to do that. It was a perfectly sincere offer," Anne replied crisply.

"And one that he must have known I wouldn't accept."

"And why not? It would allow us to live normal lives together, have children, have fun, see each other. What's wrong with that?"

"Nothing—and it will all be ours, in time. But you know I couldn't be happy throwing away this chance in my life."

"And what is that?"

"I don't know. . . . I suppose to be really good—not just a surgeon with a good life, like your father, but something else, something special."

Anne paused, and turned over on her pillow. "Five or six more years here, in this roach-filled dump of a house, living on beans for a salary, and seeing each other maybe four or five times a week and being too tired then to care—this is what you want?"

She could sense him nodding in the dark. "But why?" she asked.

He stirred and then answered carefully, "Aren't you curious to find out how good I really can be?"

"Okay," she said. "Okay."

She felt his arms around her, and she turned and put her face into his chest. She knew she loved him even more for his stubbornness, for not taking the easy way, for believing in himself. She only hoped that she would prove worthy of sharing the life of this man, her husband.

CHAPTER 7

Friday, May 17, 1985

Anne Hallam stirred in her reverie. She had often returned to this early period of her life in an attempt to analyze it, to comprehend it, to seek meanings in what had subsequently developed. She was prone to self-reproach, and found herself willing to accept guilt for mistakes that her analysis of earlier events illuminated for her, and to play the game of what would have been had she made other choices. Alcohol seemed to enhance her ability to play it.

It was clear to her, in retrospect, that her parents' visit in which her father had made his proposal to Clay was the beginning of their difficulties. Things were never really the same after that.

• • • •

There was no immediate change in their relationship or behavior to each other, but it seemed to Anne that a crack had formed in the bond between them, and that it would widen later under continuing strain. All during that fall of '38, as the days grew shorter and the few maple trees along Broadway turned to russet and gold, and Clay continued to be preoccupied and irritable on the nights he was home, she harked back to the dream of returning to Richmond with Clay and of the wonderful life they could have. Then she would put it swiftly out of mind. She had married Clay with the intention of following his lead, wherever it took them, although in the back of her mind she was sure it would be to some wonderful place and that they would be together. She was proud of what she had accomplished so far in the four or five months they'd been in Baltimore, but she wasn't at all smitten with the idea of spending another five or six years this way.

Anne and Clay talked about her getting a job, but both agreed that this would keep them even further apart, because she would not be home on those odd days when he was able to leave the ward for a few hours. She began to develop friendships with other wives of the house staff, all of whom were in the same boat and adjusting in their own ways to the training program's demands. Anne found among the wives a network of interesting gossip and rumors about hospital matters. She listened more than she spoke, however, because Clay rarely talked to her about such things. It was from the wives that she first learned of the mental breakdown of one of the surgical interns. When being queried on rounds by one of the faculty members, he began talking meaninglessly about the case. He had been admitted to the Psychiatric Division for several weeks, and then a place was found for him to continue his training in a less demanding hospital. She also heard about Ham, the assistant resident who refused to comply with the orders of an associate professor. The professor had said, "Well, Ham, if you feel that way about it, don't bother to come back to this ward again," and Ham had replied, "Doctor, you don't know how I've looked forward to somebody saying those words to me." Ham went back to his place, packed, and was gone in two days! When she asked Clay about these occurrences, he merely grunted and passed them off without comment.

One of the wives with whom Anne became acquainted was Nell Bregel, Warren's wife, who lived only a few doors from them. Nell was a nurse, as were many of the wives, and she was very quiet and reticent at first.

"Oh yes, Warren and your husband are on the same ward together," Nell said.

"I guess that's right, although Clay doesn't tell me much," admitted Anne. "Does Warren work as hard as Clay?"

"Harder," responded Nell timidly, "at least, Warren says so."

"Tell me, how do the two of them get along? Does Warren say anything?"

"I don't know whether I should talk about it, Anne."

"I'm not the enemy, Nell. It's just that I feel I need to know more about what's going on over there—in order to know how to deal with things. Clay acts as if he's locked in some great struggle, but I don't know whether it's with himself, the hospital, or what."

"Promise not to tell Clay that I told you, but I think that part of his struggle is with Warren." Nell moved a bit toward her as if glad for a chance to share a confidence with someone.

"Will you tell me more," said Anne, "so I can understand?"

"You know, Warren is a funny person. I've been married to him six months now, long enough to be able to see it. Oh, he treats me fine, when he thinks of it. I have no complaints about that. It's just that he's obsessed—he's practically on fire—with the need to win his residency here. He talks about it all the time, how he made himself look better than some of the others, how he answered questions they couldn't or made a diagnosis they missed. Unfortunately, Clay, your husband, being on the same ward, is Warren's most direct competition."

Anne listened quietly and then said, "I see."

"But that isn't all," Nell continued. "I think Warren is jealous of Clay."

"What do you mean?"

"Well, of his looks, his background. See, Warren went to a small college in Kansas, and his parents are poor. He resents Clay's . . . uh . . . easy circumstances."

"He must be very bright."

"Oh, he's fearfully bright, and he makes sure everyone knows it."

Anne came away from this meeting partly relieved, for she now understood not only the pressure that Clay must feel but also his reticence to talk about it. He was fighting a battle she didn't even know existed and was sparing her. Once again, she hoped she could give him the support he needed. She never mentioned the conversation to him, but she understood even more clearly how hard it was for him to leave the ward, as well as the guilt he frequently displayed when he came home.

In early December, when a few early traces of snow were on the sidewalks and window sills, Clay called one evening before supper to say he wouldn't get home until late that night. They had planned to have dinner with the Mateers and another couple, so Anne went anyway. She enjoyed the evening. The talk was about Christmas and New Year's holidays. Each intern would have four days off for one or the other, and Clay had drawn Christmas. She returned home around ten o'clock, left the hall light on, and was halfway up the steps before she remembered that she had forgotten to lock the front door. She was about to go back down but then realized that Clay would be coming home soon and that if she left the door unlocked he wouldn't have to stand there in the cold, fiddling with his key. She changed into her flannel nightgown and read for a while, hoping he would come, but finally succumbed to the warm comfort of the bed, switched out the light, and fell asleep. Their bed was at right angles to the room entrance, projecting into the room from the left wall about three paces from the door. She had left the door open for Clay, but the old wooden steps creaked, and it was a creaking that awakened Anne. She looked toward the entrance and saw a man framed in the light from the hall, and she thought he was Clay.

"Hi, honey," she began, but choked off quickly, when she realized that this man was too burly to be Clay. Terror swept over her in a stomach-wrenching wave, and she threw back the covers and leaped out on the other side of the bed, clutching the sheets to her.

"What're you doing here?" she demanded, her voice tight. She could hear the man's heavy breathing as he stood there adjusting his eyes to the dark. The sour aroma of cheap wine reached her.

"Get in bed," he rasped, and started around the bed toward her.

"What do you want?"

"A fuck—what yo' think I want?" He lunged around the bed at

her. She tried to leap across it, but he launched himself across after her and pulled her back onto the bed. As she began to scream, he caught her by the throat and forced her head back into the pillow, and he pressed her with his weight. He pulled his hand from her throat and produced a knife from his belt. He let her see it and then put it to her throat under the left jaw.

"Make any noise and I'll cut your fuckin' head off." Her breath came in short pants as she felt his awful weight on her like some giant beast cleaving to her and rendering her powerless. Terror exploded through her skull, shattering her senses, driving her consciousness almost outside her body until she seemed a witness to what was happening, rather than a part of it.

"You don't want to do this—get yourself in trouble—my husband will be home any minute, . . . " she was able to make herself say.

His face was close to hers now, his sour breath on her neck, and she could feel the fury in his grasp.

"You ain't got no husband—he don't come that much," he snarled, and tore the flannel nightgown up over her head.

"Wait!" she cried.

He slapped her hard once with his right hand. "No talkin'," he said, and she felt him opening his pants.

"Spread your legs, or get cut," he commanded.

She felt waves of vertigo come over her, and her breath came in gasps. She saw him raising up over her like a monstrous animal, shifting toward her, forcing her legs apart with his weight. Then she could feel his penis, stiff and hard, slamming at her vagina. Suddenly, unbelievably, she heard the front door of the house opening and closing.

She shut her eyes and screamed! "Clay—look out—he's got a knife!" She waited for the knife to descend, expecting it, steeled—but instead, the man rolled off her, and she heard him run into the bathroom, throw open the window, and leap out onto the roof of the kitchen below, as Clay rushed into the room. "My God, Anne, my God—I'm here—I'm here, baby." He rushed to her and took her in his arms as she lay, half-delirious, sobbing softly.

The painful recollection of this event almost fifty years ago was enough to rouse Anne from her reverie by the window. She poured herself another drink. But she continued to dwell on the attack, examine it, as if she were an archaeologist scrutinizing specimens from her own past. During the ensuing days after the attack, she had remained terror-stricken, embarrassed, ashamed, and angry. Raw emotions blocked her mind and kept Clay from reaching her. He arranged with Dr. Sarnoff to be home several days with her, and he had bars installed on the windows and new, heavy locks on the doors. She underwent a careful examination, and it was determined that full penetration had not occurred. The police had assured them they would begin an extra watch in the neighborhood. From what she had told them about the rapist, including his familiarity with the bathroom window and his knowledge of Clay's frequent absence, they were sure that her house had been watched and that they would eventually catch him.

Anne was seen by a psychiatrist, when it became evident that she was suffering but not able to express her feelings. The psychiatrist was unable to allay her terror. She didn't want to go outside the house, even with Clay. She lost all interest in eating and would only nibble at food Clay offered her. She refused to see any of their friends, even the Mateers, who came frequently to call on them. Despite Clay's patient, loving attempts to reassure her and help her come to grips with her emotional shock, she was unable to unblock.

Later, of course, and especially now, after almost fifty years, it became clear what the trouble was: out of the whole awful experience, the humiliation, the fear, the degradation of it, the memory of it that kept overriding all, and that she could not excise from her mind or express her anger at, were the words spoken in his impatience by the rapist, "You ain't got no husband—he don't come that much." Recalling these words enraged her, distressed her, caused her to feel depressed and alone, and she subconsciously knew it would be the same after Clay went back to work. She would hardly let him leave the house, and yet would have nothing physically to do with him when he was there, so great was her sense of aggrievement.

After several weeks, Clay said, "Honey, look, we're not getting anywhere—you're losing weight, you look terrible, and you can't talk to me about it. It seems to me that we have two choices."

Anne looked at him emptily. "What are they?"

"One," said Clay gently, "is to enter the psychiatric ward here at the hospital for a while. I think it's the best choice, and I could visit you every day."

"And the second?"

"The second would be to go home to your parents for a while—get out of this environment. You wouldn't be afraid there, and maybe you can work this thing out. I can join you at Christmas time."

Anne looked at him steadily for a moment, aware of her conflicting emotions, loving him and wanting him, yet in some way angry at him for the shock she had suffered. He didn't understand—how could he? He hadn't been assaulted, violated, shaken to his roots. She somehow felt that he, too, should suffer . . . should also give up something.

"You . . . couldn't come with me—to Richmond?"

"I could . . . I guess," his manner betraying that he was torn between his need to return to the hospital and his desire to do his best for her. It was obvious that he hoped she would make the decision for him, and it pained her even more that he could not fully make the commitment himself.

"No, that won't be necessary. I think it's best that I go home for a while and that you join me at Christmas—it's only a few weeks off, and I'll be better by then. Do my parents know everything that happened?"

Clay nodded. "I called. Of course, they wanted to come immediately, but I thought it was better for us to have some time together, though it hasn't helped, has it?"

"I guess not," Anne shook her head. "I'm sorry about all this, Clay, sorry to be a burden."

His remonstrances were sincere, but she sensed a feeling of relief in him, which was even more evident to her several days later when her mother and one of her sisters arrived in a chauffeur-driven limousine to pick her up. Anne and Clay parted soberly, uncertainly, on the front steps of their row house, with tears, pledges to write and call, and assurances of love. He doesn't understand, she thought, and I can't tell him.

Her return home was marked by warmth and understanding from

her parents, who left the door open for discussion but did not try to draw her out about the rape. They had told everyone that she was visiting for a few weeks before Christmas, and they encouraged her to go out with her friends. And gradually, in this familiar atmosphere, she felt her confidence begin to return, and her spirits to revive. Her appetite returned, too, and she began to regain the weight she had lost. Christmas came too soon, however, and, when Clay arrived to reclaim her, she found the wound reopening. His presence was a reminder that broke down superficial tissues of healing. The thought of returning to Baltimore with him, with all of its implications, with Clay's absences and preoccupations, was abhorrent to her. Her sleep was full of nightmares.

She and Clay slept in the same bed, but she could not let him touch her sexually, even though he tried and was obviously tortured by her nearness. She thought he looked older and tired, and she wanted to mother him, but the idea of sex with him was repugnant. On the third night, his last night, he tried to force her, reaching under her nightgown to seek her breasts, pulling her against him. She could feel him hard against her thigh.

"You too, Clay?" she said.

"What do you mean, me too?" he returned.

"I don't want this now—you're forcing me. What's the difference between you and . . . him?"

He recoiled in anger. "I'm your husband, for God's sake. And I love you."

She was silent for a time. She said, "You love me, Clay, but you don't love me enough. Why weren't you there when I needed you?"

"But I was," he answered indignantly. "I got there in time. I broke it up, didn't I?"

She sat up, staring at him. "I mean in time to prevent it—to keep it from happening at all? Do you know what he said? 'You ain't got no husband—he don't come that much.' All those lonely days and nights. Maybe he was right. Maybe I don't have a husband—only a part-time lover."

He was up and pacing now. "My God, that's it, isn't it? You blame me—that's what's in your head. You think it's all my fault. Do you know what kind of pressure I'm under—do you know what I'm trying to do?"

"No, because you never tell me. All you do is come home occasionally and read or sleep, eat, and make love. Do you think that's enough?"

"I'm sorry, Anne, I had no idea you felt like this. I suppose I should have talked to you more—told you more about how things are—but it won't be this way for long."

"How long?"

"A few more years maybe. But this is the worst year of all, and it's going quickly."

"Maybe for you. Look, I know you have to work hard, and I know the other wives are putting up with it, but maybe I'm different— maybe I'm not cut out to be a Johns Hopkins wife. All I know is that right now I'm full of doubt and I can't come back with you tomorrow."

He stopped pacing and stared at her, then said, "Anne, I love you. You're all I could ever ask for or want in a wife, and I don't want to lose you. So take your time about working things out—what you want to keep and what you want to let go. I need you very much . . . but I have to say that I also need to do what I'm doing. The work is hard and exhausting, but it's also the most exciting, the most compelling, that I've ever known. Every move I make there is a learning move, and every teacher has something to teach. The competition to stay in the training program is grotesque . . . but I have to try. Don't give up on us, Anne, don't throw away what we have together. Help me be what I think I can be."

She watched him leave the next day, his tall figure bent against the cold December wind.

God, what am I doing to him—and to me? she thought. But the answers weren't at hand.

December gave way to a cold, drab January, with intermittent snow and driving rain. Ice formed on the James River. Anne ice-skated on the pond near the Griers' home, went to the movies and to a few cocktail parties, and read. She felt better, but still felt no compulsion to return to Clay in Baltimore. Her parents remained very understanding, although her father did begin to mutter a bit about her going back to Baltimore soon. She tried on several occasions to talk to him, but found that she couldn't. She was afraid that his opinions were already formed. She knew that he still wanted Clay to join the Grier Clinic, and, although he loved her, his advice was bound to be colored by that desire.

May Harding was her best friend. She was willowy and blonde, and she considered herself a modernist and well ahead of Richmond standards. She went to Smith College, considered safe by her banker father, and smoked cigarettes through a violet cigarette holder. Her nose was prominent, and her green eyes were a bit too close, but her complexion was flawless. She and Anne had been drawn together through their prep school years by their style, family friendships, and what they believed was independent thinking. May had been maid of honor at Anne's wedding, and, when she came home to Richmond on her winter break from Smith, Anne's was the first door she headed for.

At first Anne was quite guarded and hesitant to discuss her situation even with May, but, as their friendship reestablished itself, she gradually overcame her hesitancy.

"It's strange how different our lives have become in just a short time," she said to May one afternoon after skating. The two were sipping hot chocolate in the Hardings' kitchen. "You're telling me about history class and dating, and I'm telling you about pots and pans and laundry."

"Well, you live life, and I procrastinate, and that's the difference. I don't think you're missing anything," May retorted, languidly. "The boys are so retarded these days."

Anne laughed and then said, "I need to talk to you a bit, May . . . Do you mind?"

"I'm delighted," May replied. "I was beginning to think we were no longer confidantes. It's obvious there's something wrong . . . that you're not just home for a visit, as your mother is telling everyone. You look like hell—even your hair looks depressed. I've been hoping you'd tell me."

"I'm sorry," said Anne. "I haven't felt up to talking about it, but now I do—to you."

May nodded, and then encouraged, "Clay misbehaving?"

Anne shook her head. "Not that—not entirely anyway. For one thing, I was raped."

"Raped! My God!" gasped May. "No wonder you don't look well—what happened?"

So Anne unfolded the story, including its aftermath on her feelings and her need to leave Baltimore.

"Terrifying, especially the knife," responded May. "Were you hurt?"

"Oh, a few bruises and aches, but nothing bad physically. Mentally, I'm still not right. I still wake up at night at the slightest sound. They caught the man but it still doesn't help. Maybe I'm just a chicken . . . "

"I don't believe that," answered May, drawing herself up and trying to look wiser than her twenty-one years. "You never lacked for courage. Remember the night at Saint Catherine's when we had to sneak back to our rooms by going over the roof and along the ledge into our windows? That was your idea—still scares me that we did it."

"Then I felt invincible," said Anne. "Now I don't feel invincible anymore."

"Like I said," replied May, "you really live . . . not that rape is a part of everyday life, but finding out that one is not invincible surely is. What does Clay say?"

"That there are bars on the windows and new locks on all the doors, and that he wants me back."

"He's being very patient, it seems. Tell me, Anne, how're you two doing, except for this?"

"Wonderful . . . when I have him. But I don't have him that often. He works so hard." And she explained their life to May.

May listened carefully as Anne talked, then she said, "Well, dear, let me say something. When you told me you were getting married, at the end of your freshman year in college, I frankly thought you were crazy. But after I met Clay and got to know him, you suddenly changed into the smartest and most sensible girl I knew. I was envious of you—still am. He's clearly a special person. But I think there's one thing you ought to admit to yourself and resign yourself to: you'll never really have a person like him—never enough, anyway. He has too much talent, too much sense of mission. You'll have to learn to be satisfied with the bits of time you do have together, and don't expect too much. Or else leave him now, while you have the chance. That's my advice."

In early February, Randolph Grier stopped by to see Anne. He seemed to have recovered from the heart attack and was back on the bridge circuit. "I must tell you about this hand we played at the Auchinchlosses' last evening. We'd been drinking champagne and were all a bit tipsy, so I decided to have some fun. Our bid was six spades, which we didn't have a chance of making. However, between us we did have a nice diamond suit, so . . . first I drew trumps, and then began playing the high diamonds from the board, but instead of following suit I threw off my club and heart losers from my hand. I got back in my hand, and led my own high diamonds. Well, Florence Auchinchloss, on my left, instead of yelling, 'Renege—renege,' said, 'Oh, my God, here come those damn diamonds again.' Believe me, it was most amusing." He giggled.

They chatted for a while about family and memories. Anne thought he looked thinner and older. Since his heart attack, his sparse hair was grayer, and his features were sharper. She thought suddenly how much she did care about him, how close to him she felt.

"Uncle Randolph, I have a problem," she said.

For an hour she talked to him, in the small study of her parents' home, as the maid served them tea, and the February wind blew against the windowpanes.

At the end of it, Uncle Randolph looked quite solemn. He said, "A terrible business, Anne. I don't know how you've gotten through it."

"It shook me a lot, Uncle Randolph . . . that such a thing could happen. It made me timid. But the odd thing is, I seem to blame Clay for the whole thing, as if it were all his fault, for not being there to prevent it—for never being there. The other interns' wives are going through the same thing, except for the rape, of course, but they're coping with it. Why should I be different?"

Uncle Randolph cleared his throat. "Well, I don't know—maybe you are different. As I've always said, you are an independent thinker— always have been—not a follower. It's why I've always felt we were a bit alike. You're not as content to sit around and mark time as some might be. Also, you're a bit younger than most of them— maybe a little impatient. But I think once you've reasoned things out, and decided what's really in the long run important to you, then you'll be fine."

"But why do I feel I can't go back to him? Why do I know I love him and want him, but can't return?"

Randolph took some tea, cleared his throat again, and said, "When I was young, about your age, I had a wonderful friend whom I loved. At one time in school I was trying for the Latin prize. I worked hard for it and thought I had won it, but I didn't. I was very hurt— and angry. My friend didn't even know how upset I was, but I needed to get his attention and punish him for my hurt. So I cut him off, wouldn't speak to him or see him for months. I was miserable. Finally, I woke up one morning and decided I'd punished him enough. My hurt felt satisfied, so I called him, and we got together, and everything went back to usual. I never knew whether I had made him suffer, but the point was that I thought I had.

"It looks to me like you're trying both to get Clay's attention and to punish him for not hurting like you hurt. After all, why should he get off scot-free when you're married and supposed to share everything? But I believe one morning you'll wake up and say, 'We're even—I've punished him enough.' And you'll go back to him."

She smiled at him and said she didn't think it was that simple. But strangely enough, several days later, she awakened, called Clay at the hospital, and told him she was coming home.

She began packing excitedly, eagerly, all doubts suddenly dissolved.

· · · ·

Anne, sitting now in her chair by the window of their stately house in Baltimore and sipping her bourbon, blurrily remembered the excitement and desire she had felt when she was preparing to return to

Clay, almost fifty years ago. Then why didn't I, why didn't I go back—stay with him?

Her mind dulled by the alcohol, she struggled to focus it. And then she remembered the letter. It arrived the day after she'd called Clay to tell him she was coming back to him. It was unsigned, but had a Baltimore postmark. It said, "Your husband is having an affair—ask him."

CHAPTER 8

Friday, May 17, 1985

Jim and Charlotte talked in the soft lantern light under the mothering branches of the Judas tree. They had spoken sporadically at first, touched on casual subjects, but gradually the topics became more personal.

"Do you have brothers and sisters, Jim?"

"I have two half-sisters by my father's previous marriage, but I don't see them much." He sipped from a brandy that Ona had served him. "So it's just Mom and me now. My father died a couple of years ago."

"What's your mother like?"

"She's . . . kind of a dingbat, a wonderful dingbat. She's into everything at once and has a great enthusiasm about it all. Everybody loves her, and she's on lots of committees. She's attractive, in her late forties, and still has her health, thank God."

"Do you think she'll ever marry again?"

"I doubt it. She says she could never get used to another man's eccentricities again, and she's got all the money she needs. I don't think she'd want to be tied down again."

"Your father sounds interesting. Was he eccentric?"

"Oh, no more than any of us male types, I think." He smiled again. "He was a broker, and he did okay in that, but his heart wasn't in it. He tried a number of things—he even owned a ballet company for a while—but I don't think he ever was really satisfied."

"That sounds eccentric enough!" Charlotte exclaimed.

"Agreed. It was called La Petite Ballet, mostly castoffs from the New York City Ballet and the American Ballet Company. He housed it out on Long Island, near our home in Southampton, and he booked performances for it at benefits and social gatherings around the Long Island area. It did all right for a while, but then one night its building burned, and all the scenery and costumes were lost, and he let it go."

"Too bad," she said thoughtfully. "I'd like to have known your father—and your mother, too."

"I can arrange the latter—but she's quite different from your parents."

"How do you mean?"

"Well," said Jim, "Your parents are statelier, much more intellectual. Your mother is still a knockout despite her age; in fact, she's almost regal. How old is she, do you mind my asking?"

"She's almost sixty-seven, but don't tell her I told you."

"Trust me! That, however, makes you arrive a bit late on the scene."

Charlotte nodded. "She was about forty-two when I came along. They wanted to make sure I was last, I guess."

" 'The last shall be the best' is the saying. Do you think you resemble your parents? You know, intellectually?"

"I suppose I might be a sort of modern intellectual. I can usually find the left of center on most social issues, but then it becomes clear that the left also has a left and right, and that left has another left and right, and I get confused." She laughed. "And you—are you like your mother and father?"

"I have moments that belong to both, I suppose. But look, it's time for me to go. And because you're going to be here in town for another few days, why don't I present you with the opportunity to have fun and also to see what I do, at work and at play, sort of the Yin and Yang of my life? I'd love to have your observations."

"How could I resist such an offer? What does it involve?"

"Well, it will involve your tomorrow. The work part takes place in the hospital auditorium. I have to discuss a fascinating case at Grand Rounds, and, if you can understand enough of the jargon, it will show you a kind of high point in what I do, or what I'm training to do."

She thought for a moment, then said, "Why do you want me to come?"

"I don't know exactly," he admitted. "I just think it would be nice."

"So this would be the Yin. What about the Yang?"

He laughed. "The Yang is a party tomorrow night, at some friends' house, near the hospital."

She laughed with him and finally said, "A Yin and Yang day—I've never had one, but I accept with pleasure. What are your terms?"

They rose and walked toward the door.

"Get a good night's sleep, and come to the hospital auditorium at quarter of twelve tomorrow. Pick a good seat and relax. I'll see you afterward, in your dad's room."

They shook hands on it at the door and parted, both excited by what they felt about each other this evening and by their anticipation of the next day.

Jim made rounds early next morning, Saturday, to Bertram Harper's great satisfaction.

"Excited about your presentation, I suppose." The sneer in Harper's voice was only barely audible. "Want to tell me your diagnosis now so I won't have to sit through it all?"

"No, Bert, I'm gonna keep you in suspense for a while, but I'll tell you right now that I think I've got it. Want to tell me yours?"

"You know mine. I think it's acute pancreatitis with abscess forma-

124

tion. What do you think we've been treating him for all week?"

"But he's no better, is he? In fact, he's worse. Of course, the operation this morning will tell us the answers, but I think I've got it worked out."

"I can hardly wait. Shall we get morning rounds over?"

They were joined by Harris, Jim's fellow intern on the ward, and the three of them went around the entire floor, visiting each patient, and pushing the chart rack in front of them, accompanied by the three floor nurses.

They found Dr. Hallam reading the morning paper in the chair by his bed. The meeting was brief, with Harper checking his left hand grip and listening to his carotid arteries.

"We're going to do that carotid artery angiogram on Monday, Dr. Hallam," Harper said.

"Fine, Dr. Harper, I'll look forward to it," Dr. Hallam said, and smiled up at them. As they turned toward the door, he winked at Jim. The latter smiled back but quickly turned away, anxious not to upset the rhythm of the rounds but knowing he would be returning later, after Grand Rounds, to meet Charlotte. He thought Dr. Hallam looked a bit paler and weaker that morning than the previous day, but his examination showed him stable and revealed nothing new.

By the time they had finished rounds it was ten o'clock, and then Jim had another hour of ward work, which took him an hour and a half, so preoccupied was he with the case he was going to discuss. He kept turning over the details of the case in his mind to ensure that he hadn't overlooked any possible clues.

Saturday Grand Rounds was the closest medicine ever got to show business. It focused on the most interesting case, or cases, in the medical services during the week, presented with some pomp in the great medical auditorium and featuring audiovisual screen projections of data relating to the case, auxiliary presentation of x-rays by a chief radiologist, and pathology by a senior pathologist. Dr. Mendel, the professor of medicine, presided over (or produced) it. It was his pet educational project, and he took a great interest in its success.

The presentation drew not only the hospital medical staff but also internists and other physicians from all over the city, who came to enjoy and learn from it.

Grand Rounds usually drew from cases in which the diagnosis was already known and treatment under way, but in special instances a case was selected in which the disease was as yet undetected and remained elusive, in order to illustrate the diagnostic process as practiced at the hospital and to point out possible flaws in reasoning. These diagnostic mysteries were to Jim one of the delights in his pursuit of a medical career, and one of the abiding reasons he had chosen internal medicine as a field, rather than surgery or some other specialty. The intellectual challenge of diagnosis, necessitating careful analyses of all symptoms and laboratory clues, weighing the special significance of each, was an exercise he never tired of. On certain occasions he became so wrapped up in the puzzle and its solution that he almost forgot that a patient's life was involved.

One week ago, Jim had admitted the present case, a forty-seven-year-old auto mechanic who had severe abdominal pain, to the medical service. Jim had been devoting much time to this case ever since. Of course, he had had plenty of help and advice from above, from Bertram Harper and the chief resident, Reggin, to various professors who had come to see this patient, but their best efforts had not provided any satisfactory answers or any definitive line of treatment. In fact, the man was worse. That morning he was undergoing an abdominal exploratory, to find the exact nature of his problem, but Jim, who was given the honor, or onus, of presenting his case to the audience, had a new theory on what the diagnosis was, and he was excited because no one had mentioned the possibility before—it was all his.

Dr. Mendel rose from his seat in the front row and glanced back over the tiered assembly as if checking the gate. Then he strode to the microphone.

"Good morning," he intoned, his voice flat, as if not to prejudice the audience. "We have an interesting case in diagnostics this morning, a man with abdominal pain. In a reversal of the usual order, his case will be presented by his resident, Dr. Harper, and discussed by his intern, Dr. Gallier. The correct diagnosis is unknown, but the patient is being explored surgically this morning, so I hope we'll know the correct answer by the time we've finished here."

Harper took the microphone. "Good morning. This is a forty-seven-year-old Caucasian male auto mechanic who was admitted here six days ago because of abdominal pain.

"The pain had begun intermittently three weeks before admission and became progressively worse; it was accompanied by loss of appetite and vomiting. Physical examination showed a temperature of 100.6 degrees, a pulse of 100, and a normal blood pressure. He was tender in the mid-abdomen but there were no other findings, and he was not jaundiced. Laboratory work included an elevated white cell count, normal liver function tests, normal pancreatic enzymes, but a CAT scan of the abdomen showed probable enlargement of the pancreas, while x-rays presented some gas distention in the intestinal tract, in the ascending and transverse colon. A G.I. series and barium enema were normal.

"The patient was placed on gastric drainage and intravenous hyper-alimentation, along with Gentamicin and Keflin. He became progressively weaker, and his temperature rose to 101 degrees. His endoscopic cholangiogram examination was negative. A repeat CAT scan showed only some thickening of the walls of several feet of small bowel. Because of continued deterioration, and no definite diagnosis, it was elected to operate on him this morning.

"Dr. James Gallier will discuss the case."

Jim rose from his seat in the front row and approached the microphone, passing the sardonic-looking Harper, who was returning to his seat. Tension swept over Jim as he spread his notes on the rostrum and prepared to speak to an audience composed not only of Dr. Mendel, senior medical staff of the hospital, and many visiting internists and practitioners, but also, although he hadn't seen her yet, Charlotte Hallam. He realized he was going out on a limb by himself in making the diagnosis he was going to propose, against the opinions of the more experienced staff who had consulted on the case, and was suddenly aware that he might be making a fool of himself. Where was the confidence he had felt last night, when like a fool he had invited Charlotte to come here?

"Good morning," he began tentatively, "you have just heard the medical history of this forty-seven-year-old man during his six days in this hospital. His case excited much interest and debate on the ward because of the paucity of diagnostic findings and his steadily downhill course. He was frustrating to treat, because his pain was so severe that he was writhing with it and could gain no relief.

"The various x-rays and blood tests ruled out such common causes of abdominal pain and fever as perforated ulcer, gallbladder disease, diverticulitis, kidney colic, and, of course, appendicitis. The initial CAT scan of the abdomen showed a possible soft-tissue mass overlying the pancreas, which the second CAT scan seemed to confirm. This led some to make a diagnosis of pancreatitis or pancreatic cancer with abscess formation, and he was treated for this with no success. Against this diagnosis, it seemed to me, were these factors: there was no evidence of gallbladder disease, which may lead to pancreatitis, and he was not an alcoholic, which also leads to pancreas disease. So, he had no obvious cause for pancreatitis. Also, his serum amylase was normal, and his endoscopic pancreatic duct evaluation was normal. Again, these are against the diagnosis of pancreas disease.

"The second most favored diagnosis made by those who saw the patient was primary ileitis, which could have produced the pain, the fever, and the CAT scan findings of the change in the walls of the intestinal tract. However, that condition is rarely so rapidly progressive as the process in our patient today, and it is usually heralded by some diarrhea, which the patient did not have.

"The third most favored diagnosis on the ward was some type of primary small-bowel lymphoma, a tumor that perforated the small intestine wall and caused swelling or abscess at the head of the pancreas."

Jim looked up at the audience for a moment before taking a deep breath and continuing.

"After being on the case all week and after much thought and reading, I suddenly thought last night that none of those diagnoses fits the case. And, perhaps because of another patient I'm attending who has had a blood clot, I began to think of it as a possibility in our present case. The more I read about this condition, called mesenteric vein thrombosis, the more certain I became that that's what this man has.

"The mesenteric vein, of course, returns the blood from the small intestinal tract and drains it into the portal vein system, which takes it to the liver and then back to the heart. A clot in the mesenteric vein would gradually produce inflammation, fever, and severe abdominal pain, as well as the swelling in the region of the pancreas, as seen on the CAT scan.

"Causes of mesenteric vein thrombosis are several: it can be seen as a result of trauma or blows to the stomach; various kinds of cancer in the liver and pancreas can obstruct and cause it; and it can be seen from blood deficiencies in various anticlotting conditions. Mesenteric vein thrombosis was first described in 1935 by Eberhard and Warren in the *Journal of Surgery and Gynecology* as a clinical entity, and in a small percentage of cases it occurs with no known causative factor.

"I believe it is the proper diagnosis in today's case."

Jim stepped down from the podium as a murmur swept through the audience. He sat down gratefully and wiped the moisture from his forehead.

With a grudging, lopsided smile, Dr. Mendel walked to the microphone. "That was an interesting discussion, Dr. Gallier, and a fascinating conclusion. I must confess that I heard about this case, although I didn't see him personally, and I leaned toward the diagnosis of acute ileitis with a perforation . . . but now we'll see. The patient has been explored surgically this morning, and I see Dr. Grossman, who was the surgeon, has kindly joined us. Dr. Grossman, can you tell us what you found?"

Still clad in his surgical green garb, Dr. Grossman said, "I heard the tail end of Dr. Gallier's discussion, and I can only say that I wish we'd been able to talk to him prior to surgery, and maybe we wouldn't have been as surprised. Our preoperation diagnosis was acute pancreatitis with abscess, and we were ready to drain it.

"Instead, at operation, we found that the pancreas was normal and that there was no abscess. Instead, there was extensive clotting through the mesenteric vein plexus, and a hemorrhagic necrosis of about a foot of small bowel due to the clot. This area of bowel was removed, and patient is doing well. I'd like to congratulate Dr. Gallier on his diagnosis."

Jim felt a warm flush of pleasure surge over him, and a wave of applause swept over the audience. He hadn't made a fool of himself. He was still glowing later on when he came to Dr. Hallam's room, and found Charlotte there.

"Jim, congratulations, that was marvelous," she said, smiling, as he came in. "I've been telling Dad about it."

"Yes, well done, Dr. Gallier. I hear you hit one on the button."

"Hello, Charlie. Hello, Dr. Hallam. I was very lucky, but I did feel confident that it was the right diagnosis—that is, up until the time I had to talk about it."

"The courage of one's convictions is courage indeed, especially in a medical institution where there are so many so-called authorities," said Dr. Hallam. "The message may be 'Don't listen to the old fogies'— at least all the time." He sank back on his pillow.

"How are you feeling today, Dr. Hallam?" asked Jim, checking his pulse. He appeared tired, and his speech was a bit thick, as if speaking took more effort than the muscles were able to make.

"Not bad—not bad, Doctor," said the older man. "Tell me, your case today—Charlie said the condition was described in 1935?"

"Yes sir, in the *Journal of Surgery and Gynecology* by Eberhard and Warren."

"Close to the year of my internship," murmured Dr. Hallam, "a long time ago." He seemed to be drifting off to sleep.

Charlotte bent over and kissed him on the forehead, "I'll see you later, Dad, and Mom will be in soon."

She and Jim left the room quietly and walked up the corridor together.

"What do you think, Jim?" she asked anxiously. "He seems so weak and tired."

"Yes, he does, but he's bound to be after an episode like he's had. I don't see any new neurological signs that indicate he's any worse, and he's still receiving his anticoagulant. I'll look in on him again shortly."

They walked in silence toward the main exit, where Charlotte's car was parked.

"I enjoyed the Yin part of the day, Jim," she suddenly smiled. "Is the Yang still on?"

He smiled back at her. "I'm glad you came, Charlie. It was great of you to make the effort. The Yang part, however, is the best part. Shall I pick you up at eight?"

He walked her out the door, then retraced his footsteps toward the ward. He, too, was worried about Dr. Hallam's appearance today. He had lost some of the acuity that he had manifested the last few days, and now, seven days after the onset of the episode, he should be stronger.

Returning to the office on Marburg 1, Jim went carefully over Dr. Hallam's chart, reading the nurses' notes, and reviewed his medications. He found nothing there that disturbed him or made him think that a change in medications was indicated. The vital signs, blood pressure, pulse, and temperature were all steady. One nurse's note indicated that his appetite was off a bit for breakfast and lunch, but that was all. Nonetheless, Jim phoned Dr. Andres, the neurology professor who was in charge of Dr. Hallam's treatment, and related his observations. Dr. Andres promised to come and have a look.

"Is his heparin dosage okay?" Dr. Andres asked. "He's not overloaded, is he?"

"No, sir," answered Jim. "I just checked it."

"Pupils are equal? Good. Look, why don't we get another CAT scan, just to make sure he hasn't bled or had a further onset? I'll be over soon."

It took the rest of the afternoon to do the studies and harvest the results. They were normal and showed no evidence of a stroke, and by that time Dr. Hallam seemed brighter. Jim was in much better spirits by the time he picked up Charlotte that night.

The party was in Will and Henny's apartment. Will was a fellow intern of Jim's, and Henny was a nurse on the surgical service and had as great a zest for life as Jim had ever seen. He thought a lot of both of them. They enjoyed a spacious apartment and a wonderful enclosed patio, which Henny had decorated with multicolored lights strung overhead.

The apartment was dimly lit, and most of the furniture had been cleared for the party, which was well under way by the time Jim and Charlotte arrived. Henny and Will met them as they entered, pushing the crowded doorway open for them.

"I'm delighted to meet you, Charlie," Henny greeted her. "Will is a great admirer of your father's. We're so glad he's feeling better. Jim, will you please get over to the piano, stat? The quiet is driving me nuts. Do you mind, Charlie? Willie'll bring you a drink."

"That is, if he can hear you in this din," laughed Jim, "but I'll be glad to help out later."

"Oh, we need you now. Charlie, will you make him play, please? We'll be friends for life if you do."

Charlotte laughed and grabbed Jim lightly by the ear. "That did it—where's the piano?"

They found it in the living room, an old upright jammed up against a corner wall. They laughed their way through the crowd, which parted willingly for them as they saw that Jim was going to play.

"You do play the piano?" Charlotte asked as both of them sat down on the seat. "You never told me."

"I don't really play, my fingers just get very excited when they're near ivory. I think it's a sexual deviation."

He began to play, nonchalantly at first, talking as he did so. The easy rhythms of the Beatles, Cole Porter, Springsteen, Gershwin emerged from under his fingers as if sprung from an old vault. The crowd gathered around them, singing for a while, then wandered off into conversation and returned. Jim played effortlessly, swinging from one tune into another, taking requests and obliging, his eyes wandering from the keyboard to the crowd and back to Charlotte, who sang in a contralto voice and watched him as if seeing him for the first time. He was obviously enjoying it all, and she saw no sign of the serious, sometimes frowning, expression that he often wore in the hospital. Excited by the nearness and beauty of Charlotte, Jim often kept the melody going with the right hand, while taking his left off the keys to put his arm around her.

The crowd's interest in singing began to wane, and Jim's attention focused more and more on the music. He began to play Scott Joplin and then the arcane but haunting rhythms of Erik Satie. His grin faded to a dreamy smile, and his gaze no longer wandered but became fixed on his own finger work as if mesmerized by the sounds his hands were evoking from the keyboard.

He had no idea how long he had played, but when he finally looked up Charlotte was gone from the piano seat. He turned around on it, feeling guilty about having neglected her, and tried to spot her in the crowded, semidarkened room. Not seeing her, and suddenly feeling disturbed, he got up and searched the next room. He found her there talking to Jonas. They broke off abruptly as Jim approached, and he could not make out what they were discussing; but much later, well after midnight, he brought up the subject as he drove her home.

She looked at him, across the intimate darkness of the small car, and said, "We were talking about you, mostly. Jonas was telling me what a great person you are, as only a roommate can do. He's very devoted to you, you know. Want to hear what he said?" Jim nodded. "He said you're more casual about your own gifts, less impressed by them, than any other person he knows. And in the next breath he was telling me how much I could do for you."

Jim gave her a quick look. "Oh? In what way?"

"He's worried about you. He thinks you're in some sort of tailspin and that you need encouragement. He thinks I could help."

Jim grinned, steering the car slowly through the darkened streets. "Jonas doesn't mess around, does he? If there's something on his mind, he gets it right out."

"Is there anything to what he said? What did he mean?"

"I guess it was something I said to him the other day—some doubts I had."

She hesitated, gazing out the window, then said, "Turn right at the next corner, in case you don't remember. Do you mind if I ask you something? Why did you want me to come to your presentation? Did your doubts have anything to do with it?"

Jim rounded the corner and pulled up in front of her house. The street was dark except for the areas illuminated by a few street lights and house lights. The scent of privet and wisteria filled the air, and a dog barked in the distance. Jim turned off the motor.

"I most assuredly wanted you there. It just seemed important to me that you be there. I don't think I was really trying to show off . . . except in a way maybe I was. . . . Did you at all enjoy being there?"

She nodded. "I was very proud of you. A lot of it probably went over my head, but I understood enough to get the gist, the fascination, of it."

"You did? You could see that? The challenge of it? The human side of it? Each case its own story, with its own set of problems. One reason I wanted you to come was to see if you could see the—the *importance* of it."

"I can see that, and I think you make an excellent problem solver. I was very happy for you."

"Oh, I was lucky . . . I was just closer to the case than the rest of the guys."

"Jonas says you're a natural—that you'll make a wonderful doctor. Judging from the way you've handled Dad, I certainly agree."

He leaned his arm up on the seat and touched her hair.

"God, you're beautiful," he murmured, almost to himself.

"Now that it's dark you tell me that!"

"You're beautiful in the light and in the dark," he laughed. "I'm so glad we had today."

"I, too . . . but you've changed the subject. I do want to know why you wanted me to be at that conference today." She pulled a pack of cigarillos from her pocket and quickly lit one.

Jim slumped comfortably back in his seat, facing her, and then said slowly, "All right. Remember, you asked. . . . I think I wanted you there because I needed someone like you, someone . . . important to me, to see what I was doing. You said that Jonas told you I was a natural for medicine . . . well, that's true only in part. I've loved the study of it, and I do feel comfortable in it. But in the last few months I've been examining myself to try to see whether I've got what it takes to be a physician my whole life. And every time I do I seem to come up short. I find I have very little desire to do research, and I may be too lazy and selfish and superficial to be any good at teaching. And finally, the practice of medicine itself seems to be getting crunched under the burden of its own paperwork and the paranoid assumptions of our malpractice generation. The nobility of medicine is in doubt, and the sublime freedoms of it are passing. Medicine is on its way to becoming a trade rather than a profession."

He broke off and then continued, "I've been asked to continue in the residency program here. It's a real compliment, I guess, given the competition, but it's four or five more years. I have to make a decision, and I needed to talk to someone."

"What about Jonas? Have you talked to him?"

"Jonas is great . . . a true friend. But Jonas is Jonas. He sees with great clarity, and he thinks that medicine is the one and only path to the Grail. I don't know whether he would truly understand doubt on the subject. 'Temporary internship melancholia,' he would probably say about me."

"And you think he believed I could pull you out of this melancholy?"

"Probably—only it's not melancholy. It's just uncertainty. But I believe he's right in thinking you could help." He leaned toward her. "I somehow needed you to, to understand . . . umm, to approve."

Charlotte leaned forward and snuffed out her cigarillo in the ashtray. "I don't know, Jim," she said slowly. "I understand that you need encouragement in what you're doing, and I think it's wonderful that you want it from me. I think . . . I think if I cared less, or not at all, I might find it easy to say, 'Wow! What you're doing is great—it's important, necessary—keep it up.' But I do care, very much, and for that reason I find it difficult to answer what you're asking. Has it occurred to you that I might be biased?"

"Biased? How so?"

"Have you forgotten that I was raised in a medical family?"

"Temporarily, yes. I didn't think it had anything to do with this."

"But you see, it does, at least in my particular case. I've seen what it can mean to be a doctor. Reputation, honor, financial rewards, but also isolation, pressures, frustration. They balance out, to me. And to the doctor's family, it means separation, estrangement. I have to tell you that quite a few years ago I swore I would never marry a doctor. I'm afraid you've picked the wrong person."

Jim was silent a moment and then said, "Not at all. Maybe I've picked the right person but the wrong life. But I'll say this . . . if you ever did marry a doctor, he would know it was for love and nothing else."

Both laughed.

"I should go in," she said.

He leaned toward her and gently kissed her in the middle of her laugh. They embraced, and he smelled the fresh perfume behind her ear.

"You marry the person, not the profession," he said.

"True of almost anyone except a doctor," she replied, "but you'd better let me out of this car anyway."

At the porch, she turned to him as she unlocked the door.

"If it helps, Jim, I don't think you could be selfish, or lazy, and certainly not superficial. You play Erik Satie too well for that."

He drove back to the hospital in silence, without the radio on, lost in thought about Charlotte, her kiss, her scent.

The huge clock in the dome of the hospital read two o'clock as he entered the front doorway. He went to the ward to make sure all was well with Dr. Hallam. At the nurses' station it was quiet, and the last report, from midnight, indicated some restlessness and some increase in pulse, but nothing disturbing. The nurse thought he was simply asleep. Jim decided to put his head in the room just to still the sense of foreboding that he was beginning to feel. As he opened the door and looked toward the bed in the dim light, he was instantly aware that something was terribly wrong. Dr. Hallam was moaning and thrashing about wildly in bed. When Jim turned up the lights, Dr. Hallam sat up in bed, eyes staring wildly, and shouted, "There— there it is!" and flopped back.

Jim called loudly for the nurse and in a second was over Dr. Hallam's heaving body, both restraining him and examining him at once. His breathing was rapid and harsh, and his blood pressure, when Jim was finally able to get it, was elevated. As the nurse entered the room, Jim cried out, "Get a rectal temperature on him, will you, while I hold him!"

He gripped the patient firmly, and she finally succeeded. Jim noted the digital readout of 103 degrees, and then examined the heart and lungs, which were clear. The abdominal examination was also negative.

Dr. Hallam probably had either a sudden infection or a cerebral hemorrhage, Jim was thinking as the nurse handed him the ophthalmoscope. He looked first in the right eye and found that the pupil was markedly dilated; the left, to his surprise, was similarly widened. He and the nurse placed temporary restraints on Dr. Hallam's arms and legs, and he started down the hall to order an immediate cerebral CAT scan.

Jim reflected that with a mid-brain bleed there would have been dilation of the pupils, but Dr. Hallam would have been paralyzed, which he wasn't, and with an infection there wouldn't have been any pupil widening at all. Jim reached the desk, and his fingers were dialing the Radiology number, when he suddenly stopped.

Realizing that he was overlooking something, Jim put down the receiver, staring ahead. Dr. Hallam had agitation, hallucinations, seizure, high blood pressure and pulse, fever, dilated pupils, and there were no other findings. What the hell does he have? Then Jim thought it couldn't be . . . and yet . . .

He checked the chart and the order sheet, and found that the patient had not been given any narcotic or sleeping pills. "It's just not there," he murmured to himself, "something's missing."

He got up abruptly and hurried down the corridor to his patient's room, where by this time a team of nurses was starting an intravenous solution and drawing blood for testing and culturing. He looked wordlessly around the room, searching for something, anything, that would give him a lead. He went to the bedside table and began to look through the drawers, finding nothing. He rummaged through Dr. Hallam's clothes in the small closet—again nothing. He began looking about wildly, trying for the moment to ignore the heaving figure on the bed, thrashing against the restraints. His eye caught Dr.

Hallam's toilet kit, on the windowsill. He tore it open—shaving cream, razor, toothbrush, empty toothpaste tube but, as he looked at it, not entirely empty. It appeared depleted at the top but full at the bottom, where there was a narrow slit. Jim picked it up, and fine powder came out on his fingers. He stared at it a moment, almost unbelieving, smelled it, tasted it, and then said to the head nurse, "Begin an intravenous injection of Propronolal, one milligram per minute, and give him two and a half milligrams of Haloperidol intramuscularly, now. I'll be right back."

He sprinted down the corridor to the telephone and dialed the number he had by now memorized.

"Hello?" said Charlotte's sleepy voice.

"Charlie, I'm sorry, this is Jim. I think I'd better talk to your mom—it's an emergency. . . . Yes, I'll wait."

"Hello, Jim," Anne Hallam finally said, "is it serious?"

"It is, Mrs. Hallam, and I have to have an answer. Mrs. Hallam, do you know . . . is Dr. Hallam on, or has he ever taken—drugs?"

Jim heard a gasp at the other end of the line, a pause, and then Mrs. Hallam's clear, low voice. "Cocaine!"

CHAPTER 9

Friday, May 17, 1985

Dr. Clayton Hallam sank gratefully back on his pillow after bidding good-bye to Bartie Mateer that Friday evening and following him to the door with his eyes. It was great of his old friend to make the effort to see him—age being a consideration as well as the fact that Bartie hated to leave his wife these days for any reason—but it was no more than other efforts that each had made for the other over the years during times of personal tragedy or strain. He himself had gone up to New Jersey scarcely less than a year ago when the nature and extent of Betty Mateer's illness became clear.

"She's better," Bartie had just informed him. "She's finished her chemotherapy and is taking an estrogen-antagonist. The oncologist thinks the cancer has been arrested, and she's well over the effects of the breast surgery. She's still weak, of course, so she can't travel so easily. We don't do much traveling these days. This is my longest expedition in several years."

"You were great to come. God, we see each other only in problem times. Not like the old days, eh?"

"No . . . well, foul-weather friends are the best, right? Both of us have been lucky, though, all things considered. I mean, some ups, a few downs, but on the whole, not bad.

"Too bad old Dan can't be here." Bartie spoke from his bedside chair, folded deeply into it, his white head almost lower than his long jutting knees crossed in front of him. He jiggled his upper foot continuously, a puppet on a string.

"You know, Bartie," replied Clay at length, "your one trouble is that after fifty years of careful coaching you've never learned how to sit in a chair!"

He was about to continue when Jim Gallier appeared in the doorway. He was just checking on his patient, he said, before going to the Hallams' house for dinner. Clay introduced Bart to Jim, then waved the intern away, bidding him not to let Clay's wife and daughter keep him up too late. Jim smiled and withdrew. Bart sat back down in his chair, although not so deeply as before.

"I didn't mention that you, too, were going out there to dinner, Bartie. I figured you'd want your own transportation, because he may be staying later than you, and you're not leaving yet."

Bartie grinned. "He's a possible suitor for Charlotte, then?"

"Oh, God knows about that—I'd probably be the last to find out. I did check on him, though, just in case," he said, smiling. "He's got an excellent reputation here and has been asked to stay on and complete his residency in medicine."

"Well, Clay, both of us know what that means in these hallowed halls. Tell you what—I'll kind of look him over at dinner tonight and let you know if I approve. . . . I guess I'd better get going if I'm to be on time at Anne's table. Any messages?"

He got up and approached the bed, and stuck out his long-fingered hand for Clay to grasp.

"How'd you ever get to be an eye surgeon with hands like that?" Clay said, grinning as he took the hand in his. "Thanks for coming, my friend—it's helped a lot to see you. Please give my love to Betty. And come down again when you can."

Bartie started to withdraw his hand, but Clay suddenly tightened his grip again. "And Bartie," he said in a low voice, "about

Dan. . . . That wasn't my fault. You know that, don't you? It wasn't my fault."

Surprised, Bart stepped closer. "Of course, I know that, everyone knows that. He was shot badly, and the equipment failed. There was nothing you or anyone could do."

Clay nodded and said, "Yes, yes. That's right. He was practically dead when I operated. His brain was a mess . . . and the damned cautery quit. I did what I could but it was no use. God, God, I tried . . . I really tried . . ." His voice trailed off in a sob.

"Clay, my friend," said Bart softly, "I know you tried. You worked on him for over four hours and even then wouldn't leave him. If anybody could have brought him around, you would have. Don't fret about it."

"It's just that . . . that . . . oh, damn it, Bartie, damn it, I wanted him to make it."

They remained for several moments with hands clasped, the giant figure of Bart Mateer stooping slightly over the bed, looking down at his friend.

At length, Clay looked up and released Bart's hand. "You'd better go. Give them my best, and tell Anne I'll talk to her on the phone later tonight. Keep in touch, will you, Bartie?"

Bart left, and Clay's head sank back on the pillow. He felt exhausted and overwhelmingly sad. The visit from his old friend, at first pleasurable, in the end had been stressful and depressing. He lay with his eyes closed, propped up on the pillow. The nurse brought his evening tray and left it by him, supposing him asleep.

He opened his eyes after a while and looked around. He was alone, and the sounds of the ward on this Friday evening were muffled and seemed far off. The thought of food repelled him, and he pushed the tray away from the bed. He knew what he needed. The need entered his awareness, waiting for him to acknowledge it. But as quickly as it rose, he put it aside. It had been years, until a week ago, since he had yielded to the temptation, even though the burning wondrous furies of it were never far from his consciousness. But it was an old affair, of many years standing, that he had become used to suppressing. He was completely aware of its seductive power, as well as its potential for destruction, and he had long since realized that, once developed, the relationship between man and drug could never truly be ended, only held in check. And in this, to a degree, he had been successful— except perhaps on one or two occasions that he no longer permitted himself to think about. They were past, but this was now, and he realized that now was not an appropriate time to indulge the old, familiar need. On the one hand, it might in some way worsen his recent cerebral damage; on the other, if he were caught, the repercussions in his own hospital would be humiliating.

Clay settled back in bed, turned out the light, and tried to sleep. Again he felt the oppressive weight of his depression, which fatigued him yet kept him from sleep. He tried to focus his mind, as if doing so would relieve his gloom. Bart Mateer had looked so old today, his hair white, his face lined and gaunt, his immense body stiffened and bent. He'd done well, though, with his life. He and Betty never had children, but they had stayed close to each other in each step of his unusual career. Bart had been not only head of the ophthalmology department in his community hospital in New Jersey but also chief of the fire department and a one-term mayor of the town. A full life. He could be damned proud!

Clay wondered if Bartie was satisfied. He compared their two careers, Bartie's alongside his own—his status, honors, degrees, and renown. He could reflect on his own life only briefly, however, before he had to break off, for shades of his failures, his mistakes, his inadequacies rose around him. His honors and titles were shams, hypocritical tin badges covering up the real truths of his life. He looked over the great divide of his life and could see the good of it stretching off like a shining river in one direction and the dark stream of his inadequacies flowing off in another. Guilt rose like mist from the dark river and enveloped him, guilt long suppressed and contained, which now swirled around him and insinuated itself in his brain. And as he brooded over that point in his life where the bad of it diverged from the good, it was clear that the forking was at Johns Hopkins, in his internship year. He drifted off . . . July 1938 . . . a hot summer.

· · · ·

During the first days and weeks that followed the Fourth of July weekend of his internship in 1938, Clay worried considerably over Anne's reaction to his absences from her. Long before and frequently during their engagement, they had, of course, discussed how demanding the training would be and how hard he would have to work, and both thought they were prepared for that. As it turned out, they had failed to anticipate it adequately. They had, indeed, even managed to romanticize it to the point where they were looking forward to the life. They had imagined that he would come home late at night, and Anne would be waiting for him, and they would have a drink and light meal and talk about the day, his patients and operations, then go to bed, sleeping in each other's arms. The unpredictability of these prospects appealed to both of them. Anne usually led the discussion of the fantasies. Clay, who had a better sense of what to expect, was himself intrigued by her expectations and went along with them.

So they were unprepared emotionally for the sheer temporal demands of his work and the fatigue it produced. He knew she was shocked by his appearance and his urgent need for sleep when he came home from the hospital the first time in his internship—three days after he had left. And during the ensuing weeks he would often be too exhausted to eat or talk or even make love. He did the best he could for her, called her frequently, and went home as often as possible, but he knew that in the end she would have to reach her own conclusions and settle on her own method of adapting, or not adapting, to this life.

He knew he could never bear to lose her, for he loved her deeply. Her warm beauty, her intuitive responsiveness, and her enthusiasm enthralled him completely. And these attributes, though compelling, were not alone why he had married her. He had found another quality—something more fancied than seen, more inferred than proved. He had seen hints of it in her conversation, nuances of it in her attitudes and bearing. He had seen it perhaps most clearly in the set of her shoulders as she bailed their hard-pressed sailboat on their honeymoon. It was inner health, soundness, steadfastness that he had glimpsed in her then, and it had made him sure that she was the woman with whom he wanted to build his life. Now as he observed her apprehensively for her reaction to the stringencies of their new life, he found himself counting heavily on this quality to bring her through.

The dog days of July gave way to even steamier days of August, and they drifted into September before Clay began to see the signs in Anne that he had hoped for, of her acquiescence to the inconveniences of an intern's life. He could hear it in her voice, when he phoned to say he would be late for dinner, or not be home at all. The querulousness, the hurt, the puzzlement gradually disappeared and were replaced by understanding and acceptance. She gave wholehearted loving attention to him when they did find time together, where before she had held back, was cool, struggled with anger at his prolonged absences. He knew she was grappling with the realities of their life: all the house officers and their families were in the situation, after all. The other wives were surviving the deprivations. He felt tremendously proud of her as he saw the difficult adjustment being made, knowing she was young, energetic, and not accustomed to restraints. In his heart he promised her that one day he would make up for the hours and days of waiting she gave to him.

As he silently pledged this, his mind itself freed more and more from concern for her and increasingly turned toward his work, a fire threatening to consume him unless he could contain it. To contain it—if indeed it could be contained—required singleness of purpose.

From the very first day of the internship Clay felt as if he were running as fast as possible on a treadmill, yet was unable to keep up the pace. Even when he felt fresh, ambitious, and eager, the sheer scope of what was demanded of him and his fellow interns was shocking. Later, looking back, he was never sure how he managed to meet that demand. He found it necessary to be on his ward by half past five in the morning or, at the latest, by six. He had to draw blood specimens, start intravenous fluids, implant nasogastric tubes and Foley catheters, perform blood tests and urinalyses, and write the necessary daily orders, in order to get to the operating rooms by eight o'clock. He was usually involved in operations until at least noon, although longer ones could go on until two or three in the afternoon. There was then normally time for a half-hour lunch, followed by post-op patient care and the afternoon surgical clinics—general, vascular, thoracic, and the like—which lasted until five o'clock. They were followed by Chief Resident's Rounds, from five to half past six, three days a week, or special lectures. If he was lucky, there was time for supper, but he had to return to the wards to apply new dressings, start new intravenous fluids, and prepare patients who were to be operated on the next day. Then it was usually necessary to read up on the upcoming operations or consult recent literature relating to clinical problems on the ward so as not to be caught out on questions from residents or faculty who were both his mentors and his judges.

At the start, Clay found himself behind almost from the moment he got to the hospital. It took him longer to draw blood specimens, longer to start intravenous fluids, longer to dress his patients' wounds, than, for example, Warren Bregel, his co-intern on Surgical Ward 4, who was not only faster and more efficient in his work than Clay but who also obviously delighted in besting him.

Once, and only once, Clay asked him for help. Early one morning in late July, both of them were on the ward, hurrying to get routine care done before an eight o'clock operation. It had taken Clay an inordinately long time to introduce a catheter into the abdomen of a patient with advanced liver disease in order to drain the fluid that had accumulated in the abdomen and was compromising the patient's breathing. As he bent to this delicate task, he glanced up and saw that Warren seemed to have finished his work and was leaving the ward.

"Warren," he called, "got a minute?"

Warren checked his stride, hesitated a moment, then walked over to the bed.

"Yes, Clay?" His voice was high-pitched and tight, and his long face loomed down at Clay, crouched beside his patient.

"Morning, Warren. I'm just finishing this paracentesis, but I've still got to put a gastric tube in, and start an i.v. on Mrs. Cours over there. We've only got ten minutes left before the O.R.—any chance you could give me a hand?" Clay hardly looked up at Warren as he spoke, intent on his work and expecting an affirmative reply.

"Sorry, Clay, I've already got plans for these ten minutes. Don't worry—you'll make it. See you over there."

Clay looked up in stunned silence as Warren strode off. Such a wave of blind rage swept over him that he could hardly steady the needle that was entering into his patient's abdomen. Indeed, the only thing that saved him from a mistake was that he glanced up into the face of his patient—an emaciated, long-suffering, yellowish, alcoholic face—and he saw there an understanding of what had occurred and a fear that vigorous reaction by Clay might increase his silent misery. Clay took a deep breath and steadied his hand. He shrugged and smiled wryly, then felt the man relax, with a hoarse intonation that undoubtedly contained "son of a bitch."

The drainage from the needle dwindled and stopped, and Clay withdrew the shaft, patched the site on the now-diminished abdomen, checked the blood pressure and pulse of the relieved man, and went to complete his other chores. He was several minutes late for the start of the operation, for which the preoccupied surgeon briefly reprimanded him as he slid into his place at the table as second assistant. It was difficult for him to control his anger, difficult to hold the retractors and hemostat for Warren as first assistant, but his anger melted as his interest in the operation increased. It was not until after Chief Resident's Rounds that evening that he had a chance to say anything to Warren, catching him in the corridor as they were returning to the ward.

"Just a minute, Warren, I want to say something to you," Clay said. Looking into the eyes of his fellow intern, Clay thought, pointlessly and absurdly, that they were the same height. "It's going to be a long year, Warren, and we can't help rubbing elbows a lot, so I thought we ought to get straight with each other. That was a lousy trick you pulled on me this morning."

"Oh? What trick was that?" Warren's tenor voice was high enough to sound perpetually mocking.

"Not giving me an assist when I asked you for it. Completely unnecessary. I would have been glad to do it for you."

Warren hesitated a moment and appeared to consider this. "I guess you would have, at that. But nobody's life was in danger, and I didn't see the need."

"You didn't see the need? When I asked you for some help?"

"That is correct."

"And that's the way things are going to be?"

"That also is correct."

Clay's jaw tightened, and a dull flush suffused his face. "Look, Warren . . . "

"No, you look, Clay. Where do you think you are, back in the lavender halls of the Ivy League? Well, this is not the Ivy League. This is the Big League. Gestures don't count here. Action counts. Ability counts. Getting the job done counts." He paused and smirked. "And letting the right people know you *can* get the job done. They can only keep on half of us in this training program, and that will not be the noble half, it will be the half with the gumption and the knowledge to perform . . . "

"Even if it means sandbagging everybody else?" Clay interjected.

"What you call 'sandbagging' I call being practical. That ten minutes you asked me for I put to good use in the surgical pathology lab. If you wanted that ten minutes, Clay, you should have gotten up earlier . . . which brings me to a piece of advice for you, at no expense. Grow up, Doctor! You're still acting like an adolescent. I'm not sure you even belong in surgery, especially at this place. You've got too much going on personally . . . attractive wife, outside interests. . . . I don't think you love it enough. You've got to love it—*first.* Did they ask you when you applied here whether you'd rather do surgery or eat ice cream? Well, I was able to answer them truthfully, right off the bat, where there was surgery and everything else in the world was ice cream, that I'd rather do surgery. Maybe you don't belong here, Clay. Maybe you belong with the horses' asses who eat ice cream."

"Warren, I ought to knock your head off," was the only remark Clay could think of. The two parted company. He did, however, know thenceforth where he stood as far as Warren was concerned. He was a little less secure, however, where he himself was concerned. He felt repelled by Warren's cold disregard for others, yet had to admit that his energy in the single-minded pursuit of his goal was already bearing fruit in terms of accomplishment and of regard by their seniors. Warren had told him to grow up, but Clay dismissed this. It was true that he permitted distractions to interfere with his surgical duties. Anne was much in his thoughts, and he wasn't about to disappoint her. However, it was possible that he was indulging himself more than necessary, sleeping a bit longer than he needed to, lingering longer over dinner than he had to, and now, sensing again the competitiveness of the training and the seriousness of the rivalry, he began to realize more than ever the need to push himself.

One thing remained clear and became clearer with each passing day, and that was his love of the world of surgery. It was as if he waded deeper and deeper into an ocean that gradually rose about him until it enveloped him completely. And he welcomed it. There was so much to know about surgery, and he yearned to know it all. He never doubted whether he was in the right place. Curiosity abounded in this hospital's corridors and operation rooms, during a time when new research and techniques were revolutionizing surgery.

He bent to his work and, despite his reaction to Warren's cynical advice, he did grow. As summer yielded to the cool days of late fall, Clay changed not only in his appearance but also in his bearing. Anne noticed it. In four months he had, somehow, lost much of his youthful look. He had a more settled facial expression. He smiled less often, but his face began to reflect authority and self-confidence. So did his bearing. Gone, or going fast, was his easy gait, replaced by a shoulders-back, chest-forward, brisk, purposeful walk. His uniform, the white pants and jacket, white shirt, and tie, seemed to fit him better, although he had lost about ten pounds. And he now wore his equipment—stethoscope, pocket flashlight, surgical scissors, rubber tourniquet, straight forceps—with the authority of someone who was prepared for and could handle anything. These were outer manifestations of a growing inner confidence in himself that Clay was beginning to feel. He put his whole mind and energy into his work and found, to his growing pleasure, that they were adequate, that he could not only do his work but also compete with his fellow interns.

It seemed to Clay during the course of those months that he had been able to tap into a lode of energy and intellect that he hadn't known he possessed. His mind seemed to absorb everything, and his body adapted to deprivation, allowing him to regain the strength from a one-hour nap that a four- or five-hour sleep would not have yielded before. Only in his eyes and complexion did he show signs of chronic fatigue. He realized that he was being pushed to his limits, but he was finding those limits to be greater than he had suspected they could be. He was enthused, confident, ready for anything.

He had reason to be pleased. His joustings with Warren, at the operating table, on the wards, and in surgical conferences, continued, but no longer were they one-sided, always ending in Warren's favor. On a late October afternoon, the surgical house staff gathered around the bedside of a middle-aged black woman who had been admitted because of a tumor in her abdomen. Burroughs, the surgical chief resident, who was conducting rounds, said, "I'd like each of you to feel her abdomen, then come and look at the x-rays, and tell me what you think she has."

Clay took his turn, noting the presence of the slight prominence of the lower abdomen, then feeling the smooth, globular, firm shape that seemed to rise somewhat to the right of the midline. It was only mildly tender, and he estimated it to be about the size of a grapefruit. He smiled slightly at the patient, who looked back at him quizzically, displaying a fine hairline along her upper lip and cheeks. He looked again.

The x-rays were put up in the viewbox in the conference room, and Burroughs cleared his throat. "There's been no weight loss, gentlemen, mild constipation, no urinary symptoms, and she is menopausal. What do you think she's got?"

After a moment's hesitation, Warren spoke up. "I'd opt for an ovarian cyst, a colloid. It's in the right location, and she's the right age."

"What type of ovarian cyst, Doctor?" asked Burroughs.

"Benign, I'd say from the feel of it, and she's lost no weight. It's probably a simple follicular cyst. I see no reason to suspect other. I could see a slight calcification on the x-ray."

One by one the others spoke up, suggesting other diagnoses, appendiceal cysts, diverticula, fibromas of the uterus, bladder tumors, and so forth. But in general, for various cogent reasons, they fell in line behind the thinking of Warren Bregel.

"Dr. Hallam, we haven't heard from you."

Clay said, "Well, there's a possibility, I believe, that this might be a masculinizing dermoid cyst of the ovary. The small calcification on the x-ray looked a bit like a tooth, which can occur in a dermoid. In addition, the lady seemed to have a bit of a mustache, making it possible that this tumor is secreting a male hormone. Besides, I believe Dr. Wood told us recently that follicular ovarian cysts are rare in this race."

"Excellent, Dr. Hallam, very good indeed," said Burroughs, beaming. "That's what I think she has also. The rest of you didn't use your eyes, just your hands. Remember, look at the entire patient for clues, not just the obvious lesion. Good thinking, Hallam. Tomorrow she will be operated on, and we'll find out if we're right. Let's go on to the next case."

In the following few weeks the surgical services were even busier than usual, and Clay discovered that his diagnosis had been correct from the bulletin board, where a terse pathology note was posted. The first day of November, rainy, cold, and gloomy, was especially hectic in the hospital, and both he and Warren had three new admissions to work up. All three of Clay's were quite ill. One had persistent nausea and vomiting with high fever, possibly from an abdominal abscess. Another had fever and a wracking cough and perhaps a tuberculous lung. And the third had painful phlebitis in his leg. It was about two o'clock in the morning before he had them bedded down and had written their orders. He had just straightened up from his task and was about to leave the ward and go home when the chief night nurse hurried up to him.

"Dr. Hallam, come quickly! One of Dr. Bregel's new patients has become acutely short of breath, and we can't locate Dr. Bregel."

"Where is he—did you try his house?"

"Yes, but he's not there. He only left here about a half-hour ago. And he doesn't seem to be in the house-staff dormitory."

For an instant Clay thought about refusing to see Warren's patient, but then he and the nurse hurried down the corridor to the patient. He was an elderly, corpulent man who was obviously in respiratory distress, breathing deeply and wheezily as he sat on the side of his bed. An intravenous line was threaded into an arm vein.

"What's that?" Clay asked the nurse, as he pulled out his stethoscope to listen to the man's chest.

"It's saline, his second liter. Dr. Bregel thought he was dehydrated."

"Dehydrated!" Clay said, as he began examining the patient's heart and lungs. It was immediately obvious that the patient was not dehydrated, but indeed had too much fluid and was accumulating it in his lungs. The man's lips were turning blue, and he breathed with all his might.

"Stop that i.v. immediately. Get some oxygen going by face mask. Give him two cc.'s of Thiomerin immediately, and six milligrams of morphine sulfate intravenously . . . *and* . . . let me look at his order sheet!"

The orders that Warren had written were clear-cut: intravenous saline to run in at a very rapid rate, as well as continuous compresses to the leg.

"I didn't see anything wrong with his leg," Clay said to the nurse. He rechecked the man's legs and again found nothing wrong. He returned and read Warren's admission physical exam, written in his clear and concise script, which detailed the case of an obese man who had been admitted because of a suspected adrenal gland tumor. There was no mention of a leg problem.

He checked the names on the order sheet and found they tallied with the names on the chart. He was puzzled. Obviously the orders were entirely wrong for this patient.

He asked the nurse, "Was there by any chance another patient admitted today with a leg problem?"

She caught his drift immediately and answered, "Not on my shift, but let me look at the roster."

She left and came back with another nurse, who answered, "Yes, Dr. Bregel had another patient who was admitted earlier, who has diabetes and a leg ulcer!" Understanding made her eyes open wider.

Together they looked at this other patient's orders, and the situation became clear at once. In his usual strong and distinct handwriting, which betrayed not the slightest sign of fatigue, Warren had written the wrong orders on the wrong patient.

It took another hour for Clay to untangle the complications of the mistake and see to it that both patients were recovering, by which time Warren appeared on the ward.

"I heard I made a mistake," was his greeting to Clay. He looked greenish from fatigue.

"Where were you?" Clay responded.

"I fell asleep in the library," answered Warren and, after a pause, said, "Sorry, I'll take it from here."

Clay nodded and realized that "Sorry" was probably one of the hardest words that Warren had ever had to utter. Clay prepared to leave.

"And Clay . . . " said Warren, as Clay turned back toward him, "thanks. I'd, uh, greatly appreciate it if you didn't say anything about this to anyone."

Clay said, "Up yours, Warren. If it needs saying, I'll say it. But the nurses . . . "

"I'll take care of the nurses. See you tomorrow."

The incident never resurfaced, neither of them ever alluded to it, and it did not even bring a thaw in their relationship. Clay did derive a certain amount of satisfaction in realizing that sheer fatigue could penetrate even the crystal-clear mind of his rival and that even he was subject to human error. He doubted that Warren ever permitted himself to think of it again.

In late November the Griers came for the weekend, and Dr. Grier asked Clay to join the Grier Clinic and finish his surgical training there. During Dr. Grier's proposal, Clay remembered Randolph Grier's cryptic warning about the subtle tenacity of Grierism, and he was also well aware of Dr. Grier's reason for making the offer at dinner with Anne there, rather than to him alone. He turned Dr. Grier's offer down flatly. He gave his answer quickly, without further consideration, or even asking Anne's opinion at the moment. Taking up at the Grier Clinic would have been like stepping off a ladder at a middle rung, when he was determined to keep on climbing that ladder as high as he could go.

Later in life he would ask himself many times about how things might have gone had he accepted the proposal, but he always realized that he would never have been able to accept, not even if Anne had strenuously argued for it. Indeed, Anne seemed to have come to understand what the Johns Hopkins Hospital was all about and why he wished to continue there. He was grateful for her tacit support of his refusal to Dr. Grier. In later years he was to recognize that the Griers' visit to Baltimore that November planted the earliest seeds of discontent in his marriage to Anne.

His own recollection of the rape was always blurry. Cold and tired, he came home late that night in early December, irritated to find the front door ajar. He entered, threw his old overcoat on the chair, and was about to turn out the hall light when he heard Anne cry out from upstairs, "Clay—look out—he's got a knife."

He bounded up the steps but stopped at the entrance to their bedroom, unable to see into the darkened room. He was able to make out the large shape of the intruder running toward the bathroom. He took a few quick steps toward him, but stopped when he realized the man was already halfway out the window, with one foot over the sill. For an instant, in glow from the street light, he and the man looked directly at each other, and then the man was gone. Clay calmed Anne, then bundled her up and took her over to the emergency room. The police came and asked them questions. They assured Anne and Clay that they would catch the rapist, despite the poor description they were given. Clay hoped that the whole incident might be put behind them quickly. Anne's emotional distress persisted, however.

The psychiatrist who had spoken with Anne, a professor on the hospital staff and a former teacher of Clay's, said, "You see, Clay, for Anne this was an entirely alien experience, her first awareness of her own vulnerability, her own mortality, the first time she was rendered powerless and unable to cope at all. She feels alone and ashamed, as if she failed at being able to handle it. I think it's the experience of utter helplessness, of knowing that she can't handle everything, that is making her unable to throw it off. I recommend that she admit herself to the psychiatric institute for a few weeks and get this resolved."

Anne elected instead to return home to Richmond, and Clay went back to his work, distracted but aware that he had lost a full week of training. He was rotated from the ward service to the Accident and Emergency Room, a twelve-hours-on, twelve-hours-off shift, which although long was at least defined in its hours. The emergency room was the front line in surgery, where the first skirmishes with acute illness are encountered, and Clay found it rewarding even in his pre-occupied state. It was a high-volume arena for patients with a large variety of problems, and it required fast, accurate judgment and effi-cient treatment on the part of Clay and the other three interns and three residents assigned there. Again, after some weeks, Clay began to get the satisfying feeling of being competent and able to handle acute surgical problems.

A few days before Clay was to leave on Christmas vacation, an am-bulance arrived with cases described by the nurses at the front desk as "two abdominal stab wounds, male, one black, one white, exten-sive." The fight apparently happened in an East Baltimore bar, and both had lost a lot of blood. The black man was shocky, and the white one was almost so. The two were immediately taken to the operating room, and blood transfusions were begun. Clay was assigned to oper-ate on the black patient, and Jeff Newball, his fellow intern, was to operate on the white one.

Clay looked down on the lurid results of the knife fight. The wounds were fresh and oozing. They were mostly in front and on the sides of the body. Some were superficial, but others were quite deep. Clay could see the man's cheekbone, several ribs were laid open, and brown and red muscle tissue was protruding from a deep slash across the left upper thigh. He was a big man, almost too large for the oper-ating table.

"Must've been some fight," Clay said reassuringly, and gazed down into the fleshy face. Despite the half-closed eyes, the gaping left cheek wound, the stubby beard, something about the face seemed familiar to Clay. Suddenly he froze. He looked into the man's eyes, and the man looked back in recognition. This was the rapist!

Rage welled up in Clay, rage at this urine-soaked, worthless hulk, who had so brutally attacked Anne—rage, and a feeling of power to revenge. It would be easy to suture over a few skin areas but leave the deeper, severed arteries bleeding. After a patch job, it would take hours for anyone to discover where the bleeders were, and by that time, the man would have bled to death. No one would be the wiser. He looked down into the man's eyes again, and thought that he, too, understood the situation. Clay waited for him to call out, to demand another surgeon. But he didn't. He just lay there looking up at Clay, and waited.

Clay backed away from the table. "Hold it a minute," he ordered the nurse. "Keep compressing those wounds. I'll be right back."

He found the surgical resident preparing a lecture in his office, and said, "Dr. Burroughs, I'm sorry to break in, but this is an emergency. I have to request being taken off a case immediately!"

Burroughs' eyebrows arched up, and he said, "Okay, come in and tell me about it."

Clay's explanation was brief. "I know you're aware that my wife was raped about a month ago . . . " Burroughs nodded. "I'm about to operate on the man who raped her. He's bleeding and could die. I've got to drop off the case. Let someone else do it. I'm afraid of what I might do . . . or not do."

Burroughs looked at him. "Are you sure it's him?"

Clay nodded.

"Good," Burroughs replied, "then get back up there and do the job you're trained to do. Christ, if a surgeon dropped out every time he was in some way emotionally involved in a case, half the surgery in the country would never get done. Remember this: that's not a particular man you're operating on—that's a human being, without personality, without sin. Leave your personal feelings at the operating room door with your clothes and your wallet. You are a general surgeon operating on a general human body. Use your best judgment and do your best job . . . and let me know how it goes."

Clay said nothing. He returned to the operating room, where the patient lay silent. It was as if each accepted the other under new rules. Clay steeled his mind, and, after three hours, he closed the last laceration and stepped back. He had done the best he could, and all his patient's vital signs were stable. Clay felt relieved. He notified the police about his identification of the man, and he telephoned Anne, hoping that the apprehension of the rapist would ease her fears enough to allow her to come back with him to Baltimore. But she seemed apathetic.

His Christmas visit to Richmond was painful for both of them. Anne had made a complete physical recovery, and indeed looked more beautiful than ever. Her brown-gold hair shone, and her color was high. She smelled irresistible to Clay, who wanted her so much that tears came to his eyes.

He returned to Baltimore without her, bitter, angry, knowing that he loved her and needed her and that she was right for him as his wife, yet deeply resentful that she needed more time to come back to him. He had, after all, done his best.

Clay returned to his internship half-heartedly, finding it difficult to do much more than the mechanical duties of his work. He wrote her letters and called her on the phone, but did not return to Richmond. His visit had been too upsetting.

In early February the hospital was wrapped in blustery winds and snow. But it was snug and warm inside. The lights from its many windows beamed out across the city almost as a beacon to the ill, a signal to which they responded in droves. This was the season of influenza and pneumonia, as well as falls and fractures.

Clay was now on the orthopedic service, and it seemed to him that he had not left the operating room, or changed out of his green surgical gear, for weeks. He had not been back to his house for days. He grabbed sleep when he could in the house-staff sleeping quarters. He was finding that he did not like orthopedic surgery, or at least did not enjoy it as much as the other surgical specialties. It seemed too rough, too crude and mechanical. He was also finding that he was getting tired—and deeply so. Indeed, the phrase "bone-tired" was frequently heard on the orthopedic service. But there were other interns who were even more tired.

Charlie Segel was ill, and Clay had to replace him in an evening hip operation under Dr. Keeler. Clay had never operated in this time slot before, and the operating team was new to him. After he was scrubbed and gowned, he took his place as second assistant at the right elbow of Dr. Keeler. The first assistant, a resident named Ohr, was directly across the table from Keeler. The fourth person at the table was the instrument nurse, across from Clay, whose name appeared on the O.R. schedule as S. Speri. Clay glanced across at her and felt his breath cut off.

She was lovely, even though her mask provocatively hid the lower half of her face. She had a creamy complexion, dark eyebrows, and clear brown eyes that were large and elliptical. Clay was sure he knew what the rest of her face would look like. Her gown partly obscured her shape, but he noted large full breasts, which tightened her gown and smoothed out its wrinkles.

He had difficulty turning back to the operation, as well as concentrating for the three hours it lasted. When it was over Clay helped wheel the patient into the recovery area. He wrote the post-op orders and made the last adjustments in the dressings. These activities helped him to compose himself. It was the first time he had been so stirred by a woman since he had met Anne. He told himself that he was being ridiculous, that he was married. He laughed at himself for his erotic feelings, and he tried to ignore them.

It was close to midnight when he finished. He was very tired, but he was also hungry, so he stopped at the small canteen that stayed open all night. He grabbed a doughnut and a mug of hot coffee and slumped down at a table, then looked around at the few other people there. At one table were two fatigued interns in need of shaves, showers, and a twelve-hour sleep. At the only other occupied table were three nurses, all dressed in the green gowns of the operating room. One of them was S. Speri.

Clay caught her eye and smiled tentatively, and she smiled back. She looked as lovely as he had expected. When she and the other nurses stood up to leave, her breasts moved softly against the thin linen hospital gown.

Clay sighed and settled down to finish his snack. He glanced through his notebook to see what his operating assignment was for tomorrow, and he was relieved to find he was not scheduled until eight o'clock in the morning.

"Dr. Hallam?" said a low voice. He looked up, and it was Nurse Speri.

"Oh . . . I thought you had gone," he said, and the way he spoke the words, they were an accusation.

"I came back . . . because you looked so tired," she said.

Clay subsequently could remember very little of their conversation or even their bustling out of the hospital and across the cold streets to his house, only their hunger and need for each other. They were in bed, clothes strewn over the floor, and he was suddenly delighting in her lips, her breasts, her moist responsive skin, and her wonderful aromas. They made love that night like two intelligent animals, not savagely but forcefully, not brutally but fiercely. They were hampered by neither guilt nor conscience—he was too tired and both were too driven.

He came prematurely, almost upon entering her, and almost immediately rolled over into a sound sleep. He woke a few hours later and found her awake and looking at him. Their hunger for each other was still there, the product of the months of abstinence, and they made love again as if there could never be enough of lovemaking. They did not speak, for intelligible speech would have ruined it. She made occasional low moans, and he exclamations of love, but otherwise their lovemaking was all touching and searching and finding until finally, full of her heat and her lushness, he came again, and they slept.

They were awakened at seven o'clock by the phone ringing, a call to tell Clay that his eight o'clock operation had been canceled, but that he was expected to show up for eight o'clock rounds. Grinning, Clay replied that he'd be there. They dressed quickly, and she found some coffee while he shaved, but determined that all the food was either stale or roach-ridden and that the ice in the box had long since melted. They settled for the coffee, and sat down at the kitchen table and looked at each other.

"You know I'm married?" he asked, finding her even more lovely this morning than he had last night.

"I do know, yes," she replied. "The nurses generally know who's available and who's attached. I've heard about you."

"Oh? What have you heard?"

"That you're very nice, polite—not like some of the others—intelligent . . . and unavailable."

Both laughed.

"What about you?" He looked at her tenderly.

"I've only been here a year. I took my nurse's training in New York, where I live. I came here to see what I could learn, and also . . . "

"And also?"

"To see if I want to get married. You see, I've been engaged for two years—a nice man, very rich, who could give me, and my family, anything we want. We don't have much money. My father's a tailor, and my mother came from Yugoslavia and still doesn't speak English well. But I couldn't decide, so I told him—that is, my fiancé—that I'd come here for one year, and that would be it."

"It?"

She nodded. "I'd come back and marry him in a year, or not at all."

"And when is the year up?"

She paused, then said, "In two days. I go back in two days."

"It doesn't sound like love," said Clay.

"No, I don't exactly love him. He's nice, but he's older, and . . . he's just not exciting to me. What do you think I should do? Do you believe in marriage without love?"

He thought for a moment, wondering if he was being maneuvered into some kind of commitment. "It depends, I guess, on how many marriages you believe in . . . "

"How many do you believe in?"

He looked at her. Her face was serious, and her brown eyes looked into his. He almost slipped then, but in the end held fast.

"One, I guess."

They were silent a moment, then stood up in unison.

"We'd better go," she said.

"Yes . . . but tell me, before we do, what does the 'S.' stand for, Miss Speri?" They laughed.

"Sheila . . . Sheila Speri. A pleasure to have known you, Dr. Clayton Hallam."

"And you, too, . . . Sheila. Good luck, and, whatever decision you make . . . I think I'll always remember you."

They went out the back door and through the alley, hoping that no one would see them at that hour. But someone did.

The next morning Anne called to tell him she was coming back to Baltimore. Her voice sounded healthy and sure and full of love again.

"I'll be there in four days, on Saturday. I'm already packing. Can you meet me? I've been such a fool, Clay, a selfish, spoiled child. But I think I've grown a little. Will you forgive me?"

Clay seemed to hear his whole life sliding into place again—her voice was reality and the rest all fiction. He knew where his heart lay, and he reached out for it. He said, "I love you, Anne. I'll be waiting for you."

He did not see Sheila Speri again, except the next day from a distance when he thought he spied her leaving the nurses' residence with her luggage and getting into a taxi. From the hospital, it was hard to be sure it was Sheila. For a few moments he felt some pangs of loss, and he wished her well, but he never doubted that things were following their proper course. He had been feeling guilty about the affair. He was now prepared to relegate it to the past.

He readied and stocked the house for Anne's return, and removed all traces of Sheila's visit. He changed the bed sheets twice, to make sure no lingering scents or pins or even hair strands remained. He cleaned the bathroom carefully, and searched the floor and rug for leftover articles. Throughout his preparations, Clay considered telling Anne about the episode. He would have liked to tell her, but he recognized that this was merely a wish to relieve his own conscience rather than to be honest with Anne. For her sake and for their marriage, already on shaky ground, silence was the right course.

It was noon in mid-February when she stepped off the train at Penn Station. The sun shone, and Clay accepted this as a good omen. He had arranged the day off, and he was excited, almost trembling, when he saw her step off the train.

He tried to take her in his arms, but she rebuffed him and allowed him only a kiss on her cold cheek.

"Darling, you look fine," he stammered.

"Thank you, Clay. You look fine, too," she returned in a clipped voice.

The porter came up with her luggage on his cart. "Where to, ma'am?"

"Oh," said Clay, "bring it along out front and we'll take a taxi."

"No." Anne's voice was preemptive. "Leave it over in the luggage area for a while. Clay, I need to talk with you for a few minutes here in the station, before we go anywhere."

They found a small table in the station restaurant, where the atmosphere was as chilly as the day outside. When they were seated, Anne reached into her purse and pulled out a letter, which she offered to Clay.

"I got this in the mail two days ago, Clay. I want you to read it and tell me if there's any truth in it." Clay took the letter slowly, already filling with premonition, and as he read it he could feel his face flushing.

"Your husband is having an affair—ask him," it charged. He read it and reread it, then looked up at Anne, who sat watching him. He hesitated. He'd never been very good at lying.

"Never mind, Clay, I can already tell that it's true. Otherwise, you would have laughed it off by now." Her voice choked, and she lowered her face.

"Honey, it's not going on—it was one night, one night only. I was tired. I couldn't think right. It'll truly never happen again . . . I love you, only you . . . "

"In Richmond, we usually say that tiredness is good for a man—keeps him out of trouble. In your case it's just the opposite. How do I know you won't get tired again—and again—you bastard! How can you sit there looking so handsome, so strong, so like everything I love, and be so false?"

"I'm not false—I love you."

"When you were making love to her were you thinking of me?"

"Well . . . no."

"Clay, eight or nine months ago we stood up in church and pledged under God to cleave to each other. I think you've spoiled it for us—for me." She stood up suddenly. "I'm taking a taxi to my parents' friends' house, and from there I'll go back home. Don't try to stop me, or call me—I'll write you when I can."

"Anne, don't do this . . . " But she was gone.

He sat for a time staring at the letter, written on hospital paper. He felt numb. Finally, he returned to his house, called the Mateers to tell them they would not be coming to dinner that night, and put on his hospital whites. Although he had the day off, he needed to keep occupied, and so he went back to work.

Clay did not hear from Anne for three weeks, and then there came a brief letter saying that she was living at home, had taken a job in the Grier Clinic, and to please send her belongings to Richmond. There was no mention of divorce in the letter.

Mid-April was the time of year when the house staff were individually notified whether they would be kept on next year or whether they would have to go elsewhere to complete training requirements for their surgical specialty boards. It was the moment of hope for all of them, what they'd all been working for—to continue on in this highest ranked of training programs.

Clay's interview was not long and not entirely surprising to him.

"I've read over these reports carefully, Clay," Dr. Sarnoff said, "and weighed, as best I could, the personal problems you've had. Your work here has been, frankly, erratic. You are capable of brilliant work, and some have called you highly intuitive. On the other hand, especially in the last month or so, you have been both inattentive and . . . uh . . . less than sharp." Dr. Sarnoff continued, his voice steady. "I have no choice but to let you go. I have made arrangements for you to continue your training next year at Philadelphia City Hospital, as assistant resident in surgery, if you agree. I have an idea, Dr. Hallam, that as soon as you get your private life under control, you'll end up a hell of a fine surgeon. Good luck." They shook hands.

That was it—the end of a dream.

CHAPTER 10

Saturday, May 18, 1985

The next afternoon, Saturday, passed slowly for Dr. Hallam. He retired early that night, hoping for a good night's sleep, but instead awoke in a nightmare, moaning in his bed on Marburg I. The bedside clock said 1:00 A.M., Sunday, May 19. His mouth was dry, and he reached over for water from his bedside pitcher. He felt confused. His nightmare had been so vivid that he had a hard time bringing himself fully awake. He felt saddened and guilty. The nightmare took him back to a time in his life that, when awake, he did not allow himself to dwell upon. Unless, of course, he was in one of his moods of black despair, and then there was nothing but to follow it through—or to take the one antidote that ever gave him momentary relief.

That antidote he had previously considered and spurned. Now all objections were forgotten in the urgency of the moment. He reached over to the bedside table, pulled out his toilet kit, and selected from it the half-full toothpaste tube. He turned on his small bed light and, getting gingerly out of bed, made his way over to the closet, where hung his clothes, including the white hospital coat that he had been wearing the day of his admission. Fumbling in the top left pocket, he removed a small one cc. hypodermic syringe that he always carried in case of having to administer emergency medication and a small sterile stoppered vial with solution in it, marked "diluent," carried for the same purpose.

He eagerly but carefully unstoppered the vial and allowed a thin stream of fine white powder to stream into it from a slit in the bottom of the toothpaste tube. He measured it by eye expertly even in the dim light, allowing himself a slightly larger dose than usual, closed off the tube, restoppered the vial, and shook it to make sure the powder was fully dissolved. When satisfied, he plunged the needle of the syringe through the rubber stopper of the vial and, turning it upside down, drew out the full amount of the fluid. After tiptoeing to the door of his room and making sure the corridor was empty, he returned to the bed, lowered his pajamas, and, after selecting a spot, bunched up the muscle of his right thigh with his left hand and plunged the needle obliquely into the thigh, and, with steady pressure, pushed the entire contents of the syringe into the tissues. He withdrew the needle, quickly recapped it, buried the syringe and vial at the bottom of the wastebasket, and returned the toothpaste tube to his toilet kit and it to the windowsill. He then returned to bed to await the delicious relief that would come in a few minutes.

Soon the curtain of narcosis closed over him, and again he dreamed . . . April 1939.

. . . .

Clay looked at Dr. Sarnoff across the desk. Clay thought that the words Dr. Sarnoff spoke in his calm southern voice spelled the end of his career. He felt numb as he left that interview, as if he were dreaming and would soon awaken. He subsequently remembered thinking how many times Dr. Sarnoff must have had to deliver this message to aspiring interns and residents, and what a good job he did of it, leaving some element of pride but no element of hope, no hope of continuing at the hospital. Clay was not entirely surprised by the decision. During the last months he had been preoccupied with Anne's departure to Richmond and with his own guilt. He worked with regularity but not with conviction, enthusiasm, or vigor, and the lack of these elements in his performance had been enough to seal his fate, especially when contrasted with the constant and extravagant zeal of Warren Bregel. Fate had somehow contrived to throw the two of them together frequently in their rotations during those months.

Clay had for a time come to enjoy the rivalry with Warren. It provided an extra spark of competitive fire to drive him. Indeed, as Warren's aggressive tactics grew bolder and his own responses increased as well, whether in the operating room, on the wards, or in the conference halls, their sparring became evident to the rest of the staff and developed into a source of amusement for them, a play within a play. Clay and Warren tried to outdo each other, and their performances became virtuoso. But in the last months Clay no longer seemed interested in defending himself, and even Warren began to reduce the sharpness of his challenges.

In the end, of course, Warren triumphed and was asked to stay on at Johns Hopkins as assistant resident in surgery. After April interviews, and after the news came out about who was to stay and who to leave, further competition seemed useless, and Clay confronted Warren only once more before he left Baltimore. On a day in mid-June, Clay had gone to the Mateer's house to say good-bye. It had been a strained parting in which both Clay and Bart acknowledged the inevitabilities of the selection process and the need to pursue their careers. They promised to stay in touch. Clay returned to his house at around five that evening and was about to go up the steps when he saw Warren walking toward him on his way home from the hospital. Clay waited at the steps.

"Hello, Clay," said Warren.

"Hello, Warren. Got a minute?" Clay stepped out on the sidewalk in front of him.

"A quick one. Nell's got supper waiting." Warren looked edgily about.

"It's okay. I only have one quick question for you, Warren, and I have to have the answer to it before I leave. Did you write that letter to Anne in Richmond?"

Warren didn't flinch, and his eyes, an icy gray, stared into Clay's.

"No, Clay, I wrote no letters to Anne. Nell did!"

Clay caught himself, and felt his ears growing red. "You mean Nell . . . your wife . . . wrote Anne about me?"

"Yes. You see, she saw you and your friend leaving your house one morning, furtively, by the back door, as I recall. Nell has come to like Anne, and feels like she's a friend. She asked me what to do."

"And what did you say?"

"I told her it was her decision and that she should follow her own conscience, as, in the end, we all must," and he looked at Clay pointedly.

"You could have stopped her. That letter wasn't really an act of friendship," said Clay softly.

"Perhaps I could have—I don't know. Nell is quiet and may seem a bit mousy on the outside, but inside she's got spunk. She would have found a way if she'd wanted."

The two stood there for a long moment, eying each other steadily and evenly. Clay resisted a desire to knock the smirk off Warren's face and broke the silence. "Good-bye, Warren."

"Good-bye, Clay. Sorry to hear you're not staying on. It really won't be the same without you. Where is it that you're going, by the way?"

"Philadelphia City Hospital."

"Of course. A very good training hospital, they say."

"And congratulations to you, Warren, on being chosen to stay here—it couldn't happen to a lousier guy. Maybe you can relax next year."

"Relax? Relax? *You* go off and relax. As for me, I've got a different thing in mind." He started to walk off, but turned back after a few steps. "You know, you're not the only competition, Clay, only the most obvious. Now that ours is over, I go on to the next level."

After watching Warren go up the street, Clay went into his house. So it was Nell . . .

He had two weeks between finishing his duties at Johns Hopkins and reporting at City Hospital on July 1st. He used it to go home to visit his parents in Bloomington. They had been kept up to date on events in a sketchy way, but they were not aware of the causes of those events.

When he saw them at dinner on the night of his arrival, Clay thought that his parents looked older and that his father would not be able to practice much longer.

"I'm fine," his father insisted on the porch after dinner. "The question is, how are you? What happened between you and Anne? Was she too spoiled to stay the course?"

Clay answered slowly. "A mess, Dad, and I really can't tell you everything, except to say it wasn't her fault. You knew about the rape attempt, of course, and that set us back a while, but then she was ready to come back, and I did something really wrong, and that may have ended us. I don't know. I haven't heard from her recently about her intentions, but I do know she's working in the Grier Clinic."

His father thought a bit, then asked, "Do you still love her?"

Clay nodded. "More than ever, but I don't know what to do."

"Kind of hard to work under those circumstances."

Clay responded to the understanding. "It knocked me off my pins, Dad. I couldn't concentrate—lost my bearings a bit."

"What are you going to do?"

"Well, I guess I'm going to take this assistant residency in Philadelphia, but my heart's not in it."

Dr. Hallam knocked the ashes off his cigar. "Well, you've had a couple of blows. Your marriage, your training. I know how badly you wanted to stay at Hopkins. Life doesn't always go the way we want it. If it did, it'd probably be pretty dull. But you're still the same son I've known for twenty-five years, you're still young, healthy, bright. You can still make a hell of a difference in this world if you want to."

Clay smiled at his father. "I'm still your son, Dad, and no complaints about that. But I'm not the same. I think I found out a few things about myself in the last year, and it's made a difference. I always used to feel at ease with myself. Now? I don't know."

"You can always come back here, after your training, and join me in practice. I'd like nothing better, and I know your mother would be ecstatic. Wonderful people and a great life here, fishing, hunting . . . keep it in mind."

"I will, Dad, I will."

Three days before he was to leave, he had a visit from Dr. Grier, who phoned ahead to say that he was coming to talk with Clay and would not have time to spend the night. He arrived in the early after-noon, in a long black chauffeur-driven Lincoln limousine, and as-cended the steps to their porch effortlessly, like an Olympian. In his efficient way, he briefly greeted the Hallams and insisted on spiriting Clay away in his car for a talk.

"Nice car," observed Clay, as they settled back into the plush seat.

"Belongs to the clinic. As you may know, we have three," said Dr. Grier.

"How's Anne?"

"She's fair, I would say, all things considered." He looked at Clay sideways. "I understand you were unfaithful to her."

Clay felt his face redden and his palms sweat. He wondered if Dr. Grier was about to shoot him or merely upbraid him.

"Dr. Grier, please forgive me. I wouldn't have had it happen for the world, and I honestly don't think it would have under any other circumstances. It was almost an accident, and it only happened once. If I could make it up to her in some way, I would. How is she . . . taking it?"

Dr. Grier listened to this without displaying emotion, but at the end of it cleared his throat sententiously. "Anne feels, well, betrayed and wronged. She's always been a terrific idealist, as you know. But I also know that she's trying to come to grips with it, understand it, digest it, if you will. In her heart she still loves you and, I believe, knows that you're the right man for her. She hasn't asked for lawyers or divorce proceedings. She's assisting the manager of the clinic and seeing some of her girlfriends, but that's about all. I don't think she'd accept your apology right now, but in six months, a year, who can tell?

"At any rate, it would be best for you to be near her during this time, that is, of course, if you want to save this marriage." He looked at Clay, who nodded eagerly, and then continued. "As far as Mrs. Grier and I are concerned, we would go along with whatever decision she makes. We have viewed this as a very favorable marriage for her, and we'd like it to continue. Privately, as someone older and more experienced, I view this thing as a human deviation and can find it in my heart to excuse you—as long as it's not repeated."

The ease of this absolution was not lost on Clay, who accepted it with the gratitude of someone badly in need of some forgiveness.

"I suggest again, therefore, that you resign the residency position you accepted in Philadelphia and instead come and complete your training at the Grier Clinic. In that way, you can keep yourself in the picture, so to speak, and be there when Anne is ready. I will personally vouch for your position in the clinic."

Clay almost gasped at the difference between what he had been expecting and what he heard.

The proposal unexpectedly opened up a possible new direction for his life and offered some hope of retrieving the most valuable part of what he had lost—Anne. His heart pounded as he considered the possibility of accepting the offer.

"Does Anne know about this, Dr. Grier?"

"Heavens, no, my word on it. In fact, you and I are the only ones who do know about it."

"I wonder how she'd feel," Clay mused, "if I came to Richmond and joined the clinic staff. She might feel betrayed, for the second time."

"I'm sure I can smooth it over with her," Dr. Grier said.

"I don't know—it would be almost like I'd gotten away with murder and was rubbing it in her face. Bound to be hard for her to swallow, my showing up there. I don't think I could look her in the eye." Clay felt the logic of his own reasoning shut off the new hope that had risen in him. "Dr. Grier, I don't see how I can accept your offer right now."

"There's something you don't know, Clay. Anne is going away. She and her friend May Harding will drive across the country this summer, visit friends, and so forth. They're heading for San Francisco, where May has a brother, and they won't come back until mid-September, when May has to go back to college. Anne has said that if she likes it, she might stay out there a while, find a job . . . live."

"When do they go?"

"Around July 1st, in about ten days. But I could prepare her for your arrival, and you might or might not choose to face her before she goes. It's up to you. But her absence would give her time to adjust to your being there. It all makes sense to me!" He eyed Clay solemnly.

Clay was silent as he weighed his longing for Anne and his happiness at the prospect of being back in her world against the undoubtedly superior surgical training he would get in Philadelphia. The latter suddenly seemed unimportant.

"Dr. Grier, if you can square it with Anne and make her feel okay about this, I . . . I'll accept your offer. I'll plan to be there July 2nd." He smiled his first genuine smile in months, and Dr. Grier smiled back. The rest of the ride back to the Hallams' home was filled with talk about the clinic and Clay's duties, salary, and living accommodations. But the possibility of seeing Anne was the most important part of Clay's change of plans. He was elated.

After Dr. Grier had gone, Clay told his father of his decision. He replied, "Well, you're the best judge of things, Clay, and I'm glad you're happy about it. Seems to me like you may be crowding Anne some, though, instead of giving her more room. And once you join the clinic, it may be hard to leave, if you ever want to. I mean, it may be long term."

Clay listened, but his heart was already made up. He was going to get Anne back. That was all that mattered. That night he wrote two letters, which he posted the next morning. The first was to the Philadelphia City Hospital, explaining a necessary change in his plans "for family reasons" and asking their understanding and forgiveness. The second letter was to Anne:

My Dear Anne,

By now your father will have explained to you his (renewed) offer to me to come to the clinic to finish my surgical training, and my acceptance. I think he wants to bring us back together again and, of course, I myself want nothing more. The possibility of our being united dominates my every thought and act. It would undoubtedly be a better life for us there in Richmond than we have had, but I do not want to force myself on you or force a decision from you about us before you are ready. I love you too much, and respect you too much, to desire anything but a free and independent decision from you about our marriage. Unless I hear from you to the contrary, therefore, I will not arrive at the clinic until July 2nd, the day after you have left for the West. Should you wish me to come earlier, let me know and I can be there almost immediately.

What happened, happened, and I cannot undo it. I would, however, like to spend the rest of my life making it up to you and showing you how faithful and loving I can be. Please give me a chance!

Hopefully,
Clay

Four days later her reply came. He recognized the scented blue envelope addressed in green ink, seized it from the mailbox, and took it hurriedly to his room, where he tore it open with nervous fingers.

Dear Clay,

I was greatly touched by your letter and your decision to come to the clinic this July, for I realize it was made for me and against your better judgment as far as your training is concerned. I hope you will never regret it.

It means a lot to me that you care this much about our marriage, but I am still full of mixed feelings about you and me and what happened. Perhaps the trip west will clear my mind. At any rate, it is still too soon for us to see each other, so please don't come before July 2nd. Write to me—I still wear our wedding ring.

I hope you enjoy being here. Dad is quite pleased and happy you are coming—it's what he's wanted all along— but what a way to get his wishes!

Anne

Clay arrived in Richmond around noon on July 2nd, and had the cab take him directly from the airport to the lodgings that Dr. Grier had arranged for him. They proved more than adequate, as Clay had suspected they would be: an ample apartment, with its own entrance and stairwell, in a large private home near the clinic. The surrounding yard was deep and so heavily treed that it seemed to absorb the house, and the swimming pool in the rear was hardly visible. Clay admitted himself with the keys left for him above the door frame. He found a note telling him that he had use of the pool, and there was also a guest membership card to the Richmond Country Club. As he looked around the apartment, he recognized that Dr. Grier had not forgotten anything.

The gracious old house, owned by a friend of the Griers, was not far from the clinic. The next afternoon Clay strolled the few blocks to it, arriving at one o'clock, the appointed time. As he entered under the wrought-iron archway, which bore in large letters "The Grier Clinic," and walked up the landscaped sidewalk toward the entrance, he saw Dr. Grier awaiting him in front.

"Ah, Clay, right on time," said Dr. Grier, advancing toward him. "I like that!"

Clay returned his greeting affably, and the two paused as they turned to enter the clinic. They gazed at the white columns of the entrance portico and the ivy and brick face of the three-storied building, and Dr. Grier said, "Your new home, Clay. I hope you grow to love it as much as I do."

He clapped Clay lightly on the shoulder, and the two went into the building. Dr. Grier steered him down the immaculate corridors to the staff dining room, where Clay found that a banquet luncheon had been arranged for him. All of the staff physicians, the nursing supervisors, and the clinic's board of directors were there—there was a one-hundred-percent turnout, which Clay found amazing, but Dr. Grier seemed to think was routine. Clay had already met many of these people at the wedding, but this time the encounters had a different tone, and Clay realized he was being sized up. Dr. Kit Grier was there, as was Dr. Laurence Grier, all eighty years showing, but "still operating four days a week and loving it," as he put it to Clay.

At the end of the meal, Anne's father rose to his feet and said, "Well, thank you all for coming to meet Dr. Hallam. I hope you've all gotten to chat with him. Of course it's only the beginning. As you know, Dr. Hallam comes to us from his surgical internship at Johns Hopkins to continue his surgical training. It is my hope that each of us will make him welcome, teach him what we can, learn from him what we can, open our minds and our hearts to him, and make him one of us." Smiling, he added, "Remember, he's my son-in-law."

Clay recalled this last admonition often during the weeks that followed. He found that his duties were light. He was given the run of the clinic and the privilege of dropping in on, and assisting in, any operation. He could stay as long as he liked or leave when he liked, and he had few actual duties, for teams of nurses and technicians were proficient in administering intravenous solutions and in doing laboratory work. He began to make friends with the staff, who were quite friendly and warm toward him—although defensive, he thought, when he tried to probe the depth of their knowledge about the surgery done in the clinic. He was too wise to be openly critical, and so he remained popular, but he began to form opinions about their individual abilities and who could teach him the most. He spent a lot of time reading in the clinic's excellent medical library. He loved reading and enjoyed being alone and having the leisure time actually to *read* the surgical literature instead of having to cram it in.

Clay had a standing invitation to dinner with the Griers almost every night. At first he went occasionally, but, as the news of the attractive and able young surgeon-in-residence at the clinic spread, he began to be asked out more often, not only by staff but also by others, and he soon discovered that the attractions of Richmond's fabled society were many and varied. After three or four weeks, he began to feel that he belonged here. He was eager for Anne to come home.

One night he encountered Randolph Grier at a dinner party.

"Uncle Randolph, good to see you again. Did you know I was at the clinic now?"

Randolph, who was weaving a bit from the champagne he was drinking, replied, "Been expecting you, Clay. You seem more real already, more like a true Grier. How's Anne?"

Clay shrugged. "I'm not sure. We're not in close communication, as you probably know."

"Oh, she'll be all right. Now that you're here, she'll come back and you'll live happily ever after, here in your gilded cage, and you'll have lots of little Grier-Hallams. It's all written in the cards." He giggled.

He seemed peaked and shaky, and Clay scrutinized him, ignoring, for the moment, his sarcasm. "How're you feeling, Uncle Randolph? Are you taking care of yourself?"

"Fine as wine, Clay, or champagne when I can get it. I'm all recovered from my heart problem, and they haven't buried me yet."

"I'd love to come and see you, sir, and take you out to dinner if you'd let me."

Randolph's face became serious. "First, tell me how you like it at the clinic. What do you think of it?"

"Well, sir, I've been here almost a month and I'm having a great time." Clay grinned. "I may be in heaven except for missing one angel."

"Very well, I will go out to dinner with you in six weeks—let's see, September 15th. I'll write it down. And you must tell me where you are then."

Some days later, Clay finished his clinic work early in the afternoon and decided to pass by the emergency room to see if anything of interest was occurring. As opposed to the E.R. at Johns Hopkins, the one here was small and inactive, kept that way by the board of directors, who during years of accounting had found emergency medicine to be unremunerative. Consequently, the availability of the E.R. was not well known, and ambulances were encouraged to pass it by. Occasionally, however, the ill and injured would see the clinic sign over the driveway and come up the road for help. This is what had happened today.

Clay was drawn toward a cubicle in the E.R. by the noise. Opening the door, he saw the staff E.R. nurses and two aides attempting to lift a patient from the examining table onto a stretcher. The patient was a white woman who looked to be in her midtwenties. She was groaning in pain and pleading to be let alone.

"Can I help?" asked Clay.

One of the nurses looked at him and said, "Oh, Dr. Hallam, yes. Help us get her onto the stretcher, if you will."

"Taking her to x-ray?" Clay asked, as he drew closer and noted the patient's stricken features.

"No, we're trying to move her out to the ambulance. They're taking her to the Medical College." She was assertive and experienced with such cases. "C'mon, hon—let's move it onto the stretcher." As she pulled on the girl, Clay saw dark blood from her vagina pooling on the bed.

"She's hemorrhaging," Clay pointed out.

"We know," replied the nurse.

"That's why we're trying to move her out of here quickly!" said the other nurse, older and less forceful.

"But maybe she shouldn't be moved," said Clay, "at least to another hospital. Here, do you mind if I examine her?"

The nurses and aides looked at each other, then left the room. Clay examined her carefully. The nurses were waiting in the hall when he came out.

"She's got a ruptured ectopic pregnancy. Stomach is hard as a rock, and she feels shocky. She shouldn't be moved! What's her blood count?"

The younger nurse looked at him disdainfully. "We already know that, Dr. Hallam, and her hemoglobin is down to six grams. We've *got* to move her out!"

"No!" Clay shouted at her. "We're keeping her. Get her typed and matched and get some blood going. Alert the operating room. Who's the gynecologist on call?"

The nurses went off, he supposed to do his bidding, while he went back into the room to complete his examination and tell the patient what was occurring. A few minutes later, there was a knock on the door, and Clay stepped out to find the manager of the clinic, Mr. Remson, nervously awaiting him.

"Dr. Hallam, the nurses tell me there's a problem here. Arrangements have already been made to send this patient to the Medical College."

"But I'm countermanding that order, sir. I think she's too sick to send out—she might not make it!"

Mr. Remson cleared his throat and looked away. "I'm sorry, Dr. Hallam, she has to go. Believe me, she'll be okay. We do it all the time!"

Clay looked at him and felt rage building inside him. "What? I hope I didn't hear that correctly, Mr. Remson. Look, you're no doc-tor—in fact, I'm the only doctor I can see here, and she's too sick to send anywhere. Where are the nurses?" His raised voice echoed throughout the corridors. "They'd better damn sight be getting that blood ready, or I'll have their licenses!"

Just then the nurses appeared with the blood, and Clay reentered the room to help them start the transfusion. He had just found the vein and gotten the blood started when again the door opened and Mr. Remson's voice came from the doorway.

"Dr. Hallam, can you come to the phone? It's Dr. Grier."

Clay came out and took the phone at the desk.

"Hello, Clay," came Dr. Grier's reassuring voice, "some trouble?"

Clay told him about the patient, her rigid abdomen, her low blood count, her precarious blood pressure, and ended by saying, "She should be operated on right away, Dr. Grier. She has peritonitis and fever. She may die."

Dr. Grier replied, "I'm in complete agreement, Clay, complete. The nurses have told me everything. I've been in touch with the Medical College. They're all set to operate. A team is ready for her as soon as the ambulance can get her there. It'll only take ten minutes, and that's a lot faster than we can get set up here—so ship her out as soon as you can, Clay. She can get transfusions on the way. Thank you for your help. Are you coming for dinner tonight?"

Clay watched as they put the moaning woman into the ambulance. He could hardly believe what was happening. The woman did sur-vive, however, as his phone calls to the hospital confirmed. Neither Clay nor Dr. Grier mentioned it again, but they were reserved in each other's company thereafter.

A few weeks later, something else happened. One of Clay's few duties was to perform physical examinations the night before surgery on patients in whose operations he was to assist the next day. A lot of hernia surgery was performed at the clinic. In fact, as he studied the daily O.R. schedules, Clay concluded that it was the most frequently performed surgery week in, week out. Hernia surgery is, in general, relatively easy surgery, so Clay had mostly ignored it, but he believed he should at least see how it was done here. They should be experts, he thought.

He looked over the schedule for the next day and picked a case with Dr. Markell, a jovial middle-aged man who operated at the clinic almost every day. The patient was a heavy-set schoolteacher who had been referred to Dr. Markell by his family doctor because of a right inguinal hernia, but when Clay examined him at length the night before his surgery, he was unable to find any hernia. Satisfied that no hernia existed, he grinned at the patient and said, "You're in luck. No surgery for you tomorrow—no hernia!"

Clay wrote a note on the chart detailing his findings, as well as a tentative discharge order for the patient in the morning, and left. He was stunned when he returned the next day and found that the operation had been done and the hernia fixed. Clay was incredulous. He found Dr. Markell in the surgical dressing room, preparing for another case.

"Dr. Markell, I was surprised that you took that patient to surgery this morning. I couldn't find any hernia there to fix."

"Well, it was mighty small," drawled Dr. Markell, rummaging around in his locker. "We tightened things up for him a bit."

"Dr. Markell, I don't think there was any hernia there."

Dr. Markell turned around. "Look, Dr. Hallam, you're young and you're new here, so I'm going to tell you something. It doesn't really matter whether there was a hernia or just a little weakness. The point is, the man thought he had a hernia. His own doctor had told him so. Both of them expected him to have surgery! I couldn't disappoint them, could I? Besides, I'm sure the doctor has already been sent his rebate." He watched Clay's face carefully, as if waiting for a puzzled look. He got it.

"Rebate? Doctors get rebates when they send patients here?"

"Of course they do. Family doctors have to live, too. We recognized this long ago. The consequence is that we get a lot of surgery patients referred to us here at the clinic who might ordinarily go elsewhere." Dr. Markell sighed, as if talking to a child.

Clay's mind was in a whirl as he left the locker room. Not only was unnecessary surgery being done here, but doctors were *paid* to send their patients to the clinic.

He went over his discovery later in the office of Dr. Grier, who smiled. "It's not as bad as it may sound to you, Clay. The clinic needs referrals to function, so we make it worthwhile for family doctors and internists and pediatricians to send us cases. For years the clinic has lent and even given financial support to students so that they can go to medical school. In some cases we even set them up in practice. Naturally, these people are grateful and refer their patients to us. So if we do an occasional, *possibly* unnecessary procedure, well, we don't disappoint anybody, and our mortality rates are as low as anyplace in the country." He clapped Clay on the shoulder.

"You'll get used to it, Clay. You'll be fine. It's our system. And it works."

For Clay sleepless nights followed, and troubled days. He was living a lie. He wasn't living by his own code anymore, but the clinic's. He ought to leave the clinic. But what about Anne? How could he explain it to her? Maybe he could stick it out, at least until she returned. He knew one thing, at least. If he ever became the head of this place, things would change.

He still hadn't heard from Anne, but that did not particularly disturb him. He felt she was looking for answers, for resolution, to the hurt his infidelity had caused. He would have liked to talk to her, but he believed that if he waited she would eventually return. Then they would see about the clinic and its problems.

This was his state of mind when, two months later, he operated with Laurence Grier, who repeatedly had asked Clay to assist him. But this was the first chance Clay had to do so.

"Just want you to see how an eighty-year-old does it, Clay," he said. "Keep your eyes open! Ever done a hysterectomy before?"

"I will, Dr. Laurence. I don't want to miss anything," Clay replied. "I've assisted on several before."

He liked the old gentleman. On this day, however, they were in trouble right from the start.

The patient, an obese, middle-aged woman who had a fibroid tumor of the uterus, began bleeding as soon as the first incision was made. Because of her abdominal fat, the team had difficulty getting and maintaining a good view of the operative field. After about an hour of trying to free up the uterus and dissect away the thick cords and ligaments that held it in place, Dr. Grier was clearly shaky. Clay saw him whisper to a nurse, who in turn passed the message to another nurse, who left the room.

"Everything okay, Dr. Laurence?" Clay asked.

"Only fair, my boy. I'm having a little trouble controlling the bleeding—she's so damned fat. Want to see what you can do?" The two men changed places, and Clay began to orient himself with what had been done. It took him about fifteen minutes to do so and to stop the multiple bleeding sites that were pouring blood into the operative field. He was about to carry the operation forward when a burly man, fully gowned and masked, and smelling of cigar smoke, appeared at his side, looked down into the operative opening, and said, "Where are we?"

Dr. Grier, on the other side of the table, looked up and said gratefully, "Linus, you're here!"

Linus answered, "Yep, I'm here, Laurence. As per your request." Indicating Clay, he asked, "Who's this?"

Dr. Grier said, "Linus, this is Dr. Clay Hallam, our surgical resident. Clay, meet Dr. Linus Quigley, surgical consultant extraordinaire. Glad to have you aboard, Linus."

"Yes, well, move aside, sonny, so I can get a look in there," muttered Dr. Quigley, and forced Clay backward as he moved into his place. Clay was at a loss as to where to go, but Dr. Grier asked him to come around the table and take his place as first assistant, then he himself left the table. So Clay found himself assisting the newcomer in finishing the operation. Clay swiftly discovered that Dr. Quigley was an excellent surgeon. He grasped the problem immediately and enlarged the operative incision, gained a better view of the area, and removed the uterus in a short while.

After the operation was over, Clay and Dr. Quigley walked together toward the dressing room.

"I enjoyed working with you, Dr. Quigley. A brilliant recovery of that case, and a pleasure to see." Clay glanced at him as they entered the room and approached the lockers. Dr. Quigley sat down on the bench, pushed his floppy cap back on his head, and began rummaging around in his locker. He made no reply to Clay's comment.

"I'd love to have the chance to assist you again sometime, if you'd let me," continued Clay, wondering if the man had heard him.

Dr. Quigley pulled a cigar out of the locker and lit it. He looked up at Clay and replied, "Look, sonny, you seem like a nice kid and you did a good job helping me today. So tell me, when's this place gonna learn? Letting a doddering old man and an untrained boy loose on that woman today was almost murder. It was a tough case. Suppose I hadn't been available at home when they called! I mean, to let that old boy continue to operate just because his name is Grier!" He shook his head, sighed, and started peeling off his gown.

"Sir, do you mind if I ask what your role is around here? I mean, I haven't seen you before, or seen your name on the O.R. schedule."

Dr. Quigley looked at him again with eyes like blue saucers. He grunted. "I'm a surgeon, sonny, a surgeon. I come when they need me. I'm not on the regular staff here. I have a crosstown office." He resumed dressing, as Clay watched.

"You mean, you come only like this? When there's an emergency?" asked Clay.

"Yup, that's it! I come when called. It's because I'm reliable—I do good salvage work. And I don't mind it. It's interesting and it helps to pay the freight."

"But how come you're not on the staff? Don't you want to be?"

Again the blue stare. "Look, I don't know how much they've told you about this place, but I'll say this. They've got some good surgeons and some bad ones. The latter ought to be let go but they're family-connected, or close to it. I guess I wouldn't mind being on the staff, but they'll never ask. I mean, my name is Quigley—not exactly southern aristocracy—but I don't mind. I'm doing all right."

He turned to finishing his dressing, and Clay thought the conversation had ended. As Clay was leaving, Dr. Quigley called, "My parting advice to you, sonny, for free: Be a surgeon. Don't be a jerk."

When he left the dressing room, Clay knew that he had to resign from the clinic. Dr. Quigley had said it right. He didn't want to be a jerk. If Clay was to continue to train as a surgeon, he wanted the best training he could get. He didn't want to have to call a Dr. Quigley if he got into trouble. Anne or not, he couldn't live a lie. He had to leave.

He walked down to Dr. Stuart Grier's office and managed to explain to him his decision to leave. Dr. Grier seemed relieved to hear this. Evidently other staff members had voiced their opinions of Clay, and he had listened. "I think you're right, Clay. In retrospect, I think you're too young to have come here to the clinic. You need a little more seasoning, a little more training, first. It's my fault. Maybe you can come back after you've finished your training. But where will you go?"

"Well, sir, I was thinking of seeing if Philadelphia City Hospital still has an assistant residency position open."

"Go to it. And let me know if I can help. And Clay, don't worry about Anne. I'll explain everything to her."

Clay didn't know whether he wanted Dr. Grier to explain his departure to Anne, but he didn't really care. After he awoke the next morning, he called City Hospital and was delighted when they offered him a spot. He was asked to arrive by September 15th. That was only two days away, but he agreed.

He couldn't leave without saying one more word to Randolph Grier. Clay finally located him having lunch at the Richmond Men's Club. He explained that he was leaving for Philadelphia, then said, "Well, Uncle Randolph, I fell out of heaven, and I'm back in limbo."

Randolph looked at him through his pince-nez glasses. "Sit down, Clay. Lunch? No? Then share some champagne with me, at least."

The waiter brought another glass and filled it, and the two tipped their drinks to each other.

"Your health, Clay."

"And yours, too, Uncle Randolph."

"And about your fall out of heaven, it was your destiny. You don't belong here at the Grier Clinic. It's too—uh—jejune for you. But of course you had to find that out for yourself." Randolph nibbled at poached salmon and sipped champagne.

"I guess. But where do I belong?"

Randolph pondered a minute and then chuckled. "Do you want to take up bridge, Clay?"

Clay laughed with him. "Maybe I should at that! But not without Anne. Tell me, do you think she'll ever come back to me?"

Randolph thought a moment and then said, "Well, she's a Grier, but she's also female and independent, and, in the long run, I'd bet on that to steer her back to you. You belong together, not apart."

"Well, Uncle Randolph, you mean a lot to Anne, and I have to say you've come to mean a lot to me. I hope you'll take care of yourself. And I hope, no matter what Anne does, that we can stay in touch." He stood up to go.

"Don't worry about me, Clay, and I want to say also, don't feel sorry for me. I indulge myself to the fullest, and, if that's taking care of myself, I'm following your advice. I'm a ghost around here. But to you and Anne, I'm as real as life itself. Write to me, dear boy, because I'm exceedingly fond of you."

As Clay departed, he glanced back at him, a frail old man with a large, aristocratic head and a pink face, bent solitarily over his meal. Clay felt a lump in his throat. They might not meet again soon.

Clay arrived at Philadelphia City Hospital on September 15, 1939, having failed to come to terms, or even come to grips, with the changes in his fortune. He felt numb and hollow at having lost so swiftly his sense of direction. He analyzed these changes and even explained to himself each step that led to his present situation, but he simply could not accept it.

Did he even want to be a doctor anymore? Maybe he should try other work. He thought about becoming a teacher—he had always found the possibility of teaching appealing, although he had never done any. Or business. Or law. . . . But no matter how many alternatives he considered, he could not abandon his desire to be a doctor. Medicine filled him with a special feeling of being and knowing something important. And he was excited about using his knowledge. In the end, there were no other choices for him. He felt right about being a doctor.

There was not much time to brood. City Hospital had a reputation as a provider of good medical care for a large segment of the indigent population of greater Philadelphia. Its pace, volume, and diversity of cases were considerable, requiring both expeditious and thorough care. A large house staff, supervised by faculty members from different medical schools in the area, provided that care. Low and ungainly, the hospital buildings stretched over several city blocks. It took about a week for Clay to orient himself to the hospital's layout.

He was actually grateful for the frenetic pace of the surgical service. He didn't feel at home here; he ultimately belonged at Johns Hopkins, but at least he was doing the work he wanted to do. As an assistant resident, he had much more responsibility and freedom in decision-making than he had as an intern. He was critical of his new environs and, as he had expected, found them in many ways inferior to those at Hopkins. This hospital was large, fragmented, and had too many different services for the training to be as thorough and focused as it had been in Baltimore. There the training had been more formal, and responsibility was added in careful increments. Much of what Clay was now learning came from "hands-on" teaching and daily experience. An assistant resident could more or less choose his own direction in reading and studying, whereas at Hopkins the search for knowledge was driven, was paramount. Little research was done at City Hospital. It was a general hospital geared to furnishing good patient care and to providing adequate training for general surgeons and physicians, most of whom would eventually enter private practice. Missing was the close-knit, almost familial elitism of Hopkins, where everyone knew his confreres and respected their capabilities. Clay was quick to note weaknesses at City Hospital, partly because he was looking for them, but his brief stint at the Grier Clinic helped him to appreciate its strengths.

Clay supervised from four to six interns on the ward service and was thus in a teaching role. He had no interest in that role at the outset, being much preoccupied with his own problems, and he gave his interns only token attention. But as time went by, and he became more involved with them, he began to take greater interest and to enjoy teaching. He realized that his grounding in surgery had been excellent and that he had much to teach—as well as much to learn.

As he became interested in his interns and their progress, some of his former drive returned. He had more time to prepare for the next day than he had had at Hopkins, and he read medical articles at night. After a month, he wrote to Anne:

October 12, 1939

My Dear Anne,

I hope this letter finds you back safely from your trip to the West Coast. I know that you went there looking for answers. Were they there? I tried to wait for you but couldn't. I don't know what you have been told about my departure from the clinic, but, in short, your father felt that I needed more training before performing any major role there. I agreed with him. But I still love you and want to remain married to you.

The things that we had together, the love, the sense of rightness, the mutuality of—what?—soul, are not easy to find in the world, and may not be found by either of us again. I believe they can still be ours, if we can hold on for a while until the cloud of what I have done clears. God grant that we have time.

As I write this, Europe seems on the brink of war. The papers are full of Germany's preparations to invade Poland. The U.S. still seems to seethe with discontent, and I wonder how we could avoid taking sides if war does break out. All of this fills me with a sense of urgency, of getting things done before it's too late. It is amazing, though, how little touched the medical world, at least the medical world here, is by world events. It's like being isolated on our own special planet. My life here so far is very quiet. I am doing a lot of surgery. I hope I'm doing a good job. But I lack "heart."

More interesting, though, is my teaching role. There are four interns on my ward. They seem so young, although I'm only a year older! They are eager to learn, and I am eager to teach them. Teaching is a remarkable thing. It is calming yet energizing, as if the exchange between us is cathartic. It may be my salvation. I am as confused as ever about the direction of my career now that I've fallen off a high place. But I believe that whatever I do will involve some teaching.

I know you will write to me, when you feel you can, about what you're doing and thinking. I hope you stay well and safe. I am here for you should you ever need me.

All my Love,
Clay

After he posted the letter the next morning, he felt better. It was a relief to have expressed himself, even if he wasn't sure of how Anne would react to the letter, or if she would even read it. After three weeks the letter had not been returned, and he knew at least it had been accepted, so he wrote again. As the months passed, he began to write more frequently. There was no reply to his letters, so he sometimes felt as if he were writing to a fictional mistress, a Beatrice. He even began to feel that there was a positive side to this, for he was not constrained by having to respond to Anne's comments and was free to express his own thoughts and feelings. He wrote of his love for her and of his certainty that they belonged together, but he also wrote about his work, his surgical cases, his patients, his colleagues, and world events. His letters contained sententious pronouncements, such as, "Wars every twenty-five to fifty years seem a necessary part of life. They provide an outlet for human tensions, like a giant game, an opiate for the population, and also evoke a sense of national purpose," and "It is the duty of every government to take care of poverty and illness, which are linked. Poor and ill people pour in through the doors of this hospital day and night, then return to the same pest holes they were born in, and the cycle repeats. Mr. Roosevelt, for all his Hyde Park buddies, has gotten this country heading in the right direction. The Tennessee Valley Authority project and Social Security concepts will someday go down as great strides for humanity."

Many of the hospital staff were curious about Clay. He lived in a room in the main residence. He told them he was married, but if so, where was his wife? He said he was separated, but if so, why didn't he go out more? Because he wasn't interested. Why not? Was he ill? He spent a lot of time reading in the hospital library and in his room. As his interest in teaching increased, so did the effort he put into it. Gradually word spread among the interns that he was a well-informed and provocative teacher. The four interns whom he supervised asked if they could bring some friends to the morning and evening rounds that he conducted. He agreed, and soon as many as eight or ten house officers were gathering under his direction, or at least his instructorship. Most of the cases presented ongoing management problems for which there was no single or simple solution, but he excelled at stimulating discussion about the best treatments. Because he kept an open mind himself, he was able to open the minds of others.

In December he wrote Anne:

. . . My life here is very simple. I work, study, and sleep, and on the weekend sometimes play basketball in the gym for a few hours. Simple. The thing is, I like it. I've come to realize that I have a very strong tendency to withdraw into a world of learning, which I am now indulging. It's very stimulating, very seductive, and probably very ego-gratifying to learn from the very latest research, to know more than some of those around me, and to impart it to them. I could easily become a prig of the first order. But I hope I am saved from such a fate by keeping a sense of balance and a knowledge that this kind of life is not enough in the long run. I hope, dear Anne, that you are my key to all the more important things that life can give. Family, home, love, and compassion are all wrapped up in my love for you. . . .

In January 1940, on a cold blustery morning, Clay found a letter from Anne in his mail slot.

January 10, 1940

Dear Clay,

It's time that I write you. When I returned home, I was very disappointed to find that you had left the clinic. I still don't know how I would have reacted to having you here and seeing you. I also don't know what happened that caused you to leave so quickly, but it's between you and Dad, and he tells me nothing. I know he was disappointed.

I am well, and I enjoy my work at the clinic, where I am assistant to the manager, Mr. Remson. I think about your letters. I feel that I know you now better than ever. It has been almost a year since that awful day, yet I find that I still can't accept what happened. But I continue to wear our wedding ring.

Anne

Elated, Clay wrote back immediately.

   . . . Your letter has meant everything to me and given me cause to hope. It seems as if life, or fate, or logic, is drawing us back together again.

I'm now spending a few months in neurosurgery. It's a curious field, so different from general surgery that it seems almost another world. It's a fairly new field to me, but I'm lucky to have an extremely bright, although eccentric, teacher. I will tell you more about him another time. . . .

The field of neurosurgery was indeed a bustling specialty at this time in 1940. Clay was on the neurosurgery service that January because he had been requested to substitute for another resident, who was ill. He was finding the service interesting, mostly because of one surgeon.

At the hospital, Dr. Maxwell Schultz was called "Little Max" and "Papa Schultz" behind his back. He was about five feet six inches tall. The top of his head was bald, but the sides were fringed with graying dark hair. He wore gold-rimmed bifocal glasses. He was in his fifties, but looked ten years older. His chin was pointed, and his large ears stuck out from his head. At the hospital, when not in the operating room, he wore either a dark brown suit or a dark blue one. He wore each one for a week, then alternated.

Dr. Schultz was self-belittling and businesslike. He was in the private practice of neurosurgery, and Clay was assigned to his service at the hospital. He had a large practice among poorer patients, because his reputation was good and his fees were low.

Dr. Schultz had a much different temperament in the operating room than outside it. His quiet tone disappeared as soon as he entered the O.R. He immediately began to fret, mutter, criticize, blaspheme, and, above all, complain. However, his complaints were not bitter, but seemed talismans against bad luck.

"Damn, look at that!" he would say, looking into an open craniotomy site. "Do you think God would put that blood vessel there, just where we need to cut? If you did, God, tell me why! Was it this patient's fault, or mine?"

Or, "Who made these scissors? What company made these scissors?" he said to the nurses. "Take a note never to buy another pair of scissors from them. I never want to see another pair at any operation I do. They're duller than Dempsey's last fight."

During a difficult case, he even called out to the instrument nurse, "For Lord's sake, Miss Friar, don't give me the instrument I *ask* for, give me what I *need!*"

Clay's operating room mask disguised his frequent smiles at Dr. Schultz's remarks. The operating room nurses alternately loved him and hated him. But they all respected him—his judgment and his operating facility were outstanding. Clay learned that he had made several significant contributions to neurosurgery in operating technique and had even designed an instrument, a blood vessel clip, that was widely used.

One February afternoon at Neurology Rounds, the case of a black man from Mississippi, whose problem was a progressive unsteadiness of gait for several months, was presented for discussion. Several opinions were offered about possible causes. The prevailing diagnosis was multiple sclerosis.

The leader of the discussion, an assistant resident, looked around the room. "All right, any more ideas before going on to the next case?" She spotted Dr. Schultz and asked his opinion.

"Well, since you ask me, I'd say I believe the odds are much higher, say a thousand percent, that he has an occipital lobe tumor, maybe a meningioma, rather than multiple sclerosis."

A murmur went through the room.

"Why do you say that, Dr. Schultz? The x-rays and ventriculo-grams were negative."

"An occipital tumor wouldn't necessarily show any changes in x-ray, Doctor. The fact that the patient is a black male puts the proba-bilities of multiple sclerosis way down immediately. He's in the least common group to get it. Second, he's from Mississippi, and people who live within thirty-five degrees latitude of the equator are less apt to have sclerosis, again lowering the odds."

There was silence for a moment as the group digested this. "Would you be prepared to operate on this man, then?" a senior neurologist asked. "It's bad to operate on multiple sclerosis."

"If he'd let me, I'd operate tomorrow," replied Dr. Schultz.

When Dr. Schultz did operate on the man, Clay assisted. As they opened the occipital bone flap, the tumor came into view, its darker pulpy matter covering and crowding the normal, whiter brain tissue.

It took them nine hours to remove the tumor, using careful dissec-tion with the relatively new electric cautery technique to shell it away from the underlying normal tissue. As they wrapped the man's head, Clay said, "Dr. Schultz, that was truly an incredible job."

Dr. Schultz shook his head. "If he talks and walks when he wakes up, Dr. Hallam—that'll be the incredible part."

They finished their postoperative assessment around eight that night, then sat down for a cup of coffee in the empty cafeteria.

Dr. Schultz pulled out a pack of cigars, selected one, and, after offering one to Clay, lit his own. He leaned back and said, "I'm get-ting too old to do this kind of operation. I get tired now, and my eyes are not so good."

"I was tired, too, Dr. Schultz," said Clay.

"You get used to it. At your age you can get used to anything. I once did a seventeen-hour procedure with only two breaks. Went through two separate operating teams." He sighed. "You married, Hallam?"

"Yes, sir."

"Lucky girl! You helped me a lot today—and stop the 'sir,' if you will. In fact, you've done quite an excellent job these last few months. I suspect you have an affinity for neurosurgery. How do you like it?"

"I like it. In a small way, in the last few months I've come to be able to see it through your eyes. It seems to combine logic with skill, more than the other fields. Like that case today—your diagnosis and your operation were terrific."

"Odds—the odds were in our favor." The two were silent for a time. "What're you doing next year, Hallam?"

"Would you believe I don't know yet? I've had an offer to stay here in General Surgery, but . . . "

"Some 'buts,' eh? Do you like general surgery?"

"Yes."

"Mmm . . . good. I used to be a general surgeon once. Enjoyed it. I switched to neurosurgery about ten years ago, some time after Walter Dandy injected air into the ventricles and allowed us to see the brain—big step, that! I used to know him. A great man. He retired eight years ago. He once asked me to join him at Johns Hopkins. But do you know what I'd do if I were a young man like yourself?" He waited for and received Clay's query, then said, "I'd go into neurosurgery. It's an exciting field, with lots going on, but so much more to come! It'd be a great opportunity to make some contributions."

"It's an interesting field, all right," said Clay. "But this young man, would he stay here with you for his training?"

"Oh, no. Me? I'm a genius of sorts," he laughed, "but I'm still basically a meat and potatoes neurosurgeon, and getting old at that. No, I'll tell you what I'd do for him. I'd try to place him for his training where I have some influence, and where they have what I consider the broadest based—as well as the best—training program around. I'm sure he'd want to try it."

"And where would that be?"

"Why, Johns Hopkins, of course."

Clay's eyes widened, and he looked at Dr. Schultz closely, to see if this was a macabre joke. It wasn't. Dr. Schultz blew a cloud of smoke into the air.

"Dr. Schultz, what would you say . . . could you get me in there this July?"

His letter to Anne a few days later was exuberant.

> . . . So it seems, astoundingly, to be settled. I will return to Hopkins in July as assistant resident in neurosurgery. For the next four months, I will finish my work here under Dr. Schultz. I am happy and excited again, dear Anne, and feel again that I can make you happy. Please let me hear from you soon. I can almost feel my arms around you. Please join me in Baltimore. . . .

A week later Anne replied:

April 7, 1940

Dear Clay,

I cannot possibly come to you in Baltimore now—too many unhappy memories. And if I did it would probably only lead in the same direction again, days and nights of loneliness. I still love you very much, which is what makes it all so hard and so confusing for me. I tell myself that, because I love you so, I want only what's best for you. If I am unhappy I cannot make you happy. In fact, I could only be a burden to you.

I am not seeking a divorce at this time. I love you too much to do it. However, you are perfectly free to do so, and I would not oppose it. But I will remove my wedding ring, and you should feel free to do the same. After all, we are young and should see other people.

I am truly sorry, Clay. I feel I have disappointed you, as much as you disappointed me, but I can't get over what happened. I still hurt.

Good luck in your new direction(s).

Anne

Clay fingered his gold wedding ring as he reread Anne's letter. It seemed the perfect time to remove it and get on with his life. Anne and he had been separated for more than a year. Now he was starting into neurosurgery, and he was returning to the place he wanted to be. Perhaps it was better to cast off the past and to start a new life. But he still loved Anne. Her perfume clung to her letter. He left his wedding ring in place. It was still his link to her. His image of what life should be included neither adultery nor failure. Experiences in Richmond and Philadelphia had led him now to neurosurgery. He had acquired an ascetic discipline. He believed he knew who he was.

In late June of 1940, as the ferocity of the German invasion brought down France and increased the threat of Nazi domination, Clay returned to Johns Hopkins. A current of foreboding that America would be involved in Europe's war ran through the hospital, but Clay's enthusiasm for his new position was dimmed only by his discovery that Warren Bregel had also switched from general surgery to neurosurgery.

. . . .

Dr. Hallam bolted up in his bed on Marburg I. He was being bitten! He looked down, and his arms were covered with bugs—large, crawling, repellent bugs with wings. And they were in the air all about him, too! He flailed at them. . . . When he awakened later that Sunday morning, unaware that he had had a seizure, Dr. Jim Gallier was looking down into his face.

CHAPTER 11

Sunday, May 19, 1985

Jim Gallier bent over Dr. Clayton Hallam as he slept in his room on Marburg I. Jim took the patient's pulse and found a rate of eighty per minute; his respiratory rate was satisfactory at fifteen per minute. Dr. Hallam slept peacefully and showed no negative effects from his wild seizure early that morning. He stirred as Jim placed a stethoscope on his chest.

"Oh, Jim . . . it's you," he said, gazing around the room.

"Good morning, Dr. Hallam, how do you feel?"

"Not sure yet . . . can't wake up," Dr. Hallam muttered, trying in vain to sit up.

"Take it easy for a while. It's probably the medicine that's slowing you down. Here comes your nurse with breakfast. Try to eat a bit."

The nurse placed a tray on the bed table, then she and Jim raised Dr. Hallam up in bed.

"I'll be back soon, Dr. Hallam," promised Jim as he left the room. Jim performed his other duties on the ward. About an hour later the chief floor nurse told him that Mrs. Hallam and her daughter were in the waiting room. When he saw them, Jim was again struck by their aristocratic beauty. Both were impeccably dressed, Anne in a dark toile dress, Charlotte in a gray sleeveless blouse and skirt. They showed some pallor, and Anne was tremulous.

Jim explained that when he had checked on Dr. Hallam around two o'clock that morning, he found him having a seizure. Because it had certain atypical features, he suspected a drug overdose. He had searched Dr. Hallam's toilet kit and had found a drug. Analysis had shown it to be cocaine. Appropriate therapeutic measures had been taken.

"This morning," Jim said, "he seems to be doing very well. His blood pressure and pulse are good. He is eating breakfast, I think. You can see him shortly."

After a brief silence, Anne cleared her throat and said, "I know you want to hear about this . . . drug-taking."

Jim nodded. "It's important in his medical history. It might well have been the cause for his illness. I realize it may be painful for you . . ."

"Yes, it is," she said, then hesitated. "Yet I can see the need for it to be brought out into the open, and it might even help him to do so."

Charlotte said, "Jim, if the news of this got around to the general public, the newspapers, and so forth, it could ruin him. Is there any way of limiting—uh—those who know?"

"Of course, Charlie," replied Jim. "His principal doctors must know, but we'll try to keep it from going any further. We are usually successful in our efforts to maintain a patient's privacy."

The two women looked at each other.

"Is he out of danger?" asked Anne.

"He's a bit drowsy from the medicine, but that should clear quickly. He'll be okay."

"In that case, Jim, I believe the best thing would be for you to get the whole story from him, and let him tell you as much as he wants you to hear. It's really his story, not mine. It wouldn't be fair to him for me to tell it. I will only confirm for you, at this moment, for your treatment purposes, that he did take cocaine in World War II, but stopped completely. He took it again, ten years or so ago, but again stopped completely. Whether he took it more recently, aside from last night, I can't say. Is that sufficient?"

"Yes, Mrs. Hallam, that will do just fine. Insofar as you know, there were no other drugs involved?"

"No, just cocaine."

"All right, I'll ask him the rest. Thank you very much for coming in. Will you all be back again today?"

Charlotte nodded. "We'll be back this afternoon to see him."

Jim smiled. "He'll be here. And I will, too."

A few hours later Jim checked Dr. Hallam's vital signs. The patient watched him in silence, then asked, "Everything okay?"

"Just fine, sir, good blood pressure, good pulse."

"I see. Can you tell me what happened last night? Everyone seems in such a flutter today."

"You had quite a night, sir, a mixture of hallucinations and seizures. We had a hard job getting you under control."

"I see. Bad hospital water again, eh?"

Smiling, Jim said, "No, sir, not this time." But then his expression became serious when he realized the significance of what he, a mere house officer, was about to say to a world-renowned neurosurgeon. "We believe it was drug-induced."

Dr. Hallam looked at him quickly. "Oh? And which drug that you're giving me do you think caused it?"

Their eyes met for a moment, then Jim said, "Dr. Hallam, to go around this would simply be playing games. I'm going to be frank with you and hope you won't be offended. We have good reason to believe it was a cocaine seizure, and that you took the cocaine yourself last night."

There was a long silence. Dr. Hallam said, "What made you suspect it? I can't remember anything!"

"At first it was your widely dilated pupils and the drenching sweat. Then, during the hallucinations, you seemed to be picking things off yourself—a typical cocaine gesture. Everything fit."

"Very good. Sounds like I put on quite a show. Were you able to—uh—confirm your suspicions?"

"Yes, sir, we got blood levels, and the results have just come back from the lab. They're right here in my pocket," he said, pulling out a folded lab report sheet. "Your blood level was point-six milligrams— not terribly high, but the stuff was definitely there. And we found your toilet kit."

"I see. Well, well. Caught red-handed, eh? A bit embarrassing, to put it mildly. I suppose the next question is, Who knows about it?"

"Only myself and the night nurses, whom I swore to secrecy. Mrs. Hallam and Charlotte know, too. I sent the blood to the lab under a false name. Of course, your doctors, Mendel and Andres, will have to know when they come in."

"Well, they're old friends, so I don't mind them so much. What did Mrs. Hallam say?"

"Only that you would tell me as much as you want to about it. She said it's your story."

"Hmm . . . hers too, really, but that was kind of her, as always. Well, you have the evidence. What more do you want to know?"

"Everything. That is, anything you'd care to tell me. If I could understand . . . "

"Well, doctor, you mean why I'm depressed? Why I don't particularly give a damn anymore? Or, how a respectable old surgeon could have survived with such a habit?"

Startled by the disclosure, Jim leaned forward. "Exactly . . . all of that. Why you're depressed, why and when the cocaine began, how you've been able to carry on and still . . . do this."

Dr. Hallam deliberated, allowing his head to sink back upon the pillow, and looked up toward the ceiling. He followed his thoughts back to that sentient time in his life. Slowly and dreamily, he said, "Okay, it goes like this: During the war, World War II, I began to experiment with drugs. It was a long time ago, but it doesn't seem that way. I was a little further along than you, a senior assistant resident in neurosurgery here at Hopkins, when Pearl Harbor was bombed. December 7, 1941. I remember it well. I was just coming back from playing basketball that Sunday afternoon in the hospital gym, and a friend—the one you met the other night, Dr. Mateer, Bartie—ran up to me, shouting out the news. God, he was excited. Well, I knew right away I wanted to volunteer. I hadn't finished my training, but I was ready. I was with the first group of volunteers from the hospital staff to go."

. . . .

He closed his eyes. He had been more than ready to go to the war. The relationship with Warren Bregel, his fellow assistant resident, was strained at best, and Warren's frantic rivalry was jeopardizing the function of the whole neurosurgical service. Clay had learned an enormous amount that year and had begun research on several projects, but they now seemed insignificant.

He had heard from Anne only once. He had written her several weeks prior to his departure.

Dear Anne,
   Well, I'm off to the war zone . . . somewhere. My only dilemma is not knowing whether you wish me to continue to write to you or would you prefer that I stopped. After several years now, maybe it's better to abandon the old dreams and find some new ones. I still love you, but you are becoming less and less real and more like a picture on a postcard I once saw.
   If I haven't heard from you by the time I leave, in two weeks, I'll assume that you want my letters, and my hopes for us, to end.
                                        Clay

Eleven days later he received a letter from her:

Dear Clay,
   Please write to me from wherever you go. I want to stay with you in your thoughts, wherever you are. I realize I'm not being fair with you, and should let you go, but I can't . . . you'd have to make that decision.
                                        My love,
                                        Anne

. . . .

Dr. Hallam roused with a start, unsure whether he had been speaking or dreaming. Jim said that he had been drowsing, then turned to leave.

"No, no, let me continue. I'm okay now, just gathering my thoughts. Let's see, where was I?"

"You were leaving your training to enlist with the first group of staff volunteers."

"Yes, yes. Well, after a two-week training period at Bainbridge, we were all commissioned and dispatched to Fiji, where the unit was to set up its first long-term base hospital . . . "

As he continued, his voice settled into a quiet monotone, becoming softer, as if at times he was talking to himself rather than to Jim, and his eyes took on the glazed expression of one who is looking inward. Later, hypnotized by his own words and memories, Dr. Hallam could never remember exactly what he had said and what he had merely remembered. The boundary between speech and thought became indistinct. Jim later said to him that in his telling he had described himself as "he" rather than "I," as if he were telling a story rather than recounting his personal experience.

• • • •

Clay quickly found, as did the rest of the Seventeenth General, that bringing modern medicine to Fiji was not a casual matter. There were no buildings for them, so canvas tents had to be set up. The nearest water supply was a river two miles away, so the Seabees channeled and piped in water from there. There was no electricity, hence no power for x-rays or lights or medical instruments, until gasoline generators could be brought in. But finally, and with little ceremony, the base hospital opened and received patients. It soon filled with casualties from the Guadalcanal and Tulagi battles. As the only neurosurgeon in the unit, Clay had his hands full.

After ten months he received orders to leave the unit and join an advance surgical group to provide speedy treatment for head injuries. The front lines were in considerable flux at that time, especially in the India-Burma theater, where he was going. The Flying Tigers were making sorties against Japanese supply lines into China across the

Indian border from this area, and the British Army was sending forays into Burma to cut and disrupt Japanese communications there. There was speculation that the Ledo Road, a partly natural, partly man-made, twisting, rutted, jungle-fringed trail that led through the hills in northeastern India, might be developed for a ground attack into China, so there was much military activity in this region under General Stillwell.

Clay had difficulty getting to his post. From Calcutta, he spent four days on a hot and dusty train rolling northward. He detrained at Rangpur on the Brahmaputra River. There, exhausted, he boarded a small river cruiser. It took another four days to reach Pandu, barely more than a village stopping point, but welcome to his eyes after his steamy, mosquito-ridden days on the river. At Pandu, he located a creaky, much-abused bus, which carried him finally to Margherita, a tiny village on the Ledo roadway. On the outskirts of Margherita, he found his unit.

They were housed in a group of ramshackle wooden buildings and green canvas tents, completely surrounded by jungle.

"Welcome to the edge of the world, Hallam," said Major Flaxner Reilly, who grinned and accepted his orders, "where ceremony is not stood upon for fear there may be a snake under it. Take a few hours to look around and get planted, then I'll put you to work. We need a good neurosurgeon here."

Well, they did and they didn't. There were between four and eight general surgeons in their group at any given time, but he was the only neurosurgeon. Battle casualties from all over the northeast India–China-Burma theaters were given emergency treatment here. Most stayed a few days and then were sent on to Calcutta or Dacau by boat up the river or by air from the small airstrip outside Pandu. Clay treated blast injuries, missile and bullet wounds of head and spine, depressed skull fractures, penetrating wounds, gutter-type through and through, brain-smashing, orbit-shattering injuries. Debridement and suctioning away diseased tissue according to Cushing were his tenets. But Clay rapidly found that the neurosurgical facilities were poor and did not fit in well with general surgical operating units. After a month or so he approached Dr. Reilly about his need for separate facilities that would always be ready and not have to be set up on a case-by-case basis.

"Fine, Hallam," snorted Major Reilly. "What're you going to do, build yourself a hospital?"

"In a way, possibly," replied Clay. He had heard via the medical grapevine about a Britisher named Eden who had set up and was operating a bus in the African theater, which he had fitted out as a motorized neurosurgical unit. Clay had already located a bus he could buy if the major approved.

The major's eyes widened. "How much?"

"Six hundred and forty dollars," Clay answered.

"Sounds like an odd amount," said Reilly.

"Six hundred buys the bus, but for an extra forty the driver comes too, and he swears he knows the motor inside out and can keep it going."

The bus was purchased, then converted at the airport repair shop. All the seats were removed, and an operating room table was fixed to the floor of the bus. Clay had a powerful antiaircraft light installed in the ceiling above the table. A gas generator was set up in the rear, to provide power for an x-ray unit, an electric cautery, and suctioning machines. At the back was a sink, as well as a cabinet area for surgical gowns, masks, and supplies. The bus motor generated electricity for the lights.

It took several months to "get the show on the road," as Reilly put it, but, once in service, having a unit always ready, and a mobile one at that, proved a huge asset. Clay was very pleased. Reilly labeled the bus "Chariot of Aesculapius" and was as proud of it as Clay was. The bus allowed independence from the surgical unit. Clay was able to set up his own operating teams. He could even go to meet his cases if need be, as long as the roads were passable and not too heavily mined.

During the dreary spring of 1944, when heavy rains came, the roads became swampy and impossible to travel. In fact, any kind of travel became difficult, so while casualty rates dropped, medical supplies became scarcer and more difficult to obtain. There were only about forty patients in their hospital building at that time, but some were quite ill and in intense pain.

"At least three of my head-injury cases are extremely restless and have severe head pain," Clay explained to Major Reilly, "and we're out of paraldehyde and almost out of morphine."

"I know, I know," said Reilly wearily, "and I don't know when to tell you we'll get more. Let's go over to the pharmacy building and see what was left behind."

The derelict wooden building that served as the pharmacy had one large room to serve most of the daily functions, plus a number of smaller rooms used as storage areas. Contents of each storage room were more or less detailed in lists on the doors, but as succeeding hospital units had come and gone from this station, each had left unused drugs and supplies, to be used by the incoming unit. But many were not used and were abandoned. By common consent, these leftovers, frequently in half-open boxes and cartons, were carried to the second floor and left, as each unit brought in its own supplies for its own special needs. On this day Major Reilly and Clay searched the second floor, hoping to find medications that might be of use to them, for the unit's pharmacist first-class had reported that their own supplies were dangerously depleted.

"Ridiculous, this," said Reilly. "Can't expect men to go out and get shot if you can't take care of them." He bent over and beamed his light into a wooden crate.

"Always look before you reach," advised Clay. "Some of these boxes look like they've been gnawed by rats."

"Or worse!" said Reilly, as the first box yielded one thousand packages of condoms. "The army must have been expecting you, Hallam."

Clay grinned, holding up his own find, three hundred tubes of spermicidal gel. "And you, Major." They found everything from toothpaste to corn plasters, from hair depilators to laxatives, but nothing to serve their purpose. They were about to leave when Clay noticed a dust-covered wooden crate, about the size of a small foot locker, in a corner. Mildew covered its nailed seams, and the names of the person and unit to whom it had been sent were faded and illegible. They could, however, make out a faint notation on the front: FOR EXPERIMENTAL USE.

They pried off the top, lifted out a carefully packed cardboard box, put it on the table, and opened the top. They found row after row of small white vials, each containing a whitish powder, and each labeled COCAINE, 1,000 MILLIGRAMS.

Reilly whistled. "And a good time can be had by all. Now what the devil is that doing here?"

"Obviously somebody here wanted to see if cocaine was usable for war wounds—possibly as anesthesia."

They looked at each other.

"Dangerous stuff," said Reilly.

"So is war. So is pain," said Clay.

"Do you know how to use it?" asked Reilly.

"That can be found out," answered Clay, "especially when we haven't got anything else to use."

Reilly shrugged, "Okay, bring it along. We'll record it and give it a try. But, Captain Hallam, whatever you do, be discrete . . . and be safe!"

. . . .

"Well, there it was, and there we were. Nobody there had ever used it, but most of us had heard about it and knew it was not usually dangerous. We'd read about how Freud took it himself, and Halsted, and so forth. I mixed the cocaine with sterile saline and injected it subcutaneously into some of the most desperate cases . . . and . . . into myself. You see, we didn't know about proper dosage, so I experimented to find it. I used one milligram, ten milligrams, one hundred milligrams. I moved right on up, with a couple of friends watching my reactions.

"I finally settled on five hundred milligrams for cases in acute pain . . . and two hundred milligrams for . . . pleasure. The results were gratifying. Men who had been thrashing about and crying stopped and seemed content—happy—even with gaping head wounds and their brains spilling out. As for me, I found that two hundred milligrams made me feel like a god for several hours at least. I felt like I could cure the whole Southeast Pacific Army. At first I only took it under observation, but as time went on I began to slip it in during the day or night, when no one was looking. I *wanted* to feel that way— joyful, potent!"

Dr. Hallam looked at Jim and said, "And now I'm going to tell you something I've never told anyone . . . except my wife. I don't know exactly why I'm telling you, but I feel impelled. Bear with me, Gallier. There's something about you that makes me want you to know. I'm telling you so you'll see the horror of it . . . something I've had to live with ever since." He stared at Jim, curiously, looking for some clue to justify his confidence. "One early evening, after we'd heard the guns and artillery going off all day, they brought in nine casualties. Well, I was on a real high—I'd taken a good solid dose an hour or so before. They mentioned that one of the cases was a doctor, who'd been up forward and got clipped above the temple with automatic rifle fire. I went to look at him. He was lying face down on the table, blood all over his hair and face. Something about him must've looked familiar to me—his figure, shape of his head, I don't know. I asked them to help me turn him over . . . gently, gently . . . careful with his head . . . watch that arm . . . " Dr. Hallam raised his hand up briefly as if to catch that arm of forty years ago. "There, he's over. Now prop his head up; never leave a head wound with head down. Watch that i.v. line." Dr. Hallam stiffened, seeing the memory he was recalling.

. . . .

"My God, it's Dan, Danny Forrester!"

"You know this man, sir?" asked one of the Marines who had helped bring him.

"Know him? Yes, yes, he's my old medical school roommate. My old friend."

The Marine held out his hand. "Well, here are his dog tags. He bought it about three hours ago up near Jayapura. Sniper, I think."

I looked at the dog tags unbelievingly and saw the name, "Daniel Forrester," standing out in bold letters, with A + listed as his blood type. He must have volunteered for service as early as I did, I thought. He always wanted something different. And then aloud, "All right, let's get some blood going through that i.v. Get some nasal oxygen going!" I examined him more closely. Dan was limp and unconscious. Only an occasional flutter of the eyelids indicated life. His breathing was slow and deep, blood pressure was low but not shocky. But pulse rate was low, about 52. The left pupil was dilated. The principal bullet wound on the left temple had stopped bleeding.

"Let's get him undressed and set the portable x-ray machine here on the double. Which O.R. team is up? Get it moving."

I felt exhilarated, powerful, completely capable. I saw some signs of being able to save my friend, and felt certain of success. I had forgotten, of course, that my feeling of invincibility was drug-induced. It was fate that had brought Danny to me, fate that was allowing me the chance to bring him back from the jaws of death.

The bullet must have been a ricochet shot that glanced off another object before entering the side of Dan's head, and much of its force was probably spent by the time of entry, for otherwise it would have gone through and out. The x-rays showed it to be in the area of the left frontal lobe of the brain not far from its point of entry, with some bony spicules around it.

"Looks as though it missed the ventricles," Clay said to Dr. Fleck, his assistant, a bright young general surgeon from Salt Lake City. "Physical signs, slow pulse, slow respirations, suggest increased intracranial pressure. Probably got a big blood clot in there. Now, let's probe the bullet tract with a catheter and see where we go." He felt driven by pent-up excitement. They introduced a small catheter into the temple wound and gently threaded it forward for several inches until it stopped. "Now," said Clay, "we'll put a small amount of dye in and see where we are." The repeat x-ray showed the dye collection in the bullet tract right up to the bullet itself, with no scatter or dissemination of dye outside the narrow tract or into the liquid ventricular system of the brain.

"Good, good," gloated Clay, "now where's that blood clot? See, on the x-ray, where there's a faint scalloping of the dye just lateral to the bullet? That's got to be where it is. No contrecoup lesion here. He's got a big blood clot in his left frontal lobe causing increased intracranial pressure and unconsciousness. Now the question is what to do about it. Do we make a simple burr hole in the skull and put a needle in and aspirate it out, or do we do a full bone-flap, open the dura, evacuate the clot, and debride?"

Dr. Fleck glanced at him, then said, "Why wouldn't we simply aspirate, give him penicillin, and send him back to Calcutta, where they've got all the time and facilities they'd need? After all, we're just an intermediate station. Stabilize and send back is our game, unless there's no other choice. Here, according to your reasoning, there is a choice."

"There is a choice, yes," Clay said, "but I think we'll go ahead with the full operation." He looked down at Dan and felt exaltation welling inside him, and he could visualize the look on Dan's face when he would awaken and learn who had saved him. He almost giggled at the thought. That alone should have stopped him, but it didn't. "Local anesthesia only," he said as the operating team assembled around the table, "but have the i.v. Pentothal ready in case Dan begins to wake up." Skillfully, he made the scalp incision and turned the bone flap up. He incised the dura mater, the tough membrane that covers the brain inside the skull, and exposed the frontal lobe. He quickly suctioned away the blood and skin and bone fragments from around the bullet entrance. Then he could easily see the frontal lobe, a part of which was clearly bluish and distended from the underlying clot.

"There we are, gentlemen," he said too brightly. "Now!" With a scalpel he carefully made a small incision in the brain tissue over the clot and, introducing the suction, began to draw off the dark jellylike clot that partly extruded itself due to the pressure it was under. Clay was gratified when Dan stirred a bit on the table, seeing signs of improvement in his condition.

"A good time to close up, Dr. Hallam," said Dr. Fleck.

"No, no, we must go ahead. Better give him a little Pentothal. I'm now going to open up the cortex, get that bullet out, and debride. He should come out of this as good as new."

He made the incision, after again studying the x-rays, down one-eighth inch, one-quarter inch, one-half inch, and there he encountered it, its hard, gritty surface grating against the probe.

"Now retract a bit for me," and Dr. Fleck pulled the incision wider. "Now," and Clay reached in with his long forceps, grasped the bullet, and teased it out of its bed. "Got it!" He held it up for the others to see, then set it aside. "Next we'll clean it out. Suction on." He used the suction prong to clear out contaminated bone fragments, hair, and skin, which might serve as sources of future infection.

"We're getting a bit of bleeding here," he said. "Let's have the cautery." His voice and his hands were becoming shaky.

Dark blood was welling up from the site where the bullet had lain.

"Looks like we got a bleeder down in there, probably opened it up when we took the bullet out. Suction!"

Clay felt sweat breaking out on his brow now, and felt his hand jerking as it carried the cautery deeper into the brain opening. He heard the popping sound as the hot cautery tip hit the bleeding points and caused steam to rise. Still the blood came, in dark red streams that were immediately suctioned away. Clay felt giddy.

"Cautery," he said, and stepped on the pedal to spark the cautery, but nothing happened. He stepped on it again. No results.

His voice shrill, he shouted, "Cautery's off. What's the trouble? Is it unplugged? No? Check the fuses. Damn. We need the cautery to stop the bleeding. I don't think I can get a clip on those vessels. I'll try a little finger pressure. Get the spare cautery machine. What do you mean, it's away being fixed? Why didn't you tell me? I'll try the clips."

· · · ·

Dr. Hallam broke off his narration, as the emotionality of the moment washed over him. "I remember my hand shaking badly. I couldn't think!" In the end, one hour later, the wound had to be tightly packed with gauze and closed over, with the intent of returning the next day to remove the packing. "But when I returned in two hours to check on him"— Dr. Hallam looked at Jim, his voice low and forced—"he was dead. Danny was dead . . . Dan Forrester was dead. The cause of death was listed as uncontrollable intracranial bleeding due to equipment failure, but I knew, and Dr. Fleck knew, that I was the real cause of death. Danny didn't need that bullet out then. He might have carried it all his life and it wouldn't have hurt him. Or he might have had it out in Calcutta, where they had plenty of reliable equipment. I had been grandstanding. I couldn't think clearly, and I was shaky. Dr. Fleck knew it, but what he didn't know was that I was on cocaine. I never would have taken such a chance if it weren't for cocaine. I would have been steadier. I might have been able to clip that bleeder."

Dr. Hallam paused. "Poor Dan. Well, Jim, I've lived with that ever since. I will to the end." He bowed his head, and tears welled up in his voice. "A few months after that, our bus was blown up by a mine in the Ledo Road. I was hurt, not badly, a hip wound from a piece of metal—that injury was in late '44, and I'd been out there since early '42, so they shipped me back home. I came home a war hero, Bronze Star, Purple Heart . . . and a drug addict who'd killed one of his best friends." He sobbed. "God . . . "

After a few moments, he continued. "I was depressed, addicted, and in pain from my wound—about as low as a person could get, I guess. And you know who saved me, Jim? My wife. I don't think I would have made it if it hadn't been for Anne. We went off for two months after my discharge, and I was able to conquer my addiction and my depression. Then I came back and finished my residency training, and never touched another drug for over fifteen years."

"And then?" Jim asked gently. "And then is a different story, Jim, and I am tired. Another time, please," Dr. Hallam sank wearily back on his pillow.

"Thank you so much for the privilege of hearing that story, Dr. Hallam. I admire you very much . . . "

Hallam waved him off. "How could you? My God! I'll sleep now."

He watched beneath half-closed lids as Jim Gallier left the room, but his mind was still on the past. He was relieved and even glad that he had told him the story that no one but Anne knew, yet evoking it was painful and without pardon. He yearned for absolution, but in all these years he had found none. It was true that Anne had saved him. She had not gotten him pardoned, but she had found a way for him to live with his guilt.

. . . .

After he had received his discharge from the service, in March 1945, Clay returned to Bloomington to visit his parents. His father, fully retired from his surgical practice, looked fit and rested. They were proud of Clay and his war record, but Clay could tell they were shocked by his appearance. He lay around the house for a few days, talking to them and catching up as much as he could on their lives, telling them about his war experience—except for the cocaine. He was now using it at least once a day, trying to fight his depression, and nursing his hip injury.

On a blustery March afternoon Clay was brooding in his room when he heard a sound, looked up, and was stunned to see Anne in the doorway.

She wore a dark-blue cotton topcoat, and her golden-brown hair had been tossed by the wind. She looked older, her features more settled and fuller, but her cheeks were radiant with color, and her eyes were full of excitement. She was dazzlingly real.

"Anne! My God, you're here!" He started to laugh. He advanced toward her.

"I'm here—at last," she said, passing his outstretched hand to nestle close to him, her arms around him. He enveloped her in his, feeling the warmth of her through her coat. He felt, suddenly, that he was home at last.

"Anne, how'd you know I was here?"

"Your parents invited me."

They embraced for several moments, not wanting to break the spell, but at last each stepped back to face the other.

"You were great to come," he said, leading her to a seat on the couch.

"Why wouldn't I? We're still married, aren't we?"

He looked at her hopefully, trying to read her, and said, "Are we? There've been some changes. I'm not the same person."

"Neither of us is, I guess, but I'm here, if you still want me."

Want her? He wanted nothing but her—being close to her—the warmth of her. They had been apart for three years. He said, "I want you and need you desperately, but . . . "

She pressed her fingers against his lips and said, "No more 'buts'—

we've had enough 'buts' in our lives already. I know you've suffered. It shows. But I'm here with you. You're still the handsomest, most exciting man I've ever met, and I'm glad we're married."

They made love then in the blustery March afternoon.

Clay said, "Anne, some things happened in the war. I'm hooked on . . . addicted to . . . cocaine."

He told her the story of his addiction and about Dan Forrester as he lay beside her in bed. At the end, she said, "You must stop the drug."

"I've known I must stop, but up to now I haven't had the will— I've been so very depressed, Danny and everything . . . "

"And now?" Anne asked gently.

"Now . . . now . . . is different," he said, looking at her. "It won't be easy. But I've seen it done. And I think I know how to do it, but I'll need help. Anne, I'll need you—above all. Will you help me kick it?"

"Of course I'll help."

Clay knew what he wanted and what he had to do, but he wasn't sure that he could. He knew that he had to come off cocaine, completely and permanently. He knew that the drug, for all its seductive euphoric powers and the illusions of mental clarity, would in the long run cloud his memory, destroy his intellect, and wreck his life. He knew that there was no middle course, that his separation from the drug had to be total and forever.

Clay had read of the experience of others who had battled with cocaine, so he knew what to expect when his own trial began. But how to do it? Clay felt that he needed isolation from temptation until he grew strong enough to withstand it himself.

Through contacts of Anne's family, they learned of an island one mile off the west coast of Nantucket that seemed to suit their purposes. Shaped like a splatter of ink, Tuckernuck was a thousand picturesque acres of sand and marsh grass. Only five or six wind-beaten houses were scattered across it at coves and inlets that afforded protection to small boats. Shifting sand shoals made approach to the island difficult for all but the smallest boats, and a heavy storm or wind kept even the most knowledgeable boatman away. The houses were owned by descendants of two families who lived on the mainland and used them mostly for hunting and fishing. In off-seasons the houses stood vacant. There were no roads, no cars, no electricity except from home generators, and supplies and mail were brought across from Nantucket twice a week, by private boat.

Clay and Anne arrived in early April with a load of books, foul-weather gear, and sailing equipment. They moved into the one-story cottage arranged for them. There Clay began his ordeal, full of black nightmares and wild, restless dreams. They began almost immediately and carried him into despair and loneliness. Anne was everywhere in his catharsis. At night by his bedside, as he thrashed himself awake, she sponged off his drenching sweats with alcohol, she talked him through his nerve-wracked, depressive days. The phantom fatigue was bone-penetrating, yet no amount of rest relieved it, and strenuous physical activity only temporarily allayed it. He rowed strenuously in the small pond at the front of their cabin, for as long as spells of nausea and weakness permitted. The water was too cold for swimming, but they sailed on good days in a catboat stored behind their house, and he fished in the surf incessantly.

After five weeks or so, Clay began to feel some increased well-being, and his intense longing for the drug began to subside. For the first time, he could wake in the morning with a feeling of having actually slept and of being almost rested. His depression began to lift.

Early one morning, he got up quietly and slipped into the bathroom, past Anne, who was sleeping soundly under the light cotton blanket in her bed across the room. It was not yet six o'clock, but already the cries of seagulls were coming through the screened windows. He doffed his navy-issue undershirt and brown shorts, stepped into the bathroom, flicked on the light, and washed his face. Then he did something he hadn't cared to do in weeks—he regarded himself in the mirror. He was bearded and scraggly.

He smiled thinly. He thought, God, is there a human in there? Poor Anne is living with Robinson Crusoe. But he didn't think he needed the drug anymore.

He set about shaving, and when he finished and straightened up, there were now two faces in the mirror, his own and another, so startlingly lovely that he turned quickly to make sure it was not an illusion. Anne's blonde hair shone, and her face was tanned from the wind and sun.

"I came up behind you as you were shaving. I had a feeling. . . . Darling, you even smell like your old self again."

They made love. Anne asked, "Darling, do you think we're . . . there yet?"

Clay looked at her intently, and nodded. "We're there, honey, we're there. You've loved me and cared about me when I couldn't care about myself." He smiled at her. "Maybe I'll never get over wanting the stuff, but now I know what I want more—you and our life together. I want to make you proud of me."

Anne laughed. "Just make me—that's enough right now."

Later that day, over lunch, they talked further. "You've pulled me out of this thing, and I couldn't have done it without you. But what brought you back? What made you do it? I mean, we hadn't seen each other for years. I expected divorce papers on my arrival home."

She was silent for a moment, then said, "It would be simple to say because I love you . . . too simple. It's more than that. You were the first, Clay, in my life, and I just couldn't get over it. I was advised to by others, and I tried, but no use . . . " She shrugged. "And then there were your letters to me. They were beautiful, so revealing. I felt like I knew you too well to just let you go. I knew you'd come back to me some day, and really need me, and I knew I would say, 'It's all right, my darling, all is forgiven. Let's get on with our lives.' "

Clay smiled and answered gently, "And now maybe we can. I want to go back to Johns Hopkins for another year or two, to finish my neurosurgical training. It'll be better this time. Will you come?"

"I'm with you now for always," she answered readily. "Anywhere. But are you sure you're ready? Are you sure you're over this thing?"

"As sure as I can be."

She smiled. "You've been great, darling. I know how you've suffered. My heart ached for you so. Several times I nearly broke down and gave you a dose to carry you over, but I'm so glad I didn't."

"A dose? You mean you've had cocaine here all along?" He looked at her unbelievingly.

"Uh-huh," she responded. "Your father and others advised me to bring a small supply in case things got desperate. I don't know how he got it, but I have it, well-hidden. I'm so glad we never had to use it."

"Yes, I'm glad too. Well, let's have a last sail, then start packing so we can leave early tomorrow."

They sailed in the cool, green waters of the briny sea pond by the house and dug clams around the shore, so it was late afternoon before they returned to the cabin, showered, and began packing. Even before they started, Clay had become aware of a vague uneasiness, a tingling sensation, as if his nerves were being stimulated. This sensation persisted and even strengthened at their dinner of the clams and the bluefish they had caught that day. He couldn't eat. He fiddled with his food and decided to retire early. Anne scrutinized him.

"Sure you feel all right? That's fresh bluefish you're turning down. Maybe you rowed too far today."

"I'm okay," Clay replied. "Maybe I am a bit tired. Do you mind if we hit the sack early tonight? Big day tomorrow."

He dozed fitfully for a while, but wakened suddenly and sat bolt upright in bed. Something definitely was wrong. He quietly arose from bed, listened for a moment to Anne's steady breathing, and walked out onto the porch. His palms were sweaty and cold, his heart was beating rapidly, and his agitation was growing. He decided to have a run along the path around the pond. He had barely started his run, however, when he stopped. He knew what he needed, and he knew now that it was here. He wrestled against his urge, but only briefly. He craved ecstasy. It was near, so near, and all he had to do was find it.

Clay quickly retraced his steps back to the darkened cabin, closed the door to the bedroom, and turned on the dim hall light. Their bags stood by the kitchen door, her duffel and suitcases next to his. He had not watched her pack, but he was certain the cocaine would be in her bags. Feverishly, and with growing urgency, he opened her duffel and began rummaging through it, trying to be neat at first, and then, finding nothing, throwing things out on the floor at random.

He then opened one of her two suitcases, becoming increasingly impatient and careless about noise. He dumped the second suitcase on the floor. He was picking through its contents when the bedroom door opened and Anne stood looking at him in silent astonishment.

He barely paused in his search, but blinked up at her, framed by the brighter bedroom light, and said huskily, "Where is it, Anne? I need it—where is it?"

Anne did not answer but quietly left the doorway and retreated into the bedroom, where, moments later, Clay found her sitting on the side of her bed. He confronted her wildly.

"Anne, where is it? I need it badly. Please, give it to me."

"Clay, please listen." She looked up at him. "You don't need it. You've been almost six weeks without it. You don't want to throw all that away. Please don't ask me for it."

"Anne. I'm desperate! You can help me. Give it to me!" His voice was rising, and he stepped toward her. She did not stir from her seat on the bed, but looked bravely up into his flushed face. "Clay, I can't. I won't. You've got to hold on."

He grabbed her roughly and pushed her back on the bed and knelt over her. His voice roared, "You bitch! You've had it here all along. You could've helped me but you didn't. Give it to me now or . . ."

For the rest of his life this scene would remain in his memory. The enormity of the act he was about to commit suddenly broke upon him: Anne's frightened face looking up at him, his left arm holding her down, his right arm drawn back about to strike her. It was in this moment, he always knew, that he came off the drug. A tremendous guilt swept over him, and in the next moment he was on the bed beside her, his face buried in his arms, asking her forgiveness. This proof of the drug's power remained with him forever. It was a constant and terrifying deterrent.

Anne absolved him immediately and, as if seared by the heat of his emotions, his intense craving dissipated. They returned to the mainland the next day and returned to Baltimore.

CHAPTER 12

Sunday, May 19, 1985

Later that same Sunday morning, Anne and Charlotte returned to the hospital to visit Dr. Hallam. Jim was waiting for them in the corridor. As they left Dr. Hallam's room, he asked them to lunch, an invitation they both readily accepted.

"Why don't we go across the street to the hotel for lunch?" Anne suggested. "It'll be my treat!"

"Not at all, Mrs. Hallam, my treat today," said Jim, "but I think it's the hotel or nothing. Fortunately for us all, the hospital cafeteria is closed for lunch by now."

They were out the front entrance of the hospital and about to cross the street when Jonas suddenly appeared, heading the other way.

"Hi, everyone," he said breezily as he approached them.

"Hi, Jonas, come and meet Mrs. Hallam," Jim said, taking Jonas's arm. "Mrs. Hallam, my roommate, Jonas Smith."

The two shook hands.

"How do you do, Jonas?"

"How do you do, Mrs. Hallam? I'm sorry about Dr. Hallam, but I'm sure he'll be okay."

"Where you heading, Jonas?" asked Jim.

"Couldn't stay in the library one more minute—too nice a day. Thought I'd see what's happening over at the pool."

"Jonas, why don't you join us for lunch? We're just heading over to the hotel," Charlotte said. "Mom's treating."

"Hmm. Maybe I will. I have to run in to the hospital for a few minutes. How about if I meet you over at the hotel? Save me a place."

He dashed off.

As soon as they were seated in the tasteful small dining room the waiter appeared, handed them menus, and asked, "May I bring you something before lunch?"

"Would you like a drink?" asked Jim.

"Mother, are you going to have something? Yes? Well, I'll have a wine spritzer, please."

Anne leaned toward the waiter and asked softly, "Do you know what a Trojan spritzer is?"

"White wine with charged water rounded off with a bit of vodka, yes, madame?"

"That's it. That will be fine." The waiter bowed. "Anything else?" he asked.

"Tomato juice for me," answered Jim. He turned to Anne and Charlotte. "I've still got to get back to the hospital for a while this afternoon. How did Dr. Hallam seem?"

"Better, I thought," said Charlotte. "Didn't you think so, Mother?"

"I thought definitely stronger. He said he'd told you the whole drug story, Jim—how it began and how he managed to end it."

"Yes, he did. It must have been a terribly difficult period for both of you. He gave you most of the credit, Mrs. Hallam, for his being able to stop."

Anne smiled. "You know, Jim, in just a week I've come to feel like you're one of our old family friends . . . it's nice."

Jim smiled back at her and blushed. He realized he was being complimented but that he was also being charged with the responsibility of knowing family secrets and caring for them. That was all right with him.

Anne said, "You know, they say cocaine doesn't create a true addiction, only a dependence. The way I would describe it, from my own observation, is that it generates an immense craving in mind and body, which can be overcome only by a counter-craving. Only the individual can decide what that counter-craving is. But there has to be something he or she values more than the drug experience, for those two things can't exist side by side. They're mutually exclusive."

The waiter came with their drinks, and Anne lifted hers to her lips.

"And in Dr. Hallam's instance, it was you he needed," said Jim, glancing at Charlotte, who was looking quietly at her mother.

"Yes, it was." Anne's expression softened as she spoke. "We were in love . . . still are, at least I with him. But I think, too, it was what I represented to him that counted a lot. I mean his career, family, respectability, all the things he ever wanted. I think I was his link to them all. And he chose to quit."

She sipped her drink.

"And then?"

"Twenty productive years. Mark, our son, was born, and then Charlotte. Clay was happy and fulfilled in his work. I was busy with the children, and . . . But let's not talk any more about us. I'd like to hear more about you, Jim. You're all set to stay here next year?"

"I think so, Mrs. Hallam," said Jim. He was about to continue when Jonas arrived and took a seat between Anne and Charlotte. The waiter appeared and asked about drinks. Jonas asked for Perrier and Anne for another Trojan spritzer, and they ordered their meal.

Jonas said, "I'm a great admirer of your husband, Mrs. Hallam. He's one of the leading lights at the Hopkins, and one of the two or three best teachers I've come across."

"Thank you for saying those words, Jonas. He'd be very pleased to hear them. He's always enjoyed teaching as much as anything he's done in his career. Are you in neurosurgery?"

"No, ma'am, I'm a general surgeon," Jonas answered, "but I was on Dr. Hallam's service for a few months."

"You are in the presence of the coming best general surgeon in the U.S.A.," put in Jim, smiling at Jonas, "by his own admission."

"Not necessary, Jim," said Jonas, squirming.

Anne laughed. "You sound like my husband . . . " She looked at him, then became more serious. "Are you? That is, driven?"

Jonas smiled at her. "Like your husband? Would that I were. He's been the best."

Anne downed her glass, and said, almost under her breath, "But he paid a price."

They began to eat, and Anne motioned for another vodka spritzer.

"Well," said Jonas, eating rapidly, "for being number one you expect to pay a price—I mean—who wouldn't? If flesh and blood could buy it, I'd be willing to pay it."

"Not I," said Jim. "I'm sure Dr. Hallam never had to go that far— but there are limits."

"No limits, Jim. Whatever you do, if it's what you do, do it. Don't play the reluctant debutante. Think about your own beloved piano playing, or tennis—Do you think those professionals begrudge practicing eight, ten hours a day? No, they know that's what it takes."

"Eight to ten hours a day? Say rather eighteen to twenty hours a day—that's what Clay used to put in. . . . Do you plan to get married, Jonas?"

"Sure hope to, Mrs. Hallam, but don't let that worry you. I'll find someone like you who'll understand my problem and stick it out."

Anne sipped her drink. "And what *is* your problem, Jonas?"

"Oh, ambition, I guess."

"Fine, fine, Jonas," Anne said, "so find someone loving and understanding . . . but please don't find someone like me."

Anne had a fifth drink as they were eating dessert. She showed no signs of drunkenness, but she became more talkative. She reminisced about her upbringing in a medical family in Richmond, and about the Grier Clinic. The clinic, she said, was defunct. "Ran out of family talent to keep it going. Broke my father's heart, having to close the clinic before he died."

Anne was about to order another drink when Jonas interrupted. "Mrs. Hallam, you're going to think I'm extremely rude and brash, but you're drinking too much, and you shouldn't have any more."

Anne's cheeks flamed, and tears of indignation sprang to her eyes. "What did you say?" she gasped.

"Jonas!" said Jim. "My God."

Charlotte was silent.

"I said no more to drink. You've had enough. Are you . . . alcoholic?"

"You don't know me well enough to say that to me, Dr. Smith. Charlotte, it's time to leave." She stood up shakily. "Goodbye, Jim, come and see us."

"I'm sorry you're taking it that way, Mrs. Hallam," Jonas persisted. "I believe in speaking out and warning someone when I see they're in danger, especially if they can't see it themselves."

"And when do you consider something none of your business?" Anne asked over her shoulder as they left the restaurant.

"When the danger is over, or at least the person can see it clearly," answered Jonas. They were on the sidewalk in front of the hotel now.

"You seem to be in the proselytizing phase of your medical training. Don't let it carry you too far," said Anne.

"It's always been a problem of mine, Mrs. Hallam. Speaking my mind, that is. I believe in facing problems, not keeping them in the closet. I'm sorry if I offended."

The Hallams left Jim and Jonas outside the hotel. Charlotte and her mother headed for their car, and the two men walked toward the hospital.

"My God, Jonas," Jim exploded as soon as they were out of earshot. "That was the rudest thing I've seen you do, attacking Mrs. Hallam like that. What came over you?"

Jonas shrugged. They walked toward the hospital entrance. The day was bright. "The woman's got a problem, Jim, why not help her with it? Did you see the way she tossed those four or five drinks down? Didn't phase her at all, and it's still only three in the afternoon. Only an alcoholic could drink like that. Has Charlotte ever said anything?"

"Of course not, and even if Mrs. Hallam *has* an alcohol problem, what business is it of ours to interfere?"

"Well, as one human being to another. And you're going to marry her daughter, aren't you?"

Jim stopped short in the hospital corridor. "How would I know that? I've only known her a week."

Jonas also stopped. "A week's long enough. You *ought* to marry her. But if you're not going to, you should get out of the way."

Jim stared at him. "Why?"

Jonas began walking away, then turned and said clearly, "Because if you're not going to, I think I will."

Jim watched Jonas hurry down the corridor. There was, he decided, plenty to think about.

Meanwhile, Charlotte was driving her mother home. "I'm sorry you had to go through that, Mother. It was the rudest thing I've ever seen—so ridiculous and unnecessary. Are you all right?"

Anne was silent. Charlotte glanced at her to see if she had heard.

"Yes, yes, I'm all right . . . But it was a shock to hear it. However, I have to admit it wasn't so ridiculous. I don't know about unnecessary. It's true what he said, Charlie. I think I could be . . . alcoholic."

Charlotte pulled the car over to the curb.

"Mother, what are you saying?"

Anne stared ahead. "I don't know. What is an alcoholic? All I can say is that I like to drink . . . and seem to need it. Have you never noticed?"

Charlotte nodded. "I've noticed some things. I've smelled it on your breath, and sometimes your speech has been a little slurry. And you've seemed depressed and weepy at times. I guess I've considered it once or twice, but then passed over it . . . "

"I don't think it's anything major," Anne said. "It's that sometimes I've been very lonely, and I haven't seen any hope for things to change."

"Does Dad know about it?"

"Perhaps, probably, I don't know. He hasn't said anything."

"No, he wouldn't, would he?"

"Charlie, don't ever blame him—for anything. Since your brother died, he's never really been the same . . . "

"Mark's death hurt us all, Mother. Why did Dad have to withdraw from us, as if he were the only one suffering?"

"He had his reasons, Charlie. He was . . . more involved . . . than we were. And that's when I began to feel sadness—for what we'd had and for what we were missing. And I began to find out that having a drink helped—helped to dream, helped to pass the time away. I didn't drink much at first, because I knew the dangers. As you probably knew, Uncle Randolph was an alcoholic. But recently I've been drinking more, and caring less about the consequences."

"Mother, you've got to do something about it, you know."

Anne nodded. "Yes, I know . . . and I guess I now have a reason to stop. Clay will need me again, won't he? I can stop—I hope I can. And Charlie?"

"Yes?"

"That Jonas . . ."

"Yes?"

"A very unusual person!"

They both smiled.

Jim finished his ward work and headed for Dr. Hallam's room. He had begun to have a vague sense that his life was at some sort of turning point; and, without knowing why, he felt that Dr. Hallam might be the key to the change. He reminded himself of their differences in station—but also that Jonas would say timidity never solved any problems.

He found his patient awake after a nap and surprisingly chipper. Dr. Hallam looked at Jim appraisingly as he entered the room.

"Oh, Dr. Gallier, come in, come in . . . sit down if you can." Jim took a straight chair by the bedside. "It's been brought to my attention by the nurses that you probably saved my life last night by diagnosing my problem and giving me the appropriate treatment. Alert of you. I want to thank you." He smiled at Jim.

"Not at all, sir, but it's kind of you to say it. You seem to have made a good recovery."

"I'm feeling better, yes. Tell me, do you think cocaine had anything to do with my stroke?"

"Quite probably, if you did actually have a stroke. That's still not clear. Had you taken cocaine anytime before you had the spell last Saturday morning?"

"I can tell you exactly. I used it only twice in the last twelve years: once last night, and once last Saturday before my retirement address. I used it several times twelve years ago. And *that* was the first time since I'd taken it since World War II."

"Then I can say that it probably was the cause of your illness. Cocaine is known to be a blood vessel constrictor, and stroke has been reported from its use."

"Hell of a thing . . . a hell of a thing," muttered Dr. Hallam, "professor of neurosurgery at this great institution, in trouble because of drugs. Do you think we can keep it quiet?"

"Of course, sir, we've already taken all necessary steps in that regard. The more burning question is how to make sure you never take cocaine again."

Dr. Hallam shrugged. "Well, the fact that I nearly killed myself with it twice in the last eight days should be enough. But I must admit, at least to myself, that I'm not entirely sure I care. I'm tired. . . . On the other hand, I've always been able to put it aside before, and I might again—God willing.

"But now about you, Jim, is there anything I can do for you, to try to repay you for all you've done for me while I've been here? I'll always be grateful to you, and I seem to feel close to you." He peered at Jim again, as if close inspection would reveal the source of his affection.

"Nothing at all, Dr. Hallam, it's been a pleasure to help. I have the same sort of feeling about you, sir, a special regard. It meant a lot to me that you would tell me about the cocaine problem."

"I wanted you to know. I wanted to tell you. Somehow, by telling you, I feel lighter. Maybe I've shifted some weight."

Jim nodded. "I had the feeling you were being harder on yourself than necessary. Maybe your subconscious instincts were telling you that the bullet *had* to come out of Dr. Forrester. Maybe he would have abscessed or hemorrhaged and died anyway, if you hadn't operated. Memories can magnify guilt at the expense of facts. Dr. Hallam, there is one thing you could do for me . . . I have a great desire to hear the rest of it—your career and your life. And I hope you won't ask me why I'm so interested, because I'm not really sure." The two men looked at each other in silence.

"My career and my life. Both the same, yet not the same. A strange request, Jim. The story would probably bore you. Are you sure you want to hear it?"

"Very much, sir."

Dr. Hallam drew himself back and stared intently at the young man looking ingenuously at him from the bedside chair, seeking to discern the thrust of the question and gauge the line of his response. He was tempted to offer Jim a few well-known superficial facts of his life and let it go at that, but something stopped him. The earnestness of the young house officer was unmistakable, and Dr. Hallam concluded that what he said was somehow of great importance to Jim; but over and above was something else, some undefinable attraction between them that made him want to tell his story, made him want Jim to hear it.

"Hmm—I guess I can tell you if you really want me to. I'll make it short." Dr. Hallam settled himself. "After the Army, Anne and I came back to Hopkins and I finished my residency. Our son, Mark, was born during this time—on June 2, 1946—and I began my work on blood vessel control by the autonomic nervous system. I was then offered a two-year fellowship to study at Gray's Neurologic Clinic in London. I accepted at once, and there I completed a research paper on mapping the hypothalamus in monkeys. It was an exciting time, living in England and raising our son, and we were associated with a wonderful group of young researchers and doctors who would blow the lid off medicine in a few years. Anne loved it, and so did I.

"My work brought me the Covington Prize in 1948, to my great surprise, and with it came an assistant professorship at the university in Boston. It was hard to leave England, but this offer could not be refused, so we returned to Boston and settled in. We were there ten years, ten wonderful years. Mark was growing up and Anne was happy. I was consumed with neurosurgery and research and teaching. My brain seemed on fire and capable of limitless ideas. I developed several new neurosurgical techniques. You may be familiar with the Hallam clamp or the Hallam-Daltor dural graft—both date to this time, as well as my first EEG studies of limbic dysrhythmias.

"Then I was offered a full professorship and chairmanship of the neurosurgical department at the Medical Center of New York, again a very distinguished post—and again I had to accept. With Anne's consent, we moved to New York, where we stayed from, let's see, July 1958 to 1972, about twelve years. Charlotte was born in 1960. It was in New York that I did my work on the radiology of brain tumors. We were happy in New York. We lived in an old brownstone on the West Side. Mark went to Columbia to college, and Charlotte was at Dalton. Anne was involved with volunteer work and the theater. Some days, we all would hardly see one another until nine or ten o'clock at night. Then we'd sit on our upper back terrace awhile, in the spring and summer and fall, and look at the lights and listen to the sounds of the city, and we'd talk, excited about what we were accomplishing. Sometimes we'd listen to classical music and, if the children weren't there, Anne and I would dance . . . " He smiled. "What a little thing to remember for years, yes, our dancing.

"Toward the end of this time, I was doing special consultant neurosurgery, cases referred to me from all over the country. I completed two books—and taught and lectured and traveled all over the globe." He paused and glanced at Jim. "As you know, the established professor in a top medical school, no matter what his specialty, gets many privileges. Like movie stars and political leaders, he has invitations to go almost anywhere in the world he wants to go, and give a lecture, or do an operation. He meets the top people in his field. He becomes a sounding board and he hears all the new ideas coming in from everywhere in his field. I used to come home with my head spinning with new possibilities for research, new operative techniques to try—maybe even the very next day. We entertained a fair amount—visiting professors and so forth. It was an exciting time, Jim, a very heady time, and it went by quickly."

He reflected a moment, and smiled vaguely. "Jim, let me tell you a story—an example of what I mean. Do you have time? Well, one Saturday afternoon, in late 1965, Anne had gone out with some friends and I'd stayed home to finish some work I was doing. I heard the doorbell ring, then a knocking at the door when I didn't respond right away. I wasn't dressed to receive visitors, wasn't expecting any, and didn't want any, so I tried to ignore it, but finally that insistent tapping got the better of me and I opened the door.

"There stood a distinguished-looking man—gray hair, dark business suit, well-groomed—who introduced himself as Mr. Oliver, of the U.S. State Department, Foreign Office, and said he needed to speak with me. Well, there I was in my plaid shirt and gompers. I don't think I'd even shaved that day. I invited him in but told him it would have been nice to have had a little warning. Oliver simply said that the matter had come up only recently and he had checked to make sure I was at home—he didn't say how.

"We sat down in the study, and he came right to the point: Did I know anything about Saudi Arabia?

"I answered not really, except that I had operated on several people from there.

"Oliver said he knew that. He said that because of those operations my reputation was known in Saudi Arabia. He told me that I was one of two neurosurgeons chosen by a member of the Saudi royal family to operate on his sister. She had some sort of brain tumor and was so critically ill she could not be moved. Therefore, the surgery would have to be done in Riyadh. The United States had certain oil interests in Saudi Arabia at the time, so naturally the State Department was interested in the case and would appreciate my taking it.

"Well, my first inclination was to turn down this offer out of hand. Why should I go to Saudi Arabia? I had enough to do.

"But then Oliver said that it would be a favor to the American government, and he told me the other neurosurgeon the State Department had asked turned it down. So I took the next step, which is always tantamount to surrender in medicine: I asked to see the case.

"Oliver dug into his shiny briefcase and extracted the medical records, which had been rushed by air to the State Department. When I took the records, I asked Oliver what would happen if I accepted the assignment. He said that arrangements would be made to leave as soon as I could assemble my team of nurses, my assistants, and whatever equipment I would need. A special Air Force plane was being readied at LaGuardia, and he hoped we could leave within two days.

"I looked quickly through the medical data, skull x-rays, spinal puncture results, ventriculograms. I concluded that the patient had a blood-vessel tumor, a hemangioma, at the base of her brain. It had already hemorrhaged twice and might do so again at any minute. She needed surgery desperately, but it would be tricky, very hazardous, due to the tumor's location and the likelihood of its bleeding. The odds were poor, but at least I could see a way that it might be attempted.

"I looked at Oliver, who sat silently. I didn't like him very much.

"I said 'If we do nothing, she dies. She might even be dead by the time we get there . . . '

" 'And if we do something, Doctor?' Oliver asked.

" 'She'll probably still die. Suppose she dies under my hands?'

"Oliver smiled his thin smile. I can see him now. 'Allah has already been consulted,' he stated, 'and says this is the way and the truth. All you will have to do is make peace with your own private deity.'

"Still I hesitated. I tried to consider my schedule, my duties and commitments, Anne, and the problems of this operation, and to balance them against the condition of this unfortunate woman. She had only a slim chance of survival even if I did the operation . . . but I knew I had to try.

" 'I accept the case, Mr. Oliver, so we'd better get moving.'

"He arose at once, probably worried that I might change my mind. 'Let me have a list of what you need—within three hours, if you can,' Oliver told me. 'We'll get it together as soon as possible. You'll assemble your own operating team? If you can't, we have plenty of backup personnel.'

"I told him, 'I only need a few from here. You can provide the rest.'

"We headed for the door, where Oliver turned, and asked, 'Well, anything else?'

"I had only one other thought. 'Oh yes, the other neurosurgeon. Do you mind telling me who it was?'

"Oliver hesitated, then answered, 'No, I guess that's okay. It was Dr. Warren Bregel. Do you know him?' . . .

"Three nights later, our Air Force 747 touched down at the airport in Riyadh," Dr. Hallam explained to Jim. "It was quite an experience, coming down in the middle of that desert at night. The air depot was a long one-story building that had only a single light outside. There was no sign of a city. You see, Jim, at that time, 1965, Saudi Arabia was very primitive. Electricity and plumbing were scarce. Few people could read or write, and most lived in mud-walled huts. Three American oil companies were there, but the oil flow was still small, and only the royal family profited from the deal. The family got huge profits, of course—and threw their money around like sand. A caravan of Mercedes and Cadillacs met us at the airport and took us to our quarters in the central palace. I'll never forget that eerie ride through those dark, bumpy streets, with our shrouded drivers, two heavily armed guards who spoke no English, and a junior American consul who could speak hardly any Arabic. It was a different planet!

"The palace was lighted, and insofar as I could tell, it was a rambling maze of corridors, rooms, and terraces. The bed was of soft goat hair and had a wonderful earthy aroma. I was so tired I had one of the best nights' sleep I've ever had. Until about half past four in the morning, that is." Dr. Hallam chuckled. I remember being wakened by the first prayer-call of the day. I thought someone had gone mad outside my window, but then I realized what it was—a muezzin calling from the palace mosque, and it seemed to echo from minarets all across the city.

"That morning I met Prince Rani, the brother of my patient. He was a small man, full of energy, and he had been educated at Oxford. He knew time was of the essence, he said, and would not spend long with me, but he wished to request that I do my best for his esteemed sister. Expense, he said, was not an obstacle. Then a limousine took me the short distance to the hospital to see the princess, Fatima. Dr. Abdul Aziz, who met me at the door of the hospital, told me he had made arrangements with the princess and her family for me to examine her without clothes or veil, for otherwise Moslem law would prohibit any such exposure. Dr. Aziz was good-natured and most appreciative of my coming, a plumpish man who spoke with the charming mixture of accents frequent among Western-educated Saudis. He was apologetic for the inadequacies of his hospital and his own knowledge and staff, but he was gratified when, later on, I was able to confirm his findings and conclusions."

Dr. Hallam broke off for a moment and looked at Jim. "Am I rambling, Jim? No? Well, stop me if I do. It's all still so vivid to me.

"The princess was middle-aged, a stout, dark-skinned woman with a lot of gray in her hair and definitely a lot of fear in her eyes.

She'd apparently been scared out of her wits by her doctors, who had probably been equally scared by her brother's power. Her doctors had kept her for a week in a darkened room—quiet, sedated, light meals, almost no visitors—in order to inhibit further bleeding from her intracranial tumor. She spoke no English, but I sensed that she was intelligent, and after my exam I told her, through an interpreter, that I would operate on her as soon as my equipment was set up, probably the next day, and that I felt we had a good chance of success. She searched my face during the translation and acknowledged what I told her with a small smile and a graceful nod. I could see why her brother esteemed her so highly. I estimated that it would be an eight- to ten-hour operation, open to close, and I felt that I had a better-than-fifty-percent chance of saving her.

"The rambling, one-story hospital had shabby stucco on the outside, but the inside had been modernized, thanks to the royal family's increasing oil wealth.

"Still, we would need the special equipment we had brought with us, which my staff now set about putting in place. They would also have to get coordinated with the aides the State Department had conscripted for me and with the hospital's support team. We scheduled the operation for 7:40 P.M. the next day. This would put it after the last prayer call of the day, during which Muslim law demanded that all activities cease, and give us an uninterrupted stretch of time to do the operation.

"Once our plan was agreed on and all preparations were in motion, I was free for the rest of the day."

Dr. Hallam glanced at Jim to see if he was still interested, then continued.

"Abbie—that's what we came to call Dr. Abdul Aziz—offered to take a few of us on a tour of the Riyadh Souq, or Bazaar. About six of us gathered at the front of the palace at three-thirty, just after the afternoon prayer call. We were given white thobes to wear—I think to keep us from being conspicuous—and were driven in three new Mercedes, led by Abbie, to the central square of Riyadh, past the main mosque and the old clock tower." Dr. Hallam closed his eyes. "I can see it still . . . We went to the souq entrance. Led by Abbie and accompanied by the two guards, we entered the market. It's a wonderful experience, Jim, entering an Arab souq, full of color, people, shops, and smells.

"We wandered a while, went into a few shops and dickered for some goods as we had been directed to do. In one store, a rug market, I became interested in a tapestry piece and got involved in a bartering session with the proprietor. When at last I lost the argument and left the store, our party was gone, but I thought I saw them down the street and rounding a corner. I hurried after them, through the crowd and onto another street—only to find it wasn't them at all. I was lost. But I hadn't time to dwell on the matter, for my attention was suddenly drawn to a woman down on the street, screaming, while an Arab man stood over her, shouting and beating her with a camel whip. His eyes were fanatical. The woman was rolling back and forth trying to dodge the whiplashes, but I could make out that she was not an Arab, for in the scuffle her heavy black veil had come off to reveal her pale complexion and Western hair style, and her long black-sleeved cloak had been rolled up to the shoulders, exposing the whiteness of her arms. Her assailant wore the traditional white thobe and gura, but his beard was orange.

"Later I was told that such sights were common in Saudi Arabia at that time. Clashes between the religious police—the Matawein—and Westerners—especially women—for breaking Muslim laws were frequent. But I assure you, Jim, there are few sights more infuriating than a woman being beaten with a whip by a man—any man! I should have known better than to interfere, but my blood boiled. I leaped at the fellow from behind, seized his whip arm and bent it back, and got his whip away from him and threw him to the ground. He was up in a second, and he had a wicked-looking knife in his hand. I looked around the crowd, but I saw no Western faces, so I figured I was in for it. The man was practically frothing at the mouth, and although I was taller, he was younger and quicker, I was sure. I whipped off my own white thobe and wrapped it around my left arm for protection. I think until then the man hadn't realized he was dealing with a foreigner, for his expression instantly changed to one of surprise and then back to rage. But his tactics changed, and instead of coming at me with the knife, he stopped and gave a wild guttural scream. He was calling for help, I guess, for only instants later I was seized from behind and hauled off to a waiting van, stuffed in, and taken to what I later learned was the Riyadh Malaaz prison.

"I was thrown into a pen with about a hundred other poor souls, all Arabs. They looked hostile, to me at least. The room was poorly lit, except for the sunlight that came in from the ventilation spaces at the roofline. The floor was dirt and the walls were thick mud. It was hot and damp, and the air stank from the single toilet that always had a line waiting to use it. That prison seemed like the depths of hell, and I still sweat when I think of it. I dreaded the thought of spending the night there. I had put my long white thobe back on, partly so as not to stand out as a Westerner, and partly for protection against the flies that were everywhere. God, what a place. I learned a lot of humility in a hurry, Jim. I have never felt so intimidated. The hours went by, and no one came. I found a place to sit and lean against the mud wall. I pulled my thobe hood over my head, and waited—for what I didn't know. My main hope was that the woman whose whipping I had interrupted had reported my arrest. But to whom? The police? That wouldn't help, because surely it was the police who had arrested me, or else what was I doing in this jail? No, she would have to have gone to the American Embassy with the story, and they might have pieced it together, or at least sent someone to identify me. But maybe she couldn't, maybe they had detained her, too. I felt terribly lonely. If only there had been someone to talk to. I would have given a lot to hear one sweet word of English.

"I must have dozed off, for when I woke with a start it was dark inside our cage, except for a single bulb that burned in a wall fixture opposite the bars across the front. I was thirsty, and it took a while to locate the single water tap, which I drank from after waiting in line. When food arrived, in a large cauldron that everyone reached into with his bare hand to extract a fistful of some kind of boiled meat chunks, I found I wasn't hungry.

"I lost my place at the wall when I got up to drink, so I finally sat down on the floor, knees drawn up, my hood over my face, and focused my mind on the operation I was to perform the next day—if

I were found in time to operate, that is. I drifted between sleep and wakefulness. I knew it was getting late, but I couldn't see the hands of my watch in the darkness. I looked for a place to lie down, but the floor was crowded with sleeping bodies. I stood up to stir my circulation, and as I did the cell door was opened and two hooded figures with small lights entered. They searched, found me, and approached.

"One gestured for silence, then they led me out the cell door. No one in the room made a sound, and I guessed that they were used to such nighttime snatchings. As I left, I felt sorry for them, for God knows how long they would have to endure that prison.

"My silent guards took me down that dim corridor, down a stone staircase, and left me in a small room with a bench and a wooden table. I sat down on the bench. I was exhausted. My watch light said two o'clock—2:00 A.M.! I was just about to stretch out on the bench and sleep when the door opened, and in came a man who looked very serious indeed. He was dressed in a black cloak with gold trim and a black turban. His beard was dyed an orange-brown, like my adversary's in the market. He made his way to the other side of the table from me, then sat down in a chair I hadn't noticed. We stared at each other a bit, and then he said in perfect English, 'I am Hasham ibn Nazer.'

"He was, he said, a member of the Committee for the Protection of Virtue and Prevention of Vice. It was his duty to handle Westerners' transgressions against their holy laws. He told me the case against me was quite grave. I had attacked one of their Matawein, or religious police, in the performance of his duties . . . His voice trailed off, and I realized it was my turn to talk. It all seemed so unreal, so outlandish, and when he said 'Committee for Protection of Virtue and Prevention of Vice' I almost laughed. But his appearance stopped me. Instead, I said, 'A helpless woman—he was beating her—I simply tried to stop it.'

" 'She was breaking one of our holy laws—her bare arms were exposed in the public market—she had to be . . . discouraged from repeating this offense.'

"He got up and began pacing, pausing occasionally to stop and stare at me as he talked. His speech was high-pitched, tight, but his English was excellent.

"He said my punishment had already been determined by the book of the Sharia. My left hand was to be cut off at the wrist—here he hesitated a moment—'So commands Allah. Now, speak if you so desire.'

"I stared back at him. The whole situation was so nightmarish that it seemed unreal, and what I had just been told detached it even further from reality. But real or not, I had to try to extricate myself from it.

" 'Yes, I shall speak,' I remember starting, 'I am Dr. Clayton Hallam. I came here from the United States as the guest of Prince Rani, to operate on his sister, who has a tumor in her brain. The operation is to begin tonight at seven o'clock. It cannot be done without me—and my left hand. Please check with him.'

"He was silent, but then became quite agitated. He got up and paced about and finally stopped in front of me.

" 'I will return.'

"He hastened from the room, and came back in about an hour. Again he stood in front of me.

" 'The Matawein,' he told me, 'are not obliged to defer to any interference from our government. We are a separate entity, and we take orders from no one . . . '

"He had checked my story and found it to be correct. They were searching for me at the palace even then, and Prince Faisal was very upset. In view of all that, he said, as a favor to their esteemed brother, they had decided to lighten my punishment. Instead of my hand's being amputated, I was to be burned.

" 'Burned?' I asked.

" 'Yes, burned. But first,' he asked, 'do you regret what you did?'

"I was able to answer truthfully, 'In light of what has happened, I can say yes, I should have handled it another way.'

" 'Will you repeat your offense?'

" 'No, I should say not.' And I certainly had no intention of doing so. But I think I gave him an out.

"He nodded and clapped his hands, and two guards entered and escorted me down to another room, where more guards were posted around the walls. The room was bare, except for a charcoal stove burning in the middle of it. I was stripped to the waist, and held there, waiting, as must have many prisoners before me, and since.

"Finally a hooded figure approached the oven and drew out a red-hot poker and, holding it in front of him, approached me like the Figure of Death.

"I didn't know what to expect, but I can tell you, Jim, he had my attention.

" 'Do you believe there is no other god than Allah?' he asked.

"I ran through all possible responses and finally settled for a simple 'No!' To this day I don't know why I said it, except I was disgusted with the whole affair.

" 'Do you believe in the Justice of the Sharia?' he intoned.

" 'No!' I answered, faster this time, because I was beginning to think it didn't matter what I said anyway. He didn't even appear to be listening.

" 'Then let the justice of Allah, the Merciful, be carried out,' he said. With that he touched my left shoulder with the iron. I had braced myself against the pain, but, incredibly, I felt only a momentary singe, and then he pulled back.

" 'Do not mistake the seriousness of the punishment,' he said into my astonished face. 'You have been burned by the Spirit of Allah, and it is our saying that if you are so touched twice in your lifetime, your body will burst apart, so filled with the Spirit will you be. Therefore, do not offend again against our laws.'

"Then he gave me a long harangue about corruption and vice in America, and he said, 'Yes, you wish to dominate us. But it shall not happen, because you are weak and we are strong, and one day you will go down before us like so many puffs of cotton in the wind. Oh, you have knowledge that we do not yet have, it is true, and you know things that we do not, but you are corrupt and weak. We are strong, for the discipline of Allah is our guide. Now, go to your operation.'

"Well, that was it. I was taken back to the palace, where I had a nap and a bath, and did the operation on schedule that evening. It went beautifully, more smoothly than I had imagined. And strangely, all during the procedure I had a feeling that my left arm was behaving much more deftly and nimbly than usual. Undoubtedly the power of suggestion—but nevertheless I have never operated better. The princess lived. Three days later, we went back with a check from Prince Faisal for three hundred thousand dollars for the university and a special commendation from the State Department for me. I learned a lot about Saudi Arabia and Islamic fundamentalism. Needless to say, I've never gone back to receive my second touch of the Spirit."

Dr. Hallam chuckled, then glanced at Jim. "Shall I continue?" he asked. Jim nodded.

"It seems the better one does in his field, the more is asked of him and the more others turn to him. In 1970 I was asked to come back to Hopkins to succeed Dr. Horace Browning, who had died suddenly of a coronary. Well, I was already pretty old to become a department chairman for the first time, but it would be a real honor and they did truly seem to want me. So after a long family discussion we left the old brownstone in New York and came to Baltimore.

"That was in the spring of 1970. We found a house we liked, Anne was closer to her family in Richmond, and it seemed we were going to be fine here. And then . . . then the horror happened . . . and nothing was ever the same again." Tears filled Dr. Hallam's eyes, but he continued. "I'm going to tell you about the horror, Jim. I don't know why, but I can't seem to stop. I just seem to want you to know these thing about me—things I've never really talked about to anyone. There is something about you . . . " He looked at Jim searchingly before going on.

"Our Mark was a wonderful son. He graduated from Columbia and then he studied humanities at Oxford, but his heart was really in social welfare, and he would probably have ended up in some international peace or health organization. He had a patriotic streak, too, and so he joined the Red Cross as a front-line volunteer in the Vietnam War. He served well, did good work in Vietnam for two years, and then he came home and went back to Columbia for a Ph.D. That was in 1973.

"In November he began not to feel well. He was losing weight, having fevers. He came home to Baltimore, and I had him looked at thoroughly. I guess we all thought it might be some parasite he picked up in Vietnam that hadn't shown itself yet. But he suddenly got a lot worse, had high spiking temperature and severe headache. His white count went up, and we put him into Hopkins. They did x-rays, sonograms, cerebral arteriograms, none of which showed anything definite. Finally, I looked him over carefully myself and concluded that he had a brain abscess. His headache seemed localizing more on the left, and he had some sinus symptoms. But he was getting rapidly worse, his temperature went higher, to 105 degrees, and he was developing signs of increased intracranial pressure, swellings and hemorrhaging in the eyegrounds—I saw them developing. I should have stepped aside, gotten another neurosurgical consultant to take a look—had Bregel flown down from Boston, maybe—but there didn't seem to be time. And I guess I was so used to being the court of last resort—and maybe so swollen with pride in my own ability and my own reputation—that I paid no heed to such ideas. My son needed me and I was the only one who could save him, I thought. So I decided to operate. I had built my own tower step by step during my career, higher and higher, and thought this would be the ultimate step that would put me up among the blessed. Then, with one bitter blow, God tore the tower down around me.

"I went in to see Mark in his hospital room. He was propped up in bed, his face pallid, and his eyes sunken and drawn from fever, but he was able to grab my hand.

" 'Mark,' I said, 'I'm going to have to operate on you. Do you trust me?'

" 'Nobody I'd rather have do it, Dad. I'm in your hands.'

"I turned down the frontal bone flap, as I had a thousand times on others, and made an incision in the dural sac covering the brain, and, God, his brain came rupturing up through the incision under tremendous pressure, all red and suffused and full of tiny hemorrhages. I probed and probed but could find no pus, and it was so swollen I couldn't get it back inside the skull. I had to leave it open and simply sew the dura together over it. He died at the end of the operation. It was the sudden change in pressure when I opened the skull that killed him. . . .

"Later, the lab brought in the diagnosis from a blood test one of the physicians had ordered. It was cerebral malaria. Have you heard of it, Jim? A fairly rare form of malaria that attacks the brain and mimics abscesses and tumors . . . cerebral malaria. He had contracted it in Vietnam. If I had only waited . . . a few quinine tablets would probably have saved him. Instead, he died in my arms. I had killed him . . . " Tears formed in Dr. Hallam's eyes.

"He . . . might have died anyway, Dr. Hallam," said Jim after a while.

"Yes, I've told myself that thousands of times during the years since, but it doesn't help. I broke the law of *primam non nocere*—first of all, do no harm. It's God's law to doctors, as passed on through Hippocrates. And I broke it . . . with my own son. . . .

"Well, that night and the following two days, I took cocaine for the first time in almost thirty years, to deal with my sorrow, but then I stopped. I suddenly realized that taking drugs was an escape. What I had to do was face my guilt, live with it, not escape it. I wanted to suffer. God, I needed to suffer. I didn't want to escape. I decided to take the punishment, naked, without the shield of coke." He looked at Jim. "The same reasoning applied to suicide, which I thought about for a time.

"Instead, I turned to the world of my work—which only later did I realize was just as much an escape as cocaine. I found it necessary to avoid my home, Anne, Charlotte, my close friends, as much as possible. Any show of affection toward me was repugnant because I could feel none for myself anymore and thought that any such feelings toward me must be false, hypocritical. I pulled my career around me like a cocoon, and it saved me from the nightmare of my own thoughts. Absurdly enough, in this mind-set, my career, my contributions to the progress of neurosurgery, thrived. My pride and my self-respect and my faith in myself were destroyed, but I worked—worked to avoid the horror of having to think about Markie.

"In the years that followed the pain eased, but it was replaced by an inner numbness, an inability to feel anything emotionally." He shook his head. "It's been very difficult for Anne and Charlotte to accept my behavior, to understand it and to deal with it. I regret this deeply, but those I loved the most were also the greatest reminders of what had happened. . . .

"My retirement meant that I would no longer have my work to hide in, and I was already beginning to feel the threat of having to face my conscience. So, the morning of my retirement speech last Saturday, I took a dose of cocaine intranasally. But this time I didn't get away with it." He stared at Jim. "I had my seizure. And here we are. . . . "

Jim thought for a moment. "But, Dr. Hallam, you've spent all these years running away from something you couldn't help. If anything, it was an honest mistake! It may not have been even that. It may have been the right thing to do, based on the information that you had."

Clay Hallam looked at him dully now, his years hanging on him more heavily.

"Two things a physician has to learn to live with, Jim," he replied. "One is the blind trust placed in him by the patient, and the second is the guilt that stems from his frequent inability to justify that trust — we all get used to those. But that guy who lives under the name 'professor,' that guy at the so-called top of his profession, the last word, the last resort . . . that guy, like Caesar's wife, must be above reproach. I was no longer that, Jim, I was no longer above reproach."

CHAPTER 13

Saturday, May 18, 1985

Dr. Warren Bregel drew himself up to his full height before the three-quarter-length mirror that was hung on the back of the door to the study of his home in Brookline, Massachusetts. The light in this room was soft, coming mostly from shaded lamps rather than from windows or ceiling fixtures. It was here that he did most of his reading and writing. He did not often spend a lot of time looking at himself, but when he did he liked to do it in this room because here he seemed to look most like himself. The mirror reflected an appropriate and attractive background—the floor-to-ceiling bookcases behind him, filled with books, more than a few of which he had written or co-authored—and the light softened some of the wrinkles and sagging lines in his seventy-two-year-old face.

He had a special reason for indulging in self-inspection today. In one hour the well-known portraitist Mrs. Wingred Gordon was to receive him at her studio to begin work on his official portrait, which the Boston Neurosurgical Institute had commissioned in honor of his fifteen years as chairman. There had been, he mused, only four professor-chairmen before him, and his portrait would hang prominently forever in the great lecture hall of the Institute. He knew it was a distinct honor, but it was not unexpected—nor, he felt, was it undeserved. For Warren was, above all else, constantly aware of his station in the upper echelon of the neurosurgical world.

The somber face that stared back at him from the mirror was that of an aging man. He was almost bald, except for gray around the sides of his face, and he had a high forehead and cheekbones and long sagging jowls. His icy gray eyes looked out from the shadows of his gray eyebrows like two deep recesses in the wall of a mountain, and the wall was full of cracks and seams. He was tall and slim, with small, hunched shoulders that nudged his head forward. He had on the long white lab coat that he always wore in the hospital. His expression was austere and cynical, condescending and self-satisfied—not a likable face, but a distinctive one.

But Warren did not see that figure in the mirror. He saw instead Dr. Warren Bregel, Templar Professor of Neurosurgery at the distinguished Boston Institute of Neurosurgery. Physician-in-waiting to Her Royal Highness Queen Elizabeth II, consultant to the Sheik of Amman, possessor of honorary degrees, titles, and awards. He saw in the mirror Warren Bregel as he wanted Warren Bregel to be.

This morning, however, there was something wrong with that image, something not quite right—nothing major, more of a nuance, something vaguely dissatisfying. He turned away from the mirror, momentarily puzzled, and gazed about the room seeking some cause of his unrest. He loved this room and loved to look at it. It was his sanctuary, his fortress. No one was permitted in without his express permission. Even the cleaning woman had specific instructions about what to dust and what not to disturb. He felt at home here, in harmony with the dark red oriental rug, the varnished oak bookcases, the generous stone fireplace with his awards and honors arranged on its mantelshelf. Here the world's troubles could not follow him. He kept his study tidy, and everything seemed in order this morning—until his searching eye reached his desk. There lay the cause of his discontent, the old vinyl-covered diary, opened.

As far back as he could remember, Warren had always been methodical and organized, traits his German mother had praised in him. With her schoolteacher husband—a retiring little man from Wittenburg with whom she had come to America—looking affectionately over her shoulder, she had taught Warren to keep a diary. She believed that the discipline of recording his days and his thoughts would help him to become methodical and organized in all other matters. She also had the idea that one day her son's biography would be written. The diaries therefore would be of vital importance. His entries were sporadic at first, but his mother persisted, and when she died, in Warren's seventeenth year, one five-year volume of the diary had been filled. His habit of diary-keeping was established, and her death fixed it in his daily routine forever.

The volume on his desk was labeled number three, which, because these were five-year diaries, included the years of his internship and early residency. He had gotten it out the previous week to find material for the speech he was to give in Baltimore in honor of the retirement of Clay Hallam, and, contrary to his usual meticulous habit, he had never returned it to the bookcase. He moved over to the desk now to do so, thinking it was the untidiness that bothered him. But as he picked up the diary to close it, his eye fell on the open page, filled with his faded, meticulous handwriting, and he realized it was the content, rather than the journal itself, that was the matter. He thought back over the events of a week ago, his own speech and the beginning of Clay's, and then Clay's collapse due to a stroke. Warren had delayed his return to Boston by a whole day, unusual for him, so disturbed had he been. He was still restless and filled with a melancholic nostalgia that followed him even into this room, and he knew the cause. There were still things he needed to say to Clay, things he had to explain, if he could. He sank down into the chair by his desk and began to read from the journal:

July 1, 1940

Began my neurosurgical assistant residency today—am very pleased with my decision to switch from general surgery to neurosurgery. I think it will be a much more precise and exact field, and one that I can make a mark in. Dr. Randolph is pro-

fessor, a good man, Drs. Overman and Gasteau and Calleus
are assistant professors, and Martinez is chief resident. Should
be okay. Only one amazing thing—Clay Hallam is somehow
back here, also an assistant resident. Don't know how he was
lucky enough to get back. Thought I'd laid him to rest two
years ago. I suppose he pulled some strings. The man's a
phony—then and now. He won't last long.

Warren flipped at random through the pages, drawn by the sight
of Clay's name as he scanned the writing.

July 4, 1940

Half-day off today. Hot in Baltimore. Nell off visiting her
parents. Things going well so far, but Hallam presents a problem. There are only four of us assistant residents, so we're
bound to work together. He looks well, better than when I
last saw him two years ago—acts more sure of himself—for
show, surely, I can't tell much yet. He is anathema to me!

July 11, 1940

Another hot one—electric system went off in our apartment—ice all melted in the box—took our food next door.
Nell working as floor nurse in urology.
Operated today with Hallam, under Dr. Overman, on a
parasagittal brain tumor using the "hinge" technique of
Krouse and Cushing. Hallam seemed familiar with the technique, and said he'd used it in Philadelphia last year under
Dr. Schultz, whom I've never heard of. The tumor came out
nicely—Hallam was lucky.

August 14, 1940

Working hard and long—a nine-hour cranial abscess
drained, and then a four-hour skull fracture repair—with
Hallam, under Dr. Calleus. We used the two-stage method of
Vincent, which I, having prepared, was able to describe very
well, and Calleus seemed impressed. Hallam said he didn't see

why it couldn't be removed all at once, which is heresy, but Calleus just said he thought the abscess capsule wouldn't stand it. He was being kind.

The skull fracture was repaired using Cushing's tenets, removing the damaged bone completely under local and sucking out dead brain tissue with a catheter. Hallam seemed very familiar with this technique, which irritated me considerably.

September 2, 1940

Another day off, the first since July 4. I'm highly satisfied with the training and with my performance, except for several clashes with Hallam on some matters of treatment and judgment, especially during rounds. Some of my points were well-taken, I think, but others, I fear, I adopted simply to be opposite his position, and in these I was clearly wrong.

I've been trying to analyze further my antipathy to Hallam. I know I resent him. He's been given too much, and he somehow makes it all look easy. It isn't easy! It's hard. And it should be hard. There should be things that you have to work hard to earn in this world. Things that you have to suffer and sacrifice for to get. So why should one person have it good? He makes me feel inferior, awkward . . . he's got to have weakness. I still think he's a phony . . . but I have to admit he's a convincing one. I'm disturbed at my attraction to him. I have to work hard at not succumbing to him. I think I could love him, if I didn't hate him.

October 22, 1940

An interesting case was admitted today, under Dr. Randolph—a 28-year-old female pianist, from the Peabody Conservatory, who had begun noticing increasing numbness in the fourth and fifth fingers of both hands several months before admission. The numbness had worsened to the point where she was no longer able to play.

She was also having bad headaches, pounding and throbbing, and had become weak in her affected fingers. Physical exam shows increased tendon reflexes and some weakness in her hand grip. Dr. Randolph admitted her, thinking she might have a brain tumor. I examined her, though, and I think she's probably got multiple sclerosis, and that the headaches are migraines from worry about losing her health. Hallam took a look, and his opinion was that I am right about the headaches, but thinks she may have a herniated intervertebral disc. Studies of her begin tomorrow, and we'll see who is right.

October 28, 1940

Goddamnit. That fucker Hallam was right. The woman has a disc in her neck, shown by myelogram. Dr. Randolph is letting him operate on her tomorrow, assisted by Randolph himself, and me. ME! Shit!

Warren stirred in his desk chair, uncomfortable with the memories evoked by the words he had written forty-four years ago. As it turned out, his rivalry with Clay wasn't that important. There was enough room for both of them. But back then there didn't seem to be.

A tapping at the door interrupted his thoughts.

"Warren," came the low voice from outside the study, "you're going to be late for your sitting."

"All right, Nell, be there in one moment," he replied, making no move to rise from his chair. There was one more entry in the diary that he wanted to read before he left, one that, his memory now jogged, he remembered having written those many years ago.

Let's see, he thought, that would have been somewhere around December 1941. He leafed quickly through the pages of the journal. Yes, there it was.

December 20, 1941

So it's settled. Hallam is going off to war, and I'm to stay as chief resident in neurosurgery for another year or so. Thank God it's over, and he's going. He's pleased and I'm overjoyed. I couldn't have gone on much longer like this, the two of us sharing responsibilities as the two senior assistant residents since last July. It's been ridiculous for us to try to work together. I can't believe he's volunteering. Doesn't he know he's throwing away his career? By the time he gets back I'll be well on my way to a professorship somewhere. Why, a year or two of chief residency here by myself and I may well be the best-trained young neurosurgeon in the country.

Why is he doing this? Patriotism? Adventure? All very nice if you can afford them. I can't! To me they are simply temptations and distractions from the main goal, and I won't have them, at least for the present. But Hallam bit on them. Well, too bad for him. Goodbye, hero Hallam. He'll look good in uniform, but I can't dwell on that!

He leaned back in his chair and carefully placed his feet on the edge of his desk in the manner of one who is succumbing to a compelling line of thought. But the rivalry *didn't* end there, did it? It didn't end with our residency. He stared toward the ceiling. It kept up until— until . . . and he smiled, last weekend. Almost lazily, he reached back up and selected another volume, labeled "Postresidency Years." He leafed through it and came almost immediately to the page he wanted:

July 23, 1948

Received news today that I did not receive the Covington Prize this year. It went to, of all people, Clay Hallam for some studies he published on the hypothalamus of monkeys—good work, I admit, but no better than my own experiments on facial neuralgia. I take comfort in the fact that I already have the Baker and Theilman awards this year—not bad. Still, the Covington would have been nice.

Warren smiled slightly. Wanted it all, didn't you, old man? I was hungry then . . . but, of course, only for what I deserved. He glanced at himself in the mirror, then reached for another volume.

September 11, 1958

Just got the announcement. Hallam selected to be head of neurosurgery at New York Medical. I can't believe they took him after my letter to the search committee, which I thought pretty well damned him with faint enough praise. He continues to rise; I've got to keep busy.

Warren grunted and shifted in his chair. Strange, he mused, how over the years, Hallam and I always seemed to be orbiting each other, like two oppositely charged bodies that are drawn slowly and inevitably together, meet, explode apart, and then the whole cycle starts again. Not without its precedents in science, I suppose, two bodies brightening each other by their own collisions, and bouncing off. Both of us made it, all right; and who knows, maybe we needed each other to compete against. Maybe if we hadn't existed for each other, we would have to have had to invent each other.

Again the tapping at the heavy oak door to the study. "Warren, may I come in?"

"Yes, yes, of course," said Warren brusquely, closing the diary and swinging around in his chair. "What is it?"

"Celeste says you'll miss your appointment if you don't go soon," said Nell Bregel. She advanced slowly into the room, taking small, careful steps. She was slender and fragile, bent a bit at the shoulders and back. Her coiffeured hair was white and contrasted with her fashionable dark blue skirt and jacket. Her face was round and earnest.

"Have you taken your Parkinson medicine today?" asked Warren as he watched her slow steps.

"Yes, just now. What are you doing?"

"Oh, just looking up a few things relating to Clay Hallam in my diaries."

"Oh yes, poor Clay, how is he doing? I must go and see him."

"Nell, you haven't seen him in forty years! He's in Baltimore. He had a stroke last week. Remember? I was there?"

"Yes, I remember," she answered slowly. "You told me. How is he?"

"Okay, as far as I know. I'm going to check today, and, if he's better, I have to go down again tomorrow. I want to talk to him."

"Oh, that would be nice. Shall I come with you?"

"No! I'll only be there a short while."

"How is his wife, Anne?"

"Good—you remembered her name." Warren gazed at her curiously.

Nell settled on the edge of a sofa near the desk. "Yes, she was my good friend."

"She's fine; but she's worried, of course."

Glancing at the desk, Nell asked, "Reading from your diaries?"

"Yes."

"Will you read me the page about our marriage?"

"Our marriage? Sure. Not much to read." He thumbed back through the pages of the same volume, then said, "Here it is."

June 20, 1938

Married today to Nell Simpson Hargrieves, from Winslow Falls, Kansas. 4:00 P.M. First Presbyterian Church. Reverend Rightmeyer.

He looked up and said, "That's it."

She slowly smiled. "Yes, that's it. I love to hear it read out loud. You have a nice clear voice, Warren."

He closed the diary impatiently and started to get up, when she said, "Now, read me about the birth of our two sons."

"That's in a whole different volume, and it's getting late."

"Please, Warren, it won't take long."

He got to his feet and went to the bookcase, reshelved the volume, and selected the next one in order. "There, this should do it." He found the entry and said, "Yes, here we are."

October 3, 1948

Warren Merrifield Bregel, Jr. Born 9:22 P.M., New York Hospital. Obstetrician: Dr. Giles Canaby. Assistant: Dr. Warren Bregel. No complications.

He leafed further.

January 11, 1950

Robert Maddox Bregel. Born 3:50 A.M., Chicago Lying-in Hospital. Obstetrician: Dr. Barney Fletcher. Assistant: Dr. Warren Bregel.

"That was during my stint at the Chicago Institute. That's when I started my work on prefrontal lobotomy for relief of pain."

"Yes," Nell answered slowly, as if trying to remember clearly. "I remember you were always busy. Always busy."

"What's that supposed to mean?"

"Nothing . . . at all. Read me something more about the boys, will you?"

"I don't have time to read you any more. I've got to go. Besides, there is no more about the boys except . . . until . . . here. Do you want me to read to you about when Warren Junior crashed out the window on drugs? Here it is, March 8, 1966. Or when Maddie had his trouble?" His voice was strained, cynical, as he watched her flinch.

"No, don't read about those things. Read something in between."

"I've told you. There is nothing in between, about them, that is."

Nell looked vacantly up at the bookcase with its neat row of diaries, as if trying to understand.

"And all those other pages? . . . "

"Are my work, my career."

"Your career, Warren, your career wrote out your children . . . and me."

After a moment, he got up from his seat and went over to her, and put out his arm to her.

"I was a lousy husband, wasn't I, and not so good a father. I wonder why you stayed with me."

"Where would I have gone? And the boys?" She shrugged. "I couldn't think of anyplace."

He looked down at her averted face.

"Do you remember when we got married I told you I'd be a poor husband because my career and my work would always come first? Do you remember that?"

"Yes, yes," she answered softly.

"So why did you marry me?"

"You knew and still know why. You were a doctor. I was just a plain nurse. I had nothing special. I used to keep wondering why you wanted me." She sighed. "My family was pleased."

"I married you . . . because I needed you, as I've told you a number of times, and, I have to admit, I found a certain charm in your submissiveness. It always gave me the luxury of being honest with you."

Nell pushed herself up from the arm of the sofa with his help and moved away from him. "Submissive, yes, too submissive, especially after the boys were born. Why were you always so harsh with the boys, Warren?"

"I set high standards for them, and it was necessary to be strict. Life is a serious business, Nell. At least it's always seemed serious to me. I was raised that way. Do you know I can never recall playing any games or doing anything with my mother that did not involve some instruction or educational point to be made? Oh, I got plenty of attention, but play? Never. That's why I kept after the boys, to make them see that life is not a game. To succeed, you've got to work."

Nell looked down. "Yes, you set high standards for them, so high the boys realized they could never reach them, and they gave up."

His voice faltering, Warren said, "I was wrong, Nell, wrong about a lot of things. Tell me, do you hate me?"

As she turned toward him her tremor increased. "Hate you? No, I'm too old to hate. There may have been times, but they passed. I think I failed as a mother, and probably as a person, by not standing up to you more, but now I'm old and sick and I need you. I guess I've always needed you. We've been married forty-seven years now, and you've kept to me." Her eyes turned toward the mantelpiece, laden with awards. There were also two photographs. In one, she and Warren were being privately received by the pope; in the other, they stood next to the president. "These are no small things in life. You never let me down, Warren, you've done the one and only thing you ever promised me you'd do, and that is to be at the top of your field. You did that."

Looking at Nell, Warren was surprised to feel a wave of great tenderness. He knew again why he had married her and why he had needed her all these years: even in his lowest moments she made him feel ten feet tall.

CHAPTER 14

Sunday, May 19, 1985

The antique clock on the wall outside the entrance to Marburg I showed half past four when Jim Gallier left Dr. Hallam's room that Sunday afternoon. The long corridors were almost deserted. Stretching away for a hundred yards in two directions, the high-ceilinged passages, when empty, as they were apt to be on a Sunday afternoon, were Kafkaesque. Ever since he had been here in training, Jim had wanted to hit a tennis ball down the length of either of these somber corridors, just for the hell of it, just to watch the ball bounce along the emptiness, to listen to the echo of its passage.

He walked up the south corridor, past the small post office on his left and the hallway to the hospital's Broadway entrance on his right. His footsteps echoed hollowly from the walls as he walked toward his room. He needed to talk to someone, and by the time he opened his door he knew what he would do.

Charlotte's voice on the phone was rich and warm.

"Hi, Charlie, hope I'm not interrupting your afternoon."

"Not at all, Jim, unless you're calling with bad news."

"Not this time, unless you consider the prospect of seeing me bad news. Your dad is doing okay. I just left him. Charlie, I wonder if I could see you tonight for a while, maybe after dinner. I need to talk with you."

"Of course, Jim. Mother and I are going to have an early dinner, and then she'll return to the hospital to see Dad. Why don't you come out around seven o'clock?"

"A deal," said Jim. He hung up, feeling exhilarated. That Charlotte had agreed to see him that evening was one more piece falling into place. For the next few hours he thought about his life. He went back over his conclusions and tried to perceive their weaknesses, and he attempted to weigh the consequences of the steps he was considering. Each time he did this, he judged that he was making the right decisions.

He arrived at the Hallams' home at twilight, just as the street lights came on. The air was still and the crickets and spring frogs were in full voice as Jim ascended the steps to the front door.

Charlotte stepped out of the door to greet him, and her cheek was warm and flushed as he kissed it. He stepped back to observe her. She looked lovelier than ever. Her dark hair was upswept, and her brown eyes were alight.

She took his arm and led him into the house and out onto the terrace, where they sat on a canvas glider near an old rose trellis.

"You just missed Mother," she said. "She sent her regrets."

"Sorry to miss her. Is she okay? I mean, after Jonas's blowout today?"

"She's fine, fine. You know, as Jonas would have predicted, the blowout was helpful. Mother and I had a good talk because of it. I guess Jonas was on the right track."

"He sure knows the value of shock therapy to make people think. He even . . . " Jim looked at Charlotte.

"He even what?"

"I . . . I shouldn't say, I suppose . . . even though I know he would."

Charlotte smiled. "You don't have to."

"No, that's okay. He even said that if things didn't work out with us . . . that is, between you and me—then he would like the chance. Can you beat that?"

Charlotte laughed. "He did, did he? Well, is that what brought you here tonight? Jonas's threat?"

Jim smiled. "In a way, maybe. That, and something else."

He felt a pulse of excitement rise in his throat. He had to say it right, he had to make her understand. "Charlie, I had a long talk with your dad today. Remember I asked you once if he would tell me something about his life, and you suggested asking him? Well, I did today, and he told me. A lot. It's a great story, Charlie. A life full of accomplishment, honor, compassion . . . and humanity. I admire him more than I can say, for what he's done, for what he's borne."

"And what has he borne?" asked Charlotte in a low voice.

"I came away from his room full of respect for him, for what he's stood for and what he's been, but I also came away feeling, well, depressed."

"Why depressed?"

"About what his career has done to him. His hard work, his achievements, everything led to unhappiness."

"What do you mean? He's been a great success."

"Tell me, Charlie, did you ever hear about the cause of Mark's death?"

"Well, he died of cerebral malaria. Dad was never the same afterward. He turned away from us. I've always been bitter about that."

"I know. But it's time you knew the truth about Mark's death. He died after your father operated on him—as it turned out, for the wrong thing. Your father had misdiagnosed him. He thought Mark had a brain abscess and instead he had cerebral malaria, but nobody could have known that at the time. Your father blames himself for Mark's death, even though it sounds to me as if Mark would have died anyway. But your father has borne the guilt of that ever since."

"My God, no one told me . . . and he turned away from us . . . "

"Because he was ashamed," said Jim, "so ashamed and full of guilt that he couldn't face you."

Charlotte stared blankly at him, as the full purport of what she had heard sank in. "I was young, I guess too young to understand. But Mother?"

"She did her best, Charlie," said Jim gently, "to reassure him that she did not hold him at fault."

"Poor, poor Dad. He's kept that all to himself all these years. If only I'd known, I could have gone to him, grieved with him, helped him survive that sorrow, instead of getting bitter myself . . . against Dad, against doctors. I'm sure you know that my feelings of being rejected by Dad have colored my thinking about all doctors?" She gazed warmly at Jim.

Jim nodded. "So I gathered, and it's one reason I wanted you to hear this tonight."

"Thank you for telling me all this, Jim. Perhaps it's not too late to let Dad know that I know."

"Charlie, I came away from listening to your dad's story thinking, 'What a man, to have been able to shoulder so much disappointment, so much responsibility, throughout life. And then I thought, 'Is this the kind of life I want? So full of responsibility for human life, so many chances to err?' I'm not sure I'm geared to accept that as a way of life. I'm not sure I like medicine enough to accept its burden." He shrugged.

"How about some minor speciality?" asked Charlotte. "Aren't they less demanding?"

"Not really," Jim said. "Each has its own problems. I really like the field of medicine. It brings you as close as one can get to what life's all about . . . and yet . . . " He shook his head. "I don't know if I can hack it."

"Have you reached a conclusion, Jim?"

"Yes. I think I've made the right one. Charlie, thanks to your father's making me aware of things, I'm going to leave medicine for a while. I don't know how long, maybe for a year or two, maybe forever . . . until I can find out who I really am and what I really want to do. I've decided to resign from Johns Hopkins tomorrow. As it happens, I received a letter from a friend a few days ago. He's bought a boat, a forty-five-foot Morgan, that he wants to cruise on for a while—New

England this summer and the Caribbean this winter. He's looking for a crew. I'm thinking I'll join him!"

Charlotte looked at him, the shadows on the terrace hiding the expression in her dark eyes. "So . . . you'll be leaving."

"Yes. But Charlie, darling, a lot of things have happened to me in this short week. I've met and come to know a great man, I've changed my destiny, and, most important of all, I've fallen completely in love. I know this isn't much of a proposal, Charlie, but here it is. Sail with me on this boat, married or engaged, whichever you like. But, no matter what, come away with me. Marry me. I love you."

At the same time, five miles across the city, Dr. Warren Bregel was knocking on the door of Dr. Clayton Hallam's hospital room. Warren turned the knob and entered the room. Clay was propped up in bed, reading by the bright bedside lamp. The rest of the room was dimly lit, and it took a few seconds for Clay to identify his guest.

"Hello, Clay," said Warren as he approached the bed.

"My God, Warren—Warren Bregel! What the hell are you doing here this Sunday evening?" asked Clay, shoving his reading aside and putting out his hand.

"I came from Boston to see you for a few minutes," said Warren, standing by the bedside and shaking Clay's hand. "Are you busy?"

"Not at all. I'm glad for the company. Pull up that chair." He laughed. "You know, when I first made you out I thought you were an apparition from our internship days coming to get me out of bed and put me to work."

"Guilty conscience, eh?" Warren's laugh was a short whinny. "Well, after all, you've been lying here a week. It's time to get going. How are you feeling, Clay?"

"Better. I'm better," said Clay, stretching back against his pillow. "It's always illuminating to be on the other end of the doctor-patient relationship. Gives one lots of insights. And that's what I've had this week, I think, a few insights into things, some medical, some non-medical. You ought to try it, Warren."

"I tried it a few years ago, Clay, when I had a coronary bypass. I don't think either of us wants those insight opportunities too often.

But speaking of insights, I . . . uh . . . came down here with an old one that I want to share."

The two men were silent for a moment. "The trouble is, Warren," said Clay finally, "we're getting old. What're we now, seventy-two? I guess we *are* old. Like two candles that have burned down. . . . But we did burn fiercely for a while, didn't we? Especially when we were around each other." He looked at Warren warily. "Do you think the insight that you've brought down from Boston is going to light us up again?"

Warren grimaced. "Not my intention, of course, or my desire. Just something I've found I have to say. I was . . . afraid for a while you weren't going to be around for me to say it. And I found that very upsetting. Hence my trip here tonight—to say it."

"Well, damn the torpedoes, full speed ahead, Warren. I don't seem to recall your ever standing on niceties. But before you speak, ask yourself one last time, Is it necessary? Maybe we should let old tales go untold. I can't think of anything that would seem relevant any longer."

Warren sat forward on his bedside chair, his back straight, his eyes somber. "Nor is relevance any longer the point, Clay. Necessity is. It's totally necessary to me that I get this off my chest. I've been wanting to say it for years and have never been able to think how. Now I know the only way to say it is to say it."

"Say on, McWarren," Clay said.

"Do you remember back in our internship year when Anne received a letter in Richmond about your, ah, romantic activities at Hopkins?"

"I remember, yes."

"And do you remember my telling you later that it was Nell who wrote that letter?"

"Yes."

"Well, Nell didn't write it. I did." He gazed at Clay to see what effect his pronouncement would have on his old adversary.

Clay considered the confession for a moment, then began to chuckle, and gradually the chuckle grew into a loud laugh, as Warren sat blinking solemnly.

"Poor old Warren—poor bastard," said Clay, between laughs. "Carried that around with you all these years, did you? A real load of guilt, eh? Weighed on you, did it?" He shook his head. "I always suspected it, you know. Nell would never have done such a thing." He laughed again. "What fools we mortals be. Well, after all, I'm glad I lived to be able to laugh at it."

They were silent a minute, then Clay continued. "I laugh now, but that letter nearly destroyed my life. God, Warren, you really wanted that residency, didn't you?"

"Most important thing in the world to me at the time," Warren said.

"More than honor, or truth, or charity. My, what the young hot blood of ambition can do, especially when considered in the cool perspective of old age. Well, it worked. You got your residency. What bothers me, Warren, is wondering how many other backs you stepped on along the way up? Was my case unique or typical?"

Warren smiled. "I've scrambled . . . scrambled all the way. But you were the only competition I ever truly, uh, respected."

"I guess I could have done without your respect, then," said Clay. "It probably kept us from ever being friends."

"Oh, never friends, Clay, we could never have been friends. But the very finest of enemies, always. . . . And in the end you won, you know. When the chair became vacant here at Hopkins twelve years ago, the selection committee got down to two names, yours and mine, and they chose you."

Clay shrugged.

"Well, I came tonight with an apology, in any case," continued Warren in his high-pitched voice. "You must let me get it out."

"Of course, but before I do, tell me, has it all been worth it, Warren? Have you had a good life? You've done some excellent work, made lots of contributions."

Warren blinked, then nodded. "It's the only life I can ever imagine living, or wanting. I'm just glad I didn't miss it. I can truthfully say I'm proud of it. I can't think of anything that I could have done that would have suited me better—never could."

He stood up and approached the bed. "I'm sorry, old man, for my despicable behavior back then. I'm sorry I hurt you."

"I survived, and I accept your apology, Warren. It was big of you to come, after so many years, to put things straight."

After a moment's hesitation, the two men shook hands, and Warren headed for the door. As he opened it, Clay called out, "And Warren, the truth of it is, you and I have probably helped quite a few people in our time, but I suspect we've been hell on everyone close to us, eh?"

Warren smiled thinly, nodded, and let himself out. The door had barely closed when it opened again and Anne came in.

"Hello, dear," she said, kissing him. "That was Warren Bregel, wasn't it? I've been waiting for him to leave. What did he want?"

"Yes, that was Warren, and he came down from Boston to unload himself of an intolerable burden." Clay looked at Anne as she settled down into the bedside chair. "I'm not sure I want to tell you what it was."

"Why not?"

"Because it brings up some past unpleasantness that's better left behind."

Anne rose and began rearranging the flowers in a bedside vase. "Our past," she said, "or your past?"

Clay smiled. "All right, our past, and you've a right to know. Remember the letter you got forty-five years or so ago in Richmond telling you I was having an affair? The letter I told you Nell Bregel had written?"

"Like it was yesterday."

"Warren came all the way down from Boston to tell me it was really he who wrote it. He was afraid I was going to die before he could tell me."

"Oh," said Anne, her eyes reflecting that distant pain. "And did you absolve him?"

"I excused him," said Clay. "It hardly seems to matter anymore."

"No, not now, but then!" She continued straightening up his bureau. "Tell me, did you ever hear from her again?"

"Who's that, dear?"

"You know, the girl, the other woman, so to speak?"

Clay looked at her tenderly. "No, never again. Not another word. Ever."

"Did you ever think about her?" she persisted.

"Oh, I thought about her once or twice over the years, but not from any desire to see her, only to wonder how she's done. I wish her well, and hope she's had a good life. Stuff like that."

Evidently satisfied, Anne returned to her seat by the bed.

"How was your lunch? Didn't you go over to the hotel with Jim and Charlie?" Clay asked.

"Yes. Tell me, Clay, have you ever noticed that I . . . drink?"

"Of course I have, Anne. And sometimes you drink too much. But why? Did you get smashed at lunch?"

"I was on my way to it, but I got stopped. By a very young, very brash, but very observant friend of Jim's, whose name is Jonas. He was quite blunt, and I had to stand him down, but it was like getting a cold splash of water in the face. He cut off my supply source, the hotel waiter, and cut off my desire, because I had thought no one could tell I was drinking. It made me face myself and . . . I just wondered whether you had ever noticed."

Clay nodded. "For quite a while now, Anne, . . . and I think I've shown my dislike for it on occasion. But I always thought you had a reason, maybe Mark, or what I did to him, that made you do it. I couldn't blame you. I blame myself too much. I thought that any-time you saw me, you saw Mark's murderer. I know how you loved Mark. He was you to a T: idealistic, romantic, sensitive, everything you are. And you and he put your trust in me, and I let both of you down. God . . . Goddamn it. I don't blame you if you hate me . . . and if you have to drink to deal with it I can't criticize you. It's all my fault."

"You're wrong, Clay, really wrong. When I look at you, I never see Mark's murderer, I see his father. And I drink not because I hate you, but because I love you and you turned from me. We could have wept together. Instead, we wept alone, and we never really acknowledged our grief to each other."

Clay snorted. "I don't believe my guilt will ever diminish."

"Well, this may come as a shock to you, but you're not God, or even a god, and therefore you are subject to making mistakes. You made a considered judgment that turned out to be a mistake. I accepted that. But you paid a terrible price for it, and that I don't find acceptable."

"And what was that?"

"The price was thirteen years of isolation, of walling yourself off from human feeling. You submerged yourself in that sterile medical world of yours, your research, your teaching and writing. You did it early in our marriage and again after Mark died—a time when we should have been together and rejoicing in our love and life. You made a misjudgment on Markie, a painful one, but understandable. Then you compounded it with another mistake, a worse one because that's the one that hurt me, and hurt Charlie. I never told Charlie all the facts of Mark's death, because I wanted it to come from you, but you never talked to her."

Clay sank back on his pillow. "Why . . . have you waited so long to say all this?"

"I tried . . . so often I tried. But you weren't there. You were off somewhere. You reached your own verdict after Mark's death: Guilty. Life imprisonment with heavy labor. You should have let yourself have a jury trial. Charlotte and I would have let you off a lot easier."

Clay smiled. "The jury would have been biased, but what the hell! I've been selfish and I've been foolish. But thank God, my dear Anne, for you. I was so lucky to have found you and to have you still. You waited for me once before during the war and now you've waited for me again, to come to my senses." He looked at her. "What made you stick with me?"

Anne paused, then said, "I guess, my dear, that I've never found a worthier cause. Remember Uncle Randolph? When we received his diary after he died in 1949, we read the flyleaf together: 'Herein is the worldly record of Randolph Grier, who followed his star, and became, by most accounts, the best bridge player on defense south of the Mason-Dixon Line.' He was telling us something, Clay—something he wanted us to know."

Clay nodded. "And we listened, I think. But you, Anne, what about your star?"

She was silent a minute, then said, "I made my decision long ago, Clay. It took me a while. When you were in your residency and I was in Richmond, I thought it out then and made up my mind. You were my star—and I would follow you. I just wanted to be with you forever."

He reached out and drew her down to sit on the edge of the bed and held her close. "Years ago we would have made love at a time like this," he said.

"Years ago we did, remember?"

"Listen to me, Anne. If anything should occur tonight—or any night—I want you to know now that marrying you was the best thing that ever happened to me. I can only hope there's still time to show you."

"You're already off to a good start." She sighed.

Later, after Anne had gone, Clay lay in his bed in the dark. He felt tired from the sheer emotionality of the last hours, but he also sensed increasing optimism. It was as if some dark spot was being washed from his soul. He thought, after all, it is true that Markie might have died anyway, from his malaria, his brain was so inflamed. Anyway, it is over and out in the open at last, and maybe I can begin to live with myself again. He felt his love for Anne and Charlotte, and he knew how lucky he was to have them.

It seemed to Clay that for the first time he might be able to find a shaky peace within himself. His life had been one of responsibility and accountability, and he had been able to make some useful contributions to the human story. He had put to good use the mind he had been given and the character he had shaped. He had enjoyed his work. In his teaching he had touched many lives, and he had seen many of his students go on to achieve distinction in their own work. If tonight, during sleep, one of the tiny blood vessels coursing through his brain were to shut off, he would die with a better conscience than he had a week ago. As if that mattered, he thought ruefully.

As Clay drifted toward sleep his mind roved back to his childhood. He saw his mother, slender and bespectacled, framed in the front doorway of their home, awaiting his return from school. And he saw his father, his cap pushed back, smiling at him as they sat on a log during one of their hunting trips, the dogs sprawled beside them, panting. Clay was suspended in the space between then and now, and he felt closer to his parents than he had in the years since they died. He yearned to reach out to them, to touch them, reassure them. They seemed so close. Almost asleep, he raised his hand toward them.

Around half past ten that May evening, Jim Gallier returned to the hospital after seeing Charlotte. The long hospital corridors were again empty and quiet. He turned to look back down their gleaming empty length, and paradoxically they seemed full of the memories of the years he had spent in them.

Back in his room, he looked irresolutely around, then went to the corner behind the bureau and picked up his tennis racket and two cans of old tennis balls, took off his white jacket, tossed it on the bed, and went out the door.

He made his way down the two flights of stairs through the small lobby of the residence, which opened onto the hospital corridors. The long north-south corridor stretched in front of him, empty for its entire length, austere and dignified.

He selected a ball from one of the cans, laid the cans on the floor, and took up his Head Prince racket. He stationed himself carefully, sighted down the corridor, and hit a tremendous forehand. The racket struck the ball with a loud "thoomp" that echoed off the walls of the corridor. Jim watched and listened as the ball bounced down the long passage and into the distance, charged with its own energy.

He looked around to see if anyone was watching, but saw no one, so he bent over and selected a second ball and fired it off, this one a bit higher, so that it grazed the ceiling of the corridor in its flight, and then a third ball, and a fourth.

He was about to loose the fifth ball when he looked up to find Jonas grinning at him. He had come up the other corridor and stood there leaning against the wall, his hands in his pockets.

Jim grinned back, and without a word, blasted the ball down the corridor. They watched and listened to it bounce down toward the other end, where they lost sight of it. Jim bent over and picked up the sixth and last ball and silently offered it and the racket to Jonas. The latter hesitated only a moment, then took them and smacked his own drive down the corridor. They watched it go, then turned and went up to their room. They sat on their beds.

"You act like a man who's burning his bridges," was Jonas's first remark.

"Very observant, as always, Jonas. That was my swan song to this place. I'm going to be leaving tomorrow."

Jonas whistled. "Sure thing? No recourse? What happened?"

"A few revelations, I guess," replied Jim. "They came while Dr. Hallam was telling me about his life. It became clear to me that medicine could be a very heavy life. I mean, one mistake, one error in judgment, one mishap could ruin your whole life. I'm not sure I'm cut out to shoulder that burden."

"It's only heavy if you're not competent to do your job, and you're very competent," said Jonas.

"It's not that simple, and you know it, Jonas. I'll have to see. I have to distance myself from medicine for a while, a year or two."

"That's juvenile," snorted Jonas. "You'll see. You're hooked! Once you've sampled meaning in life, like the pursuit of medicine, everything else becomes inconsequential."

"You're wrong, Jonas, I'm not hooked yet. You're hooked. I'm still free. And I'm going to find out what the hell else is out there."

Jonas asked, "What about Dr. Hallam? And what about Charlotte?"

"Dr. Hallam will be going home in a few days. And Charlie turned me down."

"What?"

"I said she turned me down. I asked her to come with me, to marry me, but she said she wasn't ready to marry yet, and she didn't think I was either. She said she might consider going to nursing school." They looked at each other.

"She said *that*?" Jonas asked. Jim nodded. "You're giving up a lot, Jim—your four years of medical school, your internship, your good record here, maybe even Charlotte. Are you sure it's what you want?"

"No, I'm not sure. But it's what I have to do. I have to see what's on the other side. I'll come back a lot better for having been away—if I return at all.

"Charlie is a magnificent woman, and her family is great, and I may love her, but there are no strings left between us, so feel free to call her. After all, what're roommates for?"

The two grinned at each other as the clock in the tower of the old building proclaimed eleven o'clock to East Baltimore.

CHAPTER 15

Monday, May 20, 1985

On Monday morning, Jim arose early, even before the redoubtable Jonas, to go to the ward and get his daily tasks done in order to clear the rest of the day. As he worked through his duties one by one, he found, now that he had decided to leave the hospital, each duty he performed was more pleasant than ever before, as if nostalgia was already beginning. Had he ever drawn blood from patients' arteries and veins so caringly, or started intravenous solutions so proficiently? He told his patients that, due to regular mid-month rotation of house officers, this would be his last morning with them, and he wished them well, knowing that they would be the last patients he would be seeing for some time, perhaps ever. His sense of freedom and exhilaration was tempered by a feeling of loss at the prospect of abandoning habits and techniques he had developed over so long a period.

He finished, however, in plenty of time for eight o'clock rounds with Bert Harper and his fellow intern on Marburg I, Jack Fishbein. He told them nothing of his intentions until all their patients had been visited and discussed, including Dr. Hallam, who seemed to be feeling exceedingly well this morning. As they returned to the small, cluttered doctors' office at the end of rounds, Jim waited until they were all seated, then bluntly told them of his plans to leave.

"Say what?" Bert's brittle voice seemed to echo off the metal chart rack. Bert's feet swung off the desk and hit the floor with an exclamatory thud. Fishbein's only response was to gape at Jim.

"It's true, Bert. I'm leaving. Now seems the right time, because our monthly rotation is due, and I have a few weeks' vacation time coming up anyway. July 1st is the end of the year, so I can't see starting something new. My rotation would have been in the outpatient clinic anyway, so there'll be no trouble replacing me."

"But why are you leaving? What the hell's wrong? Family trouble? Romantic trouble?" Bert's insistence demanded an answer.

"No, nothing like that. A purely personal decision, Bert. It's— well, you yourself have noticed my work's not been so good lately. I've just sort of lost my enthusiasm for medicine. I've got to go away and think it over a while."

"My God," said Bert. "Look, if it's anything I said or did, well, forget it. I was riding your ass a bit, but I do it to everybody, so don't let that bother you."

"Oh, don't worry, Bert, you had nothing to do with it. It's my own problem."

After a short silence, Bert said, "Have you . . . told His Nibs yet?"

Jim grimaced. "No, I'm going to call right now and see if I can get an appointment to see him this morning. I'm not looking forward to it."

"God, he may eat you alive," Bert said. "One of his carefully chosen house staff defecting? He might have a stroke!" A few minutes later Jim called the office of Dr. Isador Mendel, professor and chairman of the Department of Medicine at Johns Hopkins, to make the appointment. His palms were sweating as he gripped the phone and waited for it to be answered. It occurred to him that he had never called Dr. Mendel's office before, either during medical school or his internship.

Dr. Mendel was not the sort of man who invited phone calls. His appearance was imposing and forbidding. He was squat and stocky, and he walked with the rolling grace and coordination of an athlete. His complexion was dark, his large brown eyes brooding, and his mane of charcoal hair swept smoothly across his broad forehead. He wore dark-rimmed glasses. His voice was sonorous, and his speech was usually brief and to the point, especially when he was irritated. His medical knowledge was legendary, as was his propensity for sarcasm. He did not suffer fools gladly. Some said he had a marvelous sense of humor, and some said that he had a large streak of kindness, but Jim didn't believe that. Dr. Mendel was in his early fifties, at the peak of his powers, but the lines and creases in his face were care lines, worry lines, thought lines, and not laugh lines. His secretary finally agreed to give Jim an appointment for quarter after twelve that day, taking fifteen minutes away from Dr. Mendel's lunch time in order to accommodate the urgency in Jim's request.

"Fifteen minutes is all you get, Dr. Gallier," the secretary told him stiffly. "Dr. Mendel has appointments all afternoon."

"That'll be plenty," promised Jim. "Thanks very much."

He spent the next hours going about the hospital saying goodbye to friends, most of whom were too immersed in their work to do more than register their surprise and ask him to stay in touch. Already he found himself almost an outsider in an ordered land, and he felt outcast and sad. By the time of his 12:15 appointment with Dr. Mendel, he was aware of how weighty a decision he was making in leaving this familiar, secure world.

Dr. Mendel's secretary did little to reassure him. She was middle-aged, portly, and had the dignified and courtly bearing of one who was fully aware of her prestige as major-domo to the most powerful doctor in the hospital hierarchy. She was on cordial terms with most of the luminaries in Johns Hopkins medicine, and she had low regard for mere house staff. She led Jim into Dr. Mendel's office and announced, "Dr. James Gallier is here." Jim found himself looking down at Dr. Mendel, clad in his long white lab coat and seated behind a large desk. Dr. Mendel was writing, and the desktop was stacked with reference books and papers and reprints.

"Sit down, Gallier." His voice was deep and mournful. Jim sat in the small chair beside the desk. The office was not imposing. The bookcases were crammed with books and papers, and there were no photographs, diplomas, or honorary degrees. A working man's office, it was small and intimate—and perhaps more threatening because of this. Jim noted that the only escape hatch was the large window overlooking the hospital grounds. Probably locked, he thought.

"Now, Gallier, what can I do for you this morning?" Dr. Mendel pushed his writing aside, and directed his attention to Jim, who suddenly knew why the office seemed so small: Dr. Mendel filled it with his presence. His face fairly radiated intelligent energy, which now seemed to Jim to be focused entirely on probing his thoughts. He felt compromised—and silly. He drew a deep breath.

"Dr. Mendel, thank you for seeing me on such short notice. I'm sorry to trouble you. But I've been thinking about this for some time now, and, well . . . I've decided to resign here. I'm going to take some time off from medicine. That is, to see if it's really what I want to do with my life . . . " Jim tried to look at Dr. Mendel's eyes during this recitation, but found by the end of it he was gazing into the bookcase. He felt inane, irresolute, and weak, saying this to a man whose entire life had been devoted to medicine, who seemed a metaphor for medicine itself.

Mendel listened without changing his somber expression.

"You've thought it over, you say?" Mendel finally asked, leaning forward and opening a manila folder.

"Yes, sir," answered Jim.

"What happened?" he asked crisply.

"Oh, nothing specific happened—just an accumulation of things, aspects, factors . . . made me doubt that I'm really suited for a medical life."

"Like what?" Mendel persisted.

"Well, like its responsibility, its weight, and what I'd call its appetite. Medicine consumes you, it eats you alive, you and your time. I don't know . . . " Jim sighed.

"Mmm . . . hmm . . . I see in your record here you're not married. Is there a . . . um . . . romantic problem?"

"No, sir, not pertaining to my decision, anyway."

"Any family pressures? Your father died a year or two ago, I see. How about your mother?"

"No, sir, Mother doesn't know yet, but I plan to tell her today. She has nothing to do with this change."

"So it's just you . . . and your feelings . . . and no one else's . . . " Dr. Mendel spelled it out almost accusingly. He spun slowly in his chair and looked out the window. This beautiful May day was warm and breezy, but the window was closed and the hospital air conditioning was already going.

"You have a big investment in your career already, in time and money. Four years of medical school, a year of internship—are you sure you want to take a chance on losing all that?"

"I'd never consider it a loss, sir. I've enjoyed almost all of it, and I wouldn't trade what I've learned for anything, even if I never return to medicine."

Dr. Mendel sighed deeply, then got up and walked over to gaze out the window. After a moment, he spoke.

"Too bad, too bad, to have gained all that capability, then have it only for personal satisfaction—brings it down to the level of a hobby. I hate to lose a good mind from medicine, and yours is a good one."

He turned around, leaned back on the wide window sill, and looked down at Jim.

"I only want one thing today, *Dr.* Gallier, and that is the clear understanding that when you walk out of that door today you go with all the facts completely known and considered by you, so that you don't look back some day and say, 'I wish that son of a bitch had pointed a few things out to me that day.' So I'll point out a few things, not to persuade you to stay, because it sounds as if you must go, but to draw the picture clearly.

"Fact one, it's hard to get back into medicine once you've left it. Much of one's medical career is forming good routines, good habits, keeping on top of new information, new developments. The longer one gets away from these things, the harder it is to come back.

"Fact two, it would be very difficult, if not impossible, for you to return here to Hopkins for the rest of your training, if you elected to come back to medicine. You know how competitive places on this house staff are to get, so once you step aside, don't look to come back here.

"Fact three, you are not unique. We usually have one or two each year who drop out of the training program here, either to leave medicine entirely or go to a less demanding hospital. And the reason this happens is because that's what our training program is supposed to do. It's designed to weed out the uncertain, the undedicated, the irresolute—that's why it's so intensive. You see, we're trying to turn out the finest doctors in the world here, and one can't be the finest unless one is totally involved, totally immersed, at least at this stage of the game. It's like being baptized, and when you come out of this training, you are, you have to be, a good doctor. The hard work, the long hours, the intense study form the habits that stand you in good stead all your life."

He shrugged his shoulders. "Of course there are temptations; of course there are other things that seem more desirable at times. I had a few myself when I was in my residency here. You know, I was a pretty good baseball player at one time. I played in college and was drafted into the Orioles farm system. I played one summer of Class D ball and didn't do badly. But once I got into medicine and had a chance to compare the two careers, there was no option for me. One seemed fun, the other seemed . . . everything. And I've never been sorry—except, perhaps, on a day like this . . . sometimes." He smiled a crooked smile.

"True, the profession's going through a bit of a hard time right now. It's experiencing pains of maturation. It's evolving into an exact science from a childhood of anecdotes and trial and error. And the public is restless. They don't want to wait any longer, so they keep encouraging the process with malpractice suits and passing laws mandating greater and greater supervision. What they don't understand is that, for most of us, our personal ethics are higher than the standards they try to impose. What they are mandating is mediocrity." He snorted. "You can't *legislate* quality—you *teach* it, and that's what we do here!"

He stood up impatiently, then sat on the edge of his desk, staring down at Jim. "But these problems will pass! Look, Gallier, I'll shorten it up. What I want to point out to you and have you come away with today is that, despite its problems, a medical career means never having to worry about the term 'trivial pursuit' except as the title of a game. A doctor can be many things these days, and have many interests. But if you are a doctor, you have to be a doctor *first* and those other things second.

"Now, do me a favor. Get out of here. Think things over again. If you drop back up here, around five o'clock, we'll forget the whole thing. If you don't come, I'll wish you 'Godspeed.' Go on now, not another word." Jim moved his mouth to speak but stopped; clearly the interview was over. As he left the room, he glanced at his watch. It was precisely 12:30.

The corridors were full of people hurrying toward the dining rooms and cafeterias for lunch. Jim moved along with them, uncertain about his next move. He was not hungry. After the interview he felt spent; his meeting with Dr. Mendel had left him shaken. The things Mendel had said sounded right, but Jim had already pondered most of them. Nevertheless, Mendel's dominating presence as he went over these points underscored how important they were. Jim found himself heading back toward Marburg I. He knew Dr. Hallam would probably be having his lunch, but even so he wanted to see him again and say goodbye.

Dr. Hallam was indeed having his lunch when Jim entered the room, alone and eating from a small table pulled up to his bedside chair. His face brightened when he saw Jim, and he motioned for him to enter.

"Good day, Jim, have a seat. May I offer you some lunch?"

"Oh, no thank you, sir, I'll be getting something shortly. I'm sorry to interrupt yours."

"Not at all. I'm glad for the company."

"Well, in that case I'll sit for a moment. How are you today?"

"I'm feeling fine. Looks as though I'll be going home tomorrow, thanks in large measure to your kind help." Dr. Hallam continued eating.

"Not at all, sir. I'm glad I could help, and I'm glad you've made a good recovery."

"Jim, I think I've made several recoveries while here, and, again, you've helped a lot, by making me face things I should have faced long ago."

"I guess facing things is never easy, and sometimes it takes a catastrophic event to make it happen. But to tell you the truth, sir, if you think I've helped you a bit in this regard, it turns out that you've helped me to face certain truths, in return."

"Oh?" Dr. Hallam wiped his mouth with his napkin and shoved the tray away.

"Yes, sir. You see, for some while now I've been having doubts about my fitness and suitability for a medical life, and helping in your case here has made me confront those doubts."

"I'm surprised." Dr. Hallam regarded him soberly. "I had no idea. You seem so good—so natural—at it. I'm very surprised."

"Thank you."

"So have you come to any resolution?"

"I have. I've decided to leave here . . . to put medicine behind me for a while, now while there's still time. Or at least that's what I had decided until I just talked to Dr. Mendel. He sort of raised my doubts again."

"Mendel can be very persuasive. . . . But look here, Jim, why don't you tell me the whole thing? What the hell has gotten you off the track?"

Jim told him about his loss of enthusiasm for his work, his feeling of constraint in it, and his lessening commitment to meeting its demands. Dr. Hallam listened quietly, and when Jim finished, he said, "Doesn't exactly sound like I set a shining example for you to follow."

"It wasn't that, sir, it was just that you kind of underscored some of the questions I'd been asking myself. I mean, about the responsibilities, the commitment, the weight of it all."

Dr. Hallam shrugged. "I loved them—they were exciting to me, and very rewarding. The poet Alexander Pope saw the whole world in a grain of sand. Well, I could see mine in a scalpel, I guess you could say. But the life's not for everybody. Tell me, anybody in your family in medicine?"

"Nobody was a doctor. My father was a stockbroker. So was his father before him. My maternal grandmother was a nurse for a while, but my grandfather made her give it up when they got married, and she never went back to it. She was here at Hopkins for a while."

Later, Clay was never able to explain for sure why he pursued this. But he did ask the next question.

"When was your grandmother here?"

"It would have been about 1938 or '39—she was an operating-room nurse."

Clay felt his abdominal muscles contract, and a momentary giddiness swept over him. He caught himself and was relieved to see that Jim had not noticed his reaction. He willed his voice to remain steady as he asked the next question.

"Hmm, that's interesting. I was here then. Tell me, what is your grandmother's name?"

"Her name is, or was, Sheila Ellender. She died twelve or thirteen years ago, in an automobile accident."

"Ellender . . . was her married name?"

"Yes. Her maiden name was . . . uh . . . Speri, Sheila Speri. Do you think you knew her?"

Struggling to control his emotions, Clay hardly heard the question. Sheila Speri! This boy was Sheila Speri's grandson. He looked at Jim, and gradually, gradually, another thought came to him. It was absurd, ridiculous, but he had to ask—he had to lay it to rest.

"Oh, I don't think so—so far back—so long ago. But because we're on this subject, Jim, do you mind if I ask a few more questions about your family? I'm trying to get a feel for your situation."

"Not at all, sir, anything . . ."

"Your father was a broker, and I understand he died several years ago?"

"Yes, sir, heart attack. He was sixty-five."

"What about your mother?"

"Oh, she's going strong. She's forty-five now—very active and into a lot of things."

"I see, so she was born . . . "

"November 20, 1939."

Clay could control himself no longer. He stared at Jim.

Jim fidgeted under this scrutiny. "Anything wrong, sir?"

Clay shook his head. "No, no, I was just harking back to those days. Please excuse me. Well, your mother must've been young when you were born."

"Yes sir, she was nineteen. Of course, she has three younger brothers, my uncles."

"I see, well, well. . . . So your grandmother was a nurse, and right here at Hopkins—imagine. Do you think she influenced you to become a doctor? Did she talk about it some?"

"She liked to talk about it—her green years, she used to call them, referring to her O.R. gown. She kept one of them right up until the end."

"Well, Jim, it seems likely to me she had something to do with your becoming a doctor, even though you may not recognize it. Tell me, what are your plans if you don't stay on?"

"I'm joining a friend who has a new boat, and we're going to sail off New England and Canada this summer. I thought it would be a good way to get my thoughts in order. . . . And by the way, sir, I asked your daughter to come with me. I hope you don't mind."

Clay swallowed. "You . . . asked Charlie? To go with you?"

"Yes, sir. In fact, I sort of proposed to her. But don't worry, she turned me down—and she was right. She's a wonderful girl, and she deserves better than to go off with a guy as uncertain about things as I am."

"Hmm. Don't sell yourself short, Jim. It's better for you to ask career questions now than at the end of your life, or never to ask them at all. I'm glad you have the intelligence to ask them, and the courage to take action. I myself think it's better that you and Charlie go separate ways—but not for the reasons you might think. Perhaps one day that will become clear to you.

"But before you go," Clay continued, "let me share with you a thought I've developed over the years. It's a good rule to live by. Find an institution—a university, a church, a workplace, it doesn't matter as long as it has quality, integrity, tradition, and will endure—and become a part of it. If you do that, your own standards will remain high and you'll be able to take pride in what you do." He smiled a little sheepishly. "I hope I'm not being too preachy."

Jim said nothing. He stood to leave, and the two men shook hands. They held the handshake a long while. Jim said, "It's been wonderful getting to know you, sir. I'll never forget you."

"Whoa, hold on," said Clay. "I can't let you go without extracting a promise from you. Will you promise an old man—or at least an elderly one—that you will write to him and let him know where you are and what you're doing?"

Surprised and touched by Dr. Hallam's concern, Jim promised.

"And furthermore, Jim, if you ever need my help in anything—in anything at all—promise that you'll let me know."

Long after Jim had shut the door behind him, Clay sat staring at it. He was almost stupefied by what had been unfolded, and he went over it again and again. Of course, everything was probably just coincidental. It couldn't really be. Things don't work out that way. And yet. And yet. Clay couldn't shake the feeling that it was at least possible that Jim's mother was Clay's daughter and that Jim was his grandson. At least the timing was right. He well remembered his night with Sheila Speri—in February 1939. Jim's mother was born in November 1939. Sheila had probably married within a week or so of leaving Johns Hopkins, as she had intended, and so her daughter's birth would have raised no questions.

But above all that there was simply something about Jim, something about the obvious affinity between them, that such a relationship would explain. He dared to hope he was right. Now he could understand why he had felt compelled to explain to this boy the darkest parts of his own past, things he had never fully revealed even to Charlotte or Anne. My God, to think he might have a grandson. He suddenly became aware of how much he missed Mark. And now providence seemed to hint at filling the emptiness that Mark's death had created. Clay felt an impulse to kneel and pray, an impulse he hadn't felt in a long, long time.

Of course, he had found Jim only to have him leave. But Clay was certain of one thing: the two of them would not lose contact with each other. Clay would see to that.

But the ramifications were legion. How would Anne take the news? Would he choose to tell her? Or ever *have* to tell her? Thank God Charlotte had not run off with Jim. Perhaps she, too, had sensed something. And, miracle of miracles, he might have a daughter out there, Jim's mother. In some way he would have to contact her. In some careful way he would have to confirm what he wanted to believe before saying anything to anybody. His mind spinning, Clay Hallam leaned back in his chair and gazed at the ceiling of his hospital room. At seventy-two a gift had been laid at his door, and suddenly he had much to live for.

The afternoon drifted by, and the five o'clock sun bathed the hospital in glowing orange. Dr. Mendel was locking his office door, carrying home a briefcase full of case reports. Anne Hallam was seating herself alongside her husband's bed in Marburg I, about to enjoy a predinner chat. Charlotte Hallam was packing to return to her job in Washington and thinking about Jim and Jonas and the possibility of returning to Baltimore for nursing school. Jonas Smith was beginning residents' rounds, but for once his mind was not on rounds. He was thinking about Jim and about how long he should wait before calling Charlotte. It would not, he thought, be long.

Jim Gallier, his bags and other gear around him, was waiting at the front entrance of the hospital for the taxi that would take him to the train station. The cab arrived, Jim got in, and they drove off. Jim did not look back. He couldn't afford to.